D0715622
DREAMSEEKER
TRILOGY

THE DREAMSEEKER TRILOGY

SILVER CLOUD

IRON EYES

BAD HEART

JENNY OLDFIELD

A division of Hodder Headline Limited

For Kate and Eve, as they seek their dreams.

This collection published in 2005 by Hodder Children's Books
Silvercloud first published in Great Britain in 2002
Iron Eyes first published in Great Britain in 2002
Bad Heart first published in Great Britain in 2003

2 4 6 8 10 9 7 5 3 1

A Catalogue record for this book is available from
the British Library

ISBN 0 340 89322 2

Typeset in Palatino by Avon DataSet Ltd,
Bidford-on-Avon, Warwickshire

Printed and bound in Great Britain by
Bookmarque Ltd, Croydon, Surrey

The paper and board used in this paperback by
Hodder Children's Books are natural recyclable products
made from wood grown in sustainable forests.
The manufacturing processes conform to the environmental regulations
of the country of origin.

Hodder Children's Books
a division of Hodder Headline Limited
338 Euston Road
London NW1 3BH

Visit our website
www.madaboutbooks.com

CONTENTS

As flies to wanton boys, are we to the gods;
They kill us for their sport.

King Lear, IV i. 44–5

WHITE WATER SIOUX FAMILY TREE

Red Hawk m. White Deer
(Chief of White Water Sioux)

Unnamed m. River That Flies Tribeswoman
(Red Hawk's brother) (MiniConjou)

Swift Elk m. Shining Star
(Died at Thunder Ridge)

Black Kettle m. Unnamed
(Died at Thunder Ridge)

Four Winds

Hidden Moon

GOOD SPIRITS	EVIL SPIRITS
Wakanda (Maker of All Good Things)	Anteep (Source of All Evil)
Ghost Horse (A major animal spirit)	Unktehi (Guardian of Yellow Water)
Silver Cloud (Spirit messenger)	Yietso (Shape-shifting servant)

PART ONE

SILVER CLOUD

THE DREAM

ONE

The old man sat by the dying fire. He wore a blanket around his hunched shoulders and stared into the embers.

The boy, Four Winds, watched and listened sadly.

'I am very old. My sun is set,' his grandfather began. 'Once I was a warrior. *Iki 'cize waon 'kon*. Now it is over.'

A burned-out log shifted, releasing red sparks into the night sky. Four Winds followed their whirling, fading dance, then looked back at the old man.

True, it was a lined face. The skin was criss-crossed with years of struggle. The hands were gnarled like the roots of a tree.

'Soon I will lie down to rise no more.'

Four Winds leaned forward to stir the embers. He concentrated on the pattern of the sparks in the sky.

'Listen, my son. Once I was a warrior. I fought my enemies and feasted my friends. My people were around me like the sands of the shore. They have passed away, they have died like the grass in winter, they have gone to the mountains. *Hena 'la yelo*. It is over.'

Standing abruptly, Four Winds made as if to cast another log on the fire. He didn't want to hear this lamenting. He preferred the tales of his grandfather's youth, of his beaded war shirt hung with ermine pelts, of the eagle feathers that adorned his headdress. Red Hawk the warrior, Chief of the White Water band of the great Sioux tribe.

'I will speak,' Red Hawk insisted, his face lit up by a fountain of fresh sparks. 'When I look back now from this high hill of my old age, I see a time of plenty. There was food for our stomachs then, and we heard no man's commands.'

'That time will come again,' Four Winds said softly.

The sparks faded and left the old man's face in darkness. 'You are young,' he said. 'The only son of my only son.'

Here was more pain and sadness. The boy turned away from the fire. The face of his dead father came back to him in the moving shadows, his eyes dark and gentle. His mother too was there in the cold night, watching over him.

Red Hawk gazed at his grandson. 'Much has ended,' he insisted. 'The Comanches came on horseback from the south. They seized the land of White Water that the Great Spirit gave us. Our people died in the mud, our women were sold into slavery.'

Four Winds closed his eyes to block out the picture of his father, Swift Elk, slain on the battlefield. Of his beautiful mother, Shining Star, snatched away in the dead of night.

'Now winter comes and the White Water people have no home. The Wild Dog Comanches take the fish from our rivers and the buffalo from our plains. We must leave our homeland on a trail of tears and walk to our deaths in the frozen mountains to the west. *Hena 'la yelo*. It is over.'

Four Winds left his grandfather at last. He respected the years that the old man had lived and the suffering he had gone through, but his boy's heart wouldn't accept defeat.

He walked between the tipis towards the river and the great plain beyond. A million stars shone in the sky. Under the moonlight, the sea of pale grass rippled in the wind.

Why must they depart because the Comanches ordered it? It was a shameful thing to leave the homeland, cast out like dogs. And Four Winds was sure that the Great Spirit didn't wish it.

'We must stay and fight!' he said to the night sky.

You are a boy. His mother's voice whispered to him from the blackness. *You cannot fight.*

Thirteen summers have passed since you gave me life, he muttered. *I call that old enough to carry a war club!*

Against men on swift horses while you have only your own poor speed and your boy's strength of arm?

'Mother!' he whispered, angered by the reminder of the Comanche band's unfair advantage.

Two summers back, the Wild Dogs under Snake Eye had ridden their strange, deer-like beasts into the Sioux village. The creatures had carried them to swift victory over the White Water band. Swift Elk had been among the dead, pierced through the heart by a Comanche lance. Shining Star and many other Sioux women had vanished from their tipis.

Since then, the small band of survivors had taken refuge on rocky heights, driven further from the buffalo and the fish. They had grown hungry, lost more men in Comanche raids, until now only five warriors remained out of fifty, plus the medicine man, Matotope. Three boys of similar age to Four Winds longed to fight alongside their elders, but Four Winds' own grandmother, White Deer, stood between them and their wish.

'A boy must go out to Spider Rock before he can fight,' she insisted. 'He must fast and seek the powers of the Great One through a vision in that sacred place. Until then he lacks the wisdom for battle and must stay by the tipi.'

Four Winds felt angered by his grandmother's words – yet he knew it was the way of the tribe.

And now his grandfather said it was over. They must roll up their tents, strap them on the travois and have the dogs drag them high into the mountains to escape Snake Eye. But escape into what?

'We will all die,' he told the stars. He was touched by the gloom of his grandfather. It fell over him like a heavy blanket which would not let him breathe.

'How soon must we move on?' Four Winds asked his grandmother, White Deer.

It was early next morning, and the old woman had risen and was busy skinning and treating the hide of an antelope. She worked with a sharp bone tool, staking the skin on to a wooden frame then scraping it clean.

'That depends,' White Deer told him, scooping water from a wooden bowl and washing down the skin. Then she scraped some more.

'On what?' Four Winds was impatient. He'd spent a night in the tipi, rolled in his blanket, unable to sleep. He knew that his grandmother would pretend that this was just one more move, from summer camp to winter quarters. But his talk with Red Hawk had convinced him that this wasn't so. This time, it was the Comanches driving them out once and for all.

'On my husband, your grandfather,' she replied evenly, scooping and scraping. The skin, once it had been rubbed down with boiled brain, liver and fat, would be used to repair an old tipi.

'And how will he decide?'

The old woman sighed and looked up. 'Four Winds, my little Kola, who can answer that question?'

'*Kola*' had been his mother's nickname for him. It

meant 'friend'. Now the sound of it ran through him like the cold autumn wind.

'Kola,' White Deer said again. 'Come, fetch me more water, or this skin will never soften.'

So he went and brought water from a creek which ran down to meet the white water below. He held the bowl under a small waterfall and let it fill to the brim. When he looked up again, he was startled by what he saw.

The bowl dropped to the ground. For a moment he thought that Snake Eye and his people had appeared on the rocky horizon, that the Comanches had found the Sioux band's latest hideout and had come to drive them higher, above the snowline into the white wilderness.

But then he made out the shapes in the morning mist more clearly. It was the creatures that the enemy called by the name of horse – those beasts that seemed like a mixture of elk and deer, but were hornless and could be ridden by a man.

Four Winds breathed more easily. For now there seemed to be no Comanches nearby – only the creatures with long necks, and hair falling gracefully to one side. They stood still and silent in the mist, looking down on him, eleven or twelve of them lining the horizon.

He stooped to pick up the bowl and refill it. The cold water ran over his wrists, the creek splashed over the rocks. Did the appearance of the horses mean that the Wild Dogs were nearby, he wondered. Perhaps he should hurry back to the tipis to warn his grandfather.

Another glance at the horizon told Four Winds that the creatures were about to depart. Some had already turned and were melting into the mist. Others stamped their hooves and made a strange snorting noise. Only one stood in the same place as before, letting the wind tug at his mane, his eyes fixed on the boy by the waterfall.

Four Winds felt the power of the horse's gaze. Not a single muscle moved as he communicated his presence across a gap of a hundred paces. He was silvery grey with a pure white mane and tail. Strange but beautiful, Four Winds thought. He had often heard of wonderful happenings from the earliest times, of creatures that came from the sun or else out of the earth. He had learned not to do anything harmful, but to be still and wait. Surely the silver horse was part of the Great Spirit's work, and He was present in him, as He was in all four-legged creatures, and the winged birds and the mountains, the rivers, the grasses, the trees.

The boy understood this and was no longer afraid. He smiled at the pale horse in the morning mist, then turned and took the bowl of water to White Deer.

'What do you know of the Comanche horse?' Red Hawk asked Matotope.

'The creature runs swift as the elk. It has the grace of the antelope,' the medicine man replied. He'd answered the call to the chief's tipi in his own time, first dressing in his ceremonial robe of eagle feathers, then singing praises to the sacred creatures of the sky.

'I don't need your wisdom to know this,' Red Hawk replied. 'This much I have seen with my own eyes. What else?'

Matotope ignored the interruption. 'He has the strength of a young buffalo and the courage of a mountain lion.'

'This is so. And he bears the enemy of our People on his back,' the old man pointed out. The cold had made his chest heave and rattle and his hands tremble. 'He makes the Comanche all-powerful. Surely he is an evil spirit, to permit the destruction of our White Water sons.'

The medicine man bowed his head and remained silent.

'Well?' Red Hawk spoke sharply. Time was running out, night was darkening around him.

'I have been to Spider Rock and talked with the four sacred animals,' Matotope said. The medicine man was in his prime, smooth-skinned beneath his feathered robe. About his body he wore a buckskin pouch filled with animal bones, shells and beads.

'You asked them in turn about this creature?'

Matotope nodded. 'I spoke with the Mountain Lion who guards the north and the Bear of the west. They knew nothing of this being. Neither did Wolf, guardian of the east.'

'But the Snake of the south?' Red Hawk prompted.

'Snake listened and told me everything. Our brothers the Ute, the Kiowa, the Apache and the Caddo already know of the horse. Our enemies the Comanche travelled south into the desert land and found people from beyond the sea. They were full of wonder at the creatures they saw there and brought many back to the plains.'

'To use as weapons of war against us,' the old man said bitterly. 'For two years Sioux blood has been spilt on the battlefield because of the horse. I have lost my only son. What advice did Snake give about *that*?'

'I asked for none,' the shaman said. 'It is as it is, and I have told you all I heard.'

For a while the two men sat in silence.

'When I turn to the east, I see no dawn,' Red Hawk said at last. 'What are my People to do, where are they to go in the coming generations?'

'It will be as the Great Spirit wills,' Matotope murmured, uneasy because he had reached the limits of his wisdom. The bones and beads in his medicine bag couldn't bring back the dead warriors or stop the Wild Dog braves.

'What is this horse? Is he a messenger like the owl or a guard of the Great Spirit? Does he advise the gods, or is he a mere servant like the dog?'

With a proud look, the shaman dismissed the old chief's questions. 'Better not to waste time wondering. Better to tell your People to roll up their tipis and move on before the snow comes,' he advised. 'The grass is dying and the leaves are brown. Soon Snake Eye will be here.'

'We have some time – a little.' Friendly scouts had told Red Hawk that the Comanches had put up their lodges in the east, ten days' walk away. The enemy didn't show any sign of wanting to pursue them at present. 'If we move from here, know that we move to our certain deaths, away from our homeland, in the white mountains.'

Slowly Matotope nodded. This was so.

'No.' Red Hawk's voice gained strength as he made his decision. 'You, Matotope, must go again to Spider Rock.'

The medicine man's eyes narrowed and glittered.

'Stay two suns and one moon. Fast and pray. Call upon the spirit of this mysterious creature, the Horse. Ask him to guide us away from danger.'

Matotope stood. The feathers on his cloak fluttered as he moved.

'Tell the Ghost Horse that he is our only hope,' the old man insisted. 'The People need food and warmth for the winter, and the strength to fight the Comanches who use the horse with ill will against us.'

'I will do this,' Matotope promised.

'Without the help of the Ghost Horse, the tribe will vanish. I am old. A People's dream has died on the battleground. It was a beautiful dream. But the nation's hoop is broken, there is no centre.'

The medicine man nodded gravely. 'In two suns and one moon I shall return.'

Red Hawk's eyes were filled with tears. '*Maka akanl wicasa iyuha el*,' he said. Go in peace.

TWO

White Deer left off scraping the antelope skin and looked up at the sky. Trouble had taken root deep in her heart and would not go away.

Yes, it was as Red Hawk said, time and again: the hoop was broken. The dream was lost.

Her son's son appeared on the hill, carrying water. His youth pained her. A boy approaching manhood, with the slight shoulders and slender waist of a child, Kola's legs were growing long like his father's, his black hair thick like his mother's. Her heart ached for him.

'I saw horses,' he told her.

White Deer scooped water from the bowl and trickled it over the animal skin. 'How many?'

Four Winds showed her with his fingers. 'One was beautiful. He was grey like the mist, silver like the water under moonlight.'

She frowned. Taking the bone tool, she scraped the remaining blood and flesh from the hide. 'I know nothing of horses. Only that they bear our enemies.'

'There were no Wild Dogs with the herd I saw on

the hill,' the boy assured his grandmother. 'These horses belonged to no man. They were free like the elk and the buffalo.'

The old woman grunted. This water was cold, the skin stubborn. She worked flesh out of the corners then laid the side of her knife against a rock to sharpen the edge. 'When I have finished with the hide I want you to help me cut the meat from this animal into strips. We must hang it in the sun.'

Four Winds frowned over the woman's work. White Deer must be angry with him for his talk about the horses. Yet she hadn't seen them. 'They stood and watched me at the waterfall,' he insisted. 'I wasn't afraid.'

'You are young.'

This was what she always said. Meaning, your judgement is shallow, there is no wisdom inside a head that bears no grey hairs.

White Deer glanced up at Four Winds' guarded face. 'You say this animal is beautiful. But a flower may be beautiful and kill with its poison. And listen, before you defend this creature called the horse. Remember that under the skin of an animal beats a heart like a human heart.'

The boy nodded. As a child hardly able to walk, he had been taught this by his mother. That animals do not look like people, but they think like people do, and they really *are* people under their pelts.

'The heart of the buffalo is good,' his grandmother

continued. 'He came from under the earth and swam a great river. He brings us life. But the coyote bears a trickster's heart. He is cunning and greedy, sent here by Anteep, the wicked chief of the lower world.'

'The horse is not sent by Anteep,' Four Winds said stubbornly.

White Deer sighed. 'Wait and see,' was all she said.

Matotope opened the flap of Red Hawk's tipi, stooped low and went out into the morning air.

There was a rattle in the old man's chest and a slowness in his brain. Always his thoughts flew back instead of forward. He came up with solutions that led nowhere.

The shaman took a deep breath and looked around the village. There were only ten tipis now, hurriedly thrown up and clinging to a steep, treeless mountainside. Three of the tipis contained only old women and children. Five were still painted with warriors' marks to celebrate victories in battle. The ninth belonged to Red Hawk and White Deer, the tenth to Matotope himself.

Once there had been eighty lodges in the village. Smoke had risen through every smoke hole; the hearths were places of comfort and plenty. Beyond their rows of tents had stretched a green plain teeming with buffalo, elk and antelope.

Matotope's eye rested on the figure of White Deer

stooped over a wooden frame, washing and softening a single antelope hide. The meat from this one animal was all the White Water band had in store for the winter ahead.

And what had the old chief told him? Go once more to the sacred rock. Call upon the spirit of the Horse to save us!

Red Hawk had a rattle in his chest and his eyes set on death. A younger chief would have listened to advice and done what the Kiowa and Apache had done in the desert lands to the south. Fight fire with fire, they said. If the Comanches have the Horse, then so must the Apache, for how can a man on foot fight a fair battle with a man on a horse?

Two summers ago, the fathers of the Sioux Nation had gathered at Thunder Ridge. Tall Bull, Red Feather, Lone Wolf and Spotted Tail had come together with Red Hawk and heard of the White Waters' troubles. Twenty of their braves had already died at the hand of the swift Comanche enemy.

The old men smoked pipes and made empty promises. They would not hear of carrying out raids to steal this mysterious creature, the Horse, from their enemies. Wakanda, the Great Spirit, does not wish it, they said.

Matotope smiled bitterly at the memory as he slid his feather cloak from his back and strode towards his tipi. Fight fire with fire. Set horse against horse. That had been his advice. But Red Hawk set his face against it and his People had died.

So let it be.

'Matotope is to go to the sacred place,' the children whispered.

'I saw him painting his body inside his tipi,' one said. 'He put on his bonnet of eagle feathers and fastened his medicine bundle to his wampum belt.'

'Then he is going to Spider Rock,' they said in awed voices.

Four Winds listened to their chatter inside the tents of the grandmothers. Outside, a wind blew down from the mountain tops, so the women had hung the dew cloth around the walls of the tipi to keep out the cold. 'When does Matotope journey to the rock?' he asked Hidden Moon, the girl who gave most of the facts.

'Tonight,' she told him. 'When the stars are clear in the sky, with the full moon to guide him.'

'Chief Red Hawk is very sick,' a small child said. 'They say he may not see another sun rise in the east.'

'Hush!' Hidden Moon warned. 'Wakanda will be angry with you for saying so.'

The boy drew a deep breath then fell silent. He crept on to the knees of one of the old women and hid against her striped woollen shawl.

Hidden Moon saw Four Winds rise and leave the

tent, his head hanging low. Quickly she followed him. 'Is your grandfather really so ill?' she asked him.

Four Winds nodded. 'He carries a deep hurt. He suffers for the People.'

'He has done all he can to save us.' Hidden Moon was the grandchild of Red Hawk's brother who had married into the River That Flies band belonging to the Miniconjou tribe. Her father had died in battle beside Four Winds' father, Swift Elk. The boy and girl were tied by blood.

Four Winds was grateful for the kind words. He walked with his cousin through the camp, past the closed flap of his grandfather's tent. 'Red Hawk remembers the wonder of the wide open plain,' he explained. 'Now all that is overthrown. His last hope lies with Matotope and the spirits of Spider Rock.'

'I don't trust Matotope,' Hidden Moon said simply.

Four Winds looked sharply into her dark brown eyes. Then he decided to make a joke of it. 'Hush, Wakanda will be angry!'

'I don't care,' the girl said, still serious. 'I say that Matotope's medicine is not strong, to let our People die like dogs in the mud. His advice led my father and your father to their deaths at Burning Rock. Thirty men on foot against a hundred on horseback, and Matotope in his holy wisdom told your grandfather they must stand and fight!'

The boy took his cousin by the arm and led her up

the hill to the place where he had seen the horses. 'This is dangerous talk,' he warned. 'Don't let the others hear you.'

'I don't care!' With the wind tugging at her braided hair and the fringe of her buckskin skirt, Hidden Moon defied him. 'If I was a man I would fight in the name of Black Kettle, my father. I would steal at night into the camp of the Wild Dogs and kill as many Comanches as I could!'

Four Winds was amused. He laughed in the girl's face.

'Laugh then!' she scorned. 'One day you will be a man and you will fight in the name of Swift Elk, your father. Imagine how it feels to be a girl, left by the hearth with your grandmother, waiting night after night for the enemy to raid your empty camp and sell you into slavery!'

'That's how it is with me now,' he admitted. 'Left at home with the old women and children.'

Hidden Moon saw that her angry words had hit home. 'But you will be a man one day,' she insisted more gently. 'And, if it is not too late, you will be a warrior.'

Matotope was leaving at sunset, so Four Winds must hurry. His cousin's words had disturbed him deeply and made him feel ashamed.

Why did he, a boy with thirteen summers behind

him, sit at home with the old women? His spear arm was growing strong. He had trained his eye to see a target and his hand to aim true. Why accept defeat without a struggle?

Quickly he made his way down from the waterfall to his grandfather's tipi. He was about to raise the flap and enter, when his grandmother stepped out.

'Red Hawk is sleeping,' she said quietly.

'I need to talk with him,' Four Winds tried to explain.

'Later.' White Deer laid a hand on his wrist.

There would be no later, the boy knew now. This would be his only chance. If his grandfather was asleep then he must plead with his grandmother. 'I wish to go with Matotope to the sacred rock,' he said.

White Deer shook her head as if an insect had landed on her cheek. 'I must fetch logs for Red Hawk's fire,' she said, hurriedly moving away.

'I mean it, grandmother. I want to go on a dream quest.'

'You are too young.' The old woman went for her logs to the stack which Four Winds had chopped. They were out of hearing of the rest of the band, in a windy place overlooking a deep canyon.

'I want to go,' he insisted.

She lifted two logs and thrust them into his arms. 'Young and foolish,' she lamented. 'Speak no more.'

He obeyed, knowing her well. Soon she herself would break the silence.

'A seeker of dreams walks away from his childhood, he says goodbye to childish things,' she said in a sad, low voice. Her thin hands trembled as she lifted the next log. 'He can never be simple again.'

'It is time,' he insisted. 'My father told me that he walked out to seek the spirits in the fourteenth summer of his life. I have thirteen summers. What is the difference?'

'You leave behind the boy, Kola. You must become the man, Four Winds.' His grandmother shook her head and let her sorrow show. 'It is I who have nursed you, my child, I who have taught you to sing and play. How can I lose the boy that I love?'

'And how can I remain the boy when the man's voice calls?' he pleaded. 'Tonight Matotope will follow the North Star to Spider Rock. I must go with him to fast, and call on the spirits to give me the power to fight.'

'That is not a man's voice, it is the voice of foolishness!' she said as she struggled to pile more logs into his arms.

Four Winds staggered under the weight. 'I must purify my body and go to the spirits, fast and pray for a visitation,' he said stubbornly. 'Or else I will fight the Comanches without the protection of Wakanda. For I will not stay in the tipi like a coward when my arm is strong!'

'Kola!' White Deer sighed with tears in her eyes. She made him put the logs down on the ground and sit cross-legged with her in the cold wind. Then she took out a small pouch made of lizard skin from the folds of her skirt. 'I found this on the tipi floor on the night your mother, Shining Star, was taken by the Comanches.'

'What is it?' Four Winds asked. His grandmother's tears had made him sad.

'Inside is the sacred cord from her body which was severed at your birth. Shining Star kept it safe in this pouch, knowing that Lizard promises long life. Her last thought when she was taken was for you and your future. It was a message to me to guard you and keep you safe.'

He watched his grandmother turn the small leather pouch in her crooked fingers. 'Thank you,' he murmured. 'This gives me strength.'

'My heart is breaking,' she moaned. 'My husband turns towards death and my son's son takes his leave.'

'But grandmother, your teaching has always been that we must look and listen for the good of the whole People. I learned this at your knee.'

She nodded. ' "In all of your actions cast away your self," ' she quoted. ' "Have always in view not only the present, but also the coming generations." It is true, according to the Great Law.'

'And all things are the work of the Great Spirit,' he reminded her.

' "He is within all things, the trees, the grasses, the

rivers, the mountains, the four-legged animals and the winged creatures," ' she chanted, her voice halting, and sighing all the while. ' "We should understand this deeply and in our hearts, then we will fear and love and know the Great Spirit, and we will be and act and live as He intends." '

Once more Four Winds let the silence flow.

'Come,' White Deer said at last. 'We will prepare a bath of sweetgrass. When Red Hawk awakes I will tell him that his only grandson, Four Winds, is setting out on his dream quest!'

THREE

The old man slept on.

Perhaps it was his last sleep of all. Knowing this, the mood in the village was heavy. Amongst the wind battered tipis, the women went quietly about their work and the men huddled round fires, waiting.

Four Winds watched White Deer talking with Matotope. He had bathed in the sweetgrass water and taken his last food before he set off to seek his dream. With a stomach full of antelope meat and berries, he was ready to begin.

But he could see the medicine man arguing with his grandmother, and so he went closer to the fire.

'Only Red Hawk can say yes or no to a dream quest,' Matotope pointed out. On the ground in front of him lay a small blanket, and on this were arranged beads, bones, herbs and a bird's head – the precious contents of the shaman's medicine bundle. 'Until Red Hawk wakes, the boy must stay here in the village.'

'But you can take him with you to Spider Rock,' White Deer pointed out. 'My husband would wish that his son's son should seek out the vision that will make him a man.'

'Four Winds is too young,' Matotope said. Noting the boy's approach, he voiced his doubts openly. 'My own quest is a hard one and the future of the White Water band relies on it. Why should I take along a child to worry over?'

'I will take care of myself,' Four Winds said. 'No one need trouble themselves about me!'

White Deer smiled faintly. Age had taught her to accept the boastfulness of youth without comment. To be young meant to be strong and proud, bold in front of the wolf, fast as the running deer. She remembered.

'I have purified myself and eaten. I am ready,' Four Winds insisted.

Matotope shrugged. He placed the line of objects inside his painted leather pouch. 'Make your farewells,' he grunted. 'When the North Star appears in the sky, we begin.'

'So, you are going to Spider Rock.' Hidden Moon stood outside the children's tipi. Behind her, the sun set fiery red in the west.

Inside the tent, the younger ones whispered together about their friend Kola's vision quest.

'Because of the challenge you threw in my face,' Four Winds confessed.

The girl nodded gravely. 'Then, Kola, you will fight in the name of your father, Swift Elk, and you will remember my father, Black Kettle, who died at his side.'

'I will,' he promised.

Hidden Moon smiled, turned and stooped to enter the tipi.

Then, with dusk settling on the hillside and the swallows whirling and swooping overhead, Four Winds went to each of the five warriors left in the White Water band.

First Sun Dancer clasped the boy by the arm and wished him well. He reminded him of his Sioux fathers who had fought before him in generations past.

Running Fox and Little Thunder each spoke of the White Water homeland and told Four Winds to put his trust in Wakanda, the Great Spirit, He who made all things.

Outside One Horn's tent, the boy promised to open himself through fasting to the visit from the Maker of All. One Horn was the oldest of the warriors. He bore the scars of battle across his chest and arm. There was a sad look in his eye as he clasped Four Winds' hand. 'Tonight, when you are gone, we will hold a ceremony, the *Alo'wanpi*. We will sing to the spirit called White Buffalo Maiden so that only good will befall you.'

Finally the boy went to visit Three Bears in his tipi. Smoke spiralled up through the smoke hole. A war bonnet of eagle feathers hung from the wall.

'Seek in the sacred place for the wisdom to defeat the enemy,' Three Bears advised. 'Open your heart to the messengers. Come back strong and ready to fight.'

Once more, Four Winds promised. For the first time, as he stepped out into the gathering darkness to meet with Matotope, his insides fluttered as though there were birds inside the cage of his ribs, flapping to escape.

He saw his grandmother waiting quietly outside her tipi, old and thin, white-haired. She held her hands clasped in front of her and made no move towards him.

You will never be simple again.

He gazed at her across the ashes and blackened logs of yesterday's fire, then he held up the lizard pouch.

White Deer bowed her head.

Then Matotope came and pointed to the first star in the night sky. He was stripped to the waist, dressed only in buckskin trousers and moccasins, with green beads and three black feathers in his hair.

The birds inside Four Winds' ribcage fought to be free. He took a deep breath. The North Star, shining like his mother in the sky, called him.

Matotope and the boy walked in silence through the night.

They came down from the cold mountain into the warm valley of their ancestors, travelling by the water's edge through willow thickets where Coyote made a midnight meal of bobcat and Otter dammed his creek and watched for the glint of fish in the water.

As the sun rose and the birds of the air began to sing, Four Winds followed Matotope through a deep canyon where the water ran white over boulders, between black cliffs. He felt the spray on his bare skin. Suddenly he lost his footing on the wet rocks, fell, and felt the foaming stream grab hold of him. He swirled downstream, dragged under by the current. But he kicked hard, swam against the flow. With a sudden effort he lunged at an overhanging branch, caught hold of it and dragged himself clear.

Twenty paces ahead of him, Matotope didn't even glance over his shoulder.

Four Winds smiled grimly and reminded himself to include an otter's paw in his own medicine bundle when the time came to make one. He would need the animal's strength underwater if he were to survive in the white water rapids of his homeland.

Soon though, they left the bank of the winding river and cut off towards the east, climbing at first to a rocky ridge, then standing to catch their breath.

The boy felt the warmth of the sun. It shone low across the new land that faced them, casting long shadows amongst the cedar trees. He saw no sign of the sacred Spider Rock on the far horizon, but held his silence. Matotope wouldn't welcome childish questions.

The morning grew hot. The breeze that had stirred

the leaves of the cottonwoods dropped away. They were through the stand of trees, treading softly towards a low, flat horizon, feeling the sun's rays beat down on their backs.

As they made for the summit of the hill, Four Winds' legs began to grow weary and sweat trickled down the nape of his neck. Yet Matotope never broke his long stride. In fact, he chose the gruelling climb to begin to talk to the boy.

'You completed *inipi* before you came?' he checked.

Four Winds recalled his sweetgrass sweat bath and nodded.

'It is where the earth, the air, fire and water join together to cleanse your spirit.'

'I know.' The boy resented the shaman's reminder.

'And you come to the sacred site with humility?' Matotope asked, with one eyebrow raised in his high, broad forehead.

Four Winds was silent. He realised that he was proud in his heart.

'Well, the days on Spider Rock may bring you to a proper sense of your true place among the White Water Sioux. And remember, many boys seek a vision and many fail to find one. They must come again and again, endure many fasts before the Great Spirit appears.'

In spite of his weariness, Four Winds picked up speed. He walked ahead of the shaman. There was no time for him to fail and come again. The Comanches would soon roll up their summer tipis and come with their horses towards Red Hawk's hideout. It might only be a matter of days before his People were driven into the snowy wastes. 'I will open my heart and meet with Wakanda,' he insisted. 'I will be ready.'

Matotope cut off on to a new track. 'Good words,' he said. 'But good words do not last long before they must amount to something. Words do not pay for your dead father. They do not protect his grave.'

Driven into silence, Four Winds followed again. He trod in the shaman's dusty footsteps, cresting the next ridge and looking down on an exposed plain of red sand. Far off, flat layers of red sandstone rose to meet the sky and amongst them stood two tall needles of rock which drew the boy's gaze.

'Spider Rock and Talking Gods Rock,' Matotope told him. 'The spirit, Spider, lives on the highest peak.'

The flutters inside Four Winds' chest started up once more. 'Why is the tip of her rock coloured white?' he wanted to know.

'Those are the bones of children she has captured and devoured. The Talking Gods keep watch and tell her who must be taken prisoner. There is no escape from Spider's web.'

Four Winds knew that it was the craft and skill of the Spider which made her so powerful. It was from underneath her rock that the spirits might be expected to answer a human call. Still, he felt a strong fear of approaching the place.

For the first time the boy was glad of Matotope's wisdom. As they descended on to the plain and trudged through the wasteland of stone and sand, he put questions about the animal spirits whose help they were seeking.

'When I call to Wakanda in the great sky above, which name shall I pray for?'

'I can't tell you. You must judge what is best.'

'How can I judge without guidance?' Four Winds needed more knowledge than he'd gained from stories at his mother and grandmother's knees.

'Very well. Each creature possesses a quality that a warrior might desire,' Matotope explained. 'When I made my dream quest many summers ago I called upon the Hawk because he is the surest bird of prey. Others call for the Deer because she can endure thirst in the desert. Or for the watchfulness of the Frog, or for the Crow who is swift and direct in flight.'

'Then I might call for the Eagle?' Four Winds asked. 'For he flies highest of all and sees all things.'

But the medicine man shook his head. 'Only the boldest may call upon the Eagle. The Master of Life, the Great Spirit, has warned that although all creatures gain power from the Sun, the Eagle is set above the rest. His help often brings added danger.'

'Then perhaps I will ask Wakanda who my best messenger would be,' Four Winds decided.

Matotope shrugged and said Four Winds must do as he chose. Meanwhile, they walked across the hot plain.

At midday the shaman took his place. He raised his outstretched palm to the sun and began his chant.' "*Tate ou ye topa kin*". The four winds are blowing. In a sacred manner I call to them!'

Four Winds watched the solitary figure under the tall column of red rock. He examined the circles of white stones placed at its base and recognised them as medicine wheels. The pattern of stones protected the traveller and guided him in his quest.

It was time to begin. Turning his back on Spider Rock, he examined Talking Gods Rock.

The tower was shorter and thicker, with a ledge at its base which faced west. Four Winds chose the ledge for his own search. Far away, through a shimmering haze, he made out a line of blue mountains.

He climbed up to the ledge, threw back his shoulders and reached out his hand to the blue sky.

' "*Wakan yan*
mica kelo
nagi ksa pawan
maka hewaye
wakan yan

mica kelo
kola
wanma yanka yo." '

Four Winds described how the Great One made a wise spirit especially for him. How he, Four Winds, had come to a sacred place, and behold, he had come in search of the spirit.

Then he waited. He waited without food or water, as the sun sank low in the sky. 'I am patient,' he told the Maker of All Things. 'I will be here when the sun sets and the stars appear. I will remain through the cold night and call again at the dawning of the day!'

Chanting and praying, the boy remained strong.

On the second day, at the foot of Spider Rock, Matotope continued to ask the questions that the old chief had sent him to deliver. '*Wakan tanka*, oh Great One, I call upon the spirit of this mysterious creature, the Horse. I ask him to guide us, the White Water People, out of danger!'

The shaman was stiff and weary. Once before he had come to this rock and talked with the four sacred animals. He had learned little and feared that his powers were fading. His return had taught him that this was indeed so.

But Matotope would die before he would go back to his People and admit his failure.

Maybe it was because his heart was no longer pure. There had been other times when he'd spoken good words and committed bad acts. And once, in battle, he'd betrayed the Sioux custom of the *Cante Tinz*, the Strong Hearts. Fighting beside Black Kettle and Swift Elk at Burning Ridge, in his medicine man's helmet of buffalo horns and eagle feathers, he had shown cowardice. While the others fought and died in the mud, he had run away into the forest.

Swift Elk had seen him and with his dying breath had repeated the no-retreat chant. '*Tuwa nape cinahan opa kte sni ye.*' Whoever runs away shall not be admitted.

How could a warrior who had fled remain wise in the ways of the spirits? It was impossible, and yet Matotope was too cowardly to admit his fault. Instead, he'd performed the ceremonies and sought for advice. Advice which had never come since that day in the battle. And so, Matotope had made up the messages and offered to Red Hawk his own poor human wisdom as the Voice of the Great One.

And so the White Water people had died.

'I call upon the Horse!' he cried out. His heart beat with a hollow sound. He willed himself to see and hear the vision sent by Wakanda.

At midday a wind began to blow from the south west. It swept across the open plain to the ledge where Four Winds stood.

The wind was warm and carried with it clouds of red dust which whirled around the boy's face. It tugged at his unbraided hair and whipped strands into his eyes. But still he stood facing the dust storm, arms stretched in prayer.

His stomach was empty now, and his mouth dry. His legs were weak. He stared into the sky, waiting for the messenger to be revealed.

Would it be Elk bringing him the gift of courage? Or the Fox with its cunning? Its brother, the Wolf, for hardiness, or the Night Owl with its wisdom? Whoever appeared would become Four Wind's guide for the rest of his life. He would wear with pride the creature's emblem – feather or claw, tooth or horn.

The wind blew and the sky darkened under the hot, southerly dust storm. The boy stood his ground, though his head spun and the noise of thunder filled his ears. He swayed forward towards the edge of the ledge, unable to see the ground beneath, his heart racing.

'*Wanma yanka yo*!' he yelled above the wind. 'Behold me!'

In a rush of dust and warm air a pale figure appeared above his head.

Through his eyelashes and half-closed lids, Four Winds saw the blurred outline of a four-legged creature. Surely this was his wise spirit, appearing in a cloud from the south. Something large, but not as immense as the buffalo, strong, with a long, graceful neck like the antelope. And long, white hair that fell to one side of the neck, and also formed a flowing tail.

Head swimming, outlines blurred, Four Winds leaned back against Talking Gods Rock.

The creature came and stood beside him. Its large, dark eyes stared calmly into the boy's own.

'I am swift as the Deer, strong like the Buffalo, brave like the Elk. I will not fail you.'

'Who are you?' Four Winds whispered.

The creature tossed his head. 'I am Silver Cloud.'

FOUR

Through the cloud of red dust and the rattle of thunder, the pale horse spoke.

'I am Silver Cloud, sent by Ghost Horse.'

Four Winds pressed himself against the tall rock. He knew this creature. It was the one who had stood on the mountain while he collected water in the wooden bowl. Tall and graceful, separate from the rest.

This dream horse had the same silver grey coat, like morning mist. He carried his head high and arched his strong neck. His ears listened to all the sounds of the world, his dark eyes saw what was invisible.

Still, the boy didn't step forward. He recalled White Deer's warning that a flower may be beautiful, yet kill with its poison. Was this a good spirit, or one sent by Anteep the wicked chief of the underworld?

He reflected, remembering that he had performed the *inipi* and opened his pure heart to the Great Spirit. He had fasted at the sacred rock. All was as it should be.

Besides, he had been sure on the mountain, across a

gap of a hundred paces, that the Great Spirit was present in the pale horse.

'I am Silver Cloud,' the horse said again. The dust storm was dying, the thunder rolling into the distance. 'I will be your guide.'

'My name is Four Winds, of the White Water band, member of the great Sioux nation,' the boy said, his voice shaking. For many winters, since he'd sat among the women in the tipi with warmth from the fire playing on his cheeks, he'd longed for this moment.

'My little Kola, one day you will go out to the sacred rock and seek your dream,' his mother had promised. 'Your vision will guide you and guard you in all that you do.'

Four Winds' fingers lightly touched the lizard skin pouch hanging from his belt. He smiled in gladness at the arrival of Silver Cloud. 'You bring me the wisdom that I need to be a warrior.'

The horse lowered his head. 'Wisdom and courage, strength and speed. I bring all these.'

'*Nagi Ksa pa wan.*' Wise spirit. The boy spoke the words and the beating of wings inside his chest ceased.

'Above all, I bring you loyalty,' Silver Cloud continued. 'I will never fail you. Love sits in my heart.'

Swift as the elk, strong as the buffalo, brave as the mountain lion, loving and loyal like the horse. Four Winds' smile broadened. 'Now I can fight our enemy, the Comanche Wild Dogs!'

Silver Cloud was silent.

'That is the reason for my vision quest,' the boy explained. 'The people of my village are dying in battle. Those who remain are too few. Also, my grandfather, Red Hawk, is old and weak. I must fight in his place.'

Still the dream creature said nothing.

'The medicine of Matotope cannot overcome the troubles of our People,' Four Winds ran on. 'Even his great wisdom fails.'

'All may still be well,' Silver Cloud murmured. 'I bring a message from Ghost Horse. But do not be too eager to enter into battle. Sometimes it is wise to take another way.'

Four Winds went close to the creature. 'I want to be a warrior,' he insisted. 'I wish to walk with my quiver and bow beside One Horn and Running Fox.'

Silver Cloud drew a deep breath through his wide nostrils. He saw the eagerness in Four Winds' eyes. 'Wait. Listen. When I have spoken with Red Hawk who lies sick in his tipi, then you will understand.'

But this answer wasn't enough. 'I must fight Snake Eye on the battlefield. I must fashion my bow strongly and make my arrows fly straight into the hearts of my enemies. In the name of my father, Swift Elk, and that of his cousin, Black Kettle.'

For a moment, doubt crept like a fox into the boy's heart once more. What need did he have of a guardian whose advice would bring shame? For he knew the

Cante Tinz saying, 'Whoever runs away shall not be admitted.'

'Come.' In turn the boy's eagerness to kill saddened the horse. He began to make his way along the ledge under the shadow of Talking Gods Rock.

Four Winds sighed angrily, then followed on unsteady legs. Silver Cloud's hooves clattered against the rock until he reached level ground. The harsh, grating sound brought Matotope down from Spider Rock.

The boy saw the medicine man emerge from the settling dust cloud. Matotope's face was weary and smeared with dirt, his body scratched with thorns.

But when he saw the horse, his hand sprang to his wide belt and he drew out his scalping knife. He raised it over his head, ready to ward off the animal's approach.

Four Winds scrambled to the ground and ran between the man and the horse. 'This is Silver Cloud. The Ghost Horse sent him to protect us,' he explained quickly, afraid of the zig-zag blue lines painted along the blade of Matotope's knife. Such a blade, combined with a bear's head carving on its wooden handle, brought instant death.

The medicine man roughly pushed the boy to one side. 'The Horse is the enemy of the Sioux,' he reminded him. 'Once, long ago when ice covered the earth, this creature roamed with the bison and the bear.

'When the ice melted, the bison became our friend, to feed and clothe us. The bear remained and gave us medicines. But the horse vanished into the underworld, along with Anteep, Thadodaho and all the evil spirits and monsters who had roamed the earth. They descended through a yellow pool in the base of a vast canyon, near to the home of Wakinyan, the Thunder Spirit. Now these spirits return only to destroy our People. Be warned, the Horse is a Killer of Men!'

Though Matotope spat out these words and kept the knife raised above his head, Four Winds sprang up. His head reeled from hunger, his lips were cracked by thirst, but he refused to believe what he had just been told. 'Who taught us that the Horse was evil?' he demanded, stepping once more across the medicine man's path.

'It is written in the Great Law.' Matotope jabbed scornfully at Four Winds with his knife.

The boy dodged sideways, then ran to Silver Cloud. 'Speak the words you have spoken to me,' he pleaded.

'I come from the spirit world to guide you,' the horse told the man, looking him in the eye. 'Trust me.'

Slowly Matotope let the knife drop to his side. But a dark scowl remained on his face. 'Give me proof that you were sent by the Great Spirit,' he insisted. He was angry that Four Winds had succeeded on his first vision quest. Jealousy twisted his heart.

'He who asks for proof does not truly open his mind,' Silver Cloud reminded the shaman. 'The shadow of suspicion clouds his judgement.'

Matotope wondered what to do. Since the creature

had first spoken, he knew that Four Winds' search had been successful and that, as usual, his had not. This was what he had feared when White Deer first approached him. If the boy came to the sacred place in purity and simplicity, then surely he would succeed where Matotope himself had failed.

Red Hawk would lose faith. Matotope would look small and foolish in the People's eyes.

But the medicine man carried the sharp tooth of Coyote among the beads and bones of his medicine bundle. He prided himself on his cunning and trickery. So he disguised his jealousy and returned his knife to its beaded sheath. 'You are right,' he told Silver Cloud. 'I see now that I was mistaken. We welcome you as our guide. What message does the Maker of All Things send?'

'Those words are for the ears of Red Hawk only,' the dream horse replied, looking deep into the shaman's soul. 'We must return to your village on the mountain before the sun goes down and rises again.'

Disappointed, Matotope grunted and cast a glance across the desert plain. In the distance, the dust storm gathered on the ridge, rising and smudging the clear blue sky.

'I will take you to speak with Red Hawk,' he agreed. 'If there is still breath in the old man's body, he will hear you.'

FIVE

The journey home took Matotope, Four Winds and Silver Cloud across the plain by day and into the dusk. Through the night they travelled among rocky foothills and by the winding bank of White Water.

As before, the medicine man made his own way in silence, his face guarded, his thoughts more hidden than ever. The silver moon sailed across a cloudless sky; the river ran deep and treacherous.

In the beginning, Four Winds walked strongly. Now he had cast away childish things and must keep up with the man who walked ahead. Even when Silver Cloud offered to let him ride on his broad back, he shook his head.

'Tell me of the place where the Great Spirit lives,' he said, wanting to hear tales of a world beyond his own.

Silver Cloud began. 'Wakanda lives under the same sun and moon as you,' he explained. 'You can see him in the blue of the sky and the colours of the rainbow.'

Four Winds looked up to the heavens, at the stars and crescent moon.

'And in the night sky,' Silver Cloud said. 'He breathes life into all you see and is not separate from it.'

'He is all around,' Four Winds agreed.

'He binds your spirit to every part of the universe. Your strength, your blood is from the fish and the deer, from the roots and the berries. You were put here beside the White Water by the Great Spirit.'

'He is all around and he is not separate from us,' the boy repeated. He felt cheated of the magical tales his grandmother had told him of a secret entrance to a place where the spirits lived. But he was no longer a child, he reminded himself.

Silver Cloud walked safely by the banks of the rushing river. 'Your grandfather grieves because your People were born into a place of plenty. While you are in it you fare well, whenever you are out of it, whichever way you travel, you fare worse. The White Water country is in exactly the right place.'

'You know all this?' Four Winds was surprised by the dream horse's understanding.

'It is why I answered your call,' Silver Cloud said simply, waiting a while as the boy struggled between boulders. 'Climb on my back,' he said again. 'The way ahead is hard. There is no one here to see.'

Four Winds looked around and found that Matotope had made his solitary way along a different path. There was a streak of grey dawn in the sky behind them, and a desire built within him to reach the village in the mountains before the sun rose.

So with difficulty the boy climbed on to the creature's back, straddling his weary legs wide and holding tight to a piece of the long white mane. He felt high from the ground and strange.

'You are ready?' Silver Cloud asked.

'I am ready.'

The horse set off at a slow walking pace, aware of the boy's fear. He picked his way with care, sure-footed and steady.

Silver Cloud clutched at the mane as the horse's back rolled. His own body slipped from side to side, his legs hanging uselessly as they moved on.

Because of the night and the lightness of his head, he began to tell himself that this was a dream, riding on a strong creature's back, being carried as if he were a child tied warmly inside a blanket to his mother's back, sleeping while she worked.

The boy and the horse entered the village at dawn. Four Winds was slumped against the horse's neck, floating between sleep and waking.

Dimly aware of the tipis on the hill above, he tried to raise himself. But the trees and rocks spun dizzily and his head lay heavy against the horse.

Around them a cold mist swirled. It swept down from the peaks, across the tipis perched on the mountainside and on into the valley. For a time Silver Cloud and

Four Winds vanished from sight, appearing again as ghostly pale grey figures, then melting away in a new surge of cloud.

A hundred paces from the first tipi, Four Winds lifted his head. A sound from behind a rock had startled Silver Cloud and the horse had frozen, ears flat against his head, legs stiff and splayed. Yet, to the boy's dizzy senses there seemed to be nothing there. He urged the horse on.

Still Silver Cloud stood, fixed to the spot between high rocks. He braced his whole body and refused to move.

A loose stone rattled down the hill. The mist came and hid the rocks. When it cleared again, there were five warriors standing high on the rocks, bows strung, arrows aimed at the enemy.

Five arrows aimed at his heart – Running Fox, Little Thunder, Three Bears, Sun Dancer and One Horn! Their bows were strong, their aim true. And they towered over Silver Cloud and Four Winds, their feathered headdresses fluttering in the breeze.

With an effort to steady himself, Four Winds pushed against the horse's neck to raise his body. But weakness overcame him. He fell forward and slipped to one side, feeling his hands lose their grip on the horse's mane. With a slide and a sudden jolt he hit the ground.

And now he was staring up from under Silver Cloud, watching the men he'd known all his life take a new aim at him lying on the earth. He lifted his hand to stop them loosing their arrows.

But the men were afraid. A lookout in the village had come running to their tipis in the grey dawn, telling of the enemy approaching on horseback. The sole Comanche was riding up from the valley surrounded by mist, maybe wounded or sick, though the Horse, the *Shonka Wakan*, was strong. One Horn and the others had taken up their bows and waited behind the rocks.

Four Winds rolled from under the horse. Surely they must recognise him. Facing the ground and hauling himself on to his hands and knees, he felt his arms shake and cursed the weakness of his body. A moment later, his arms gave way and he slumped on the ground once more.

One Horn loosened his bowstring. He saw now that the enemy was young, no more than a boy. And the strange silver grey creature stood alert but not angry, seeming to want neither to attack nor flee. He gestured for the others to lower their aim.

Running Fox frowned. Straining for a clear view of the unknown enemy, he questioned One Horn's decision.

'There is no danger from the boy,' the older brave insisted.

'But from the *Shonka Wakan*?' Running Fox grumbled. 'Why don't we kill it?'

'This horse is not to be feared,' One Horn insisted. He leaped down from the rock and approached quietly.

'Draw your knife!' Little Thunder warned, following him. He took his own blade from its sheath and held it high in the air.'These creatures are one with our enemy, the Wild Dogs. Do not trust it!'

As the mist swept on and the air cleared, One Horn made out the shape of the boy more clearly. He breathed out and let his body relax. 'Put away your knife,' he told Little Thunder. 'This is no enemy.'

Four Winds heard the man's voice as if from a great distance. He felt asleep yet not asleep, conscious of the cold earth against his face, but not able to say who or where he was. Then yes, he remembered danger, and as the man tried to turn him on to his back, he lashed out with his arm

One Horn took the feeble blow with a smile. He lifted the boy in his arms. 'Run to White Deer's tent,' he called to Sun Dancer. 'Tell her to wake Red Hawk from his sleep. This is the boy, Four Winds, back from his vision quest. And say to her that her grandson has brought with him a strange guest!'

White Deer asked them to lay her grandson in the tipi next to Red Hawk's. She covered him in soft skins and built a fire to warm him.

'Where is Matotope?' she asked.

'He did not return,' One Horn replied. 'The silver horse followed us into the village. I have tied him to the cedar tree.'

The old woman nodded. 'He brought Kola back among us. We owe him thanks.'

'I will set the girl, Hidden Moon, to stay by the horse,' One Horn promised. 'It is a strange creature, strong but not angry. It is content to stay close by.'

'Leave me now.' White Deer needed to give Kola medicine. Since Matotope was not here to cure him, she must rely on her own herbs and skills. But she said one more thing to One Horn. 'I believe that this creature is part of the boy's vision quest. Let no one harm him!'

The warrior promised and left the tipi.

'Now, my son, we will make you strong again,' White Deer promised. She stroked the boy's brow and dipped a cloth in pure water from the creek. She wiped his dust-covered face.

So young, she thought. Young and smooth-skinned, with dark lashes closed over his clear eyes. Many times she had sat over him while he slept. She prayed that this would not be the last.

Then she turned to heat a small pot of herbs and water over the fire. Soon a sweet steam rose and she took it to Four Winds where he lay. Cooling the liquid, she dipped in a spoon and trickled the contents between his dry lips. Then she waited.

From his faraway place, Kola tasted the medicine on his tongue. It was sharp yet not bitter. There was a faint sweetness to it. He licked his lips and felt gentle hands pour more liquid into his mouth.

White Deer watched him lick then swallow. She smiled as the boy opened his eyes.

He saw blurred patterns of light and shade, the shape of a face bending over him. He remembered a dust storm at Talking Gods Rock, a wind and thunder overhead. He threw aside the skins and sat upright. 'Where is Silver Cloud?' he demanded.

'Who is this of whom you speak?' White Deer asked, quietly putting aside the dish of medicine. She had already guessed the answer, but she wanted the boy to explain.

'The creature sent by Ghost Horse to guide me. I saw him in my vision. I rode on his back by White Water. Where is he?'

'Hidden Moon is taking care of him. He is tethered by the cedar tree.' The old woman calmed his fears. 'So you succeeded in your quest?' she said with a faint smile.

Four Winds grasped her by the hand. 'Beyond my hopes! The dream horse appeared and spoke to me. He carries a message which he must deliver only to the ears of Red Hawk.'

'Stay!' As Four Winds struggled off the bed, White Deer held him back. 'There is no reason to hurry. Your grandfather sleeps.'

'But when will he wake?' Four Winds could see through the flap of the tipi that the sun was already high in the sky. He wondered if the old man had been sleeping through all the days of his journey to the sacred site.

'He wakes in his own time. When you are old as he is, sleep is a blessing not to be broken.'

'But he must hear Silver Cloud's message!'

'Not now. Soon,' White Deer insisted. 'Rest now. Recover your strength.'

Four Winds realised that no argument he could make would change his grandmother's mind. He lay back on the bed, watching the smoke from the fire curl its way up through the hole in the tipi.

After a while of watching and waiting, White Deer relented. 'You have been patient long enough,' she conceded. 'Now I will go and wake your grandfather.'

The boy got up and went to the door of Red Hawk's tipi with her. There she bade him wait. As she stooped to enter, he looked around and noticed the children staring at him from a distance as if afraid to approach. The women went about their work of grinding grain to eat, and over by a tall tree which stood at the heart of the encampment was his cousin, Hidden Moon, guarding their guest.

Spotting Silver Cloud, Four Winds went across. The horse appeared peaceful despite his rope tether, and there was a look about him which seemed glad to see that the boy had recovered.

The girl too smiled. 'White Deer's medicine was good,' she greeted him. 'When One Horn carried you into the village, the children thought you were dead!'

'Only hungry and thirsty,' he told her. 'Though I would have died truly if an arrow had pierced my chest.'

'One Horn is sorry. They believed you were the enemy because of the creature. They expected to see you return with Matotope, not with the Horse.'

Four Winds shrugged. 'You are not afraid of Silver Cloud,' he noted.

Reaching out her hand to stroke the horse's neck, Hidden Moon shook her head. 'He brought you home,' she said simply.

Just then, a lookout came running from his high rock overlooking the valley. 'Matotope returns!' he cried.

His call was quickly followed by the appearance of the medicine man himself. Matotope strode up the hill full of news. As the men and women rushed to meet him, he swept them aside. 'I must speak with Red Hawk,' he announced. 'Asleep or awake, I will go to his tent.'

'He has had a vision!' the women whispered.

'The vision will save us!'

'The Great Spirit has spoken!'

Knowing this to be untrue, Four Winds ran to catch up with the shaman. As they approached Red Hawk's tipi, the boy stepped in front of the man. 'Your reason for speaking with my grandfather cannot be so great as my own,' he protested. 'We must wait for him to be ready.'

Matotope's eyes narrowed. His expression said that he would waste no time arguing with the boy. Instead, he thrust him aside and entered the tent.

'The Comanche Wild Dogs have broken camp!' he announced in a voice that travelled through the village. 'They are moving through White Water from the east. Snake Eye has vowed to destroy our People!'

There was a silence, then Red Hawk rose from his sickbed and spoke. 'Who has told you this?' he demanded.

'A scout from our brothers, the Oglala Sioux,' Matotope declared. 'I met with him on my journey back from Spider Rock. He is certain that this is true. The Wild Dogs are only ten days away from our village. With horses it will be less.'

'Name the scout,' Red Hawk said, wanting not to believe. 'Give me the reason that you met him on your journey.'

'His name is Nightcloud. I saw him from a high hill and went to cross his path. He carried this news from the Miniconjou, who gave it to him two nights before.'

As Red Hawk listened and considered, Four Winds peered into the tipi. He saw his grandmother supporting the arm of his grandfather, who stood face to face with Matotope.

'We must prepare to fight,' the shaman insisted. 'Though we may all die, we cannot run in the face of the enemy.'

'I hear you,' the old man sighed. He had wished for more days before the final battle. There was perhaps the hope that the Great Spirit would offer His help. 'What news do you bring from the sacred rock?' he asked Matotope.

The medicine man lowered his gaze.

'Did you speak with Ghost Horse?' Red Hawk insisted, leaning heavily on White Deer's arm.

At this, Four Winds entered the tipi. 'I have brought back a messenger from Talking Gods Rock,' he told the old man proudly. 'Ghost Horse chose Silver Cloud and sent him in a vision to me. He waits outside.'

Red Hawk turned his ancient eyes to Matotope. 'This too is true?' he asked in disbelief.

The jealous medicine man raised his head. 'I spoke with Wakanda from Spider Rock,' he lied. 'We agreed that it was good to send a vision to your grandson. That is how it was!'

Staring at his advisor from under hooded lids, weighed down by the passing of years, Red Hawk shook his head. 'How can this be? Why did the Great Spirit choose a boy over the wisest of my band?'

Angrily Matotope drew his painted knife from its sheath and pointed it towards the roof of the tent. 'I have stated the truth!' he declared, then drew the blade between his lips.

Only Four Winds noticed that the shaman prevented the blade from touching his tongue, as was the custom. It was a false oath he had sworn.

The chief turned to his grandson. 'I will come to the door of my tipi. Bring me this messenger,' he ordered.

So Four Winds ran quickly to the cedar tree and untied Silver Cloud. 'It is time,' he whispered, leading the horse to Red Hawk's tent.

The dappled grey creature trod lightly through the camp. There was a spring in his stride and the carriage of his head was noble. He came to a halt where all the people had gradually gathered, in front of the chief's lodge.

'You have a message from Ghost Horse,' Red Hawk began.

Silver Cloud nodded. 'He knows your grief,' he replied. 'He is sorry that our kind have been put to evil use by your enemy the Comanches. He would have you know that the Horse is a loving animal who means well.'

Red Hawk bowed. 'When we leave this place of the White Water for the final time, the valley will ring with our cries,' he lamented. 'It will be a terrible howling when we leave the home that has been ours through all time.'

'It may not be so,' Silver Cloud replied.

Matotope stepped forward to interrupt with his dark scorn. 'So Snake Eye and his Wild Dogs will simply turn their horses away? They will give us our valleys back without a fight?'

'I know nothing of Snake Eye,' Silver Cloud said. 'I come only to deliver the message of Ghost Horse and to put to the chief of the White Water band a new path for the future, without hard times and the trail of tears.'

Once more Matotope laughed without gladness from the hollowness of his spirit.

But Red Hawk silenced him. 'For the welfare of my People and the coming generations, I am happy you have come,' he told Silver Cloud. 'Tell me of this new path without tears and how it can be achieved. But remember, our enemies have rolled their tipis on to their travois and their horses move towards us. There is little time.'

It was Silver Cloud's turn to bow. 'Ghost Horse knows this. Still, he promises a way of saving your people without spilling more blood. He will give you the freedom to live in White Water, the land of your forefathers.'

'Show me this way,' the old man invited, a glimmer of hope lighting his features. He held on to White Deer to steady his shaking limbs.

'Ghost Horse has given me a task which I must complete with the help of your People. You must give me the one you love the most to accompany me on a hard and dangerous journey. If you believe in me with all your heart I will not let you down.'

Red Hawk nodded eagerly. He saw nobility in the dream creature and truth in his large, clear eye. 'Say what is the nature of this journey.'

'It will take me through fire and ice, through thunder and the raging waters to the farthest corners of the earth.' Silver Cloud did not diminish the difficulty of his challenge.

'And what is the task?'

'Following the command of Ghost Horse, through whom the Great Spirit Wakanda speaks, my quest is divided into three. Each part must be completed to save your People. First I must bring back to you a diamond from the deepest mine. Then I will search for an eagle feather from the highest mountain and return it here to you. Last, my journey will be to find a breath of wind from the furthest ocean.'

'And if you do this, my People will be free?' Red Hawk's hand shook and his breath came short.

'Ghost Horse says it is so,' Silver Cloud replied. He gazed at the circle of faces – young and old, all wary, each caught between doubt and the desire for his words to be true. 'Trust me,' he told them. 'I came in a vision to the boy called Kola. My heart is true.'

The sun shone from high in the sky on the painted walls of Chief Red Hawk's tipi. Overhead an eagle soared.

'A diamond from the deepest mine?' Red Hawk whispered.

Silver Cloud bowed his head.

'An eagle's feather from the highest mountain?'

'That is the second task of three,' the messenger confirmed.

'And a breath of wind from the furthest ocean?' The old man sighed. He considered the blue of the sky and the green of the valley below.

'Yes. And you must give me the one amongst you whom you love the most,' Silver Cloud reminded him, preparing to withdraw from the circle of onlookers. 'Think now, and before the sun goes down give me your answer.'

SIX

As was the custom, Red Hawk called a gathering of all his warriors. One Horn, Three Bears, Little Thunder, Sun Dancer and Running Fox came to his tipi, along with Matotope and Four Winds.

The women and children watched them with uneasy hearts. Such a council was usually a preparation for battle. From the cedar tree where she watched over Silver Cloud, Hidden Moon saw with pride her cousin, Four Winds, stoop to enter the painted tipi.

Inside the tent, scented smoke filled the air as a pipe was passed between the men.

Four Winds took in the faces of the braves. There was One Horn wearing the scars of battle with quiet dignity, Running Fox sitting by Matotope, both with thirty summers. They looked tensely at the floor and passed the pipe swiftly between them. Then there was Three Bears with his broad shoulders, the skin of his cheeks and brow tattoed. He was a man who had never known fear. Little Thunder and Sun Dancer were younger, with scarcely twenty summers each, yet their glittering eyes told of things that Four Winds had not yet witnessed.

Sitting in a circle with them, the boy felt humbled.

Red Hawk began to speak. 'You understand well that a spirit horse waits by the cedar tree. You saw the creature come from the valley, from the sacred site called Talking Gods Rock.'

The men bowed their heads and waited. They respected their chief's age and wisdom.

'Silver Cloud travelled with Four Winds to our village. He brings guidance from Ghost Horse, who is close to Wakanda, the Great Spirit.'

Hearing his own name, Four Winds held up his head. He, after all, had been chosen on his first dream quest. He could sit alongside Little Thunder and Sun Dancer without shame.

Across the circle, Matotope looked stern and impatient.

'My brothers, Silver Cloud has described a difficult task. He must face great danger for us and bring back certain sacred objects to bless our band and save us from our enemies. More: I must send the one I love the most to accompany him on his quest.' Red Hawk's gaze travelled around the circle, resting on no one. He knew that each and every one of his warriors would offer themselves for the task, for it would save the People and bring great glory.

In the silence, Matotope took the pipe from the

centre of the ring, a signal to speak. 'What if the creature should fail in his quest?' he asked. 'What then?'

Red Hawk listened and showed with a gesture that his medicine man should continue.

'I was present when the silver horse told of his task,' Matotope explained to the rest. 'He must find a diamond from the deepest mine, a feather from the highest mountain and a breath of wind from the farthest shore.'

A murmur went around the circle. Running Fox and Little Thunder shook their heads.

'We hear from Nightcloud of the Oglala nation that Snake Eye has broken camp and swears destruction on our People,' Matotope continued.

The mood inside the tipi grew darker. This was bad news. Each warrior prepared his mind for the last great battle.

'If we take the advice of the silver horse and wait for his return, Snake Eye draws ever closer. We are few. They are many. Do we sit in our tipis and lay aside our weapons? Do we die in shame?'

'No!' Running Fox declared his opinion without taking the pipe. The word exploded from his lips and he shaped his hand into a fist. 'I will die with my war club raised, not in my tent like a woman!'

'Matotope advises well,' Red Hawk sighed. 'There is this great risk in trusting Silver Cloud.'

Four Winds felt a tightening in his throat. He wished

to speak, but he did not hold the pipe, and besides, his thoughts were confused.

He remembered his desire to fight – the pride of battle carried out in the steps of his father, even the thrill he'd felt at the thought of danger. Tomahawk against tomahawk, blade against blade. There was bloodlust in him which could not be hidden.

But now it was not so simple. Silver Cloud had said there was another way – a great journey, a seemingly impossible mission. And Four Winds felt honoured by the visitation. His vision quest had succeeded and he'd learned to believe his dream horse. So bloodlust gave way to trust and he was left speechless in the circle.

'There is more to say,' Matotope continued, addressing Red Hawk directly. 'Remember how we spoke together three suns since? We know that the horse bears the enemy of our People on his back, that he has sought our destruction along with the Comanche. You believed that this creature had an evil spirit. How is your mind changed so much since then?'

There was a deep frown on Red Hawk's brow. 'I sent you in peace to Spider Rock,' he reminded the shaman. 'The boy went with you. He was cleansed and his heart was pure. So we must believe that the vision is true and the horse, Silver Cloud, is good. Or what is the worth of our beliefs and the beliefs of our fathers before us?'

One Horn took the pipe and spoke. 'This is right,' he declared in a low, steady voice, his eye upon Four Winds.

'But my heart tells me to follow the wisdom of Matotope,' said Running Fox, seizing his turn. 'I would fight like with like, take out a raiding party while Snake Eye sleeps and seize his horses. With these creatures on our side, we will then have a hope of victory!'

Four Winds glanced at Little Thunder, Sun Dancer and Three Bears. Their faces were set in gloomy lines as the arguments flew to and fro. Inside his own head he held the picture of the silver grey horse. So he took the pipe from Running Fox. '*Nagi Ksa pa wan*. The horse is a wise spirit. I know this. He brings us wisdom and courage, strength and speed, but above all he brings loyalty. Love sits in his heart.'

The boy lay down the pipe in the centre of the circle and no one took it up. His words went deep and moved the warriors.

'Do we wait or fight?' Red Hawk asked at last.

'Fight,' said Running Fox.

'Wait,' said One Horn and Sun Dancer.

'Wait,' said Four Winds, feeling the birds beat their frantic wings inside him.

'Fight!' Matotope cast his vote.

'Fight,' Little Thunder echoed.

All heads turned to Three Bears, who sat in deep thought. He had never been defeated in single combat; he wore the ermine pelts and eagle feathers of a great warrior. He was proud and strong.

'Do we take up our bows against Snake Eye, or

do we send Silver Cloud on his quest?' Red Hawk repeated. 'Fight or wait?'

Three Bears kept his eyes closed and head bowed. 'Wait,' he breathed. 'And may the Great Spirit go with him!'

'It is good,' Red Hawk sighed. He had dismissed his warriors from his tent and spoke only to White Deer.

She helped him lie on his bed in the darkened tipi, stroked his brow and soothed him. She saw that the life force had ebbed further. He was an old man clinging to this world hour by hour, minute by minute. But she would not weep.

'Four Winds has done well,' she murmured.

Red Hawk nodded. 'His words must have spoken deeply to Three Bears. For who would have believed that our boldest warrior would hold back from battle?'

'The boy is pure, the horse is true,' White Deer said. 'All will be well.'

So the old man closed his eyes with a peaceful mind. It was good to hold back from sending his braves into what must surely be the valley of death. Instead, Silver Cloud and his companion would guide and save them. When he woke again, Red Hawk would choose the one he loved the most.

'Who will go with the ghost horse?' the children asked. 'Will it be the strongest among us, or the wisest?'

'Perhaps Three Bears, because he wears most pelts on his war shirt,' one suggested.

'Or my brother, Running Fox, for his swiftness and cunning,' another said.

'But Little Thunder and Sun Dancer are younger,' one of the girls pointed out. 'They will not tire as an older man would.'

Hidden Moon sat some distance away, guarding Silver Cloud. She noticed that the children were no longer afraid of their visitor and that the horse regarded their play with interest. He turned his head to watch them run, swished his long, silken tail and snorted softly.

'One thing is certain,' she murmured with regret. 'Red Hawk will not choose me.'

'Because he does not love you?' Silver Cloud asked.

'No. Because I am a girl.'

Her answer surprised him. 'Amongst my people, this would not be so. Many times the mare is leader of the herd.'

Hidden Moon sighed. 'You will find it strange here.' She looked out to the west at the sinking sun. 'Red Hawk sleeps while the warriors fight to go with you. Look.'

Silver Cloud turned to watch Little Thunder arguing with his cousin, Sun Dancer. The two men had emptied their medicine bundles on to the ground and each was claiming greater power.

'I carry a feather necklace!' Sun Dancer cried. 'With

this around my neck, I run light as a feather.'

'And I have this pouch of herbs. When my legs grow weary, I place the herbs in my nostrils and I gain new strength!' Little Thunder boasted.

Sun Dancer seized a bear's claw. 'With this, I can never be weakened!'

'Here is my swallow's head. I fly speedily through my enemies without being touched!' Little Thunder refused to be beaten, and the squabble continued until Matotope himself strode between them.

'Wakanda, I will give you my blood to save my People!' he proclaimed. He made his vow with his right hand raised towards the sun.

His loud voice sent the children running and brought the other warriors from their tipis. Three Bears and One Horn frowned as they approached, while Running Fox looked puzzled by his former ally's swift change of mind.

'So now Matotope wants to accompany the horse,' One Horn said.

'Only to prove that he is above us all,' Three Bears muttered. 'They say that he consulted the skull from the White Sister Medicine bundle. That skull has great power to tell the future.'

'And no doubt the White Sister Skull foretold that Matotope would accompany the spirit horse on his quest,' One Horn grunted, prepared to show openly his growing dislike of the shaman.

'No doubt,' Three Bears agreed.

'I am most powerful among the White Water People!' Matotope swaggered around the cedar tree, knowing that all eyes were on him. 'I talk with the birds of the air and the four-legged creatures. They tell me their secrets so that no man shall defeat me!'

Until now, Four Winds had been talking quietly with his grandmother, waiting for Red Hawk to wake and give his decision. But the sound of the shaman's bragging brought him running. He saw the tall figure strutting around Silver Cloud, who was tethered to the tree, and immediately he grew angry.

Wasn't this the man who had argued against the journey? His doubts had almost swayed the vote and sent the warriors into a hopeless stand against the enemy. Now here he was proclaiming himself fittest to be the horse's friend.

Four Winds slipped through the gathered crowd and went to stand beside Hidden Moon and Silver Cloud.

'I will fight the fiercest enemy and slay the monsters of the underworld!' Matotope shouted, his back to Silver Cloud. 'I will guide this spirit creature to the diamond in the deepest mine and I will return it here to you, my People!'

'Good words,' Three Bears grumbled. 'But deeds must follow!'

Matotope challenged him. 'Who has the most wisdom amongst us?' Delving deep into a goatskin bag slung across his shoulder, the shaman drew out a skull covered in green feathers and smeared with sacred red paint. Dark beads glistened in the hollow eye sockets.

Some in the crowd gasped and cowered away.

'Behold the White Sister Skull!' Matotope shouted. 'Through it I hear White Sister prophesying the future. She has told me that it must be I, Matotope, who guides the dream horse on his quest!'

The boastful words took away Four Winds' breath. Yet who could stand up against the shaman's superior wisdom? Who except for Chief Red Hawk, who was at this moment coming out from his tipi towards the cedar tree.

The boy thought that he had never seen his grandfather look so angry. There was a fire in his pale cheek as he strode ahead of White Deer, who came running after.

'Let the medicine man be silent!' Red Hawk commanded. 'Let this foolishness cease!'

The sight of the tall old man wrapped in a blanket, his white hair braided, his eyes sparking with fury, stopped even Matotope. He had thought him close to death, unable to stand and argue over who should go with the horse. This was why he had come out to swagger and boast.

'I should strike you down with my own war club!' Red Hawk threatened. 'But this old arm is shrunk and I have no strength.'

Matotope drew breath as if to speak.

'Silence! You believe that in my head I am as weak as in my arm? I am Chief Red Hawk still, and though darkness steals over me, I will not give way to empty words and hollow vows!'

'Sit, my husband!' Seeing that Red Hawk staggered, White Deer drew him towards a rock where he could rest.

He stumbled against Silver Cloud, who stood steadily to support him. 'I will stand!' he insisted, his arm around the horse's neck. 'Matotope, I have long prayed to the Great Spirit for guidance. I have fasted, I have held faith in you, wise man of my band of brothers, even though my People fell on Thunder Ridge and at Burning Rock.'

The chief's great anger held the people in a solemn hush. They looked from Matotope to Red Hawk, seeing the shaman shrink back.

'You have brought false word from the sacred site,' the old man went on bitterly.

'No!' Denial set into the shaman's features to hide his shame. 'I have told only what the spirits said.'

'And would Wakanda lead us into battles we could not win? Would he permit us to be driven from White Water into the wilderness? No, you have betrayed me, Matotope. I see with clear eyes that I have been foolish to follow your word!'

'I will not stand and hear these insults!' the medicine

man vowed. He thrust the sacred skull back into its bag and whirled around as if to stride to his tent. He caught a glimpse of satisfaction on One Horn and Three Bears' faces and snarled at them. 'Who has talked against me?' he demanded. A thought struck him and he turned on Four Winds. 'You have spoken evil of me. It was you!'

Four Winds shook his head. 'I have said nothing.'

'It is so,' Red Hawk insisted. 'Matotope, it is your actions only that have brought this shame. Your wisdom has failed this people since the day in battle at Burning Rock when my son, Swift Elk, fell at your side. I do not know the reason and I do not wish to know. The Great Spirit sees all.'

'I am shaman to this People. They trust me,' Matotope insisted, appealing for friends to step forward. 'Running Fox, speak!'

But the warrior drew back and remained silent.

'Matotope, you will leave this place,' Red Hawk said in a slow, sorrowful voice. 'You will not return.'

The shaman recoiled as if from a sharp knife.

'You will go before the sun sets and speak to no one in this village. From this day we cut all blood ties. You have shown the cunning of the coyote and the venom of the snake, and you are no longer brother to the White Water Sioux!'

SEVEN

The sun set slowly over the jagged mountain tops, turning their snowy peaks pink. At the darkening of the day Matotope rolled up his tipi, loaded it on to a travois and harnessed his dogs to drag it out of the village. Then he slung his medicine bundles across his shoulder and set out.

His brothers shunned him, turning their backs in a show of scorn. The man who had sat at the chief's side had proved false and driven their People to their deaths. There was no forgiveness in their hearts.

The shaman drove his dogs between the tipis, his head raised in defiance. He was a tall, thin figure, still splendid in his buckskin war shirt which hung with pelts and was trimmed with beads and porcupine quills. But his face was dark and his mouth bitter.

'Where will he go?' Hidden Moon asked Four Winds.

Matotope stalked past the cedar tree where they stood with Silver Cloud. He stared straight ahead, determined to hide his feelings. A man travelling alone at the approach of winter had much to fear from the mountain lion and black bear. And besides, Snake Eye and his Wild Dogs were sweeping across the plains on horseback.

'He will go into the mountains,' Four Winds guessed, watching the two black dogs strain between the shafts of the sled. However, his whole mind was centred on the choice that his grandfather had to make.

'But he will die,' the startled girl said. 'The cold will kill him.'

Four Winds shrugged. It was as it was.

So Matotope was cast out from the White Water people, to perish in the snowy wastes.

The boy stood closer to Silver Cloud while Hidden Moon went in search of warmth from her tipi fire. She was suddenly cold to the bone in the gathering darkness.

'My grandfather must decide now who will go with you,' Four Winds murmured to the horse. 'There is no putting it off since the sun has sunk behind the mountains.'

'Ghost Horse bid me wait until the North Star appears,' Silver Cloud told him. 'After that I must leave your People and return to the spirit world. You will be left without guidance to face Snake Eye.'

'It is a hard decision.'

'Not to make it is harder still.' The creature spoke kindly, without impatience.

And then White Deer emerged from Red Hawk's

tipi. The whole village had been waiting for the flap to be raised and an announcement to be made, so they followed the old woman's movements as she wended her way through the tipis. She came past the painted war tents of Sun Dancer, Little Thunder and Running Fox without looking. Then she seemed to hesitate close to Three Bears' home.

So Red Hawk had chosen the strongest of all the warriors. Four Winds sighed and bowed his head. He felt heavy with disappointment. His grandfather had chosen strength over youth to aid the dream horse in his quest. Had he, Four Winds, ever stood a chance, he wondered.

White Deer looked at Three Bears sitting outside his tipi, his eyes raised towards her. She shook her head and turned away, walking on to meet One Horn, the wisest and boldest of the White Water warriors.

Four Winds watched his grandmother speak with One Horn. He saw by the sag of the man's shoulders that he was not the chosen one. White Deer reached out her hand and touched his arm, then walked on towards the cedar tree.

Flames from the tipi fires played across her face as she approached Four Winds. A wind tugged at her long woven shawl which she clutched close to her chest. And he could see tears in her eyes when she reached him and stopped.

'Kola, you are the chosen one,' she whispered.

* * *

The boy stood in his grandfather's tipi and felt his lack of years. He remembered the summers playing on the banks of White Water River, the winters spent in this tipi listening to White Deer's stories of Micabo's Island, when Hare took a grain of sand out to sea and made a small island to keep his children safe from Wolf. When Wolf swam after them, Hare made the island bigger. It grew so vast that even Wolf couldn't find Hare and his family, who lived happily and forever on their beautiful island.

Now he couldn't believe such things. He was a warrior and had been chosen.

'You are young,' Red Hawk began in a solemn voice. 'Your war shirt carries no pelts, your bow arm is untried.'

Four Winds lowered his head.

'Yet I will send you out on this journey to find a diamond from the deepest mine.'

The boy felt his heart jump and jolt. He glanced up and met his grandfather's gaze.

'Many voices counselled me inside my head,' the old man confessed. 'There are those here who are stronger than you, my son, and those who are wiser. I have five warriors who might succeed in this task, in whom I would place absolute trust. Wisdom tells me to choose one among them.'

Standing silently in the background, White Deer wrung her hands.

'Then I listened closely to my heart,' Red Hawk continued. 'Silver Cloud comes from Ghost Horse with a message that tells me to choose the one I love the most. I sought in my heart and cast away anger, bitterness and fear. I let only love remain. Then I slept. And when I awoke, there was only one name on my lips, and that name was Four Winds, the son of my son.'

The boy's own eyes were bright with tears. 'May my arm be strong in the service of my People!' he declared.

'Kola, my boy!' White Deer moaned.

'May your spirit be strong also,' Red Hawk counselled. 'You are my blood, my future. You carry with you the lives of all your brothers and sisters, to make amends for my own foolishness.'

'No!' His wife came forward, determined to speak. 'It was not your foolishness but the treachery of Matotope that led our sons to their deaths.'

'I was weak,' Red Hawk insisted. 'For two summers I have secretly questioned the wisdom of Matotope's war medicine, yet I did not speak out. I have paid for that with the blood of my brothers.'

'And must we also sacrifice our son's son, who is little more than a boy? Must we now send him to his death?' Beside herself, moaning and sighing, the old woman pleaded for Red Hawk to change his mind.

'I will not go to my death,' Four Winds argued. 'I will go with Silver Cloud to fetch the diamond. After that,

I will bring back an eagle's feather and a breath of wind. Our people will be saved.'

His words only made White Deer weep the harder.

'Listen, grandmother.' Four Winds spoke again. 'Silver Cloud came to me at Talking Gods Rock. He chose to appear to me there, and now it is right that grandfather sends me on the journey.'

'You say this because your boy's heart is proud. It is a great honour to be chosen. This alone does not make you more likely than another to succeed.'

Four Winds weighed her words. 'I say it is right to be chosen not for that alone,' he insisted. 'But because Ghost Horse demands it. I am the one Grandfather loves the most. Besides, I trust Silver Cloud and he trusts me.'

White Deer looked at him with anguished eyes. 'Kola, there are dangers that you do not know. Evil men and evil spirits will work against you, and your horse protector may not be strong enough to save you.'

But he shook his head and turned to Red Hawk. 'The sun is set,' he reminded him. 'We must leave before the North Star appears.'

The old man nodded and drew the boy towards the fire. 'Come, we must offer a pipe to Wakan tanka.'

Taking up a long-stemmed pipe with his trembling hand, Red Hawk made a rapid chant. 'Wakan tanka, behold this pipe. I ask you to help me.' Then he handed the pipe to Four Winds.

The boy took up the chant. 'Wakan tanka, behold me. I do not want to kill anybody. I only want to save my People. I ask you to help me.' He then returned the pipe to his grandfather.

Red Hawk completed the chant. 'Wakan tanka, I have let my breast be pierced in battle. I have shed much blood. Now I ask you to protect my son's son from shedding more blood. *Wakan yan mica kelo canon pa wan tokeca.* In a sacred manner he made for me a pipe that is different!'

'Now may I go?' Four Winds asked.

'Wait, there is a gift I must give.' Shaking with weariness, Red Hawk crossed towards a wicker box and lifted out his own buckskin war shirt. Adorned with blue and red beads, with a fringe of hair, it was blue on the upper half and yellow below. 'There is honour and authority in this shirt,' he explained to Four Winds. 'I pass it on to you now, my grandson, before my last sun sets. Wear it on your journey and remember me.'

Four Winds took the warm garment and slid it over his head.

Red Hawk delved into the chest and brought out a second object. 'This is my medicine bundle, which I also give to you, my dead son's son. May it protect you as it has protected me.'

The boy slung the bag around his shoulder and made ready.

'Last of all, take this knife from my medicine bundle. Its blade is sharp, its power great.'

With the knife in its beaded sheath strapped to his waist, Four Winds was at last equipped for his journey. His heart hammered against his ribs, his throat was dry.

'*Maka akanl wicasa iyuha el*,' Red Hawk said from deep in his throat. Go in peace. He grasped the boy's arm and looked steadily into his eyes. Then he released his hold.

Four Winds turned to White Deer. 'You are a mother to me. Give me your blessing,' he pleaded.

'My heart breaks,' she wept. 'It cracks in two.'

'Then I will go without,' he decided.

But, seeing that his mind could not be altered, White Deer quickly dried her tears and followed him across the tipi. 'Kola, beloved child of our only child, we love and honour you above all else,' she said in a clear voice. 'Go strongly, my son, and bring back the diamond. In the name of your father, Swift Elk, and of your mother, Shining Star, may Silver Cloud guide you and return you safe to our arms!'

THE SEARCH

EIGHT

'We must go,' Silver Cloud said. The sky was clear, a pale moon was rising.

Four Winds turned from the village and its people and followed the horse down the mountainside.

The eyes of the White Water band were upon him, watching his progress. White Deer stood murmuring at her tipi door, while Red Hawk sat inside. He called upon the Maker of All Things and chanted low and long.

'Return soon,' Hidden Moon whispered, though Four Winds and the horse were already tiny figures moving into the valley below. She pictured herself at Silver Cloud's side, setting out to fetch the diamond. She would be brave as any warrior, she would not tire. Now she stood alone on a rock, her eyes glittering, until the travellers faded into the distance.

Four Winds walked close to the horse, breathing in his warm sweetness. He fell into the rhythm of his companion's movement – a slow, even roll with a steady clip of hooves against the hard ground. Soon his eyes were attuned to the fading light.

'The way is long,' Silver Cloud warned. 'When you tire, I will carry you on my back.'

'Later,' Four Winds insisted. For the moment he was glad to walk under the canopy of stars, listening to the small creatures of the bush startle at their approach. A ground squirrel darted out from under Silver Cloud's heavy feet. The eyes of a ring-tailed raccoon glittered from a tree.

'We must travel south,' the horse explained. 'Bear, guardian of the west, has told me that diamonds lie in the hot lands where the sun is strong. They are deep beneath the earth. We will leave the air and descend into tunnels of rock to find the stones that glitter.'

Four Winds' skin prickled at the idea of being closed in, with the earth resting on his head. But that was far ahead, he told himself. There were many miles to travel before then.

As they gained the valley and trod alongside the river, Silver Cloud grew used to the boy's actions. Studying the slender, black-haired figure closely, he saw that two legs were not so good as four for carrying a creature's weight, but that two arms helped for pulling aside branches and taking hold of rocks and casting them from the narrow gulleys through which they passed. He found that the boy was agile and could swim across water where the current was less strong, and that he could climb nimbly and reach lookouts that his own size and weight prevented.

It took the horse longer to begin to understand the workings of the boy's mind, however. Why, for instance, did he want to walk when it only tired him? The reason seemed to be linked with a thing called pride, which puzzled Silver Cloud. It also amused him to see Four Winds stumble in rocky places where the ground was uneven. Yes, there was no doubt that two legs held you back on a long journey and to be needlessly proud was a kind of blindness.

'Will we cross the plain and pass by Spider Rock?' Four Winds stopped to catch his breath on the bank of the river. He stopped to scoop water into his palm and drink.

'No. Our journey takes us along Thunder Ridge and by Burning Rock, where your father fell in battle.'

Four Winds frowned. 'Snake Eye came in the night and raided our old village. We had thirty men against a hundred Comanches. The blood of our People stained the earth.' He recalled the time of thundering hooves and raised tomahawks. He had hidden in the bushes and watched the slaughter. The world had wept rain, the wind had howled.

In the morning, One Horn, his face freshly bleeding, had brought Swift Elk's war bonnet to him. The warrior had been pale as the grey dawn, except for the slash of scarlet on his cheek. With two hands he had placed the slain brother's headdress across Four Winds' outstretched arms.

'Why does your grandmother give you a different name?' Silver Cloud asked now. He had read the pain in the boy's silence as he drank by the river.

Four Winds broke out of his thoughts. 'Kola? That is my childhood name. It means "friend", and she teases me with it still.'

'Teases?' the dream horse inquired.

'She makes people smile to remember that I was once a child at her knee, now that I am grown tall.'

'Kola,' Silver Cloud repeated. He waited a while then spoke again. 'It is a good name.'

Little Kola. Little friend. Four Winds stood up and drew in the fresh night air. Moonlight shone on the horse's dappled coat and shot streaks of silver through his white mane. His calm, kind eye looked straight at him. 'You may call me by that name,' he said shyly. 'For I am your friend, and you are mine.'

Matotope stood by the medicine wheel on Thunder Ridge. He had not walked west into the mountains, as the people of his village had expected, but south east towards Snake Eye and his Wild Dogs band. In one hand he held his long shield of buffalo hide, in the other his blue painted knife.

The clear night sky lit up the circles of white stone which marked out the wheel. One spoke pointed south towards Spider Rock, another east, far across the plain. The shaman walked slowly into the centre of the circles and raised both arms high.

'Thadodaho, behold me!' he chanted. 'Oh, priest of death and revenge, great spirit of Anteep of the underworld, come to me!'

A wind blew the fringed sash which he wore across his bare, broad chest. There were strips of decorated leather around his strong wrists, and a string of sharp mountain lions' teeth hung from his neck. On his head, falling low over his brow, its pelt trailing down his back like a cloak, Matotope wore the hollowed head of a wolf.

'I call upon Thadodaho. I swear bloody revenge on my enemy, Chief Red Hawk of the White Water band of the Sioux nation. Bring death to the People who have flung me out into the wilderness. May their children and their children's children be wiped from the earth!'

In the sky above a low wind moaned.

'Come!' Matotope cried.

The air whirled around him. Dust rose along the ridge and the noise of thunder rolled through the heavens.

The outcast's heart beat louder. The vision gathered force, the spirit of Thadodaho was about to appear.

Out of the gloom a shape appeared. Three times the size of a man, it towered above Matotope. On its head a thousand black snakes writhed. 'Anteep has sent me to hear what you say,' the monster whispered. 'Speak then.'

Terror beat the breath out of the medicine man's body. He felt that his heart would break through his chest. Yet hot revenge conquered his fear. 'I wish to follow the spirits of the underworld. I will enslave myself to evil, since Wakanda, the Great Spirit, has turned from me.'

Thadodaho's snakes curled and hissed. Their tongues spat venom. Where it fell, it burned into the rock and made it crumble to dust. The monster reached out its claw like that of a giant bear, forcing the shaman to kneel. 'I look into your heart and I see evil has taken root.'

Matotope's wolf head bowed towards the ground. He felt drops of the monster's venom fall on his shoulders and eat through the skin. He flinched but didn't move. 'I hate the White Water people. Their chief is old, weak and foolish, their warriors waste to nothing. And now they have sent a boy of thirteen summers to seek a treasure which will save them!'

Overlooking the shaman's scorn, Thadodaho gripped his arm and raised him from the ground. 'You speak of treasure!'

'A diamond from the deepest mine. It is as Ghost Horse wishes.' He trembled helplessly, knowing that this monstrous vision could slay him in an instant. 'Ghost

Horse has sent his messenger, Silver Cloud, to help the boy named Four Winds. If they succeed in their quest, Wakanda will return Red Hawk to his White Water homeland. Snake Eye and his Wild Dogs will be pushed back whence they came.'

A cruel smile crept over the monster's face. 'Don't be afraid. This boy will not succeed, even with his spirit guide.'

Finding himself flung to the ground, Matotope scrambled to his feet and begged for an explanation. 'What is to stop Silver Cloud and the boy from entering the mine?'

'All the serpents, lizards, ghosts, frogs and owls of the Yellow Water,' Thadodaho roared. His breath swept along Thunder Ridge, blasting autumn leaves before it. 'The deepest mine is far south from here, where the sun scorches the earth. There, in the Black Mountains, the water monster whose name is Unktehi keeps guard. His power belongs to the water. Even the spirits of the air cannot trouble him. He is all-powerful.'

This answer pleased the shaman, yet he knew that powerful monsters might still be beaten by trickery. If Silver Cloud and Four Winds could outsmart Unktehi, then the route through the dark earth to the diamond would lay open. 'Will you go with me to this place?' he pleaded. 'That between us we might kill the boy and destroy the dream horse?'

Thadodaho raised a mighty wind to lift him into the

night sky. 'Go alone,' he advised. 'There is a strong evil in your heart, bitter enough to poison a boy who has only thirteen summers. Kill him and leave Silver Cloud to me.'

Matotope nodded eagerly, though the wind made him cower against a rock. 'I will go!' he promised.

'I am there already,' Thadodaho hissed from under his halo of snakes. Thunder shattered the night sky and he was gone.

Daylight stole into the valley where Kola and Silver Cloud walked. A small herd of antelope grazing in a green clearing raised their heads and stared at the two intruders. Their strange appearance frightened a young doe, who bounded away and set the others leaping after her. White rumps flashed between the thin trunks of the cottonwood trees, and they were soon gone.

'When the sun rises in the east and climbs in the sky we will leave this valley,' Silver Cloud told Kola. 'We will come out on to a vast plain, where the grass grows like a great ocean. We must cross it as fast as we can. By nightfall we will reach the Black Mountains.'

The boy recognised that this was the horse's way of saying that he must ride on his back. And now he was not too proud to accept, knowing that the horse, like the antelope, could travel at speed across the flat, open land.

So when the heat came and the hills were behind them, Kola rode again. Once more he sat astride Silver Cloud and felt the horse cover the ground at a walk. The sway of his broad back was easy, though his head was alert to every movement and sound on the way ahead.

'Take hold of my mane,' Silver Cloud told the boy as he prepared to gain speed.

Kola obeyed, seizing the silken white hair and holding tight. Suddenly the horse picked up his hooves in a smooth trot which took Kola by surprise, then made him smile to himself. He was glad there was no one to see his clumsiness. He wondered for the first time how the Comanche people had learned to be so graceful on horseback when they swept to victory in battle.

The thought made him study the problem more closely. He found that if he kept his torso upright and sat down deep in the curve of Silver Cloud's back, leaving his legs relaxed, then the motion of his own body didn't fight against that of the horse. In fact, he was riding smoothly again, finding his balance and letting Silver Cloud take a longer stride.

'At last!' the dream horse commented. The jolting on his spine had bothered him. 'Now can we go faster still?'

Kola took a deep breath then agreed. He took in the sea of grass ahead and what looked like small clouds gathering on the horizon.

'If you fall, land softly,' Silver Cloud warned. 'Choose a place where there are no rocks and plenty of grass!'

The horse broke into a lope, rocking to and fro in a motion that ate up the ground beneath his feet. His tail streamed out behind, his head was thrust forward, ears pricked to pick up hidden signals ahead.

A thrill went through Kola's body. This was how it felt to be an elk or deer running free across the plain. And now, quite close and growing louder, he heard the beat of buffalo hooves cutting across their path. So it had been dust gathering on the horizon, not rain clouds – a huge herd of bison moving over the land.

The boy knew how these great animals travelled. There would be many of the huge, woollen-headed, horned creatures gathered together, as far as the eye could see. Their passing would not be quick, unless they stampeded, and then there would be danger for all in their path. 'We should choose another way,' Kola advised Silver Cloud, who had also recognised the herd.

'Why? The buffalo is a friend to your people.'

'That's true. Their meat is our food. With their skins we clothe ourselves and build our tipis. They are givers of life.'

'Then we can meet with them without fear,' Silver Cloud decided. Instead of slackening his pace, he broke into a gallop which made Kola feel as if they were flying through the air.

A warm wind caught in the horse's white mane and in the boy's braided hair. Kola leaned low over Silver Cloud's long neck and held tight.

Soon they could pick out small groups of buffalo grazing apart from the main herd. The creatures raised their heavy heads to sniff the air and went back to their sweet, dry grass. Then Kola and Silver Cloud were in amongst them, surrounded by the flat-backed creatures whose hooves raised a cloud of grey dust wherever they went. Kola felt the heat rise from their bodies, could almost reach out and touch their tough black hides, except that Silver Cloud picked his way swiftly between them, leaving Kola no time.

At last they were through the herd and travelling on. A faint outline of hills appeared in the distance and a new river snaked across the plain. 'Are those the Black Mountains?' Kola asked eagerly.

Silver Cloud said that they were. 'The first place we come to is Crow Ridge, and after that is Burning Rock. Beyond the foothills, the Black Mountains begin. And there, in a great canyon, is Yellow Water and the entrance to the deepest mine.'

Kola felt his heart race. He wondered about the dangers that the dream horse had described. Where were the storms, rock falls and fires that came out of the mountains? Might they still have to face these, and waters that roared? For the moment, all was calm and the sun shone over their heads.

At midday, Silver Cloud drank from the river. He rested amongst willows while Kola strode up a grassy hill and stared towards the mountains.

The boy tried to make out details among the jagged, pale purple hills. His keen eyes saw snow on the highest peaks and many dark shadows that meant deep canyons split the rock. But he didn't remember in which of the foothills his father had died.

His attention was caught by a movement far to the east. A spit of rock rose from the plain and formed a low ridge along which a large creature was moving. Kola shaded his eyes from the sun and looked more closely. Could it be a buffalo cut off from the herd? Perhaps an elk which had wandered far from the highland passes?

But the boy saw with a shock that it was a man on horseback, who had stopped his brown-and-white mount to stare across the prairie in his own direction. Kola shrank back as he realised that he might have been spotted by one of Snake Eye's men. He was about to run and warn Silver Cloud when a second figure appeared on the ridge.

This man was on foot. He drew the rider's attention and walked towards him, demanding to be heard. The rider stopped to listen and look in the direction in which the second man pointed. Something in the manner of both figures suggested urgency.

Then after more talk, during which the rider seemed

to forget all about Kola, the man on foot vaulted on to the back of the horse. Both were now mounted, turning down the ridge on to the flat grassland, where they set the horse off at a gallop towards the mountains.

The boy stayed just long enough to make sure that they didn't wheel back and pick up his trail. When he saw that their path was straight, he ran down to the river to join Silver Cloud and describe what he'd seen.

But his companion had other things on his mind. His head was up and he was smelling the air attentively, looking towards the grassy hill and the spit of rock beyond. 'Did you see fire up there?' he asked the boy.

Kola shook his head. 'I saw two men.'

'There is smoke in the wind,' Silver Cloud insisted. He told Kola to climb on his back and together they went up the hill.

This time, when Kola looked towards the spit he did see smoke. A thin trail rose from behind the rock and drifted on the wind until it entered his nostrils.

'The men set a fire,' Silver Cloud concluded. 'It will reach over and around the rock, and eat all in its path.'

Sure enough, the smoke soon thickened and curled around the spit of high land. Flames appeared, licking at the dry grass and roaring as they consumed sagebrush and willow. Wind buffeted the fire, feeding the flames, which now rose three men's height into the air and advanced towards Kola and Silver Cloud.

Kola felt fear twist inside his belly. This meant that the Comanche enemy had spotted them and chosen fire as their weapon to drive the travellers back. Already the smoke had entered his lungs. The wind carried fire faster than any animal could run; the flames ate trees and left nothing but charred black land.

Silver Cloud was also afraid. Fire was the thing which a horse feared above all. It choked and blinded, roared in the ears, ate flesh. So his instinct told him to flee in the face of flames. 'Hold tightly,' he ordered, whirling around, only to discover that the fire had run quickly along the river bank and cut off their retreat.

Water would have saved them. They could have swum across the river and watched in safety as the land on the opposite bank burned. But the sly Wild Dogs had judged the wind correctly, knowing that their victims would first seek the higher land as a lookout point, before they withdrew to the river. By then, the flames would have surrounded them and there would be no escape.

Silver Cloud carried Kola down the hill, towards the only gap in the flames. A screen of hot, black smoke met them, too thick to see through. The horse put his head down to the ground, feeling Kola fall forwards on to his neck but still cling on, as they made for the ever narrowing gap.

Orange flames licked and roared. They were all around, the ground crackling and sparking, the sap from the trees hissing and spitting. Overhead, a huge plume of smoke gathered.

Silver Cloud galloped on through the scorching heat. There was still a way out, if only they could hold their breath long enough. Behind and to either side, the flames leapt. Tall trees cracked and their burned branches crashed to the ground.

Kola felt sparks shower down on him. He saw Death hold out his hand in welcome.

And then Silver Cloud was through the dark gap, clear of the circle of fire. The flames were behind and they were galloping on, almost blind, sucking in clean air at last. Rocks towered to either side, fencing them in, and a barrier of trees slowed them to a trot.

Kola raised his head from the horse's neck and took in the narrowing cliffs, the slender trees reaching skywards from their gloomy canyon. He felt Silver Cloud slow to a cautious walk through the cottonwoods, saw tumbleweed roll and drift against the bare rock walls. Then the shadows closed in and the horse and the boy came to a sudden halt. A cliff cut across their path.

They turned to see giant flames engulf the rocky entrance to the canyon. Smoke billowed behind them and tongues of flame reached into the gulley. There was no way out.

NINE

Now Kola experienced the true meaning of fear. He was a boy who had known hunger and thirst, the cold of the snow and the glaring heat of the summer sun. He had seen killing and he had hidden in bushes to escape being killed. But still he wasn't prepared to meet death by fire.

He gasped when he saw the flaming entrance to the canyon and slid from Silver Cloud's back. His first thought was to find a way to climb to safety.

The dream horse saw the boy dart in panic to the cliff and search for footholds. He glanced upwards towards a deep overhang. Climbing was no solution, even for a boy with nimble hands to grasp the rock. For a creature with four legs, the way was impossible.

It was time to call on help from the spirit world, he decided. If the *kachinas* came quickly, then all might be well. So he spoke through the thickening smoke to the spirits of the air. 'I call to the clouds and the rainbows, bring me speedily to he who wears a mask of green jade, bring me to Olmec, the great spirit of the desert!'

Straight away a fresh wind came to hold the flames at bay. It blew strongly down the canyon and fought against the fire. With it came a gathering of white clouds overhead and an arching rainbow of reds, yellow, green and blues.

Silver Cloud stood in the bottom of the canyon, grateful to the friendly air spirits, the *kachinas* upon whom he had called. He watched their clouds grow thicker and thanked the power of Olmec, half jaguar, half man, he of the jade mask who lived in the south. 'Give us rain to kill this fire,' he pleaded, 'for our journey is great and our enemy strong.'

The cool wind blew. Kola looked up from a narrow ledge and saw the rainbow, saw the magic of the sky and a faint jade face in the clouds. He clung to the rock in awe.

'Bring us rain!' Silver Cloud called to the powerful spirits of the air.

The invisible *kachinas* heard and breathed raindrops into the clouds. The drops began to fall on the baked earth inside the canyon. They spattered on the dry rock and in the leaves of the trees. Then they fell faster and a wind drove them down the gulley towards the flames. The hot earth hissed, the host of rising sparks was deadened.

Kola felt the cold rain on his hands and shoulders. He turned his face from the sky to watch the battle between rain and fire at the entrance to the canyon.

'More rain still!' Silver Cloud pleaded. The flames had fought back with a hot roar that had reached them and made them cower against the rock. Kola closed his eyes.

The separate drops became a drenching torrent, blown in sheets by the breath of a thousand *kachinas*. The fire died back, flared up and fought again in the shelter of boulders and overhanging ledges.

But both Kola and Silver Cloud knew that the flames were weaker, that they might dart through the dry grass and catch at tumbleweed, but that the water would defeat them. They heard the angry hiss of the dying flames, saw the grey, powdery ash turn black under the downpour.

They breathed freely, watching the rain ease and the rainbow fade from the sky.

Matotope looked down with disgust as the boy and the horse travelled on through the scarred landscape.

He stood alone on Crow Ridge in the foothills to Black Mountains, awaiting the arrival of Snake Eye.

For now, the shaman's anger concentrated on Anteep's servant, the serpent-headed monster, Thadodaho, who had promised that Silver Cloud and Four Winds' quest for treasure would end in failure.

After his chance meeting on the plain with Snake Eye's scout, Wicasa, Matatope had had high hopes. He had told the Wild Dogs' messenger that a boy from the

White Water band was travelling across the plain by horse. Wicasa had gone to his chief and told the story of the boy's journey to the deepest mine. And Snake Eye had swiftly devised a plan to destroy the travellers with fire.

Matotope had taken delight in the grim death which lay in wait for the grandson of Red Hawk.

But then he had watched the rainbow appear in the sky and immediately he had known that the *kachinas* were at hand. The rain had fallen and Thadodaho, for all his fine words on Thunder Ridge, had done nothing to prevent it.

So now the shaman had demanded to meet the great warlord, Snake Eye, face to face. If the evil spirits would not provide the power that was needed, then Matotope's revenge must be completed by the hand of man.

He grew impatient as he waited, knowing that Silver Cloud and the boy were moving on, growing closer to the mine by the Yellow Water. His memory flitted back to the arrival of the spirit horse at the sacred site, how his heart had twisted with envy of the boy. Then he recalled Silver Cloud's message from Ghost Horse, and how it had happened that Four Winds had been chosen above him once more. There was disgrace in that and shame had pierced him.

The sun sank low in the west as Matotope bitterly remembered. He forgot that he had tricked Red Hawk with false wisdom and dwelt only on the black anger he had felt when his chief had exiled him for ever.

How long would proud Snake Eye keep him waiting here? Was this another insult to add to all those that had been heaped upon him? With narrowed eyes and a deep scowl, he awaited the approach of horses' hooves.

The Black Mountains loomed larger as Silver Cloud and Four Winds left the plain and entered the foothills. They were no longer a hazy purple, as from a distance, but a dark red like the red of war-paint smeared on the faces of Comanche warriors. The shadows lengthened and the air grew cool.

Silver Cloud entered the mountains after a long day spent crossing the plain. He and Kola had survived the fire set by the Wild Dogs, but the effort had tired them both. Fear had drained their energy, and still the acrid smell of smoke lingered. It was in his coat and mane, and on the clothes of the boy – a charred, dead smell that brought back to mind the leaping flames of the canyon.

They needed to sleep, but the mountains offered little shelter. Trees were scarce, scattered up the rocky slopes, their roots twisting out of the dry, crumbling earth. Deepening shadows of rocky pinnacles spread across the narrow valley, and overhead a black raven soared.

'We must rest at the first water,' Silver Cloud told

Kola. 'We have journeyed through the night and the day without food. Now it is time to stop.'

Reluctantly Kola agreed, sliding to the ground and easing his legs. They would find a place by a creek and he would pick berries. Grass would be there for the horse to eat. 'Tomorrow will we reach the lake called Yellow Water?' he asked anxiously.

'Perhaps.'

'How deep into the earth must we travel?'

'We will not know until we arrive.' Silver Cloud's ears picked up the sound of running water to the east. As he made his way towards the water, he warned the boy that there were many obstacles still to overcome. 'I must tell you of evil spirits guarding the place, and of Unktehi, the water monster who lives below the lake. He will not let us pass without challenge.'

'Does he guard the diamonds?' Kola asked.

'Yes, he and his spirits bar the way. Many men have tried to enter, but most die at Unktehi's hand. The others return to their People with empty eyes and horror fixed in their hearts.'

Kola felt his courage flicker and fade.

The horse saw this. 'Don't be afraid. I am here to guide you.'

'Then I will be strong,' the boy decided.

But that night, as he lay on the ground beside the creek, staring up at the stars, his heart would not be still.

* * *

'Give me a reason why I should trust you.' Snake Eye drew Matotope towards the fire burning inside a circle of stones. His face was painted white with narrow black streaks running from his forehead to his chin. A slash of red crossed his mouth and stretched from ear to ear.

His men had ridden to Thunder Ridge and seized the shaman. They had bound him with strips of hide and dragged him back to the camp behind their horses. Then they had shown him, bleeding and covered in dirt, to their chief.

'Take off these ropes!' Matotope snarled. Wicasa, the messenger, had betrayed him with false promises of a meeting on the ridge. Instead of Snake Eye himself, a group of four young riders had returned and overcome him. Now all of the Wild Dogs band had gathered round the camp fire to look and listen.

'Give me good cause,' Snake Eye repeated, taking his knife from its sheath. He dug the blade into the earth and studied the outcast closely.

'I come with news of the White Water People, to tell you of their plan to defeat Snake Eye and send him back across the plains.

'Ha!' Grey smoke rose from the fire and hid the chief's face. But there was scorn in his voice. 'Red Hawk has few warriors, his People are weak. Soon Snake Eye will drive them into the snow and they will die there.'

Matotope felt the leather strips bite into his wrists.

There were many men here who would raise their knives and strike. He must talk with a smooth, silver tongue to escape death.

'That was so,' he admitted. 'But now there is a dream creature sent by Ghost Horse. Wicasa has seen him, your People have set fire to the grass to drive him back.'

Snake Eye looked around the circle, at men with braided hair and painted bodies. Beyond the thin screen of smoke, their faces scowled with suspicion at the disgraced shaman. The chief picked out his scout who sat cross-legged, leaning on the long staff of his tomahawk.

Wicasa nodded and said this was so. 'The dream horse brought rain from the *kachinas* to quench the flames. He travels south into the mountains with a boy.'

Quickly Matotope laid out more facts. Then he demanded a second time to be untied. He felt that here, in the heart of the enemy camp, he could seal new alliances that would lead to his final revenge.

Snake Eye gestured to the nearest man, who leaned forward and cut roughly through the bonds. The news that the White Water band had earned the help of Ghost Horse troubled him. Now his plan to drive Red Hawk into the mountains would not be so easy. 'Why do you, medicine man to the White Water People, come here to tell me this?' he demanded.

'They are no longer my brothers,' Matotope said

hastily. 'They have poured shame upon me and my thoughts are black.'

'You would help us?' The red slash across Snake Eye's mouth stretched into a cruel smile. His hair hung in many beaded braids. He wore crow feathers at his waist and a loincloth of antelope hide.

Matotope raised his head proudly. 'Without my help you will fail,' he warned.

Snake Eye let a silence hang in the smoky air. He knew there was no honour in this man, and yet he could be useful. So he bade one of his men to begin a slow beat on his drum. Another, who wore a cap of wolfskin and rings of silver in his ears, chanted in a low voice.

The rest rose and began to dance, raising their arms to the night sky, calling on Anteep, great spirit of the underworld.

'Come,' Snake Eye said to Matotope, guiding him towards his tipi. 'We will speak more.'

TEN

Two nights had passed and now the sun rose on the second day of Silver Cloud and Four Winds' journey. Instead of open plain they faced narrow canyons between rugged cliffs. For soft grass underfoot there was stone and dust.

Kola woke from a shallow sleep. His dreams had been filled with suspicion and uneasy dread of creatures invented by his own imagination. The monsters were shadowy beings who lurked in the darkness. They had sharp teeth and claws, matted hair and slimy, scaly skin. They crushed their prey between powerful jaws.

So his head spun and his limbs ached when he stood to find the silver horse already feeding by the water's edge. The sight of him helped calm the boy, who recalled Silver Cloud's promise that he would never let him down.

The horse was graceful in its habits. Every swish of his long tail and twist of his supple neck were beautiful to behold. How could such a noble animal harbour disloyalty?

More ready now to continue the quest for the diamond, Kola went down to the water where he washed his face and drank deeply. He seemed to Silver Cloud vulnerable as he stooped there. A boy, not yet fully grown, with smooth skin and dark, clear eyes. His body still had to put on muscle, his legs were as long and thin as a colt's. And yet Red Hawk had honourably chosen him for this journey, according to the condition that Ghost Horse had laid down. It had been the greatest sacrifice that the old man had had to make, to risk the life of his only son's son. The grandmother had wept bitter tears.

Silver Cloud gave Kola time to finish bathing then search for berries and roots to fill his stomach. At last he told him that it was time to move on. 'We have far to travel,' he reminded him, inviting the boy to climb on his back. 'Yellow Water lies in the heart of these mountains, at the bottom of a canyon so vast that it seems the whole world must split in two. It is a hard journey in the heat of the sun.'

Kola prepared himself. By now he had grown used to the sensation of riding the horse and felt that by minute changes of balance he had become part of the creature's rhythmical motion. There was a harmony between them now.

Silver Cloud's hooves clipped against stones and crunched over sandy gravel. All around, sharp pinnacles of rock rose, their layered bands making strange patterns on the silent landscape. This was no place for antelope or buffalo, Kola thought, but for small lizards basking in the sun and for snakes who hugged the shade.

Yet he felt after a time that he and Silver Cloud were being observed. He would look up at the nearest ridge and there would be no one there, only a suspicion that hidden eyes were looking down on them. This went on for many hours, as the fierce sun went on climbing in the deep blue sky.

At last Kola confided in Silver Cloud. 'There are eyes in the mountains. I don't see them, but I feel them.'

'You are right,' the horse agreed, without showing any concern. 'A man has followed us since dawn.'

Kola's gaze raked the horizon. The observer, whoever he was, was softer than a shadow, swifter than the wind. There was nothing to see except ravens wheeling overhead.

'He is to the west, in the shade of the overhang. He knows the mountains well,' Silver Cloud observed, as calmly as before.

The boy shot a look in that direction. The overhanging rock was only two hundred paces away. 'What does he want?'

'We cannot tell until he has spoken with us.'

'When will that be?'

'When he chooses.' Silver Cloud stopped, perhaps to invite the hidden observer to show himself.

As the heat beat down upon them in the still air of

the canyon, Kola grew afraid in spite of Silver Cloud's untroubled words. Who but the Wild Dog Comanches knew they were here? Why would anyone shadow them without showing himself? Slowly wrapping his fingers around the carved handle of his grandfather's knife, he grew ready to use it.

But almost before he prepared, the man appeared from under the overhang. With hair braided simply, wearing no war paint or war shirt, but only fringed deerskin trousers and soft moccasins, he bounded down from the shady rock into the full light of the sun.

Kola saw at a glance that this could not be one of Snake Eye's men. No enemy would show themselves in this way without wielding a tomahawk or bow and arrow. Nor would he be alone.

'I am Nightcloud of the Oglala Sioux!' the man announced. 'I am your brother.'

Thankfully Kola removed his hand from his knife. He relaxed as Silver Cloud walked up to the man called Nightcloud, who was nimbly scrambling down the rocky slope to meet them. 'You bring us news from the Oglala People?' he asked.

Nightcloud nodded. Hardly breathless, he offered the hand of friendship to Four Winds. 'It was I who sent word to Red Hawk to warn him that Snake Eye had broken camp.'

'I remember.'

'I watched the Comanches and their horses, knowing that they planned to sweep west into the mountains beyond White Water.'

'My grandfather thanks you,' Kola told him. 'But this is nothing new. What else?'

Nightcloud frowned. 'Now I am puzzled,' he confessed. 'The Wild Dogs rolled up their tipis and began to head west as I expected. But then they changed direction. Snake Eye ordered a new camp by Thunder Ridge. He sent men to set flames to the grass and make a great fire.'

'He hoped to trap Silver Cloud and me,' Kola explained. 'But he did not succeed.'

'This I also saw,' Nightcloud said, looking with respect at the dream horse. 'But surely this would not be enough to delay Snake Eye more than one day in his eagerness to defeat your People. Yet still he stays by Thunder Ridge and does not move west.'

The news surprised Kola. He decided to trust his cousin, Nightcloud, by telling him of the reason for his journey with Silver Cloud. 'The lives of my People depend upon our success,' he explained. 'With the diamond, we will be stronger. And then we will bring back the feather and the breath of wind, and Snake Eye will have no power over us.'

'Then the Wild Dogs have learned this,' Nightcloud pointed out. 'Why else would they delay over a mere boy and one horse?'

'But how could they know?' Kola felt a cold shock run through his body. His skin began to sweat.

Nightcloud shook his head. 'I only tell what I see. I watch from afar, I do not listen to their reasons.'

Kola thought hard. 'If you, Nightcloud, can follow our trail, then so can Snake Eye,' he said slowly.

'Yes, but I have not seen Comanches enter the Black Mountains,' the Oglala scout assured them. 'I have waited since dawn for them to follow you, but no man has set foot in these canyons. My warning is only that Snake Eye rests by his tipi and has not travelled west.'

'We thank you,' Kola told him. The bad news meant that he and Silver Cloud must hurry ahead. 'We hope that one day the White Water People will be able to repay our debt to our Oglala brothers.'

Nightcloud bowed his head. He had treated Four Winds as an equal, yet he wondered at his youth. To learn that the future of Red Hawk's band sat upon the shoulders of an untried boy had caught him by surprise. It was news he must take back to Skidi, leader of his band. Raising his head again he spoke the words that meant, 'May the good spirits guide you,' then he stepped back and melted into the shadows.

Four Winds and Silver Cloud journeyed on towards the great canyon in the heart of the Black Mountains. Water grew scarcer as the creeks dried to narrow trickles, and nothing except cacti grew in the sandy earth.

Silver Cloud knew that in the heat of the early afternoon Kola was tiring. He sensed too that the scout's message had raised fresh fears and that the boy was tensely waiting for the Wild Dogs to appear. So he thought to amuse him with a tale.

'There was once a Chief who had a vain and beautiful daughter called Proud Girl,' he began. 'The father chose for her a husband whose name was Bold Eagle.'

'I have heard this story at White Deer's knee,' Kola interrupted impatiently. 'It is for children when they sit around the fire.'

'And for weary travellers and all who care to listen,' Silver Cloud instructed. 'There is laughter in the story to raise a smile, and to carry us on our journey.'

So Kola let the horse continue.

'But Proud Girl did not want Bold Eagle for a husband, though he was serious, strong and brave, and each eagle feather in his headdress signified a bold deed. So she taunted him and called him a man of ice who could not smile.'

Talk of ice made Kola long for frozen mountain streams to slake his thirst and cool his skin. He sighed and listened as the story unrolled.

'Still, her father arranged the marriage between Proud Girl and Bold Eagle. But Bold Eagle thought he would have revenge for being called a man of ice. He went out and sang six Power Songs, to the north, south, east and west, and to the sky and the earth beneath. Then he took stones and animal bones, and around them he kneaded snow into the shape of a man. He dressed the man-shape in a beaded shirt and a robe of coloured feathers. He gave him bracelets for his wrists and a splendid headdress, then told him he was the mighty chief, Moowi. "You are rich and handsome," he said to the ice-man. "And no woman can look upon you without longing." '

'I remember!' Kola interrupted eagerly this time. Already a smile played on his lips. Though the story was an old one, he found that it took his mind away from present dangers. 'Though women loved him, Moowi had no heart, no love and no pity. Bold Eagle sent him to Proud Girl's village and watched her fall in love with Moowi!'

'Moowi spoke little, and was cold and haughty,' Silver Cloud went on, glad that his tale had won his rider's attention. 'But still Proud Girl went to her father and demanded to marry him, and her father agreed. There was a wedding feast which Bold Eagle attended. He watched with interest, noting that Proud Girl continued to scorn him. And he smiled when Moowi refused to be drawn close to the camp fire.

'The next morning Moowi and his new wife set out on a journey to the far north, as if to meet his People. He walked swiftly over mountains and through rivers, and Proud Girl wore out her moccasins running to keep up. She grew cold in the wind and snow and begged to rest, but Moowi would not hear of it.

'As long as the snow fell and the wind blew from the north Moowi walked strongly, but then the sun shone through the dark cloud and he began to tire. At last he sat down in the shade of a tree. "My husband, are you sick?" cried Proud Girl.

"Yes, wife, I am very sick," he replied.

'So she ran to a stream to fetch water, but when she returned the sun shone strongly on the tree and there was no sign of her husband.'

'Proud Girl called Moowi's name!' Kola jumped in, his eyes sparkling as he remembered the end to the tale. 'She searched and called out, but found only a little pile of bones and stones and some rags, beads and feathers. So she cried and went home, thin and hungry and no longer beautiful.

'And as she passed by Bold Eagle she saw him smile. "Is it anything to smile at?" Proud Girl asked through her tears. "Yes, it is something to smile at," Bold Eagle replied. And he took his dog and his sledge, and he went back to his own tribe.'

Time passed this way, with more tales and reasons to smile, so that Kola forgot his fears and told Silver Cloud Sioux stories which he had not heard. The sun was high in the sky and Kola had ceased to suspect every rock they came to and every shadow down every dry and dusty gulley.

It was only when the two came to a stream running deep through a narrow gulch that they began to pay attention to their surroundings once more. They each took the chance to drink, then went quickly on, finding to their surprise that the path of the stream was blocked by a giant boulder. The boulder dammed the stream so completely that the water had been forced underground, and beyond this spot, the bed ran dry through the gulch and out into a wide valley.

'What is this place?' Kola asked, looking round the huge, dish-shaped area and picking out deep holes in the sides of the cliffs.

'This is Kooyama,' Silver Cloud explained. 'Home of the cave-dwellers.'

Kola was astonished. He was used to the wind blowing around the skin cover of a tipi on the open plain and had never heard of such a thing. 'The people make their homes in the rock? But they must live surrounded by earth on all six sides. It is all around them, above their heads and beneath their feet!'

Silver Cloud agreed that it was strange. 'We will meet the people as we pass through,' he predicted, moving closer to the holes carved into the rock.

There were a hundred square entrances linked by stone steps and walkways – a village built into the cliff. Each was finely decorated with carvings and inlaid with rich turquoise. But instead of finding that Kooyama's cave-dwellers came out of their strange honeycomb of houses to investigate the strangers, Silver Cloud and Kola discovered that the caves were empty and the whole valley deserted.

'Where are the people?' Kola asked, peering up at the dark entrances. There was no smoke from fires, no dogs barking or children playing.

'Gone away?' Silver Cloud suggested.

Kola thought of a worse possibility. 'Perhaps they are dead.'

'I have not heard.' His guide too was puzzled. Here and there he saw small pieces of broken pottery lying on the ground, and stone circles containing the ashes of long-dead fires.

'Maybe Snake Eye has been here too,' Kola went on. He didn't like the stillness of the air and the thick layers of yellow dust lying undisturbed on the walkways.

'There is no blood,' Silver Cloud pointed out, 'and no sign of battle.' He thought back to the boulder which had dammed up the stream. 'No, I think the water to the village has been taken away. The Kooyama people could not live without water, and so they were forced to move on.'

Sadly Kola accepted the explanation and sympathised with the people. 'They have lost their homeland, the place where they belong.' He wondered long about a tribe like his own White Water band who must wander without roots, and how the boulder had arrived to dry up their water supply. Perhaps it had been angry spirits determined to teach the cave-dwellers a lesson who had dropped the giant rock from the sky.

In any case, there was no time to linger. The sun had run more than half its daily course and the shadows were lengthening. They had to leave Kooyama Valley and press on towards the south.

Kola was glad to be away from the deserted village and travelling on to their goal. As Silver Cloud trotted briskly through the next narrow canyon, he was wrapped up in thoughts of the diamonds which lay deep under the ground beyond Yellow Water. He tried to picture the size of the precious white stones and wondered how they would find their way down the tunnels without light to guide them. And he remembered White Deer, his grandmother, waiting at home, the five warriors around their fires, and Red Hawk lying ill on his bed.

The cry, when it pierced the silence of the valley, froze Kola's blood. It came from the back of the throat, full of bloodlust, filling the heavy air.

He looked to right and left, saw men driving their horses down the hills into the canyon, carrying shields, wielding tomahawks. The boy's heart stopped dead, then restarted with a rapid, uneven beat.

The Wild Dogs were upon them before they had

time to flee – six men in full war cry descending at a gallop, trapping Silver Cloud and Kola.

The horse reacted in an instant, rearing up in front of the first warrior to attack. His flailing hooves sent the Wild Dog sprawling from his horse, leaving a gap for Silver Cloud and the boy to charge through.

But the five other riders were in hot pursuit. One launched his tomahawk as they charged. Kola felt it fly close to his head, saw it strike a rock and fall harmlessly. He glanced over his shoulder to see the enemy horses bunch together down a narrow gulley, jostling each other as their riders urged them on. Then he let go of Silver Cloud's mane with one hand and quickly seized his knife.

Ahead, the gulley widened and the Wild Dogs spread out. They raced alongside Silver Cloud, leaning to swipe at Kola with their tomahawks. Swiftly Silver Cloud swerved to avoid them.

With an extra shock, Kola realised that there was a face among the enemy that he recognised. The features were long and thin, the mouth cruel and downturned, the eyes black with bitterness beneath a wolfskin helmet.

Matotope! Kola couldn't believe his eyes until the treacherous shaman leaned in towards him and whispered cruel words above the beat of horses' hooves.

'You think you are strong, Four Winds,' he snarled. 'But let us see now how the boy stands up in battle!'

Kola struck out in anger with his knife. He caught the blade in the mane of Matotope's horse and felt himself wrenched from Silver Cloud's back. Meanwhile, Snake Eye himself had charged ahead and rounded on Silver Cloud, who, free of his rider, raised himself high on his hind legs and pawed the air.

Silver Cloud's hooves smashed down close to the Chief's head. Snake Eye ducked to avoid them, clinging to the side of his black-and-white mare. From under her belly, he reached out and swiped the blade of his tomahawk down Silver Cloud's side.

As Kola rolled clear of other horses' thundering hooves, he heard Silver Cloud scream in pain and twist away from Snake Eye, only to clash with Matotope. Now the dream horse was hemmed in and bleeding from his side.

He fell to his knees then struggled up again. With a stagger he turned to fetch Kola, but Snake Eye blocked his way. Blood streamed from Silver Cloud's wound and stained the ground. Kola darted towards him but was flung aside by the charging fury of another Wild Dog horse. Then he watched in horror as two of the men threw ropes which circled around Silver Cloud's neck. They drew the lassos tight. Silver Cloud fought back, twisting and writhing to be free. But the ropes strangled him and stole his breath.

Then Snake Eye cried out a command and led his small band down the gulley. His men surrounded Silver

Cloud and dragged him after their leader, letting out triumphant yells. Last of all, Matotope circled his horse on the spot where the dream horse's blood stained the ground. He raised his knife to the sky in cruel exultation.

'Return to Red Hawk and tell him that his sun is truly set!' he cried to Four Winds. 'The quest is ended, and his People shall die!'

ELEVEN

Kola tasted the bitterness of defeat.

All the hopes of the White Water Sioux had rested with him, and now they were dashed to the ground where Silver Cloud's blood seeped into the sand. What was left but for the boy to return to the mountains and tell how he had failed?

He stood alone in the valley where his hopes had died, bleeding a little from a cut on his arm and wishing for death.

For a while he sat in the dirt. The sound of hooves had faded, but Matotope's last words still rang in his ears. The sun beat down on him, a small, solitary figure sitting slumped in the dirt.

Though Kola's body was still, his thoughts whirled. Ahead lay an impossible journey into the deepest mine, guarded by monsters, protected by the fearful Unktehi. But behind lay defeat and the deaths of all his band.

He saw the faces of the warriors, One Horn and the rest, and recalled the battles they had fought. Then there were the children: three boys of his own age, the girls and the small ones. The women would weep over them and bewail their fates.

Most of all Kola thought of Red Hawk and White Deer waiting by their tipi, watching as he climbed the mountain alone. Their old hearts would feel the stab of pain when they realised he had returned without the diamond. And was this the way that he, Four Winds, should repay them for the blessing of life?

No, he would go on, he decided. Snake Eye and Matotope believed that he was too weak to face the bad spirits of Yellow Water alone, and perhaps he was. But Kola knew that one did not always need to be strong to defeat the enemy. He could call instead upon the trickery of Coyote and the wisdom of Raven to outsmart Unktehi. If he kept his wits about him, then he might still succeed.

But meanwhile he grew weak. The sun was draining his strength and he was losing blood from the cut on his arm. So, seeking out the shade of the nearest rock, he untied his medicine bundle, the gift from his grandfather, and laid the contents on the ground.

First he took up a necklace of turquoise beads from which hung an eagle's feather. Putting this around his neck, he knew he would run faster than ever before. Then he opened a small bag of herbs, took out the dry, strong-smelling powder and rubbed it into his wound. The cut burned like fire, then the pain died away. Kola retied the pouch and returned it to his medicine bundle.

'May the power of this bundle be great,' he muttered, rolling up the contents and slinging the pack across his shoulder.

He began a chant as he walked back into the sun.

> '*Sumka ismala*
> *miyelo ca*
> *maka oka winhya*
> *oma wani.*'

I am lone wolf, I roam in different places. The sight of a lizard watching him from the rock where he had sheltered put him in good heart, for after all, it was as his grandmother had said: Lizard brings long life.

Kola walked on through the valley. He grieved as he went for the loss of Silver Cloud, his friend. The beautiful creature had been cut down, ropes choking him, and the dust had risen into a dark cloud as Snake Eye, his warriors and the treacherous Matotope had dragged him away.

The sight of the disgraced shaman flashed before the boy's eyes. He had snarled like a wolf from under his helmet, his black eyes glittering as he held his lightning knife to the sky and sent his own People into oblivion.

Soon, if Matotope had his way, there would be none left of the White Water Sioux. Their bones would become dust and sweep from the mountains into the valleys of their homelands. Their dead voices would call in the wind.

'Four Winds, wait for me!' a girl's voice cried from the jagged horizon.

At first Kola mistook it for the wailing of his People when they learned their fate. He walked on solemnly without looking up.

'Four Winds!' Hidden Moon called again. Hot sand blew up from the deep valley and stung her bare legs and arms. For two nights and almost two days she had trailed her friend and his dream horse. Often she had lost their tracks and had to speak with the birds of the air and the creatures of the plains and the hot mountains to discover where the travellers were headed. She talked to the grazing buffalo and to the wheeling crows, and they had taken her the way she needed to go.

Seeing that he did not answer, she left the ridge and dipped into the valley, her feet sliding over the loose earth, which sent larger stones peppering down the hill. Soon her descent had set up a small landslide which Kola couldn't help but notice.

He shaded his eyes and looked up into the sun. Was this friend or enemy?

Hidden Moon slid and scrambled down the slope, reaching for handholds in the rock. From her vantage point on the ridge she'd seen Snake Eye and his riders sweep into the valley and capture Silver Cloud. With a shock she'd recognised the wolfskin helmet and cloak of Matotope.

'Wait for me. I will join you. Together we will find the diamond!' she promised.

Kola knew her voice first. The she stepped into the shadow and he could make out her figure. Smaller, more slender than he was, younger still. 'Go back!' he told her angrily. 'This is no place for children!'

The girl ran to his side. 'I will not return. I will go with you to find the precious stone!'

He stopped in his tracks. 'This is foolish. You are my cousin, the granddaughter of my grandfather's brother. I will not let you give up your life.'

Prepared for this answer, Hidden Moon stood in his path. 'I have told you that I did not trust Matotope, and left the village and travelled alone by night. I have swum rivers and braved the buffalo. I saw you almost killed by fire and the great gift of rain that came with the rainbow. I do not stand here now, your equal, only to be told to return to my tipi.'

'Why did you come?' he demanded.

'For the same reason as you.' She stood defiantly in front of him. 'Because I cannot stay in the village and wait for Snake Eye to drive us out.'

'But I went on my dream quest to Spider Rock,' he reminded her. 'Only then did they permit me to make this journey.'

'I am a girl. They would not send me to seek a vision.

That is how it is.' Hidden Moon held her head up. 'I came in any case.'

Kola puzzled over what to do. Should he tell his proud cousin that her help was not welcome, or should he accept it? Back in the village, the women would worry over Hidden Moon's absence. They would fear that a mountain lion or bear had stolen down from the mountain and taken her. There would be much weeping. On the other hand, he recalled her anger at being made to live a life in the tipi and by the cooking pot, where she would weave baskets and sew beads on to war shirts until she was old.

'I am sad about Silver Cloud,' Hidden Moon told Kola. 'I quickly learned to love him when I guarded him by the cedar tree.'

'Did you see where Snake Eye took him?' Kola asked sharply. He thought that perhaps she had seen more from high on the hill.

But she shook her head. 'They vanished into another gulley. The horse fought them but he could not break free.' She glanced at Four Winds' pale face and bloodstained arm. 'Are you weak from the wound?'

'A little,' he confessed.

So Hidden Moon drew an object from the beaded pouch she wore around her waist. It was a long, white plaited band, woven in with small silver discs. 'Wear this around your wrist,' she told Four Winds. 'Silver Cloud bade me take hairs from his mane and weave it into an amulet to protect anyone who wears it.'

Kola grunted and held out his wrist. He imagined the power that the silken, silvery band would bring.

'Let us go,' she murmured, as if it was useless for him to argue further.

He looked into her determined, dark eyes. Here was his match. 'Yes', he conceded, 'let us go.'

Snake Eye, Matotope and the rest took Silver Cloud back to where the main band waited in the baking hot desert.

A hundred Comanche warriors got to their feet and raised their voices in praise of Anteep of the underworld. 'Oh, Great Spirit be praised that he has delivered this gift of the dream horse to us! May our enemies perish. May the Wild Dogs flourish!'

Their chief dragged the prisoner into their midst. Silver Cloud's coat was dull with the red dust of the desert, there was dried blood down his side. He did not resist as men threw more ropes around his neck and legs until he was tied fast and unable to move.

Then Snake Eye called for the War Bundle to be brought from the Tent of War. He took out the skins of birds and held them up in the still air and appealed to the war gods to bring them victory. 'For the swallow and the hawk are messengers of war!' he cried. 'And we invoke their power!'

His warriors chanted in support, gathering around

Silver Cloud in a tight circle several men deep.

Then Matotope took off his wolfskin headdress and handed it with much ceremony to Snake Eye. 'The life of the warrior is like that of a wolf!' he cried. 'We lie in wait, we prowl through the bush, we pounce! I give this sacred robe and my spirit powers to you, my new chief, that you may succeed in battle against my sworn enemy, the White Water Sioux!'

Snake Eye took the robe and placed it around his shoulders. His men began a dance of war, creeping low and springing forward like the wolf they worshipped.

At the centre of the circle Silver Cloud stood hobbled. He gazed out over the men's heads, across the desert into a shimmering heat haze. The pinnacles on the horizon quivered, the sun was blood red.

'Death to the spirit horse!' the Wild Dogs yelled. 'He bears the enemy on his back and is sent by Ghost Horse to punish us!'

Silver Cloud saw the men take up their spears wrapped with otter skins and trailing eagle feathers. They held them aloft, crying for his blood. He was saddened at the spectacle.

Snake Eye stood apart with Matotope. His heart beat coldly and slowly as he raised his right hand, its palm towards the heavens. 'Kill the dream horse!' he ordered.

The Wild Dogs aimed their spears.

* * *

At a certain moment, as Four Winds and Hidden Moon left the steep canyon and came into a wider valley where trees grew and some buffalo grazed, the boy felt a strange breath of wind across his face. It cooled and soothed him, and brought with it a whispering voice.

'*Wisdom and courage, strength and speed. I bring all these!*'

Four Winds looked around to find that the voice had tricked him, for there was no one nearby.

'*Above all, I bring you loyalty,*' the spirit voice murmured.

'What is it?' Hidden Moon asked Four Winds. She saw that he was transfixed by something which she could not see or hear.

'Silver Cloud is present,' he warned. If no longer in body, then still in spirit.

'*I bring you loyalty. I will never fail you. Love sits in my heart.*'

The boy walked on thankfully, the girl at his side.

As the second day of his journey ended and the sun faded into the west, a Raven came to talk with them.

'Where are you travelling to?' The bird had alighted on a stricken tree, made bare and twisted by a lightning strike. He had watched them approach, his shiny black head cocked to one side. Then he had spoken in a cheerful voice.

'To Yellow Water,' Four Winds replied. 'To find a diamond in the deepest mine.'

'Alone?' the bird asked in some surprise.

'Why not?' The boy tried to sound confident, but his

body shook. He knew the raven as the wisest of birds and so feared his advice. 'Can you tell us: are we walking in the right direction?'

The bird nodded. 'You are almost there. Tomorrow, when the sun rises, the giant canyon will appear and the lake will spread before your eyes. To the east of Yellow Water lies the mine you speak of.'

Four Winds thanked him, then made as if to hurry on.

'Unktehi's monsters guard the entrance,' the raven said, slowly flapping his wings and rising from the blackened branch. He flew lazily above their heads. 'They are many and dangerous.'

'Do they know we are coming?' Hidden Moon asked. She too was nervous of the raven.

'They know everything,' he replied. 'And remember, no one has ever passed through the entrance, though many have tried.'

Four Winds frowned and quickened his pace.

The raven floated on an airstream to their right. 'Unktehi himself resides there. Only the foolish dare approach.'

Or those with the cleverness of the coyote, Four Winds thought to himself.

'And can we be certain that this is the entrance to the deepest mine in the world?' Hidden Moon asked.

'You can be sure of that,' the raven cawed. 'Just as there are diamonds in the ground. But you must travel far with the earth above your heads to find them. I hear from the chipmunk and mole that sometimes rocks fall and block the tunnels. If you do outsmart Unktehi and his guards and enter the mine, then you must take great care that the roof doesn't fall on you.'

Hidden Moon shuddered. But then she remembered the bracelet of hair which she had made for Four Winds. 'We draw our strength from Ghost Horse,' she told the raven bravely. 'He sent his spirit, Silver Cloud, to protect Four Winds. The roof will not fall!'

'But Ghost Horse has allowed his messenger to be taken and tortured by your enemy,' the bird pointed out, wheeling slowly around. It seemed that he'd almost finished what he had come to say. 'I have a vision of Silver Cloud staked to the earth, facing a hundred sharp spears.'

'Stop!' Kola begged. 'I don't want to know!'

'Would Silver Cloud wish you to continue this way?' The raven's last remark was designed to leave the boy and girl in grave doubt. Slowly he flapped his ragged wings.

The question brought Kola to a standstill. He stared ahead, towards the south and the canyon that split the world in two.

A breath of wind spoke. '*I will never fail you. Love sits in my heart.*'

'Yes, he would wish us to continue,' he told the raven. 'Tomorrow we will go to Yellow Water, come what may.'

TWELVE

Four Winds and Hidden Moon walked through the night towards the Yellow Water Canyon. The stars guided them and the light of the moon showed them where to put their feet.

They shared their journey with the mountain lion and coyote who stalked through the bush and crept along moonlit ridges. Once or twice they heard the sudden snap of twigs and the rustle of leaves, the high cry of a helpless victim drowned by a loud snarl and a snap. In the silence that followed, life ebbed and a meal was made.

The sound of the hunt made the travellers' flesh creep. They could picture the glistening white fangs of the coyote and the bright yellow eyes of the lion. Worse still, Hidden Moon spotted an owl circling above them, a soft prophet of doom.

'Look!' She held Four Winds by the arm and pointed to the pale shape floating in a current of air.

The owl circled, tilting its broad wings to catch another breath of wind, wheeling high above their heads.

It was an ill omen – but Four Winds put the vision to one side. He did not want to speak with the owl, for nothing was going to prevent him reaching the canyon and the entrance to the mine.

Before dawn they entered the place which split the world in two. There were many valleys cut by a turbulent river, sided by sheer cliffs rising high into the sky. It was as if the water had smashed its way through mountain after mountain, wearing away the yellow rock, finally finding its bed on harder, darker granite deep in the earth's crust.

Kola saw this in the grey dawn and was overcome by the splendour of the canyon. He wondered how water could cut through rock and how the wind and rain could wear away the mountains. He felt small and humble, and far away from his homeland.

Hidden Moon too realised that they had almost reached the end of their journey. She followed the route of the wild white water, searching for the place where the river ran into the lake, Yellow Water. But a mist rose from the mighty river and curled around the base of the canyon, drifting up the rugged sides until the sun appeared at the rim of the highest ridge. There, where the golden pink rays met the white mist, was an explosion of rainbow colours, which gladdened her and gave her the heart to go on.

As the sun rose, Four Winds and Hidden Moon stopped to drink. The water from the mighty river was cool in their dry mouths. They let it trickle through their fingers, scooped again and splashed it on to their tired faces. Then they looked up at the sun and took courage from the dawning of a new day.

They hadn't walked on more than a hundred paces from their watering place when a sound and a movement from a shallow cave on the opposite bank caught their attention. A weak human cry rose above the swirl and lap of the water against the banks.

Startled, Four Winds scrambled on to a high rock and peered across. He made out the figure of a girl crouching inside the entrance to the cave, her hands stretched out as if pleading for rescue. She was young – perhaps seven or eight summers – with her long hair coiled strangely around her head, and wearing a woven shawl and skirt of deep sky blue.

'Who is there?' Hidden Moon asked, climbing on to the rock. She gasped when she saw the solitary child.

'We must go and speak with her,' Four Winds decided.

'How? By swimming across this great river?' Hidden Moon held back. 'There could be danger in the water.' Monsters like Yietso who ate human flesh and Tehotsodi who could flood the whole world. 'And what if the girl is a vision created by evil spirits to trick us?'

Four Winds knew this was possible. 'You think that Unktehi and his master, Anteep, know that we approach the mine?' he asked.

Hidden Moon nodded. 'Raven told us so.' She stared at the girl crouching in the cave. 'This is an evil vision,' she insisted. 'We must ignore her and go on our way.'

But the boy was not certain. The child looked ill, as if a fever had raged through her small body. It seemed that she couldn't stand or even crawl out of the cave towards the water's edge. 'We can't pass her by,' he insisted. 'Let me swim across and speak with her.'

Hidden Moon sighed. Time was precious. 'Then do it quickly,' she urged, still afraid that the child was other than she seemed.

So Four Winds took off his medicine bundle, but kept the feather necklace and band of silver horsehair around his neck and wrist. As he prepared to dive into the yellow water, he touched the lizardskin pouch on his belt. Then he threw himself head first into the river.

He plunged underwater and gave a strong kick. The river was deep and the current powerful. He had to swim against it so as not to be dragged too far downriver. After two more strokes through the murky depths, he pushed for the surface.

Hidden Moon waited anxiously for Four Winds' head to break clear of the surface. Her heart beat fast and uneven. She was sure that Yietso was down there on the muddy bed, gloating over the trick he had played.

But then her cousin appeared, his black hair smooth as an otter's against his skull, swimming hard for the opposite bank. The child cried louder as rescue approached.

Four Winds fought the current to stay even with the cave. He felt it tug at his legs to slow him down and drag him back towards the river bed, so he kicked harder than ever, using his arms to pull him towards the bank.

At last he made it and hauled himself out of the water. Now he could hear the girl sobbing and pleading for help, still crouched inside the dark cave. So, with water streaming from him, he climbed up beside her.

'Don't be afraid,' he said softly.

Now that he had arrived, the girl cowered back into the cave, which was low and dark. This was no evil spirit who had shape-shifted into a helpess child, he decided, for these were real tears she was weeping.

Four Winds waited for her to grow less afraid, then said, 'Tell me your name.'

'Gilspa,' she answered, shaking with fear. 'I am a child of the Tesaktumo People of the Hopi nation. Our home was Kooyama.'

The boy recognised with a start the name of the cave village through which he and Silver Cloud had passed. He recalled the carved doorways and empty steps. 'What happened to your people?' he asked.

'We left our homeland when the spirits took away our water,' she explained. 'Our Chief Hatali died of a fever and our People were scattered.'

Four Winds listened with sorrow. 'Tell me how you came to be here.'

'My mother hid me in this cave when the Comanche war party came amongst us,' Gilspa explained. 'There were a hundred spears and many women and children died.'

'Where were your warriors?'

'Gone to fish in the Yellow River and to hunt buffalo on the plain. Snake Eye chose his time well.'

Anger rose in Four Winds' throat. His hatred for Snake Eye grew stronger than ever. 'What happened to your mother?'

'She hid me here and promised to return. I grew hungry, my hands shake, I am afraid.'

'I know Snake Eye and his Wild Dogs,' Four Winds said bitterly. 'He is sworn enemy of my people, the White Water Sioux. He slew my father and took my mother.'

'Then you will help me?' Gilspa begged. Her round, dark eyes were full of tears, her small mouth trembled.

He nodded. 'I will take you across the river and search for what is left of your People, the Tesaktumos. We will not part until I have found your cousins.'

She wept now for gladness, climbing on to Four Winds' back and clasping her hands tight around his neck. He climbed down from the cave and entered the river slowly, keeping above the surface and swimming steadily to the shore where Hidden Moon waited.

'We must go back to Kooyama,' he told his cousin. 'Gilspa is sick. She needs to be with her People, the Tesaktumo Hopis.

The news made Hidden Moon frown deeply. 'We cannot go back to that place,' she protested. 'The village is empty. What would we gain?'

Four Winds knew that Hidden Moon could not bear any delay in their quest for the diamond. 'I know, it is difficult,' he admitted, setting the girl gently on the bank. 'But I cannot leave her here.'

'Why not? Is not the future of the White Water People more important than the life of one small Hopi girl?' Hidden Moon argued. 'Why must you delay by returning to Kooyama?'

'Because it is not in my heart to let her die. She is sick and helpless. She has wept enough.'

Hidden Moon's voice rose. 'Then you are a fool!' she cried. 'You have been tricked by a spirit who has taken the shape of a pretty girl. Unktehi is cunning. He knows how to divert you from your quest now that Silver Cloud is not here to guide you!'

Four Winds took a deep breath. 'I do not think this is Unktehi's work.' He looked again at the girl who shook and wept all the more as the two cousins argued. 'I must take her back to her People.'

'This is not flesh and blood!' Hidden Moon shouted. She flung open Four Winds' medicine bundle and delved into the pouch containing herbs.

Gilspa shied away, back against a rock.

'See, she shrinks from your medicine as though from poison. Only an evil spirit from the underworld refuses to be made better, knowing that to take the medicine will change him back into the evil monster that he is!'

'Stop. Do not frighten her.' Four Winds came between Hidden Moon and Gilspa. 'I have made up my mind to do what my grandmother, White Deer, has taught me. I must cast away self-interest and look and listen for the welfare of others.'

He spoke calmly. Hidden Moon knew that she had lost the argument. 'My cousin,' she said in a broken voice. 'Kola!'

'Will you come with us?' he asked, taking Gilspa on his back once more.

Hidden Moon shook her head. 'I will go forward.'

'Then stay by the river until you reach Yellow Water,' he instructed. 'The canyon will be broad and deep. Wait there by the lake until I return.'

'I will do all I can to seek the mine,' she insisted.

'But you will not enter alone.' Four Winds was afraid for her now. 'Remember, it is I who must fetch the diamond, as Ghost Horse ordered. If we are to save our People, it must be me.'

Reluctantly Hidden Moon bowed her head in agreement. 'Your heart is kind and true,' she told him sadly.

It was hard for Four Winds to turn away from the

cousin he loved, for she walked alone into danger. But he found her headstrong. He thought she lacked judgement and kindness towards the Hopi girl. '*Maka akanl wicasa iyuha el.*' Go in peace, he told her.

'So with you,' she replied, making one last silent appeal with her eyes.

He turned away with the burden of the child. Gilspa's arms almost choked him as they set off back towards Kooyama. She weighed more than he'd imagined and his steps were slow.

'Where did your people go after they were driven from the cave village?' he asked. The sides of the great canyon closed in on him as they re-entered the smaller gulleys of the night before. The coyotes and the lions kept watch once more.

'They fled far,' Gilspa replied. 'When Chief Hatali died and Snake Eye attacked, they were driven into the dry hills, away from the water. I do not know where they are now.'

'And your mother. After she hid you in the cave, where did she go?'

The child on his back wept. 'She went away, who knows where. Perhaps the Wild Dogs caught her and put her to death.'

'They also took my mother, Shining Star,' he confided. His heart had broken in two and never mended. He knew how Gilspa must feel.

After many paces, as the sun reached its height, Four

Winds tired. He stopped by a creek and eased the child from his back. She sighed and moaned and said her whole body shook with fever.

'You must drink,' he told her, showing her a way down the steep bank of the stream. 'If your head is hot with fever, then you must bathe it in the cool stream.'

But she held back and refused to take his hand. 'I cannot walk,' she whimpered.

So he went alone and drank, then held his palms together and filled them so that he would have water to take to the child. She lay on her side on the ground as if sleeping, her back turned, her black hair coiled in a strange, snake-like design over her head. The water trickled slowly through Four Winds' fingers as he bent over her.

A drop landed on her woven shawl and sank through, another on her blue skirt. There was little left in his hands as he sprinkled it on the girl's hair and face to cool her fever.

The water splashed. The figure on the ground writhed and coiled, rearing up as a giant serpent, high above Four Winds' head.

Four Winds staggered back. He gazed up at the snake's flat, scaly black head and soft yellow throat. It had eyes like emeralds with a slash of black pupil; its thin, forked tongue flickered towards him.

The snake laughed as Four Winds drew his knife. 'This is the boy who comes to steal a diamond from the deepest mine!' he cried. 'Poor fool; he is easier to trick than a newborn baby. What chance then of outwitting Unktehi and taking the stone back to save his People?'

And Four Winds cursed and cried out against his own childish simplicity. He swiped with his knife at the serpent, who slid beyond reach, his black scales glistening. 'Kill me, then!' he yelled, sick of being the plaything of the cruel spirits. 'Crush me to death, poison me with your tongue!'

The snake dipped its head and began to coil its body around the boy.

Four Winds felt his arms being pinned against his side, felt the pressure of the snake's body against his ribs. He did not resist. *Forgive me*, he prayed to Red Hawk, his grandfather. And to all the others among his People whose futures he had destroyed.

THIRTEEN

The canyon walls rose to meet the sun. They were immense, bare cliffs which dwarfed all objects and made the mighty Yellow River which ran through the yawning gap seem like a slow trickle.

Hidden Moon held her breath as she entered the canyon. It was as they said: this crack in the rock could split the world in two. Sighing deeply, she went forward, a tiny, fearful figure in the hot, deserted landscape.

The sun beat down. There was no wind. Hidden Moon ventured on in a storm of fear, anger and confusion.

Four Winds had been drawn away from his quest to save his People because of the kindness in his heart. Hidden Moon saw danger in his rescue of the girl, Gilspa. On the other hand, she recognised that the child, if she *was* who she claimed to be, was, like them, a helpless victim of evil spirits and Snake Eye's band. But her cousin's tender-hearted action had left her alone in the desert to continue the search for the diamond. That could not be right.

'He is foolish!' she cried out loud to the birds high above and the water rushing by her feet. 'If he must save Gilspa, why doesn't he bring the girl with us on our journey, and afterwards take her to find her People?'

She was sick, she could not walk, came the answer.

'I do not believe that,' Hidden Moon said aloud.

That is because you are hard-hearted.

'She would not take medicine for her fever.'

Children are afraid of medicine. Gilspa had been alone in the cave for two nights, praying for her mother to return. Her fear was great.

'Mine also,' Hidden Moon sighed. She gazed ahead to where the rushing river widened and curved across the flat bottom of the canyon, eventually flowing into the largest lake she had ever seen.

The sight of Yellow Water slowed her pace. There was her journey's end, there lay the diamond that would save her People. And yet she felt fear rise within her. Four Winds had gone. The dream horse was no more. She must face Unktehi alone.

Raven saw the girl stop by the edge of the lake. He picked her out as he wheeled over the canyon, knew that she was alone and afraid.

So he flapped his wings and sailed on an air current close to the ground, alighting on a smooth rock close to where Hidden Moon stood. He hopped to a place where she could easily see him, settled his feathers and spoke.

'Where is the boy you were travelling with?'

'Gone,' Hidden Moon muttered.

'And left you alone?' the bird cawed. 'What was he thinking of?'

'You must find him and ask him yourself,' she replied angrily, 'for I have no idea why Four Winds put the Hopi girl before the future of the White Water People.'

'Hmm.' Raven ducked his glossy head. 'Tell me more.'

So Hidden Moon described the girl in the cave and her cousin's brave rescue. 'Now he carries her back to Kooyama in search of her People,' she reported, noticing that the bird grew agitated as she spoke.

'This Hopi girl – she was small, with her hair wound about her head, and wearing a coloured shawl?' he asked.

Hidden Moon nodded fearfully. 'Her name is Gilspa.'

'This is not her name!' Raven announced. 'Neither is she from the village of Kooyama. In truth, this is Yietso, dread monster who guards the mine with Unktehi. He takes many shapes to fool his enemies, and one of these is the girl, Gilspa!'

The news made Hidden Moon cry out. 'In my heart I knew!'

'You are wise,' Raven commented. He admired the girl and wished to give her advice that would save her own life. 'Know then that it is dangerous for you to continue alone, without the guidance of Ghost Horse's messenger, Silver Cloud, and without the help of the boy, Four Winds.'

Hidden Moon nodded. Tears sprang to her eyes as she imagined Four Winds' fate at the hands of Yietso, the flesh-eater.

'Then you will give up this quest,' Raven insisted.

'I cannot!' she cried. 'While there is a chance that I might find the diamond and take it back to my People, I must go on!'

'But this is only the first of three quests,' Raven reminded her. 'The task is too great. Go home and tell your Chief Red Hawk that it is impossible.'

'I cannot!' she said again, shaking her head while the tears fell.

Raven regarded her sadly. 'You have a brave heart,' he told her. 'You would not sit waiting in the tipi, but came after your cousin and the dream horse.'

'Why must I sit and wait because I am a girl?' she cried. 'I have as much courage as a boy, my brain is quick and my body is strong.'

The bird continued to gaze at her with his bright, black eyes. 'Go home,' he repeated, more quietly than before. 'Follow my advice before it is too late.'

But Hidden Moon dried her tears. 'I will go forward,' she decided. 'And what will be will be.'

* * *

The shadowy rocks were still cool in the morning sun when Hidden Moon came to the entrance to the mine. It lay on the eastern shore of the vast lake whose water was an intense blue under a clear sky. She studied the opening carefully. It was the height of two men, but the width was narrow. A ledge of yellow rock overhung the opening, casting a dark shadow.

The girl stood in the sun, gazing all around. The surface of the lake rippled under a hot breeze. In the distance, a small herd of antelope stopped to drink before they hurried on down the bare canyon to good grazing land beyond.

Taking in the peaceful scene, her sore heart eased. Instead of the monsters she had been warned about, there was calm and beauty beneath a pure blue sky.

Soaring high, Raven looked down sadly.

Perhaps she had caught Unktehi offguard, Hidden Moon thought. The dreaded guardian of the mine had not been expecting her and had used all his energies to help the Wild Dogs trap Silver Cloud and send Yietso to cheat Four Winds. Now he was sleeping.

And so it was possible for Hidden Moon to creep unnoticed into the tunnel that lay beyond the quiet entrance. She entered the shadow of the overhang and peered inside, waiting for her eyes to grow accustomed to the darkness.

A small lizard ran clear of the tunnel, its pale, thin body passing close by the girl's feet.

Hidden Moon braced herself and stepped inside. The sudden cold hit her and made her shiver. A silence deeper than she had ever known enfolded her. She gritted her teeth and made herself go forward.

Darkness pressed in on her. She breathed in its dampness, smelt decay all around. Feeling for the walls of the tunnel, she discovered that they were rough and close together, though the roof was still higher than she could reach.

I am surrounded by rock, she thought. *It is above my head and beneath my feet.*

And then Unktehi, who had been silently watching all this while, acted. He laughed to himself at how easy it was to defeat these puny enemies. What need was there of a storm and a great disturbance of nature when a mere loosening of rocks above the girl's head would be enough?

Hidden Moon could see nothing, but she heard a stone dislodge and fall at her feet. Dust sprinkled on to her face, then another stone fell. The roof of the tunnel was cracking.

Fear gripped her heart. She turned back, only to find that stones were loosening and dropping on all sides. She stumbled on one, turned again and again until she lost all sense of which way to run. And now the dust came down like rain and choked her, the rocks overhead grating and shifting with a huge, grinding shudder.

Hidden Moon tried to run, but falling rocks prevented her. She gasped and went down on her hands and knees, scrambling back towards what she thought was the entrance. There was dirt in her mouth; stones bruised her as they dropped. A light glowed a little way ahead. She was sure it was the sun and she struggled past larger rocks and boulders that blocked the way.

Unktehi smiled again. Then he released a final shower of rocks.

It is not yet time!' Yietso declared with a cruel smile as he loosened Four Winds from his coiled grip.

The boy fell to the ground, dazed and breathless. He gazed in bewilderment at the giant black serpent rearing over him.

'Go!' Yietso hissed. 'Unktehi has said that you must live!'

Four Winds groaned at the aching of his ribs. The monster had curled around him, intent on crushing him to death. And yet, suddenly, as the darkness began to close in on him and the world swam from his grasp, the snake had released him.

Yietso stared down with cold, cruel eyes. He was growing larger, filling the narrow gulley where the stream ran its course. As he increased in size, his black scales grew indistinct, as if melting into a cloud hovering above the boy. Yet his emerald eyes remained clear.

'I don't understand!' Four Winds gasped. 'Why not kill me now?'

'Because your time has not come,' the monster sneered. 'Unktehi has spoken.'

Four Winds rose from the ground, taking up his medicine bundle and bear club knife. He was weary, his heart sickened by the shape-shifting spirit. With an angry gesture of defiance, he raised his knife. 'I will not give in!' he declared. 'While there is breath in my body I will search for the diamond!'

Yietso melted into a dark cloud, his green eyes flickering. 'You give us good sport,' he mocked. 'One boy alone against the might of Unktehi!'

One boy and one girl! Four Winds remembered that Hidden Moon was by Yellow Water, waiting by the deepest mine.

There was laughter in the sky as the cloud dissolved into the air.

The thought of his cousin sent Four Winds running back through the narrow gulleys and across streams that led in time to the great canyon and Yellow Water. He forgot the weariness of his legs and the aching of his ribs, ignoring the signs in the landscape that would have told him that Hidden Moon had passed by. So he leapt creeks and overlooked footprints, then ran by the cave where he had foolishly stopped to rescue Gilspa. For Hidden Moon had sworn that she would go forward, and there was proud stubbornness in her heart.

As a child of four summers she had said to him, 'Teach me to hunt.' At six she had learned to fashion a bow of hickory, at seven she had brought back rabbits and a small deer. Now she had proved herself his equal by travelling alone in the footsteps of Silver Cloud.

Four Winds had told Hidden Moon to wait by the lake until he returned, but he could not be sure that she would heed his advice. Her eyes had begged him not to take the girl to Kooyama, but he had refused. Why then should she wait as he had asked?

Fear for his cousin and the eagle's feather which he wore around his neck gave speed to the boy's feet. He should have given her the silver horsehair band to keep her safe, he thought now. As it was, she had gone unguarded.

Shortly after the sun had reached its height, Four Winds entered the canyon of Yellow Water. His feet caused a thin trail of dust to rise as he made for the eastern shore and sought the entrance to the deepest mine.

'Hidden Moon!' he called. His voice drifted against the sides of the canyon and came back as the faintest of echoes. 'Hidden Moon, I am sorry! You were right about the Hopi girl!'

The water in the lake rippled and sparkled as it had done when she had passed by. Far above, the Raven watched.

The eastern shore was made of soft sand sloping

gently to the water's edge. Four Winds easily picked out Hidden Moon's footprints, which he followed as far as a cave with an overhanging rock shading its entrance. Here the trail stopped.

'Hidden Moon!' he shouted, cursing the dull echo which tricked him into thinking that she had replied. He closed his eyes and groaned when he saw that she had entered the mine alone.

No! he told himself. *She would not! This is another of Unktehi's tricks to lure me inside to my death!* He spun round, expecting to see Yietso laughing behind his back, or the dreaded guardian of the mine himself, taking a monstrous shape. But no; there were only faint clouds on the horizon, rolling into the canyon and screening the high sun behind a white haze.

A wind fluttered through the long fringes of Four Winds' war shirt as he turned to look once more at the tall, dark entrance to the mine. There was a gloomy feel about it, with the overhanging ledge, and the air inside seemed thick with dust. As the boy looked and listened, he heard small rocks fall from the roof and rattle to the ground.

They fell with a dull, light echo and made the startled observer's eyes open wide. He went forward jerkily towards the entrance, then stepped over stones that had rolled clear of the mine and now blocked his path.

'Hidden Moon!' he whispered.

He picked his way into the tunnel. Hope flared when

he tried to tell himself that the rockfall had been slight. These rocks were not big, and surely the roof was strong.

But though the dust still swirled, he could see that the tunnel ahead was blocked. Shielding his eyes with his hand, he crouched low and stared into the gloom.

Three paces ahead, Hidden Moon lay on the ground as if sleeping. Her eyes were closed, her cheek resting against the cold rock.

Four Winds crept towards her. He brushed the dirt from her face and leaned close. There was no breath. Her spirit had passed.

So he lifted the rocks from her body and carried her out of the mine into the sunlight. He laid her by the shore of the lake, then sat by her side. She was pale and cold as he unbraided her long hair and spread it about her shoulders.

'*Iki 'cize waon 'kon.*' It is over, he whispered.

His heart ached, but he did not cry.

FOURTEEN

Four Winds buried his cousin, Hidden Moon, on the shore of Yellow Water. He knew that she must cross the mountains and return to their White Water homeland on her way to the land of the dead.

'Behold!' he cried to the heavens. 'May her spirit rise to the stars and travel peacefully into the hereafter!'

Then he took his knife and scratched the shape of a mighty Thunder Bird into the smooth rock close to where he had buried her. The bird, Wakinyan, had wide, flapping wings. He brought thunder and lightning which the travelling spirit might harness to clear obstacles out of her way.

In his heart Four Winds grieved for his cousin, but still his eyes remained dry.

Hidden Moon had followed the way of *Cante Tinz*, the Strong Hearts. She had not been a coward and run from danger. Instead, she had found the courage to go forward alone into the mine. Four Winds honoured her and chanted as he withdrew from her grave. 'He who turns away shall not be admitted.'

As he looked towards the dark entrance, he was aware of clouds gathering. Thunder Bird was getting ready to flap his wings to assist Hidden Moon on her journey. Four Winds heard the low rumble in the sky and was satisfied.

But as he left the grave and walked towards the mine, the rumble grew to a roar which rolled through the bruised sky, then echoed as an ear-splitting crack directly overhead. Instead of preparing to guide the spirit of Hidden Moon on her way, it seemed that the Thunder Bird was angry and about to unleash a cruel storm into the dusty canyon.

Sure enough, the crash of thunder was soon followed by a flash of lightning which ripped the sky apart. It shot to earth, its forked path reflected in the lake, sending a shock wave that would paralyse all who saw it.

Four Winds felt a huge dread pass through him. Already plunged deep in grief by the loss of Silver Cloud and Hidden Moon, the ill omen of the approaching storm almost made him sink to the ground.

All is against me. The world is my enemy, and I must fight Unktehi alone! he cried to himself.

Overhead, a second flash of silver lightning tore the sky.

Then the rain began. It fell as slow, cold drops on Four Winds' upturned face. Then it came down faster, heavier, until, blown by a fierce wind, it lashed his skin and blurred his vision. The cold force of it made him seek shelter under a ledge of rock, staggering there across sandy soil which was already criss-crossed with muddy channels made by the downpour. Eventually he found refuge and huddled against the rock.

Four Winds took a deep breath. He must prepare himself to enter the mine and risk everything to find the diamond. The stone was deep underground, at the end of many dark tunnels, protected by Unktehi and his evil spirits.

Perhaps this storm was the work of Unktehi's demons, who had gathered the forces of nature to fling them against Four Winds' first attempt to enter the mine. As a child he had learned of the monster, Tehotsodi, who came armed with floods to drown his enemies.

Yes, Four Winds thought to himself, *Tehotsodi will send a wall of water into the mine so that no man will reach the diamond!*

Or else, Yietso has returned to his master, Unktehi, and this is another of their games to frighten me and send me running back to my People!

Soaked to the skin, his grandfather's war shirt dripping and clinging to his skinny body, Four Winds stared out into the raging storm.

Then, in a roll of thunder and a searing lightning flash, Silver Cloud returned.

He appeared on the lake shore, a small, misty figure

in the far distance, growing larger as he galloped towards the mine. His hooves pounded the ground, splashed through water, kicked up spray. Sometimes he would vanish from Four Winds' vision, hidden by a flurry of rain and wind, or by a rock which came between them. And then the boy was afraid that he had imagined the horse and he would sink back under his ledge. 'This is another trick,' he would tell himself. 'A false hope to torture me.' Then he would curse Unktehi and stare into the distance to make doubly sure that his guardian dream horse wasn't there.

Silver Cloud sped through the rain and wind. He ignored the lightning, sent by Unktehi, which landed at his feet, and the blasts of thunder which cracked over his head. He had been away from Kola for more than a day and night, during which much had taken place. Now the boy took refuge from the storm at the entrance to the deepest mine. And he, Silver Cloud, was needed more than ever before.

The grey horse appeared again out of the rain. Four Winds saw that he was closer, more solid than before. His drenched mane was whipped back from his head, his neck stretched, his legs splashing and speeding towards the mine. Was this real, or was it another of Unktehi's cruel spirits in disguise? Still Four Winds would not allow himself to believe.

Braving the worst of the thunder and lightning, Silver Cloud reached the entrance to the mine. He shook his mane and endured the torrent, turning towards Kola and speaking as he had spoken before. 'I have returned.'

So Four Winds sprang from his shelter and raced towards the dream horse. He reached to touch Silver Cloud's neck and run his hand down to his streaming shoulder.

'Believe it,' Silver Cloud assured him.

'But how?' Four Winds was almost unable to speak. He had seen the horse roped and tied, dragged away bleeding by Snake Eye and his band.

'Through the strength of Ghost Horse, messenger of Wakanda, I was delivered,' Silver Cloud replied. 'The Comanches hobbled me and thrust their spears into me. They left me lying dead on the earth.'

Four Winds gasped.

'They carry hate in their hearts. But Ghost Horse sees everything. He returned me to the Other World to meet with Wakanda and be healed by his power, which is greater than all others. Look, I have no wounds in my side!'

Four Winds saw that it was true. Silver Cloud was whole and strong. The boy's heart swelled with solemn wonder. 'My cousin, Hidden Moon, followed us,' he reported sadly. 'Unktehi's spirits killed her as she entered the mine.'

The horse nodded. 'Her name will live amongst the brave. And now we must honour her and complete the quest.'

Four Winds looked through the rain towards the dark, overhanging entrance of the mine. Silver Cloud's words had stirred him and rekindled his courage. 'Without you to guide me I have made many mistakes,' he confessed.

'And you have also come far, and shown much courage,' the horse reminded him.

'You will stay now until we find the diamond?' Without Silver Cloud's calm presence, Kola doubted that he could succeed.

'I have sworn to stay by your side.'

The boy sighed. 'Then together we will defeat Unktehi as you have defeated Snake Eye,' he said in a low voice. 'First we must move the stones which crushed Hidden Moon.'

So they trudged through the storm to the cave which led into the mine and began to push aside rocks to clear the way. Rain still beat down from a leaden sky, slowing Four Winds down in his work of lifting and dragging the heavy debris.

As they worked, Kola looked over his shoulder at the dismal lake and the great canyon sides. He thought of Yietso and his huge, writhing coils of snake flesh, and of Unktehi, as yet invisible. A cold shudder ran through his body as he made himself lift the next stone and carry it with scraped and bleeding hands.

Silver Cloud sensed Kola's deep dread. He wished he had words to take away the fear and soothe the boy's grieving heart. But he knew that the answer lay beyond what he could say, deep in the mine beneath their feet.

At last, Kola rolled away the last rock which blocked the tunnel. He looked at Silver Cloud then stepped inside.

His footfall released a flash of lightning and a roar of thunder. They came at the same instant – the blinding light and the rumble – making Kola spin round and raise his arm to shield his eyes. He saw the dark outline of Silver Cloud framed in the entrance and beyond him, casting a great shadow, loomed the evil serpent shape of Yietso.

Fear came then and battered at Kola's heart. He saw the grinning jaws and the glaring emerald eyes, the shining black scales of the monster who had tricked him. And the taunting words came back, 'It is not yet time.'

Now though, Four Winds was closer than ever to discovering the diamond, and Silver Cloud was with him. So it seemed certain Yietso had returned in earnest.

Still, Silver Cloud didn't flinch as he stood between the serpent monster and the boy. Even when the waves on the lake behind Yietso grew rough, as if troubled by a mighty wind, the horse faced the enemy without fear.

Holding his breath, Kola stole back towards the entrance. The waves on Yellow Water rose high up the sides of the canyon, hitting the rock with enormous force and casting spray back into the water. It was as if something underneath the surface was causing it – a mighty force heaving up towards the light from the dark depths.

A wave rushed up the near shore, tall as ten men. It crashed on the stony slope, over Hidden Moon's grave, then ran and leapt as white spray as far as the entrance to the mine. Silver Cloud felt it swirl around his legs.

Then the creature below the lake surfaced. It heaved itself into view, so huge that it took away Kola's breath. The horned giant spewed water from its mouth, rising on to two legs and surveying the canyon.

'Unktehi!' Silver Cloud breathed.

The monster rose slowly, letting the water run from its broad back. It was pale gold, the colour of the land around it, and its burning red eyes were set in dark sockets.

Four Winds crept alongside Silver Cloud.

'Don't be afraid. Unktehi cannot leave Yellow Water,' the horse told the boy. 'In the lake no one can trouble him, for he is too powerful. But on land, Wakanda's force is stronger.'

'So why has he come?' Kola trembled at the sheer size of the water monster, who filled the base of the great canyon and whose eyes shone like red fires in the hissing storm.

'To talk with Yietso and guide him.' Silver Cloud watched the grinning serpent withdraw towards the shore. His black body writhed low on the ground, with only his flat head erect, until he reached the water.

'Then this is our chance!' Hurriedly Kola ran back to the mine, followed more slowly by the dream horse. 'Come!' he urged. 'What is the matter?'

'I hear horses galloping,' Silver Cloud replied, searching up and down the canyon.

'It is nothing but the rain!' Kola insisted. Their head start on Unktehi and Yietso must not be thrown away.

So he entered the mine a second time, only to find that his guide did not follow. 'Come!' he called again.

For a few moments Kola tried to find his own way down the rough, narrow tunnel. He touched the cold sides, felt the darkness close in on him and imagined the distance he must walk to find the diamond. Turning back towards the exit, he heard movement and expected to see the dream horse coming to join him.

But the figure he saw was that of a crouching man moving stealthily towards him. He trod soft as a mountain lion, holding a raised spear above his head.

And now Kola too heard the sound of galloping horses, and saw men and riders swarm around the entrance, led by a figure in a wolfskin headdress. Silver Cloud was quickly surrounded by whirling warriors on horseback.

This was Snake Eye and his band. They had followed footprints in the loose earth, ridden through the storm to find the Sioux boy. And now, amazed and angry that the spirit horse had returned, their war cries filled the air and they threatened to bring their raised tomahawks crashing down on Silver Cloud.

As Kola hesitated, so the warrior on foot crept nearer. In another flash which lit up the dark tunnel, Kola recognised the face of his hated enemy, Matotope.

The man who had betrayed his People paused and sneered at the boy's startled glance. 'Close your jaws and do not look so foolish. I am sworn brother now to Snake Eye. He is my Chief!'

No words formed on Kola's lips. There was a bitter taste in his mouth as he stared into Matotope's narrow eyes.

'Stand aside!' Matotope ordered. 'I travelled ahead of my new brothers. It is my task to go into the deepest mine and bring back the diamonds for Snake Eye and the Comanches!'

'Never!' Kola stood firm. He took out his knife, given to him by Red Hawk. 'You must kill me first.'

Matotope laughed and made a stabbing gesture with his spear. He sprang towards Kola, who quickly stepped to one side. The lunge took the medicine man past him, into the darkness of the mine.

'I have Silver Cloud to guide me!' Kola warned. 'He has escaped you once. His power is strong.'

Once more Matotope cast aside the warning. Crouching again, the blade of his spear flashed and then he spoke. 'The power of Unktehi is stronger, and Snake

Eye has called upon the master, Anteep, to guide him. Your dream horse will never defeat the might of the evil ones!'

Outside the tunnel, thunder crashed and horses' hooves clashed against the rock. Matotope's mocking words rang loud in Kola's ears.

But then, in a sudden flash from out of nowhere, Yietso was there. The black snake reared over Matotope's head, his yellow throat glowing. The medicine man spun round, leaving his back unguarded.

Kola was poised, ready to plunge his knife between Matotope's bare shoulder blades. He saw the place where the blade should enter, to one side of the backbone, between the ribs.

Yietso's fierce gaze held back his arm and he couldn't strike. Then the monster turned his eyes towards Matotope. 'You dared to enter Unktehi's mine!' he challenged. 'What is your purpose here?'

'To kill the boy and prevent him from stealing the diamond.' Matotope's answer was cowed. He shrank back against the wall and let his spear drop to the ground.

Yietso swelled out his form until it blocked the way completely. 'This is a lie,' he hissed. 'I am everywhere in this mine. I know that you plan to cheat Unktehi and take the stone for yourself!'

'No! I swear to you that we are in the service of

Anteep, leader of Unktehi. We would not steal the stone!'

'But I heard you confess your greed to the boy,' came the challenge. 'You cannot unsay what has already been said!'

'Then it was because Snake Eye ordered it!' Matotope's voice grew high and soft as he twisted his way out of the blame. 'Believe me, I would not have undertaken the task if my life had not been in danger. The leader of my enemy, the Comanche Wild Dogs, made me do this!'

Yietso regarded him with a cold, cruel eye. 'You are not a newly sworn brother to Snake Eye, after all?'

A groan came from Matotope's throat. 'Yietso!' he pleaded. 'My heart is with you. Forget about the diamond. I will do anything you ask!'

The serpent monster lowered his head so that his flickering tongue played around Matotope's cheek. 'How is this? Betrayal is your nature,' he hissed.

'Believe me, I am your servant!' The medicine man fell to his knees.

' "Believe you"?' Yietso mocked. 'As Red Hawk, Chief of the White Water band, believed you when you ran from the battle at Thunder Ridge? As Snake Eye believed you when he sent you to fetch the diamond?'

'I came to do Snake Eye's work!' Matotope whined.

'No. You came for the stone. But your plan was to flee from Snake Eye once you had found it. There is no loyalty in you. You would betray all men!' Yietso delivered his judgement in a harsh voice, his face close to the man's.

'I give you my word!' Matotope cried.

The serpent drew coldly back. 'Your word is less than nothing,' he replied.

Saying this, he fixed his eyes on the guilty man, who felt the stare penetrate deep beneath his skin into his spirit. It ate into him like a bitter poison, hollowing out his body, leaving nothing but the shell.

Matotope rose in terror. As his body was eaten away from the inside and his heart stopped beating, he opened his mouth to speak.

'No more words!' Yietso commanded, increasing the intensity of his stare.

Kola saw that Matotope suffered great anguish, yet he could not understand why. The man seemed whole, but his mouth was twisted into a silent scream, and he clutched his chest, wildly beating his fist against his ribs. Only the gaze of the serpent held him in its power.

The beating of Matotope's fist grew weaker, he staggered and fell to his knees.

'Stop!' Kola pleaded with Yietso to end the traitor's pain.

But still the invisible poison ate away at Matotope. It seared him and made him raise his arms in silent plea.

There was nothing left of him, only bones that wasted to dust even as he sank. Yet still his eyes saw the serpent.

Until his last breath was taken, the man knew his tormentor and shrivelled under the glare of his green eyes.

FIFTEEN

Words had failed Matotope. The lies he had lived by were no more use. His life had ended in agonised silence.

Through his horror, Four Winds saw that this was fitting. But he was afraid for his own life now that Yietso had turned the medicine man to dust. So he fled from the mine, stumbling into the thunderstorm and the frantic whirlwind of horses and men.

The Wild Dogs had surrounded Silver Cloud and were racing their horses in an ever tightening circle. Their spears were raised and their wild cries rose above the low, constant roll of thunder.

With Yietso behind him in the tunnel, the boy had no choice but to dart between the circling horses in an effort to reach his guardian. Risking his life, he lunged forward between two of the mounted Comanches, feeling the hot breath of their horses and the swipe of a tomahawk close to his skull.

'Kill him too!' Snake Eye snarled the command, wrenching the reins of his black-and-white horse to steer it out of the tight circle and ride to a nearby hill. Here he reined his mount to a standstill to look down on the destruction he had ordered.

Four Winds found Silver Cloud trapped in the centre of the warlike circle, still untouched by the weapons of the enemy. Time and again he reared on to his hind legs, striking out with his front hooves to ward off attack, but when he saw the boy he stopped for an instant to let him climb on to his back.

Gratefully Kola made the leap, then held tight to the silver horse's mane. He felt the strong body lunge forward as if to break through the circle, only to be driven back again by a jabbing spear. High on the hill, Snake Eye looked down with a dark frown.

Then Yietso the shape-shifter charged from the mine. He had chosen the new form of a mighty black stallion, stronger than any horse ever seen, with wild eyes, flaring nostrils and ears pinned flat against his head.

The Comanche horses saw him and shied away.

'Hold the circle tight!' Snake Eye cried.

His band forced their horses to keep their positions while Yietso approached. When the black stallion veered to one side and charged through the rain down to the lake, they closed in on Silver Cloud and Kola once more.

Kola watched Yietso reach the shore and saw with renewed horror that Unktehi himself still squatted in the water, his vast bulk filling the canyon. As the two monsters met and planned their next move, he appealed to Silver Cloud. 'Must we die?' he whispered in terror.

His horse reared and struck out at the Comanches. 'We need powerful magic,' he replied. 'You must call quickly on the memory of your mother, Shining Star, while I turn day into night.'

With no time to question, Kola fulfilled the strange command. In the midst of the storm and the charging circle of enemy horses he closed his eyes and brought to mind his beautiful mother. She appeared with the soft look of love which he remembered, dark eyes melting as she gazed into his cradle, lips smiling, long dark hair falling loose over her shoulders.

As he remembered, so Silver Cloud called upon Ghost Horse to drive away the storm clouds. The powerful spirit brought a wind from the south which swept into the canyon and rolled the clouds over the northern ridge and dried up the rain. Ghost Horse made the sky dark, sending the sun behind the mountains to the west. Night fell, to the wild consternation of the Comanches and their horses.

'Day has become night!' they cried, letting their mounts shy away from the circle, making a space through which Silver Cloud could charge.

'The dream horse has defeated the Sun! Death has come to the day spirits of the sky!' The Wild Dogs broke away in fear.

Kola held tight as his horse charged through the

weakening ring and set off at full gallop along the shore of the lake. He saw the moon appear as a pale crescent and the stars prick holes in the dark blanket of the night sky.

'Pursue them!' Quickly Snake Eye rallied his band. He led them in a race to capture Silver Cloud, leaning forward and urging his horse to cover the ground.

Meanwhile, Yietso had talked with Unktehi, whose dark presence still towered over the scene.

'Destroy the dream horse and the boy!' Unktehi passed a sentence of death. His red eyes glowed like giant coals through the black night. 'And do not let the Comanches live. They plotted with Matotope to steal the stone from deep in the mine. Though they swore allegiance to Anteep, they follow only their own desires!'

So Yietso kept the shape of the stallion and set off like a dark shadow in pursuit of all.

Hearing Comanche horses close on their heels, Kola glanced over his shoulder to see Snake Eye at their head. The chief's moonlit face was set in cruel lines beneath the wolfskin headdress. His spear glinted and a round, buffalo-skin shield swung loosely by his hip. Shouting the order for his band to fan out along the width of the shore, Snake Eye looked as though he would never give in.

'What now?' Kola breathed. Looking ahead, he saw that the giant canyon narrowed where the lake ended and that the plan of the Comanches was to overtake them and block their escape.

'Call once more upon Shining Star!' Silver Cloud told him. 'For though I can outrun Snake Eye, Yietso follows behind, and his power on land is stronger than mine.'

A second glance showed Kola the swift, strong shape of the black stallion drawing level with the Wild Dogs.

'In the air Yietso cannot touch us,' Silver Cloud promised. 'Call now upon your mother!'

Kola clung to Silver Cloud's mane and spoke to the night sky. 'Behold!' he cried. 'I am Four Winds, son of Swift Elk and Shining Star, from the band of the White Water Sioux! It is two summers since my father gave up his life for his People and my mother was taken by the Comanches. I call now upon Shining Star whose home is the night sky. Take us out of danger, into your arms!'

The time was right, and as he spoke, the silver stars in the heavens gathered together in a shining chain which lowered itself gently towards the earth. The chain spread its rays over Silver Cloud and his rider, enveloping them in a glow which separated them from their pursuers.

'Take hold of the end of the chain,' Silver Cloud told Kola, who reached up and touched the stars.

At that moment, the dream horse's hooves left the ground and rose slowly out of reach of Snake Eye. The Comanches looked on helplessly as the boy and the horse floated clear of the earth, high above their heads.

Yietso too halted his swift stride and gazed in anger at the magical sight.

'Higher!' Four Winds begged the stars. He searched for his mother's face in the blackness overhead, but only heard her voice tenderly calling his name. 'Kola!' she sighed. 'My son!'

The chain of stars drew them higher. 'Mother!' Four Winds replied, his heart melting at the soft sounds.

'You have done well, my son!' she whispered.

Silver Cloud and Kola drifted into the sky, leaving behind their earthbound enemies.

Yietso turned then on Snake Eye. 'You are a fool!' he cried. 'You cannot destroy a mere boy of thirteen summers!'

'And you!' Snake Eye retorted. 'Your power is weak, in spite of your proud bearing.'

'A fool and a deceiver!' Yietso challenged, raising himself on to his hind legs. 'Yet your cunning wins you nothing except shame and defeat!'

The taunt drove Snake Eye into cruel action. Raising his spear, he chose his target and with deadly accuracy plunged the tip into the stallion's chest.

The Wild Dogs gasped and reined back their horses. As their chief drove his spear deep into Yietso's flesh, they saw the shape-shifter spill black blood. He fell to the earth and writhed, returning to the form of a serpent. From the lake, Unktehi roared out his anger.

Snake Eye jerked back his spear and drove his horse forward. Before Yietso could recover, he ran at him and trampled him, making him writhe and hiss.

Now the band of Comanches saw that the bitter actions of their leader had brought upon them a great trouble. They were full of dread and their cowardly hearts drove them away from the place where Snake Eye fought with Yietso. Reining their horses towards the end of the canyon, they set off in confusion, leaving Snake Eye to his fate.

Still Snake Eye attacked the monster, beating him down until he lay without movement, his blood spreading as a black pool under the horse's hooves.

Then at last the Comanche chief withdrew, raising his decorated spear into the air and yelling his defiance. 'I curse Yietso and his master, Unktehi! I will not follow Anteep! From this time Snake Eye will call upon no spirit to help him. For I am strong. Alone I will defeat my enemies!'

His voice echoed down the canyon and into the night sky where Silver Cloud and Four Winds were held by a swaying thread of stars. 'I am strong. Alone I will defeat my enemies!'

Snake Eye wheeled his horse around to follow his fleeing band. Rearing him up, he shook his spear one last time. Then he galloped away, the hand of revenge gripped tight around his heart.

Four Winds heard the proud, bitter message. He

looked to the heavens to hear Shining Star's tender voice soothe away his fear, but though he listened hard, he met with disappointment. There was silence over his head as the night sky faded into dawn and the gentle stars lowered him slowly back to earth.

SIXTEEN

'Two have died,' Silver Cloud warned. He stood with Kola before the dark entrance to the mine.

The boy already knew the danger of entering. With his own hands, he had lifted the stones from Hidden Moon's body. He had seen Matotope fade into dust.

'I have the plaited bracelet which my cousin made,' he told Silver Cloud. 'And the lizard skin pouch with the sacred cord. Lizard means long life,' he said with a brave smile.

'You will have need of good omens and the gifts of your grandfather, Red Hawk.' Silver Cloud watched Kola open his medicine bundle and lay out the objects at the entrance to the tunnel.

Once more the boy chose the feather necklace for speed and this time a knot of sweetgrass to purify his cause. He rubbed the grass against the skin of his face and arms, saying, 'Behold me. The diamond we seek is sacred. May our enemies sleep, may the journey end in reward, for our quest is just!'

Then he rolled up the bundle and slung it across his

shoulder. 'Snake Eye has smitten Yietso with his spear. At least we have one less enemy to fear.'

But his wise guardian shook his head. 'As with me, so it is with Yietso. He will return to Anteep, head of the underworld, to be renewed. A ceremony will make him whole again.'

'Then we must begin our journey into the mine before he returns,' Kola said, clenching his fists in an effort to master his fear.

'Unktehi has many other spirits who guard the diamonds,' Silver Cloud said, looking intently along the length of the lake. Daylight had returned, together with brooding clouds which had settled along the high ridge marking the edge of the canyon. At the death of Yietso, Unktehi had withdrawn below the surface of the lake, no doubt to make another plan aimed at defeating the intruders.

Following the horse's gaze, Kola couldn't pick out any sign of danger. Yet he knew that the smallest creature could present a hidden threat, even the spider who wove her webs in cracks in the rock.

'We will not succeed by the knife and spear,' Silver Cloud predicted. 'Unktehi will send spirits too strong and cruel for us to overcome. So it is as I said in the beginning: sometimes battle is not the way.'

'What then?' Kola was ready to give all his boy's strength to the fight, and eager now to begin.

'We must be wiser than our enemy, and trick him.

Unktehi watches us from his underwater lair. As soon as we enter the mine, he will set his monsters upon us to draw us back.'

Kola felt his skin crawl at the notion of Unktehi's red gaze fixed upon them. 'How do we prevent them?' he asked.

Silver Cloud walked slowly under the dark overhang and peered inside. His silver grey coat made him look ghostly, his noble head was raised, his ears pricked and listening. 'We will take a risk,' he decided, casting his gaze towards the rocks strewn down the slope. 'We will let Unktehi see us enter and send his spirits after us. But before they reach us, I will bring down another great fall of rock.'

The danger was so great that it took away Kola's breath. 'You will block the tunnel?' he gasped.

'Yes, and make Unktehi believe that we died like Hidden Moon, crushed under the collapsing tunnel.'

'But we will stay ahead of the rockfall!' Though the risk was great, the plan was clever. 'Then we can go deep into the mine without Unktehi's spirits giving chase. But when we return to the rockfall, what then? Won't our way be blocked and all our efforts wasted?'

Silver Cloud turned kindly towards the boy. 'When you hold the diamond in your hand, then our journey is ended,' he explained. 'Ghost Horse will return us to Red Hawk and your People faster than the lightning strikes the earth.'

★ ★ ★

With this hope in his heart and complete trust in the dream horse, Four Winds accepted the plan. They entered the mine together, under Unktehi's jealous gaze.

The water monster summoned Washoe, the great bird of Lake Tahoe in the south west, and the white water buffaloes from Bull Lake to the west. Then he called upon the myriad of water babies from Yellow Water itself, small people with long hair that swept down from their heads and cloaked their bodies, whose task was to guard the hot springs. He called from the mountains a great giant with one eye which glowed in his forehead, called Numuzo'ho, the Crusher of Men. Lastly, he gathered his many serpents, lizards, frogs, owls and eagles. But he did not call on anyone who might break through rock.

'Follow the horse and the boy,' Unktehi told his servants. 'The horse is messenger to Ghost Horse and has many powers. Crush them both!'

So Washoe the giant bird flapped his heavy wings and took flight towards the mine, ahead of the buffaloes and the water babies who clung to the thick hair around their necks. Numuzo'ho, with his glowing eye, strode after them, ready to destroy.

Kola stepped into the darkness with Silver Cloud at his side. They heard the rush of a giant bird's wings beating the air and the thunderous steps of their many pursuers.

'Make ready!' Silver Cloud urged Kola forward. 'Take ten steps and then wait.'

With his heart thumping hard against his ribs and his mouth dry with terror, he obeyed the command. Five paces into the blackness, he paused and turned. Behind him was the square of daylight and his connection with the world he knew. Ahead was the dark unknown.

'Walk further!' Silver Cloud commanded.

Still Kola hesitated. He pictured the rocks falling from the roof, cutting out the light. What if the way ahead was also blocked? He would be imprisoned in stone and breathe his last breath in darkness. Every instinct cried out against it.

But he loved the horse and trusted him with his life. 'I will never fail you. Love sits in my heart,' Silver Cloud had promised at Talking Gods Rock. This then was the greatest test.

So, with trembling legs, Kola did his bidding, feeling the darkness throw its damp cloak around him, following in the footsteps of poor Hidden Moon.

From the lake, Unktehi watched his horde of evil spirits surge towards the mine. Washoe alighted on the rocky ledge above the entrance, sending in the small water babies, who scuttled into the darkness, their long hair streaming behind.

Silver Cloud saw the creatures enter. Summoning all his power, he forced the rock above his head to crack. It split with a grinding shudder, sending a fault line shooting along the roof of the tunnel towards Unktehi's followers.

Fatally weakened, the roof straight away started to crumble on to the water babies, piling rock upon rock so that soon Kola could only see a narrow gap through which daylight entered. He put his hands to his ears to dull the crack and thud of falling rock. 'Silver Cloud!' he called out, as the last rays of light disappeared.

All was dark and quiet. The last rock had wedged itself into the final gap. The wall was complete. Kola could hear his own breath. 'Silver Cloud!' he cried again.

A silver white glimmer appeared at his side. 'It is done,' the horse said.

Unktehi rose from the lake in anger once more. He raged at Washoe and Numuzo'ho. 'Clear a path!' he roared.

'But the horse and the boy are dead,' Washoe protested. He'd heard the howls of the water babies and pictured the scene of destruction inside the tunnel.

'How can you be sure?' Unktehi needed proof. 'Dig through the rockfall!' he commanded Numuzo'ho. 'Bring me their crushed and lifeless bodies!'

As the giant began to heave at the rocks, Silver Cloud and Kola set off on the last stage of their journey. Instead of pitch blackness, the silver glow from the horse's body cast a pale light – enough to show the uneven ground underfoot and the twists and bends in the sloping tunnel.

'It is as if the earth has swallowed us!' Kola whispered, picturing the weight of rock above their heads. He kept his hand on Silver Cloud's neck and took his pace from him.

'Yet men tore out this rock and dug this mine,' the horse reminded him. 'Many exhausted slaves lost their lives in the search for the glittering stone.'

Kola examined the rough marks on the rock walls. It was true: the tunnel had been gouged out with flint blades, step by step. The path to the diamond was stained with dead men's blood. But he did not have time to wonder, as every step took them closer to the end of their first journey.

Soon the sloping ground gave way to steep steps cut into the rock, taking them deeper. Water began to trickle through the roof and form narrow streams, falling as small waterfalls down the worn steps. They ran into a pool in an underground cavern which widened out before Silver Cloud and Kola.

The boy shook his head in wonder. He had not known that the rock beneath his feet contained streams and caves, nor that the stone could form strange icicles which hung the height of a man from the roofs. His feet splashed through shallow pools as he held firmly to Silver Cloud's mane.

'The trick of the rockfall worked well.' Kola's voice echoed through the eerie cavern. He could hear no footsteps behind them and his fear began to ease.

'Unless Unktehi suspects and orders his giants to remove the stones.' Silver Cloud knew his enemy well. But he realised that the trick had given them more time.

They passed through the high cavern, back into a tunnel, and followed more steps deeper into the earth.

Kola wondered how far they must continue. He stumbled in his eagerness.

'Do not fall now!' Silver Cloud warned.

Down they went. The tunnel grew narrower, so that Silver Cloud had to lower his head. His sides swayed against the walls, his hooves clattering on the uneven stone.

'Dig faster!' Unktehi told Numuzo'ho. He grew certain that the horse and the boy were not dead after all.

The giant clawed at boulders and tore rocks from the entrance to the mine, which the buffalo spirits rolled down the hill into the lake. Washoe circled overhead, swooping to pick up rocks between his great claws and let them drop into the water. The bird saw black clouds gather on the ridge and welcomed them as signs of ill omen. He circled higher and cried out a message to Unktehi below. 'Behold, Yietso is here!'

The guardian of the mine looked up and saw the black serpent appear at the edge of the canyon. The ritual to renew him in the World Beneath had been speedy; he had returned life-side to help defeat Silver Cloud and the boy.

'Let me enter the mine!' he hissed at Unktehi, seeing that Numuzo'ho had opened up a narrow gap into the tunnel. 'For I am the power that can defeat the enemy!'

Unktehi gave his assent. 'Go quickly!' he commanded. 'For the boy grows close to the diamond!'

Deep under the earth, Kola crouched as the tunnel narrowed.

'I cannot go on!' Silver Cloud told him. 'You must continue alone!'

So the boy stooped and edged forward, hoping that the way ahead was not long and that he would soon reach the bottom of the mine. There was rock all around him, no sky or sun. Only the darkness leading to the diamond.

He went on to his hands and knees, feeling his way. Cold water trickled on to him and the rough stone scraped his skin. And then at last he reached the end.

It was a small chamber lit by a dull green light. Kola found that he could stand, and looked around, wondering about the source of the light.

On a ledge there was a buffalo-skin bundle bound with thongs, much like the medicine bundle he carried across his shoulder. The boy's heart leapt when he saw it. He ran towards it.

But a shadow hovered by the ledge, resting on a rock, coiled and dangerous. A snake raised its head, its emerald eyes glowing.

Yietso! Kola's hand had almost touched the bundle on the ledge before he saw the serpent and recoiled.

The snake's tongue flickered, ready to strike.

The boy's hand went towards his knife. Yietso would not stand between him and his prize! He would fight the evil spirit with all his might.

The serpent hissed and writhed towards him.

Drawing his grandfather's blade, and calling out the name of Red Hawk in a clear voice, Kola felt no fear. This blade would strike like lightning. It would overcome the worst of enemies.

And yet he had never struck in anger in all his thirteen summers. He felt his hand tremble as the snake began to wind its body around him. Then he thought of all that had passed on this journey, and the prize that was still to be won. So he brought the knife up in the name of his father and all who had been slain by the Comanches, and in the name of all his People who were to be saved.

The blade slashed against Yietso's soft throat. But it was not the force of the knife in his flesh that paralysed the creature and made him slide to the ground. It was the power of Swift Elk, who was treacherouly slain, and the strength of the White Water People, whose spirits were greater than the evil of Yietso and his lord, Unktehi.

Kola withdrew his knife and watched the serpent sink lifeless to the ground.

He turned to seize the bundle from the ledge, then ran from the chamber, scrambling through the tunnel to rejoin Silver Cloud. He held up the leather parcel, untying it with trembling fingers, using his knife when his fingers proved too weak.

The dream horse stood by silently and watched.

At last Kola opened the tightly wrapped bundle. He spread it on the ground in the pale silver light, turned it this way and that until he realised that it was empty.

'No!' he gasped, and searched again.

There were no glittering stones.

Four Winds looked up at Silver Cloud in dismay. He felt a tight band of sorrow around his chest. The picture of his grandfather, Red Hawk, and his grandmother, White Deer, wringing their hands in despair, struck him to the heart. And he thought of brave Hidden Moon.

The boy slumped bitterly to the ground. '*Hena 'la yelo.*' It is over.

As he bowed forward in defeat, tears welled from deep within. They rose through his wounded heart, washing it clean. And they appeared in his brown eyes, shining in the light.

Silver Cloud watched and waited.

Kola's tears brimmed over and fell on to the empty bundle. They turned into bright, glittering diamonds – the purest and most perfect ever seen.

The boy reached out and took up one of the

glittering stones. As his finger closed around the diamond, he smiled at the dream horse through his tears.

Then Four Winds and Silver Cloud called upon Ghost Horse, and the spirit took them home.

THE RETURN

'I will speak again,' Red Hawk said. He held up the diamond from the deepest mine for his People to see.

Four Winds stood by his side.

'The son of my only son, Swift Elk, has made his journey with the dream horse. They have sought out the first prize of three and suffered much to bring it home.'

White Deer's face ran with tears of pride. 'Praise the goodness of the Great Spirit, Wakanda,' she murmured. 'That he has brought my grandson safely back to my arms.'

Red Hawk's gnarled fingers closed around the precious stone. 'Now there is a gleam of light in the east for the White Water band. Though frost whitens the trees and ice freezes the streams, there is hope that we may yet overcome Snake Eye and his Wild Dogs.'

Four Winds heard the sigh of satisfaction that passed between the warriors, the women and the children. It was like wind amongst pale aspen leaves.

'We have lost our brave child, Hidden Moon,' Red

Hawk went on. His old eyes searched the evening sky for the first pale glint of stars in the heavens. 'She is with Wakanda, where the noble spirits of our fathers rest.'

The People murmured their praise of a girl who had given her life for their future.

In Kola's mind's eye, her brown eyes flashed. Her voice said, as if from a great distance, 'I will go with you to find the precious stone!' When they were children, playing by the tipi, he had taught her to pull a taut bowstring and aim true. Now Thunder Bird stood guard over her grave.

Tomorrow, at dawn, as he stepped out of the village with Silver Cloud on his second journey to find the feather from the highest mountain, he would carry the memory of Hidden Moon with him.

Gravely his grandfather took an eagle's feather from his own war bonnet and gave it to Four Winds. '*Iki 'cize waon 'kon*,' he said softly. 'Once I was a warrior. Now it is the turn of the young and swift.'

The boy took the feather and ran his thumb along the soft, silken edge. Then he tied this badge of honour to the leather thong which bound his precious medicine bundle.

He looked up and met the dream horse's wise gaze. *Now I am a warrior too.*

PART TWO

IRON EYES

PROLOGUE

The warrior boy stood proudly at his grandfather's side.

'Though frost whitens the trees and ice freezes the streams, there is hope that we may yet overcome Snake Eye and his Wild Dogs.' The old man clasped the diamond which his grandson had brought home. He spoke of a gleam of light in the east for the White Water Band; a faint hope that his People would survive.

Four Winds felt the strong beat of his heart. It did not falter, though he had another journey to make, a second test of his courage to undergo.

'Now it is the turn of the young and the swift,' Red Hawk insisted. With gnarled hands and trembling fingers, he took an eagle feather from his own war bonnet and gave it to Four Winds. 'May it carry you further and faster, may it give you power over your enemies.'

Four Winds tied the gift to his medicine bundle which hung at his side. Tomorrow he would depart, strong in Chief Red Hawk's trust.

Tomorrow with his dream horse, wise Silver Cloud, sent by Ghost Horse, true servant of Wakanda, the Maker of All Good Things.

Tomorrow, to the highest mountain, to bring a feather home. Guided by Silver Cloud, gladly facing danger for the sake of his grandfather, Red Hawk, and his grandmother, White Deer. He would carry with him the hopes of his small band of White Water Sioux.

Through his weariness he saw plains to cross, hills to climb. He saw winter's icy grasp, felt the raw wind, breathed in cold death.

Alone he could not make this journey. But with Silver Cloud's strength and swiftness, with the goodness of the great Wakanda to give them courage, he would set out to find this feather.

Tomorrow, after he had rested.

'Kola, sleep now.' Using his childhood name, his grandmother came forward with her hand outstretched. 'The moon is high, the day is done.'

'I am a warrior, not a boy,' he whispered.

He had seen battles, slain Yietso with his grandfather's knife. Now no one could call him boy. He had cast off his childhood name.

'You are the only son of my dead only son,' White Deer told him gently. 'I have held you in my arms. Only I can call you boy.'

So Four Winds softened and allowed himself to be led to the tipi. He took a blanket and wound it around his shoulders, heard his grandmother draw the dew cloth, felt the darkness settle.

THE DISCOVERY

ONE

Four Winds slept.

In his dream he heard the voice of his cousin, Hidden Moon. It came to him through the flapping of enormous wings that raised thunder in the heavens, and the night sky flashed with lightning.

'Four Winds!' Hidden Moon breathed over him in his dream. Her black hair, glossy as a jay'swing, hung loose over her shoulders. Her face floated so close to his that he could see only the dark pools of her eyes.

The boy turned in his sleep.

'I am with you still,' Hidden Moon consoled him. 'Though the rocks fell and I could not reach the diamond, though you buried me by the lake under a great stone, I will not leave you.'

Dream thunder roared, lightning split the sky.

'I am part of all you see, along with your father, mighty Swift Elk, and my father, Black Kettle, who fell at Thunder Rock. We are inside the great hoop, the circle of life which cannot be broken.'

Four Winds sighed and turned on to his back.

'I am in the stars and the moon, the tall forests and the fishes of the oceans.'

Thunderbird crashed his wings. His eyes darted forks of silver light into the sky.

'Do not be afraid.' Hidden Moon whispered in the boy's ear. 'Going always brings return. The air is crowded with the words of those who have gone before. Listen and you will hear them.'

Four Winds threw off his blanket and sat upright. His body ran with cold sweat, and yet the words his dead cousin had spoken were comforting.

No, it was something else that had woken him. Perhaps the autumn mist that had crept through the heavy, painted dewcloth? Or some disturbance by the cedar tree which stood in the centre of their camp.

He listened hard. The cedar tree was the place where Silver Cloud kept watch while the tribe slept. The dream horse never closed his eyes, was always watchful, ready to act. And Four Winds could hear him now, shifting restlessly under the great tree, whinnying softly.

So the boy crept out of his tipi. He felt ice crackle in the clear air. A twig snapped underfoot.

The horse turned. His long neck was arched, his ears pricked. 'Make no sound,' he warned.

Four Winds halted. He listened again. Way below, the White Water River rushed by. Overhead, a keen wind whistled.

'There is a man in the valley,' Silver Cloud told him. 'His foosteps are swift.'

The message startled Four Winds. At night no one moved alone, for fear of the mountain lion and the bear. 'Which way is he running?'

'Towards the tipis. He stumbles in his haste.'

'How far from here?'

'A thousand times a man's stride.' Silver Cloud didn't hesitate.

'I don't hear anything.' The boy peered into the darkness. Who was this man: friend or enemy?

'He is coming,' the horse said.

Then the flap across another painted tipi opened, and the great Sioux warrior, One Horn, stepped out. The oldest and wisest of Red Hawk's braves, he had seen many battles and brought back Swift Elk's bloodied war shirt from Thunder Ridge. He saw Four Winds staring into the valley and quickly strode across. 'My sleep was disturbed. What is the matter?'

'A man is running through the night,' the boy informed him.

One Horn went back to his tipi for his bow and tomahawk. Then he vanished through the trees into the valley.

The wind blew and the moon sailed in the sky.

'Two men are coming,' Silver Cloud warned Four Winds at last.

Soon the broad figure of One Horn reappeared on

the brow of the cold hill, accompanied by a slighter, younger man, whose feathered headband and quilled shirt showed that he was a member of the White Water tribe.

'Sun Dancer!' Four Winds murmured. He recognised the young man's bearing, his springing step and the forward thrust of his head.

And now the arrival had brought other sleepers from their tents. They gathered beside the cedar tree, close together for warmth, wondering what news their messenger brought.

'Sun Dancer set out with my brother, Running Fox, two suns ago,' the squaw, Burning Tree, told Four Winds. 'Red Hawk wanted news of your search for the diamond. He sent his two youngest braves across White Water, into the desert, to meet with Nightcloud of the Oglala Sioux and ask how you and the spirit horse had fared.'

Four Winds nodded at the young woman. He sensed her fear. Where was Running Fox now? What news had Sun Dancer brought?

'Don't worry; Running Fox will be close behind,' another woman assured them.

Four Winds turned to Silver Cloud. 'Are there more footsteps in the valley?'

The horse shook his head.

Then Sun Dancer broke away from One Horn and sought out Burning Tree. His eyes brought sorrow before he spoke his words.

'Your brother, Running Fox, is gone from life-side. He is with your father and your father's father, and all who have gone before.'

Burning Tree cried out. She clung to Sun Dancer's war shirt, tugging at it as though to make him send the words back, to swallow them and tell her that her brother lived yet.

'The Comanche Wild Dogs took him,' Sun Dancer insisted. 'Five men came from behind and pierced his side with their spears. Their horses trampled him into the dust.'

Four Winds stiffened at the name of Wild Dogs. The Comanches put their horses to evil use, they were in the service of Anteep, the Source of All Evil.

'Believe me, your brother is dead,' Sun Dancer said softly, taking Burning Tree's hands in his.

And the women set up a wailing and moaning that soared into the night sky. 'May the great spirit, Wakanda, embrace him. May he live in the memories of the White Water People forever!'

White Deer came from Chief Red Hawk's tipi. She was old and stooped, her bones stiff. But she received news of the young warrior's death calmly. 'We have seen much suffering,' she told Burning Tree. 'The Lizard of Long Life visits few of our People. It is as it is.'

And the old woman let the girl weep in her arms, knowing that the tears would soften her grief.

'How did the Comanches steal upon you?' One Horn asked Sun Dancer.

'We were talking with Nightcloud of the Oglala Sioux. We learned that Four Winds was alive, but that the spirit horse had been captured by the Comanches. All this Nightcloud saw. We feared for the boy in his solitary journey into the mine.'

Now Four Winds shuddered as he recalled the worst of times; how he had been tricked by shape-shifting monsters as he'd travelled alone to find the diamond. And how he'd turned away from the wise advice of his cousin, Hidden Moon, and sent her to her death.

'And then?' One Horn prompted.

'There were many buffaloes on the plain. They came swiftly in a cloud of dust. Behind them hid the Wild Dogs on their horses. Before we knew it, they were upon us. The Comanche war cry filled the air. Soon Nightcloud and Running Fox lay in the dirt. I stepped in the path of one horse and wrestled the rider from his back. The creature stopped and let me take the place of the Wild Dog. He bore me to safety.'

One Horn grunted. 'I will carry this news to Red Hawk,' he decided.

'Wait.' Sun Dancer laid a hand on the old man's arm. 'On my journey home I learned that Snake Eye lives. The monsters of Yellow Water did not defeat him, and he is still determined to drive our People from our land.'

'This I know,' Four Winds confirmed gravely. He told the gathering how he and Silver Cloud had seen Snake Eye slay the snake monster, Yietso, shedding his blood as a black pool upon the ground. Then the leader of the Wild Dogs had cried out his defiance: 'I curse Yietso and his master, Unktehi! I will not follow Anteep! From this time Snake Eye will call upon no spirit to help him. For I am strong. Alone I will defeat my enemies!'

And the people murmured in fear under the stars. With such a foe, how could their small band hope to survive? Among the White Water People there were four warriors left out of fifty. Five including the boy, Four Winds.

'Tomorrow, I will depart with Silver Cloud,' Four Winds promised. 'I will fulfil the second part of my quest and bring the feather from the highest mountain.'

'The way is long,' someone sighed. 'And the boy is young.'

'I will succeed!' Four Winds vowed.

'Words!' a second doubter murmured. 'Words do not pay for our dead people. They do not protect our father's graves, nor our homeland. Good words will not give us back our children.'

And Burning Tree cried again. 'Oh, my brother!'

'What will become of us if the boy fails?' came the cry. And the lamentations of the women reached the stars.

TWO

'Not so fast,' Silver Cloud counselled the impatient boy. 'There are wise words to receive, ceremonies to perform before we depart.'

Four Winds strode restlessly through the camp. It was almost dawn. 'We must go now,' he insisted. 'If we wait, the women will delay us with their tears and fears. We have no time for ceremony.'

The horse waited quietly under the cedar tree. The boy was like a young colt, eager to try out his speed and power. But those who hurried heedlessly into danger had to be checked. 'The mountain will not move,' he advised. 'It will still be there for us to climb.'

'But Snake Eye has sworn to defeat us and winter closes in,' Four Winds protested. The leaves were gone from the aspen trees and ice formed on the surface of the tumbling streams. He knew that his People would not long survive the loss of their White Water homeland.

'Wait,' Silver Cloud insisted. His eyes were untroubled as his white mane lifted clear of his face in the wind.

'We will depart at the right time, with the blessing of Red Hawk.'

So Four Winds was forced to linger amongst the tipis until the sun rose. The first signal was the call of birds, almost before grey dawn had streaked the sky. Then the silent mule deer appeared at the edge of the camp, picking at the bark of trees, wandering on, heads to the ground, in search of food. Soon, the women came out of their tents, built fires and prepared flat bread from the band's scant supply of maize, which they ground between two stones.

The smell reminded Four Winds that he must eat in preparation for his journey to the highest mountain. He would need all his strength to walk and climb, to face the Comanches and outwit the forces of Anteep. So he sought out his grandmother, White Deer, and humbly asked for food.

The old woman bowed her head and set about her task. Sixty years had not broken her and, though her face was sunken, her hair was still black, parted and braided in two long ropes down her back.

'Did you sleep with your dreamcatcher over your bed?' she asked him, as mothers and grandmothers did.

'Yes,' he replied. It was not bad dreams entering through the woven web of threads, beads and feathers that had kept him awake, but the weeping of Burning Tree.

'And did you bathe in sweetgrass?'

'Not yet, grandmother.'

'Then you must. The water is ready. Go now while I bake the bread.'

Reluctantly, Four Winds did her bidding. He lay in the scented bath, eyes closed, undergoing *inipi*, the purification ritual which would prepare his spirit for the new journey by taking away the stains of the old one. Breathing in the steam, eyes closed, he grew calm.

'Good,' White Deer said when he reappeared by the fire. She gave him bread and stood over him to watch him eat. 'You have changed,' she told him.

He nodded. 'I have seen many things on my journey.'

She remembered how he'd leaped to cast off childish things; his pride when he had been chosen by Red Hawk to perform the three tasks; her fear for him as he'd set forth with his spirit guide. And now she wanted to counsel him again.

'Remember, the White Water Sioux are the people who do not die. We may pass from life-side and our world may change, but we change with it. We accept the new.'

'But not the mastery of Snake Eye,' he retorted.

White Deer regarded him steadily. 'We accept change, as summer turns to winter, and the spring returns. All that is within nature we embrace.'

Four Winds grunted, then nodded. The bread was warm and good. It filled his empty stomach.

'I must tell you who we are, who we have been and

who we may become,' his grandmother went on, her back to the wind, a thick shawl around her thin shoulders. 'We are the Sioux people of the plains, we weave our stories into our dewcloths, we celebrate the bravery of our warriors and the air is crowded with our words. Remember.'

Four Winds stood up from his meal. 'I remember that I am son of Swift Elk, who fell at Thunder Ridge, grandson of Red Hawk, our chief, who lies sick in his tipi. Of the White Water Warriors who are left; One Horn, Sun Dancer, Little Thunder and Three Bears, I was the chosen one.'

'And the youngest by many summers,' she sighed.

'Because I am the one who Red Hawk loves the most.'

This time, White Deer bowed her head. 'It is so. But you must heed your elders, Kola, including the ones who lived before. We only exist because our ancestors loved, cared and prepared for us. And now we too love our land and our way of life.'

'Which is why Snake Eye and his Wild Dogs must not defeat us,' he said angrily. 'To be cast out from White Water breaks the precious circle, the Hoop of Life.'

Then he looked into his grandmother's eyes and read the wisdom of her years. He recalled how she wore her apron tied around her waist to clean deerskins drawn tight on to a wooden frame. How she cooked eggs for him and knew which herbs cleansed, which were good to eat, and which beautiful flowers were poison. He knew that she had never cut her hair since she was born and that she had shared her stories with him from the time when he lay in his cradle.

'Yes,' he said. 'I will listen to the words of my forefathers.'

His answer made White Deer glad. 'You must meet with our warriors before you leave for the highest mountain. You must perform *Tokaklah* with them, to forgive our enemies, or else the bitterness for Snake Eye will burn into your heart.

So Four Winds quelled his impatience. He waited for the sun to rise fully and the mountain mists to clear. He saw his grandmother as she truly was: a lover of the land, the people and the quiet nights full of fireflies and the smell of cedar trees. At one with the tarantulas and rattlesnakes.

He spoke to her again as the warriors came from their tipis. 'I will listen to the words of those who have gone before,' he promised earnestly. 'But I must also listen to my dream at Spider Rock, when Silver Cloud was sent to guide me. The vision sent by Ghost Horse tells me when I am doing the right things for my People. It keeps me on the path of the heart. It is the one thing that I know can never be taken away from me.'

White Deer listened intently. Yes, Four Winds had changed. He grew up and away from her. All that was within nature she accepted. 'Your vision is good,' she told him. 'May it keep you safe.'

Then One Horn came to fetch Four Winds and brought him into the circle formed by Sun Dancer, Little Thunder and Three Bears. A pipe had been prepared, and the men passed it between them. 'Wakanda, we forgive Snake Eye and his Wild Dogs,' each one murmured, breathing in the scented smoke and releasing hatred from his heart.

'Wakanda, we forgive Snake Eye and his Wild Dogs,' Four Winds repeated, though his heart did not go with his words.

One Horn took the pipe and passed it once more around the circle. The cloaked warriors breathed deep. 'We forgive our enemies.'

Through the rising smoke, Four Winds caught sight of Silver Cloud. The horse watched and listened to only the boy.

'We forgive our enemies,' Four Winds vowed. The hatred lifted from him and ascended with the curling blue smoke.

'*Maka akanl wicasa iyuha el*,' One Horn said. '*Walakata no woawicin waste*.'

Peace on earth to men who carry no hatred.

'Now we may go,' Silver Cloud said.

The dream horse had seen the boy struggle with his impatience and abide by the customs of his People. He knew the depth of White Deer's fears for her grandson, and sensed that there was one large farewell still to be paid before they departed.

'Your grandfather, Red Hawk, waits for you in his tipi,' White Deer told Four Winds.

The boy went obediently, bowing his head at the entrance, preparing to face the old chief's frailty. Four Winds longed for Red Hawk to be standing tall and upright, wearing his war bonnet with pride, as he had been five summers ago. Instead he found him in the gloom of his tent, laid low by the years, propped on a travois of buffalo skins. His breathing was uneven, his eyes almost shut.

'My son,' Red Hawk murmured, hearing Four Winds approach. 'The time has come to travel to the highest mountain.'

'I am ready. Silver Cloud is here to guide me.'

'You will have need of the dream horse. It is a hard journey you must travel together.'

'He bears me on his back,' Four Winds explained. 'His legs never tire. He has the eyes, the speed and the shyness of the antelope.'

Red Hawk sighed. 'A good guide. Do not go separately from him, but stay together.'

Four Winds gazed at the lined face surrounded by furs, at the dim eyes and the trembling limbs. 'Grandfather, what do you know of the highest mountain?' he asked.

'It is in the north, where the brightest star rises in the night sky. Far from here, where the world is always winter and the People live in tipis made of wood.'

'But then how do they roll up their houses? How do their dogs draw them on the travois?' Four Winds' gaze moved to Red Hawk's own tent, up towards the smoke hole, around at the four poles of cedar which supported the painted skins. He saw his grandfather's precious medicine bundle hanging from one of the poles, containing all the beads, bones, animal skins, pipes and arrows which had given Red Hawk his great wisdom and power.

'I do not know. In my long life I have seen the splendour of the Crow People and the fierceness of the Blackfoot. But none of my People have travelled to the winter land of the wolf, to the highest mountain whose name is Mount Kivioq.'

There was a pause as Red Hawk struggled for breath. Then he asked in a weak voice for his medicine bundle.

'Take out the moccasins decorated with quills,' he instructed.

Four Winds' fingers fumbled with the leather thongs which bound the bundle. He laid it out on the earth floor of the tipi, running his hand over the yellow skull of a small bird, picking amongst the bead pouches and lizard skin purses which contained the strong medicinal magic of herbs and finely-ground roots. Finally he picked up the soft leather shoes.

'They were made for me by my grandmother when I completed my first vision quest,' Red Hawk explained. 'Each quill of the porcupine is a captive prayer prepared by the old women of the tribe for young ones just setting out as warriors. Now, as my days disappear furiously into time and my sun is setting, this gift is yours.'

Four Winds took them and put them on his bare feet. He would tread more bravely on the prayers of his grandfather's grandmother, which had carried Red Hawk to victory.

'Know one thing,' Red Hawk continued. 'There is nothing more certain than the death I am about to face. As the sun sets and the seasons change, I am drifting towards my end.'

'But you will still be here when I return,' Four Winds murmured. 'I will bring the feather back to you.'

His grandfather reached out for his hand. 'This may be the last time we meet, here in this world, life-side.'

Four Winds' grip tightened. Tears burned his eyelids. 'You have taught me all I know. You have guarded me and guided me.'

'And now you are a warrior. Follow your vision, trust your dream horse, for he is a messenger of Ghost Horse, follower of Wakanda, the Great Spirit and Master of Life.'

'I will follow him. I will succeed in the two tasks remaining.'

Red Hawk closed his eyes and nodded. 'The White Water country is good country. It is a place of grass and rivers. We hunt game and gather berries, nuts and roots. There is food for all our band.'

As Red Hawk recalled the days of plenty, Four Winds too flew back in time to the days of the *piksun*, when his father hunted and built the drive lanes for the buffalo, leading to the sheer cliff face of Thunder Ridge, where Swift Elk himself had later fallen in battle.

Days of plenty, when the women skinned the buffalo. And every part of the creature had its use. The White Water People would use the rawhide for shields and shoes, for rattles and drums, for ropes and buckets. The buffalo tail became a brush to sweep the tipi, its horns were turned into cups and fire carriers. Even its bones had a dozen uses, as clubs, sleds and knives.

'Those wonders that we then beheld are overthrown,' Red Hawk lamented. 'When the battle was lost at Thunder Ridge, our dream was buried in the bloody mud and burned in the fire set by the Comanches. The march from the valley by those who remained was terrible to behold, leaving the home which had been ours through all time . . .'

The defeat had almost broken the old man's spirit, Four Winds knew. 'It was the fault of Matotope,' he said bitterly. The false shaman had betrayed the People. He had led them to their deaths.

But Red Hawk sighed out his disagreement. 'It was

the work of the Great Spirit, the moving force of the universe, seen in the blue of the sky and the rainbow, who willed it to be so.'

'But why would the good spirits wish us to be cast out?' Four Winds demanded. 'Why do they wish us to die in the mountains?'

'We must not question,' Red Hawk replied, raising himself on to his elbow, anxious to make his grandson understand. 'We should know deep in our hearts that Wakanda is within all things, then we will fear and love him, and act and live as he intends.'

Four Winds bowed his head.

'You and I are bound by blood,' Red Hawk reminded him, sinking back. 'And the child and the old man are close . . .'

'I am no longer a child!' Four Winds interrupted.

'. . . We are close because you have just come from the Great Spirit, and I am about to go to Him.'

Once more, Four Winds grasped the old man's hand. 'Wait for my return,' he pleaded.

'It is as Wakanda wills.' Red Hawk soothed the boy with his words of acceptance. 'My son, I have no more gifts to give you, only my prayers. Remember to use your medicine bundle well, and to keep my knife slung from your wampum belt. May the quill shoes take you swiftly to Mount Kivioq. May you bring back the feather for our People. Now farewell.'

'I will come back and show you the feather from the

highest mountain,' Four Winds insisted. 'You are chief of the White Water band. You will return at the head of your People to the land where we were born.'

The old man lay silent and exhausted in the scented darkness.

'Kola,' a voice said gently from the door of the tipi. It was White Deer, using his childhood name, easing him softly away from his dying grandfather's side.

As Four Winds stood, he brushed the tears from his eyes. 'Going always brings return,' he whispered. They were the words that he would carry with him, on this his second quest.

THREE

A mist hid the sun in the sky; a grey start to Four Winds' second quest.

Before he left, Burning Tree came to him. Her face was pale, but she had taken care to dress finely: her deerskin shift was heavily fringed and decorated with a shawl of beadwork, and she wore embroidered moccasins. The grieving woman handed Four Winds a birch-bark box filled with pemmican, a paste made from meat, fat and berries. 'Take this for your journey with the dream horse,' she said quietly. 'And may the spirit of my brother, Running Fox, go with you.'

Four Winds took the food and thanked her. He rolled the box into his medicine bundle and slung it across his shoulder.

Then Burning Tree gave him a necklace made from bright, shining, wolf's teeth. 'My brother, Running Fox, gave this gift to me when our father, Slow Bull, died. May it protect you from the forces of Anteep and his evil spirits.'

Gratefully, Four Winds took the second gift. He was

moved to tell Burning Tree how much her brother had taught him. 'From Running Fox I learned to chip and flake flints to fashion them into arrowheads and spearblades. He taught me to carve a sacred pipe and paint a shield to protect myself in battle. His arm was straight and strong when he drew a bow, his aim was true.'

Burning Tree smiled. 'Today One Horn and Three Bears will return to the place where Running Fox fell. They will bring his body to the village. They will paint and oil him and dress him in his best robes; they will wrap him in buffalo skin. Then they will build a frame of branches high into the sky and offer his body to the night sky. Tomorrow Running Fox will dwell with the Morning Star.'

It was good. Four Winds was glad for her. 'Take care of my grandmother, White Deer, for she has much sorrow,' he asked.

'I will love her like my mother,' Burning Tree promised.

So Four Winds left the village with Silver Cloud.

He trod behind the graceful creature, whose head was raised and neck arched, the graceful flow of his silken mane falling along it. The strength of his broad back contrasted with the slenderness of his long legs but Four Winds knew neither would fail him when the time came.

He looked back and down at the tipis, almost

swallowed by mist. His band had no homeland, no shaman and only four warriors remaining. Their chief was close to death. What chance for him, then, a boy of thirteen summers, on this journey into the frozen north? For a moment, Four Winds' courage failed him and his heart beat wildly inside his chest.

Silver Cloud too paused and turned. He sensed the boy's altered heartbeat and understood the reason. 'The sun will burn off the mist,' he promised. 'Soon we will see our way ahead.'

And Four Winds took the spirit horse at his word. They would see the way ahead, and the quest would unfold. So he followed Silver Cloud across the mountain, each step taking him away from his grieving People.

As Four Winds and Silver Cloud travelled, the mist began to lift and the boy's spirits rose. To be walking beside the spirit horse through the aspen trees was a reason to be glad. The sun was on their backs; the mountains stretched ahead to the north and west. Underfoot, green moss and lichen softened the hard grey granite, and on the rocky outcrops, many round-eared pika kept careful watch.

The presence of these tiny creatures calmed Four Winds. He smiled to see the ground squirrels standing tall on their hind legs, as they peered over the top of the grass in the small meadows which lay between the hills.

And he walked happily alongside a spiky porcupine, ambling by a creek, stopping to nibble at bark then snuffling off into the undergrowth.

But after a while, Four Winds began to sense other watchers in the shadows beneath the rocks. He heard the throaty bark of a vixen, and the dog fox's shrill reply, and caught sight of sly bobcats hiding in willow thickets by the creeks.

Silver Cloud too began to tread more warily, keeping his ears erect, listening to distant sounds.

They came out of a green valley, along a high ridge. A north wind drove light clouds across the sky, carrying with it a warning of the snow already falling above the tree line.

'A man is following us,' Silver Cloud told Four Winds.

The boy looked and listened. Was the man friend or enemy? His mind was racing, his body tense. Was a Comanche scout already on their trail? Had Snake Eye ordered a constant watch on the White Water band? Four Winds feared the end of his second quest almost before it had begun.

'The man stops when we stop,' the dream horse reported.

Enemy, then! A friend would surely reveal himself and share his news.

So Four Winds took refuge under a granite outcrop while Silver Cloud went silently through the tall pine trees, his footfalls soft on the bed of pine needles. The horse would see and hear much more than any man. He would soon return and recount what he had learned.

Settling into the shadowy overhang, Four Winds thought out a plan. If the news was bad, there were only two choices: to flee far and fast from the Comanche brave, or to stay and fight. On no account must he be allowed to escape and return to Snake Eye, for then the Comanche chief would know that Four Winds' second journey had begun.

If the Wild Dog came by foot, then the boy's choice would be to climb on to Silver Cloud's back and gallop away. The dream horse would run swifter than the deer until the enemy lost their track and had to return to Snake Eye empty-handed.

But if their follower came by horse, then the race would be even, and flight might not succeed. After all, the Comanches, along with the Shoshone and Nez Percé tribes of the southern deserts, as well as the Cheyenne and the Crow, had captured the wild horses of Mexico, brought by boat, by men with pale skins. No longer content to stay in their homelands, those warlike tribes had tamed the strong, peaceful creatures, taking to their backs with spears and shields, and now rode the horses to swift and cruel victory over tribes to their north.

That was how defeat had come to Red Hawk's people at Thunder Ridge; and how Four Winds' father,

Swift Elk, had been slain, along with many other Sioux warriors.

Waiting now in the shade of the outcrop, Four Winds recalled the first time he had ever seen such a wondrous creature. It was two summers back, when the leaves of the aspens were beginning to turn to gold. He and his People had been breaking their summer camp on the bank of the White Water River when two of Snake Eye's men had appeared on the horizon. Four Winds and his cousin, Hidden Moon, had been collecting water in skin carriers, ready for the journey to more sheltered winter quarters.

Hidden Moon had looked up at the approach of what sounded like elk. She had gasped and whispered Four Winds' childhood name. 'Kola, look!'

At first he hadn't recognised the shape or the meaning of the approaching riders. It had been mysterious and he was afraid. But he hid his fear from his cousin, and watched and waited. He had heard from his grandmother and his mother, Shining Star, of wonderful things that had happened from the earliest times. So he thought these creatures with two heads and many limbs must have come down from the sun, or else out of the hill on which they stood. He knew he must not try to hurt them, or something bad would happen.

Then, as the horses and riders had drawn nearer, Four Winds had made out that the riders were men and were separate from their mysterious creatures. Still, it made no sense to see a man on a strong and beautiful animal who bowed to his will. The men wore headdresses with tails of feathers, they painted their faces with chalk and red dye, and held their spears aloft.

'Hide!' Hidden Moon had whispered. And they had concealed themselves in a cave by the river.

The two men had looked down upon the White Water People as they loaded their tipis on to their travois. Then they had reined their creatures away from the ridge and vanished out of sight.

And those were the first horses Four Winds ever saw. They came from south of the river, from the flat land where the Wild Dogs lived. Later, they returned and, with their horses, the Comanches began to slaughter all who bore the name of Sioux. It was a battle Four Winds would never forget. One which had left him an orphan.

Lost in these thoughts, Four Winds only vaguely saw the silver-grey shape of Silver Cloud descend from the ridge and retrace their recent steps. Sometimes the horse disappeared from sight behind a rock or in amongst a thick copse, soon to glide clear, glance up towards the boy, then continue in his search.

It was only when a ground squirrel broke from the cover of some nearby sagebrush that Four Winds came back to the present moment. The creature chattered and scurried away, annoyed by an unseen disturbance which put the boy on his guard. He listened, but heard nothing. Then he peered out from under the overhang.

Silently a figure dropped from the ledge above the boy's head. Four Winds drew his knife. The man whirled to face him, crouched and ready to spring.

A cry escaped Four Winds' lips. 'Sun Dancer!'

The White Water warrior stood up straight. 'Lucky for you I am your brother!' he reproached. 'Were you sleeping while I crept up on you?'

Four Winds felt flames of shame fan through him at the just criticism. He had been caught off-guard, remembering past times. 'How did you pass by Silver Cloud?'

Sun Dancer shrugged. 'How do I hunt the deer and outwit the elk?'

Through patience and skill, Four Winds knew. By using the direction of the wind and the cover of rocks and bushes. By being one with the landscape.

'Even the spirit horse cannot know all the ways of the White Water Sioux!' Sun Dancer said, with a touch of pride. 'But know for certain that you would have died three times over if I had truly been your enemy.'

The boy hung his head. What kind of warrior was he, that he had fallen at the first hurdle? Then his shame turned to anger. 'What right had you to trick me?' he demanded. 'Why skulk like an enemy and waste our precious time?'

'I wanted to shame you and sharpen your wits,' Sun

Dancer told him. 'You are young. You have much to learn.'

Four Winds frowned. 'And you so heavy with the weight of years,' he said scornfully. After all, Sun Dancer had only seven or eight more summers more than he. He had still to gain the full stature and strength of One Horn or Three Bears.

And Sun Dancer had always been proud. He had not shared his knowledge like Running Fox, but had hunted alone and kept a distance from the children at the tipi doors when Four Winds had been amongst them. A tall, slender man, he held his head high and rarely smiled.

'You have shamed me,' Four Winds acknowledged, noticing Silver Cloud returning up the mountain. 'Now you may go back to the village and say that the boy has no skill, that his wits are dull and that he will never return with the feather from the highest mountain.'

'I will not go back,' Sun Dancer answered firmly. 'I must go with you.'

'Who says?'

'Red Hawk, our chief. He has sent me to guide you north, through the lands of the Blackfoot and the Gros Ventres, where I have travelled two summers ago. I know Sarsi Ridge and Arikara Valley, where you must pass on your journey to Mount Kivioq. I know the tall Cree nation and the handsome Arapaho; their medicine men and their warriors, their dances and their ceremonies.'

'But this is my journey. I was chosen as the one Red Hawk loved the most,' Four Winds insisted. It was as Ghost Horse had commanded.

'Though the old man is close to death, his wisdom has not deserted him,' Sun Dancer reminded the boy. 'He has sent me as your guide.

Four Winds frowned stubbornly. He didn't know whether to trust this new situation; after all, why had his grandfather waited until after he and Silver Cloud had begun their journey before deciding to send Sun Dancer as their guide? Was it possible that the young warrior was not what he seemed? Perhaps this was some shape-shifting spirit, a servant of Anteep, sent to lure them away from the right path.

'You must prove to me that your purpose is good,' the boy insisted. He wished that Silver Cloud would hurry to join them, but the horse seemed relaxed, stopping every now and then to graze.

Sun Dancer agreed to the test. He unslung his medicine bundle from his shoulder and quickly unwrapped it for Four Winds to see. 'Here is my medicine pipe, gift of the great Thunder Bird. Thunder Bird made peace with me on my vision quest, and the power of the pipe is great in my family.'

Four Winds nodded. A man's medicine bundle was secret and sacred. He kept it with him and never let it go from him. Its contents were known only to the small band of warriors to which he belonged. So, seeing the beads and feathers alongside the Thunder Bird pipe, he was content that this was no false spirit, but Sun Dancer himself.

'Red Hawk has sent us a guide,' he told Silver Cloud. 'Sun Dancer has travelled among the People to the north. He knows their ways.'

The horse bowed his head. 'We must journey on. The sun has reached its height. By nightfall we must reach beyond those distant hills.'

So the two warriors and the spirit horse set off, the boy still angry at his own dull wits and resenting the need for a guide.

They walked silently, following Sun Dancer's directions through deep canyons and out on to gentler slopes. They passed Sarsi Ridge and trudged through Arikara Valley with the wind in their faces and heavy clouds gathering on the horizon. The land was alive with jack rabbits and antelope, with prairie dogs and, in the distance, great herds of buffalo eating the short grass. This was Cree land, Sun Dancer told them. There was no threat.

So they made good progress until the sun began to sink, when they were hailed by a tall Cree scout belonging to the Okeepa band. The scout emerged from a copse of aspens, bare-chested and unarmed. He greeted Sun Dancer and announced that he was Buffalo Bird, sent to fetch the weary travellers into the Okeepa village.

'We will give you food, and shelter you from the night frost, then send you on your way,' Buffalo Bird promised. 'But first you must delay your journey until our shaman, Big Snake, has performed our hunting ceremony. Until then, no man may pass through our land.'

So, reluctantly, Four Winds accepted the offer, following the scout down into a valley where a hundred tipis stretched along the banks of a creek. Dogs lay at the entrances to the tents, while children played and the women fed the fires with cedar logs which gave off a rich scent.

The scene filled Four Winds with envy. This was how it had been with the White Water People, before the Wild Dogs had driven them from their homeland. Then, everyone had plenty to eat and no one was cold.

'Come,' Buffalo Bird invited.

They followed him towards his tipi, and the three men entered, while the horse stayed close to the pole by the door which supported Buffalo Bird's medicine bundle and war shield.

In the centre of the tent, Four Winds made out the comfort of a fire glowing red. Smoke rose through the smoke hole, past racks of drying meat. Kettles, pans and water stood near the door. Weapons hung from the supporting cedar poles.

'All is in its place,' Sun Dancer commented with satisfaction.

Then Buffalo Bird requested they join Big Snake in

the hunting ceremony. 'Tomorrow we hunt buffalo,' he told them. 'Big Snake has the power to make the buffalo come. But first he must make a sacrifice to the wind.'

Full of curiosity, Four Winds and Sun Dancer followed their guide out to an area in the centre of the tipis, where the Cree medicine man had placed a pole topped with a strip of scarlet cloth. At the foot of the pole he had placed buffalo skulls painted red and decorated with feathers; a gift to the buffalo spirits. Then Big Snake smoked his pipe and began to sing the Bull song, accompanied by a drum.

'He will sing all night long,' Buffalo Bird explained. 'Then the buffalo will come.'

'May your people have food for their stomachs all winter long,' Sun Dancer said. While Big Snake sang and the sparks rose into the dusk sky, he told his friend of the troubles of the White Water People.

'It is because the Comanches have the horse and you do not,' Buffalo Bird pointed out. 'I fear they will defeat you and move north, sweeping aside every band who stands in their way. Soon the Cree and the Assinboin will be driven away from their valleys and streams, into the frozen mountains.'

'You think we should capture their horses?' Sun Dancer asked eagerly.

Four Winds scowled. It didn't seem right to talk of the beautiful creatures as objects to be stolen and possessed.

'How else will you defeat them?' Buffalo Bird replied.

'Yet Red Hawk is old,' Sun Dancer reported. 'He clings to the ancient ways, where the dog is the only servant to the People.'

Here was another reason for Four Winds to be angry with Sun Dancer, hearing him talk of the chief of their tribe with too little respect.

'Who will replace him as chief?' Buffalo Bird inquired.

Sun Dancer shrugged. 'It is between Three Bears and One Horn, the oldest and best of our warriors.'

'But still my grandfather is chief,' Four Winds reminded him. 'He has sent me on this journey. I have completed my vision quest, found my guardian spirit, and that dream horse, Silver Cloud, will accompany me for the rest of my life.'

The two older men smiled at the boy's raw pride.

'We do not need to steal and tame the horse, because he has appeared to me in my vision,' Four Winds insisted. 'In this way we will defeat our enemies.'

Buffalo Bird nodded and grew serious. 'You are young, but you have a good heart and courage to go with it. May the great Wakanda guide you in your journey.'

Then they left off talking and went to eat meat and berries until their stomachs were full. After this, Oki cize-tawa, an ancient Cree warrior, passed around the smoking calumet, decorated with green duck feathers and the carving of a woodpecker's head, and began to entertain the visitors with stories.

'*Tate ou ye topa kin*,' he said. 'The four winds are blowing. Once, the coyote stole the flame from the black god of fire, who was asleep. The coyote travelled with the glowing coals through the house of the Sun, which is guarded by the eagle spirit. He continued through the house of the Moon and finally came to the house of the first man and woman, where he gave them the fire. So the coyote became the helper of man and allowed him to prosper.'

'It is good,' Sun Dancer, Buffalo Bird and Four Winds murmured.

'Once, the world contained only animals who spoke like humans,' the old man continued. 'A fierce monster kept all the animals in fear by devouring them, until bold coyote jumped down the monster's throat and sawed up his heart with a flint. Then coyote cut the whole body into small pieces, and each piece created a different tribe.'

The listeners smiled and said that this was also good. This was the wisdom of the Plains People, they all agreed.

And, when the story telling was done, Four Winds retired to sleep in Buffalo Bird's tipi while Silver Cloud stood throughout the silent night, under the stars.

FOUR

Soon after dawn they set off again.

The Cree buffalo hunt had already started, with two warriors hiding under wolf-skins, creeping towards the unwary herd. Then, sensing danger as the wolf-men drew close, the bulls formed a semi-circle to guard the cows, until the hunters leaped up and brought down the nearest bull with their tomahawks.

'Big Snake makes powerful medicine,' Sun Dancer commented, as he; Four Winds and Silver Cloud paused on a hilltop to watch the successful hunt in the valley below.

As one bull fell, so the thousand-strong herd set off to the east, racing headlong through trees and over boulders, where the weaker creatures stumbled and were pounced upon by other waiting Okeepa hunters. But most of the heavy-headed creatures stampeded to freedom, raising a huge cloud of yellow dust until the far horizon disappeared and the thunder of hooves faded.

'Today we must pass through the land of Wahnistow

and his Blackfoot band,' Sun Dancer said. 'Beyond that is White Buffalo River and the limit of my wisdom.'

'Must we cross the White Buffalo River to travel north?' Four Winds asked. Part of him wished for the adventure of travelling on without their guide, but another part had already grown to rely on Sun Dancer's experience.

'Yes, and it is a difficult crossing,' came the reply. 'Though now the water is not deep, as it is in the spring when the snow thaws from the mountains.'

'Do not think of tomorrow,' Silver Cloud warned them quietly. 'Look around and think of today.'

His words put them on the alert. What had the dream horse seen or heard which warranted this?

Four Winds studied his surroundings. The trees here grew more sparsely; the wind cut more keenly through his fringed leather shirt. Yet there were still many places to hide; behind the fingers of rock which lined the ridges and down dark ravines where daylight never penetrated. Knowing he grew too tense, he began to ask Sun Dancer what he knew of Wahnistow and his Blackfoot warriors.

'I know little, except that they wear the wolfskin headdress, because the life of their warriors is said to be like that of the wolf. And that these Blackfoots collect scalps on their war journeys and are to be much feared. Wahnistow himself, though of slight build, has killed three enemy chiefs and taken fourteen scalps, which hang in his tipi.'

Four Winds felt a shudder run through him. His pace quickened.

'Do not run from shadows.' Silver Cloud gave his advice sternly. 'That way, you flee into danger.'

So the boy slowed again, looked around, saw nothing. He felt small in the midst of the bare mountains, as if a gust of wind could take him and cast him into the air, then dash him down and smash his bones to dust. He found himself wishing for a real enemy to face, instead of this uneasy passage across the empty spaces.

'Look behind,' the horse said quietly.

Four Winds and Sun Dancer spun round. Three men stood on a rocky ridge, their hair-fringed war shirts blowing in the wind. They wore grey wolf-head bonnets and were armed as if for war.

'We come in peace!' Four Winds cried, his voice thin and high.

The Blackfoot warriors leaped to the ground, wielding their knives. 'You are enemies of the Comanche Wild Dogs,' one snarled. 'We have heard of your journey to the deepest mine, and of your silver spirit horse who calls upon the gods to aid you.'

'Our journey is just,' Four Winds reasoned, though he trembled at the glinting knives and the blood-red war paint on the faces of the Blackfoot. 'Snake Eye has driven my People from our homeland. We fall and die like leaves from the trees.'

The nearest warrior slashed his blade towards him, curving a broad arc through the air.

Four Winds snaked away from its path, his reaction swift and lithe. Then Sun Dancer drew his tomahawk and stepped in front of the boy. 'Why talk to men who will not listen!' he cried. 'Wahnistow's warriors think only of scalps and the trade that can be done with the treacherous Wild Dogs!'

Silver Cloud was amazed by this angry talk, which could do no good. 'Climb on my back,' he whispered to Four Winds and Sun Dancer. 'I will carry you away from here.'

But Sun Dancer would not hear of fleeing. Instead, he stepped forward and swung his heavy tomahawk at the second Blackfoot, slicing the bow from his grasp and sending him reeling against a rock.

Four Winds too would have stepped in beside him, but Silver Cloud reared up in front of the boy. The delay gave the three Blackfoot men time to recover and close in on Sun Dancer. This time, their blows landed and their knives cut deep into his flesh.

'Now come with me!' Silver Cloud ordered, as Sun Dancer bent forward, bleeding from his chest. He stood guard as Four Winds caught hold of his wounded brother and laid him across the horse's back. Sun Dancer slumped face-down as the Blackfoot set up a war cry and threatened to attack again.

'Now!' Silver Cloud said. This was their last chance to escape.

So Four Winds vaulted up beside Sun Dancer. The horse reared, threatening the enemy with his hooves, then whirled away and set off at a gallop.

Only the yells and cries of the Blackfoot braves pursued them. As Silver Cloud ran to safety, Four Winds clung on to his mane, leaning forward over Sun Dancer, who lay motionless and with his eyes closed. When the horse finally stopped by a mountain stream, the boy quickly slipped to the ground and hauled his fellow warrior after him.

'Why did you come between me and the enemy?' he demanded angrily of Silver Cloud. Because of the horse's action he had not been able to help Sun Dancer.

'Your purpose is to find the feather,' Silver Cloud reminded him. 'What would it serve to be injured or killed by the Blackfoot?'

The horse didn't understand the ways of the Sioux nation. 'A mare would defend her colt to the death in the face of wolves, wouldn't she? So I must help my Sioux brother.'

Silver Cloud fell silent.

Four Winds examined the wounds which Sun Dancer had received. There were many gashes across his chest; one deep and wide. Blood poured from the wound on to the earth.

The boy leaned to listen to the heartbeat of the wounded man. It was faint. Life was ebbing.

So he unwrapped his medicine bundle and pressed herbs into the worst wound, which he covered with a pad of soft kidskin, then bound the leather tightly with a strip of cloth to stem the flow of blood. Then he took Sun Dancer's sacred medicine pipe from his own bundle and laid it across his chest. 'May Thunder Bird bring back your strength,' he murmured.

Soon Sun Dancer's eyelids flickered and he looked out on to the world. 'I must follow my brother, Running Fox,' he whispered.

Four Winds scooped water from the stream and made Sun Dancer drink. 'Do not talk of dying,' he implored.

'I am not afraid.'

'But do not die. Understand that the spirit horse meant you no harm and that I would have offered my own life to save yours.'

'The horse was right,' Sun Dancer acknowledged. 'To stay and fight was wrong. Sometimes it is better to flee.'

A hard way to learn this lesson, the boy thought. 'I have used strong medicine,' he promised. 'No more blood will flow.'

Sun Dancer nodded weakly. 'Leave me here and continue your journey,' he told them.

'No!' Four Winds countered. There were many

creatures with sharp claws and teeth. Sun Dancer would be at their mercy.

The wounded man saw that the boy was in earnest. So he fumbled for his knife in its beaded sheath, drew it and pointed it at his own heart. 'I will plunge this blade into my body,' he threatened, 'rather than keep you and the dream horse from your journey.'

Four Winds fought for the knife, but Sun Dancer used the last of his strength to push him away.

Covered in the other man's blood, desperate to save him, Four Winds fell back. He saw that Sun Dancer meant what he said. 'Wish us well on our way,' he implored.

'Go in peace,' Sun Dancer replied. '*Maka akanl wicasa iyuha el.*'

Heartbroken, Four Winds took up his medicine bundle and climbed on to the horse's back. 'May Thunder Bird protect you, my brother,' he whispered.

'You are son of Swift Elk, grandson of the great Red Hawk,' Sun Dancer reminded him in a faint voice. He kept the knife point pressed against his flesh. 'Be strong on your journey. Ford the white river and journey into the snow. Seek the help of the Nez Percé and the five nations of the Hodenosaunee: the Mohawks, the Oneidas, the Onondagas, the Cayugas and the Senecas, fishers of the great lakes. The Sioux have traded copper and flint with these people. They know our ways.'

Four Winds wished that Sun Dancer would conserve his precious breath. 'Speak no more,' he begged, still hanging back instead of continuing. He bitterly regretted the feelings of pride he had lately held against his wounded brother.

As Sun Dancer lay back, his sacred carved pipe rolled to one side. Four Winds dismounted to put it firmly into his grasp. When he looked up he saw that they were surrounded by six Cree men.

He sprang to his feet in surprise.

Buffalo Bird stepped out of the group. 'We will carry Sun Dancer back to our village,' he told Four Winds.

'But this is Blackfoot land, home of Wahnistow. The way is full of danger.'

Buffalo Bird nodded. 'We will go the way we came, silently through the shadows. We would not leave Sun Dancer here to die.'

'How did you know we needed help?'

'We followed the buffalo. They brought us to the mountains. Our scout, Red Crane, kept watch over you. Now go, while we carry your brother home.'

'Give him strong medicine,' Four Winds begged, springing lightly on to Silver Cloud's back. 'The wound is deep.'

'His heart is strong. Big Snake will tend him. When you return from your journey, Sun Dancer will be made new.'

Gratitude almost burst the cage of bones in Four Winds' chest. He bade farewell to Buffalo Bird and Sun Dancer and he and Silver Cloud continued on their way.

FIVE

White Buffalo River snaked between two high ridges at the edge of Blackfoot land. A few pine trees straggled across the hillsides, their roots struggling to find soil and nourishment. They leaned away from the biting north wind, swaying and creaking as Silver Cloud and Four Winds passed through them.

The boy looked up at the darkening sky and decided there was time to cross the water before night fell. They must choose a good place, away from the white water rapids directly below them; perhaps downstream around the next bend.

Four Winds dismounted for the steep descent. Silver Cloud let him pick his own way, watching him scramble over boulders and cling to tree roots to stop himself from falling. The horse's way was more sure-footed but slower, his hooves sending loose grit showering over the edge and blowing in the wind. Below them, the rushing water roared.

'We need the wings of a bird to cross this river,' Silver Cloud said. He saw that the current was strong and treacherous and that it would take all his strength to swim across.

As they picked their way downstream, hoping to find a calmer stretch, Four Winds realised that Silver Cloud was fearful in a way he hadn't seen before. This must be because the horse was a creature of the land, not water. On land he was sure, steady and swift. But water slowed him and threatened to pull him off course. No wonder then that he was unhappy about crossing the rapids.

There was no way of avoiding them, however; no calm stretch where the water flowed gently, only torrents and waterfalls, swift twists in the river's course and steep cliffs to either side.

'We will cross together,' Silver Cloud decided. 'Cling fast to my mane and don't let go.'

Gingerly he approached the water's edge. He lowered his head to smell possible dangers, stepped forward, retreated, then tried a second place.

Four Winds saw the white water foam between Silver Cloud's legs. He held tight to the strong, silky mane as they stepped deeper and the horse stumbled on the rocky bed.

'Stay still and hold on,' Silver Cloud warned. He got ready to plunge out of his depth and swim across the current.

Four Winds drew a sharp breath as the icy water splashed his legs. He felt the blast of the wind and breathed in the spray that came off the fast-running river.

Then Silver Cloud struck out into the current, swimming strongly, head clear of the water, neck fully stretched.

Downstream the river twisted out of sight between two pinkish-grey cliffs. Upstream, two black-tailed deer stood on an outcrop, silently watching.

They had reached the middle of the river, water swirling and foaming all around them, when Four Winds saw a danger which he hadn't expected, in the shape of two giant logs speeding towards them. They were pine trees, uprooted by the force of the swollen river. They had toppled into the current and were being carried downstream at great speed, smashing and splintering against rocks, but still tumbling along the surface.

Four Winds gasped. One log had pushed up against a huge boulder and lodged itself against the river bank. But the other sped on. And Silver Cloud was giving all his strength to battling the current; there was no way of him changing course to avoid the log.

The river pulled at the horse, sweeping him this way and that. Four Winds clung to his mane, praying that the log would swirl clear. But no, the water was bringing them together, and now Silver Cloud had seen the danger and was powerless. He swam in vain.

Four Winds saw the log roll sideways. There were

jagged stumps of branches all along its length; it was a massive pine, its bark blackened by the water. Then it hit them. Silver Cloud took the brunt on his shoulder, but the force threw Four Winds from the horse's back, sideways into the river.

He sank under the surface, swam clear of Silver Cloud's thrashing hooves and tried to resist the current. But he was dragged deeper under. Fight! he told himself, as his limbs were tugged this way and that. He kicked hard, aiming upwards for the surface before his lungs burst. His head broke clear, he sucked in air, then was sent tumbling down again. Down amongst jagged rocks and wild currents, his hair streaming, his body thrown about like driftwood. Down between slippery boulders, his hands clutching to grab hold of a surface that would steady him and let him kick clear again.

Then, suddenly, he was over a ledge and falling, falling. Slipping down a long waterfall, tossed clear and dropping through mid air, Four Winds cried out as he fell. He landed in a deep, green pool under a torrent of falling water. The pool broke his fall and, recovering himself, he swam clear.

The boy had dragged himself out of the pool when Silver Cloud looked down from the top of the waterfall. The horse saw that, though Four Winds was exhausted after his battle with the water, he wasn't injured. Silver Cloud himself bled from the wither where the log had crashed into him, yet he too was able to continue the journey.

So he raised his head and whinnied to draw the boy's attention. Slumped forward, trying to regain his breath, Four Winds looked up and saw with joy that Silver Cloud had escaped from the rapids. He began the steep climb to rejoin him, the water thundering in his ears, his feet often slipping on the moss-covered rocks.

At last, the horse and the boy met again. Four Winds shivered, his teeth chattered and his lips turned blue.

'May that be the first and the last river we have to cross!' he gasped.

'You must make fire to warm yourself,' Silver Cloud decided. 'We will rest.'

So Four Winds used the old way of taking a dry stick and grinding it against a stone until a spark flew and he could ignite a handful of the straw he had ready. The straw was set under more sticks which caught light and then more wood was carefully placed on top. Within minutes, the fire glowed red and Four Winds basked in its warmth.

Silver Cloud watched and was satisfied. 'Sleep now,' he suggested, 'while I discover the path we must take.'

Gratefully, Four Winds lay down by the fire. He brought his knees to his chest, curled up and fell asleep.

In his dream, Four Winds saw a circle of elms and some snowy, sloping hills. Overhead the stars were glistening.

Some stars seemed so big and close that he could touch them if he reached out his hand. But instead, the stars reached out to him, and a being robed in red appeared before him, with eyes large and almond-shaped and as black as the night. He motioned for Four Winds to look and see the spirit breath of his people fading. Then he motioned again, towards a woman as old as the Earth. She spoke about the danger of his journey and gave Four Winds a book of stars. Her ancient finger pointed to a certain place amongst the stars, and the being said, 'This is your People's place. Do the right thing for your People and the land. Let this vision keep you on the path of the heart. It is the one thing that can never be taken from you.'

Then the old woman and the red-robed figure melted into the night sky.

Four Winds woke with new strength and courage. He had sought out and discovered his place in the Mystery. He rose and kicked earth over the fire to deaden the embers. Soon the dream horse would return.

'I have visited the Blackfoot village,' Silver Cloud reported.

Daylight had faded, snow was in the air, and Four Winds could tell from his guardian spirit's excitement that there was much more to say.

'Wahnistow feasts with Snake Eye and the Wild Dogs,' he said urgently. 'The Comanches are here!'

Four Winds felt his heart jolt. Wahnistow and Snake Eye together! The Blackfoot and the Comanche; both with horses, both war-like, now teamed against the White Water band.

'Show me!' he said to Silver Cloud.

They went at dusk through the ravines. Snow dusted the rocks with a fine white powder; clouds hid the moon and stars from sight.

Yet Silver Cloud could pick his way through the shadows. His eyesight was keen, his hearing acute.

So they came to the village when only night creatures roamed. The owl, messenger of misfortune, glided quietly through the trees which encircled the Blackfoot village, his wings beating softly, his sharp eyes fixed on the intruders. From the thick sagebrush on the hillside, half a dozen pairs of yellow wolf eyes glowed.

Four Winds could see his own breath on the freezing night air. Silver Cloud carried him downwind of the Blackfoot horses and made no noise.

There was a fire burning in the centre of the circle of tipis and many men gathered round. The Blackfoot warriors wore their wolfskin headdresses while their visitors, the Comanches, wore the flowing feathers of their tribe. At their sides they carried tomahawks, knives and spears.

Two men stood out from all the rest. One stood with his back to Four Winds and Silver Cloud, the other faced them. This was Wahnistow in his wolfskin headdress; tall and lean, his face streaked with red.

'Whoever wishes to succeed in war against the White Water Sioux must join the Sun Dance!' he proclaimed in a loud voice. 'What sacrifice will you make to the great sun in the sky?' he asked the men standing around the fire. 'Will you give him silver and flint, will you offer him your flesh and blood?

And the warrior with his back to the onlookers replied, 'I, Snake Eye, will give my flesh and blood that I may conquer my enemies' And he raised his spear so that his Wild Dogs would join in the chant.

'What is this?' Silver Cloud asked a terrified Four Winds.

'This is the *uci tapi*, the tribe's war dance,' the boy whispered, watching as the Blackfoot and Comanche warriors mounted their horses by the light of the fire, separated and went to the outskirts of the village. Then an old man beat a drum and sang a song, while the horsemen dismounted and began to prance by the side of their horses, imitating their mounts' high-stepping walk.

'*Kola tuwa nape cinahan opa kte sni ye!*' the warriors cried from the darkness at the rim. 'Friends: whoever runs away shall not be admitted!'

Then Wahnistow called his horsemen back to the fire in a splendid procession. 'Now we are ready to carry out the final scalp raid against our shared enemy, Red

Hawk and his White Water Sioux!' he proclaimed.

And Four Winds felt a tight band of terror across his chest, as Snake Eye grasped Wahnistow's arm in a gesture of friendship. Now he could see the Comanche chief's evil face, and he recognised the broad, cruel features, the hook-like nose and the eyes that were merely dark slits under a heavy brow.

'First we must stop the boy, Four Winds, and his powerful spirit-guide!' Snake Eye announced.

'My warriors have ambushed them,' Wahnistow acknowledged. 'They slew the boy's companion, Sun Dancer, and left him dead on the ground, but the mighty dream horse carried the body away.'

The reminder caused a superstitious murmuring among the Blackfoot braves. They had been robbed of their precious scalp by the magic of the horse. And now they were afraid of Silver Cloud and his power.

Four Winds smiled grimly to himself. His friends, the Cree, had done a good job of ghosting Sun Dancer back to their village. Now he prayed that their medicine would restore his friend.

'Silver Cloud and the boy warrior have outwitted us on their journey to the deepest mine,' Snake Eye admitted now. 'Even the great Anteep and his servant, Unktehi, who lives beneath Yellow Water Lake, could not bring forth a power strong enough to overcome Wakanda and his servant, Ghost Horse.'

Wahnistow considered this. 'Then perhaps we should

carry out our scalp raid against Red Hawk and ignore the boy?'

But Snake Eye shook his head. 'If Four Winds returns with a feather from the highest mountain, then the White Water band might one day reclaim their homeland. This much was told to us by Matotope, treacherous shaman of the White Water People.'

The Blackfoot chief frowned deeply. He was beginning not to relish the fight. Then again, he had traded silver with Snake Eye in return for new horses which the Wild Dogs had brought up from the southern plains. Besides, he could not appear a coward.

As the drumbeat died and the old man fell silent, Four Winds heard Wahnistow agree with Snake Eye that their first task was to track down and destroy 'the boy and the spirit horse'. The chief glowered out from under his wolfskin headdress, taking a pipe and offering it to the sky. 'Anteep, behold this pipe. I ask you to smoke it with me and help me kill the boy, Four Winds. That is why I speak to you with this pipe.'

As he lit the fragrant tobacco, Snake Eye grunted. 'Anteep, Lord of the Underworld, was no help to the Wild Dogs by the side of Yellow Water. I swore then to defeat the boy warrior without the spirits' help!'

'These two chiefs differ on many things,' Silver Cloud remarked.

But Four Winds replied that together, the Blackfoot and the Comanches presented double the danger. The red-robed figure had been right to show him the fading spirit of his White Water band. There had never been such a threat to his People – not even when Matotope had betrayed them or when Unktehi rose out of Yellow Water – as the one now presented by Wahnistow and Snake Eye.

The drum started again and the singer chanted. Comanches and Blackfoot joined together in their war dance, their cries rising and echoing back from the bare mountains, their faces lit by the flickering flames.

'We must journey on,' Four Winds said, his throat dry with fear.

'We must think what to do,' Silver Cloud insisted. 'Remember that Evil must be outsmarted, for the sheer force of Evil is always stronger than Good.'

The boy recalled this lesson from his first journey and knew that it was so. But still he shook with fear, and the desire to run gripped him.

'What makes Wahnistow and Snake Eye stronger than Red Hawk?' Silver Cloud went on.

'Their number,' Four Winds said. The warriors of the White Water band had dwindled to a handful, while the enemy numbered over a hundred.

'What else? Are they braver and more cunning than your People?'

Four Winds drew himself to full height, but he scorned to reply.

'No,' the horse said for him. 'Then what gives them their strength in battle?'

The boy thought for a long time. From his hiding-place he saw the dance grow wilder, the shrieks and cries of the warriors louder still. Outside their war-like circle, the women and children watched in silence. 'The Comanches and Blackfoot ride their horses into battle,' Four Winds concluded. 'That is why they defeated my People at Thunder Ridge.'

'So, without their horses they are less strong?'

Four Winds nodded. 'Slower. They cannot outrun us. They are the same.' For many summers, until the coming of the horse from the Land of the Sun in the south, it had been so. And the White Water People had held their homeland.

Silver Cloud liked the boy's answer. He knew now what they should do. 'We will set free the enemy's horses,' he declared. 'Tonight, while the warriors sleep. By dawn they will be gone.'

SIX

Four Winds needed patience, cunning and courage to complete the task of setting free the horses. He could not appeal for help to the band's medicine man so, instead, he opened up his medicine bundle and took out an eagle feather which had once adorned his grandfather's ceremonial headdress. Then he took a handful of dirt from a place at the edge of the enemy village and a handful of snow which powdered the rocks. Crouching in the dark over a dish-shaped stone, he mixed the two together. Then he dipped the plume into the mixture.

The dream horse watched the strange ritual. The heart of the village was emptying as men went into the tipis to sleep. Women came and doused the fire. A dog barked in response to a wolf's long, thin howl.

'Now it will snow during the night,' Four Winds explained. 'The enemy will stay in their tents and we will have no difficulty setting free the horses.'

And, sure enough, the snowflakes thickened. They floated to the earth, covering rocks and weighing down the branches of the trees until low ones touched the ground. And the snow brought with it an eerie light, in spite of heavy clouds, so that the boy and the horse could see the cold watch kept by three Blackfoot braves – the pacing to and fro around the corral where the horses were penned, the ice-stiffened limbs, the beating of arms against their chests in a vain attempt to keep warm.

Then, just before sunrise, the three sentries gave in. They had done their duty and seen that the horses were safe throughout the night. Now, surely, it was time for them to retreat into their tipis.

So they trudged off before other life was stirring and the sky was only faintly streaked with the pink light of the rising sun.

Four Winds faced the east and raised his right hand. 'Wakanda, I pray you to take pity on me,' he implored. 'I am now between life and death. For the sake of my People, I ask your help to set free these horses.'

He chanted the prayer and then spoke more words: '*Shonka wakan, wanla ka nunwe.*' The medicine dog, may you behold. '*Mita sunke, wakin yan iye ceca wanla ka nunwe.*' My horse like the Thunder Bird, may you behold.

'I am ready,' he told Silver Cloud, climbing on to his back and easing himself down one side of the horse's deep body. In this way, the grey creature could steal around the rim of the village without the boy being seen. Then, even if one of the sentries were to return, he would probably mistake the lone horse for one who had escaped from the corral. He would not set up an alarm.

By the doors of the tipis, dogs awoke from their sleep. Wisps of smoke from the fires of the night before curled out of the embers. Softly, Silver Cloud and Four Winds made their way towards the corral.

The horses stood in the grey light. They swished their tails. One or two snorted nervously at the soft thud of Silver Cloud's hooves on the snow.

As they approached the fenced area, Four Winds drew his knife. The fence was made of pine stakes driven into the earth, with one narrow exit blocked by ropes made of plaited leather. The plan was to cut through these ropes and drive out the captured herd.

But a black dog outside the nearest tipi grew alert. He stretched and padded towards Silver Cloud, his hackles rising. When he picked up Four Winds' scent, he snarled.

The boy held his breath. All now depended on them reaching the corral and swiftly cutting the rope before the dog woke his master. So he swung himself up into full view and urged Silver Cloud into a trot.

The snarling dog ran at them, setting up a mad bark. Others joined in and soon the intruders were surrounded by savage, yapping beasts.

Men with spears emerged from their tents. Sleep dulled their eyes and it took some time to make out the shadowy shapes of Silver Cloud and Four Winds at the gate to the corral.

The dogs closed in and the Blackfoot men ran to join them as Four Winds leaned out to slash at the ropes. Vicious jaws snapped and closed around his ankle, dragging him from Silver Cloud's back.

Then the horse reared up and struck out with his front hooves, driving the dogs back. They whined and cowered, while the Blackfoot raced through the snow.

Four Winds fought off the nearest dog. He cut through one rope. Inside the corral, the frightened horses tossed their heads and reared.

'Come!' Silver Cloud cried to Four Winds. He saw that the horses could not be freed before the men were upon them. They must give up the plan or die.

Four Winds stumbled on his bleeding foot. He fell to the ground, raised himself and grabbed the dream horse's mane. With difficulty he swung himself on to Silver Cloud's back.

He was scarcely balanced before Silver Cloud leaned back on his haunches, then surged forward through the dogs and men.

The Blackfoot jabbed spears and swung tomahawks, but none found their target and Silver Cloud swept by.

Angry at his failure, Four Winds cursed the wakefulness of the black dog. He gritted his teeth and clung to the horse as they wove between the tipis, past the tall cedar pole at the heart of the Blackfoot village.

They were almost clear. Four Winds' ankle dripped with blood and the pain went deep. But they would soon be out of the village, in amongst the pine trees. Silver Cloud would gallop to safety.

Until a tall figure stepped from behind a rock, wielding a tomahawk decked with feathers and red horsehair. Red paint smeared his cheeks, his plaited hair was parted down the middle and there was a cruel smile on the harsh features. Snake Eye!

The Comanche chief lifted his tomahawk behind his shoulder, aimed and threw. The heavy blade flashed towards Silver Cloud's head. The horse swerved and threw Four Winds from his back. The boy thudded to the ground, rolled in the snow and sprang up, knife in hand.

Then Snake Eye laughed, his dark eyes full of hate for the young boy who had dared to undertake Ghost Horse's quest. 'Where are your gods now?' he gloated, drawing his own knife in return. 'What good is the magic of the dream horse to you now?'

Before Four Winds could reply. Silver Cloud came between the man and the boy. He reared on to his hind legs and struck out with his hooves, bringing them crashing down on the Comanche chief who had jeered and expected to defeat the boy with one swift throw of his tomahawk. The hooves caught Snake Eye on the side of his head and sent him sprawling against the rock. The knife slipped from his grasp and he slid motionless to the ground.

There was an instant when Four Winds heard and thought nothing. His mind and vision were full only of the sight of Snake Eye's crushed skull, his blood in the snow and the blade half buried, his body sprawled oddly.

Then, out of the terrifying silence, Blackfoot warriors came yelling and screaming at the horse who had destroyed Snake Eye. And all was chaos again.

'Come!' a voice said to Four Winds. A hand reached out and drew him unseen behind the rock while the men attacked the dream horse.

The boy found himself face to face with a girl younger than him. She held him tight by the hand, crouching out of sight, looking for a chance to escape.

'Who are you?' Four Winds gasped.

The girl was dressed in the garb of the Blackfoot, in a beaded robe and long deerskin boots bound with thongs. She wore a silver medallion around her neck and a blue bandanna around her jet black hair.

'I am Black Tail Deer,' she whispered back. 'You must not talk, but come with me.'

His heart told him that this was the right way, that Silver Cloud would be able to use strong magic to survive the attack of the Blackfoot braves. So he followed the girl, creeping away from the place where

Snake Eye lay, towards a tipi on the edge of the village.

Black Tail Deer took him inside and bound his injured leg. Her small fingers worked deftly to stem the blood.

'They will kill you if they find me here in your tipi,' Four Winds warned. 'Why did you come to help?'

'I do not like Snake Eye and his Wild Dogs,' she confessed. 'I would not see him defeat you and the beautiful silver horse. I am glad he is slain.'

'Why?'

The girl refused to say more until he pressed her. 'If you really want to know, the Comanches trade in more than silver and horses,' she told him grudgingly.

The answer still didn't satisfy him. 'What else?'

'In battle, Snake Eye orders the Wild Dogs to capture women and children. He brings the prisoners to the north and trades them with Wahnistow for more silver than ten horses can buy.'

Four Winds studied Black Tail Deer closely, guessing now at her reasons. 'You are not Blackfoot?'

She shook her head. 'I am Oglala Sioux, daughter to Nightcloud and Summer Rain. I was brought here three springs ago. But my heart is in my homeland still.'

So Four Winds understood and his heart softened towards the girl. 'I am White Water Sioux. We are brother and sister.'

Black Tail Deer smiled back at him. 'I will come with

you and the horse. Wahnistow will not keep me from my People.'

There was no time for Four Winds to explain his quest, only to promise that he would return for Black Tail Deer when his journey was done.

Tears sprang to her dark brown eyes. 'I will not stay!'

'Only for a few days,' he begged.

'You will not come back. Wahnistow will keep guard, you will not re-enter the village.'

And, however he promised, she would not be satisfied.

Meanwhile, outside the tipi, the war cries of the Blackfoot warriors were joined by the wailing of the Wild Dogs over their fallen chief.

'Behold, the dream horse has destroyed Snake Eye!' they cried. They lifted the crushed body and carried it to the centre of the village, where the women made a fire to warm him, for they found that the man's heart still beat, though his eyes were closed and his body twisted and broken.

By the corral, Silver Cloud fought to escape the spears of the Blackfoot braves, not with magic but with cunning. If only he could release the imprisoned horses and let them loose on to the hillside, then Wahnistow's men would be forced to follow.

So he swung away from the men and lunged with all his might against the spiked stakes which fenced the horses in. His weight crashed through two of the stakes, creating a gap just wide enough for a horse to escape through. Then he whirled to one side to leave the captive horses room to flee.

Only one of Wahnistow's men saw what was happening. Straight away, he stepped in front of the gap, his arms raised.

But the terrified horses would not be stopped. Their instinct to flee from danger was strong, and now they saw a way. The lead mare, a dark bay with a black mane and a white star on her forehead, charged for the gap, smashing down and trampling another stake as she passed through. Then others followed, stampeding after the leader, churning up the snow and throwing aside the Blackfoot brave who barred their path.

Silver Cloud too joined them and made good his escape.

And Wahnistow appeared and ordered his men to run after the horses, for neither the Blackfoot nor the Comanches were strong without them. Then he strode to the new fire where Snake Eye lay.

He bent over his brother in treachery and listened to his breathing. When he stood up, his face was hard and grey as stone.

'Would that Snake Eye had died under the horse's hooves,' he said sternly. 'For the life that remains to him is not worth living.'

SEVEN

'Where is the boy?' Wahnistow demanded, in the midst of the fleeing horses and grieving warriors. Women snatched children and took them back into the tipis for safety. The snarling dogs retreated to the edges of the village.

No one had thought about Four Winds since the moment when Silver Cloud had struck down Snake Eye. Now, though, the nearest men began to search in the snow.

'Here is his blood!' cried one, tracing a crimson trail behind the rock where Black Tail Deer had concealed herself.

'But perhaps this is the horse's blood,' another said, 'or the blood of Snake Eye himself.'

Through the trees, the baying of wolves and the sound of horses galloping heightened the confusion. An early sun struggled to penetrate grey snow clouds, casting a wintry gleam on the village.

'Find him!' Wahnistow ordered. 'Without the spirit horse he cannot go far!'

A search began among the tipis. Piles of logs for fires were overturned, dewcloths pulled down and every corner ransacked.

'I must go!' Four Winds told Black Tail Deer. 'Soon the dogs will smell me out and all will be lost!'

The girl seized a striped blanket from the bed in the tipi. She flung it around Four Winds' shoulders; a poor disguise, Four Winds knew. But he would rely on his speed, given to him by the eagle feather which he carried in his medicine bundle. And he would not leave the tipi by the entrance facing into the village. Instead, he would take out his knife and make a slit in the painted skin at the back. Then he would creep away as soft and stealthy as a mountain lion.

Black Tail Deer cried to see him go. But the searchers drew near and Wahnistow's angry commands reached every corner of the village.

'Find the boy! We will tie him to the cedar pole in the bitter cold. The horse will return to save him and we will put them both to death!'

Black Tail Deer let out a small cry, then took a deep breath. 'Go then!' she said to Four Winds. 'Take the slope to the west. I will send them a different way.'

So he sliced through the buffalo-skin wall and stepped out into the open. He heard the searchers burst into Black Tail Deer's tipi, heard her declare in a frightened voice that yes, she had seen the Sioux boy, and that he had headed south, back the way he had come with the horse.

Four Winds wrapped the blanket tight around him. There were no tipis between him and the trees perhaps thirty paces away. But it was an open, rocky space without shelter – thirty footfalls when a dog could bark or a searcher could let an arrow fly from his bow.

He would run swift as the deer. He would make no noise.

Twenty paces, and the tall trees beckoned. Their boughs were laden with snow, the undergrowth thick and frozen.

Twenty-five paces and he saw a figure emerge from the trees. It was a woman and he was not afraid. She didn't call out a warning to the searchers or step across his path. She simply watched from a distance, her head covered by a shawl, a container of water resting on her shoulder.

Four Winds ran towards her. He knew this woman, though she did not yet know him.

But was it a trick? Were his thoughts so muddled that he saw shapes that were only dreams?

The woman put down the water. She stared into Four Winds' eyes.

'I am Four Winds of the White Water Sioux,' he whispered, against the howl of dogs and angry cries of men. 'Son of Swift Elk, grandson of the great chief Red Hawk.'

She sighed and closed her eyes. Then she touched his face with her fingertips, as if she thought he would melt like the snow. 'I am Shining Star,' she murmured. 'Wife to Swift Elk, taken from my village by Snake Eye after Thunder Ridge, sold in slavery to Wahnistow. I am the lost mother to Four Winds of the White Water Sioux.'

Four Winds' mother was even more beautiful than he remembered. Her eyes were warm, her murmuring lips soft and full. He knew the gentle curve of her chin, the smoothness of her neck and the slope of her shoulder from the countless times when he had nestled against her as a young child, and now he was speechless with wonder that they should meet again.

'It is you, my son!' she whispered.

He nodded, unable to speak.

'You are grown strong and straight. I would hardly recognise you.'

'I am a warrior,' he told her proudly.

'Like your father and grandfather.' She was glad and sad at the same time, reaching out to him again. 'But you must go now. Every moment you delay brings the men nearer.'

Four Winds' heart was joined with Shining Star. Her blood was his blood. He could never leave her.

'Go!' she urged.

How many times in this life of the warrior would his

heart tell him one thing and his head another? As with Sun Dancer, now with Shining Star. 'This is too hard,' he told her.

'I am happy now that I have seen you, my son,' Shining Star said through her tears. 'Every night I have dreamed of such a moment, yet never hoped that it would come.'

'I have seen your star in the night sky,' he whispered. 'I have heard your voice.'

'My son!' she cried, putting her arms around his neck and resting her head on his shoulder.

'Come with me!' he begged, forgetting all caution. 'I will not leave you with Wahnistow.'

She pulled away. 'But the Wild Dogs say you are on a quest. You must travel far with the spirit horse.'

'And you will go with me!'

'I cannot.' Glancing around, Shining Star saw that danger drew nearer. The chief of the Blackfoot tribe was himself searching the outer tipis. She pushed Four Winds into the shelter of some undergrowth and impulsively stepped forward to show herself.

'Prisoner Woman!' Wahnistow called in his own language. 'What are you doing? What have you seen?'

Shining Star picked up her water carrier and trudged to meet him. 'I am bringing water,' she answered quietly. 'I have seen horses fleeing up the mountain.'

Wahnistow pushed her roughly against a tree. 'But not the boy?' he demanded.

She shook her head. 'I have seen wolves, but no boy.'

The chief's eyes narrowed. 'He is Sioux, like you. You would lie to save him!' And he thrust his arm against her throat, pressing her head back against the rough bark. 'Is it true that the boy has not passed this way?'

Shining Star struggled to push him away. 'Why ask if you don't believe me?' she challenged.

'I see the lie in your eyes!' he retorted, forming his hand into a fist. 'You are a false Prisoner Woman, fit only to be struck!'

Four Winds sprang out of the bushes and leaped on to Wahnistow's back. He pulled him down and rolled in the snow, fierce as a mother bear in defence of her cubs.

The Blackfoot chief gripped Four Winds' torso with his legs. He punched his body and squeezed the air from his lungs. But the boy fought back until Wahnistow called out for help.

Then men came running up the slope, slowed by snowdrifts, but bound soon to break up the fight and take Four Winds prisoner.

Shining Star cried out to the sky. 'Wakanda, I offer you my life to help Kola, my son!'

And at that moment the spirit horse returned. He thundered across the mountain, mane flowing, tail streaming behind. His hooves scarcely touched the ground. He was dappled grey and white like the clouds and the snow; part of mighty Nature's force.

Silver Cloud reached the place where Wahnistow and Four Winds fought. The Blackfoot warriors were frightened by his power and stopped short. They recalled how the horse had struck down great Snake Eye and left his twisted body on the ground.

'Come!' Silver Cloud said to Four Winds in a way that must be obeyed.

The boy rolled free of the Blackfoot chief, powerless to resist. He climbed on to Silver Cloud's back, knowing this was the path he must follow. There was a mountain to the north and a feather to bring back.

'Good!' Silver Cloud murmured, preparing to sweep on across the hillside.

Four Winds glanced behind, to his mother, Shining Star, standing alone under the trees. Her hands were clasped to her breast in prayer while the Blackfoot warriors surrounded her.

'Mother!' the boy cried.

But his voice was lost on the wind.

'My heart is broken.' The boy spoke to Ghost Horse from the top of a high ridge. Snow blew all around him. 'It is torn in two.'

'Time will mend it,' Silver Cloud promised.

But the boy knew that the wound of separation could never be healed. 'For two summers I have believed that my mother was dead along with my father, Swift Elk. We did not dream that she had been taken prisoner and brought to the cold land of the north.'

Four Winds drew a small object from his medicine bundle and showed it to Silver Cloud. 'This is the lizard skin pouch left by Shining Star on the floor of the tipi when the Wild Dogs came on their war raid. My grandmother found it and gave it to me. It signifies long life.'

The horse bowed his head. 'A mother always thinks of her son.'

'She thought only of me when the Comanches came. Now I have found her, and I think of other things: the feather, the future of my People.'

Silver Cloud listened.

'Wahnistow will punish Shining Star,' Four Winds predicted. 'He knows that she lied to protect me. She is his slave. He will put her to death.'

For the first time, Silver Cloud understood that he had ordered the boy to sacrifice his own mother for the sake of the quest, and that the boy had obeyed. But now his heart was broken and weak. 'It is the work of Wakanda, the Great Spirit,' Silver Cloud counselled softly. 'He is within all things. You are a warrior, and act and live as he intends.' But, secretly, he understood the depth of Four Winds' grief.

'You have time to call on the spirits for help in the next part of our journey to Mount Kivioq,' Silver Cloud said, after a long silence.

So Four Winds sat cross-legged in the snow and asked for the Eagle to visit him here on that ridge, for the Eagle flew higher and saw more than any other creature.

The bird came through the snowstorm, circling above the ridge. His wingspan exceeded a man's arms; his eyes saw every rock, and, below him, the boy sitting on the ground.

'Must I make this sacrifice?' Four Winds pleaded, his face turned up towards the great bird. 'Is it as the Great Spirit wishes?'

The Eagle swooped low into the valley. He soared high and pushed back the huge snow clouds, bringing blue into the sky. The last flakes drifted down and melted on the boy's cheeks.

'You see each blade of grass, every silver fish in the mountain stream. Must Shining Star die at the hands of Wahnistow?'

The bird came and hovered close by. His curved beak was black, his shiny wing feathers marked with white bands.

'We will follow where you lead,' Silver Cloud told the bird spirit, inviting the boy on to his back.

So the bird flew ahead and, with the spirit's help, the horse and the boy took to the air to follow him; over rocky peaks, into valleys; looking down on the tall pines and icy streams which grew small, like bands of silver glinting in the sun.

Four Winds soared high above the land, like the Eagle,

like a great bird of prey. His heart swelled and beat faster as the air grew thin.

Then the Blackfoot village was beneath them, its circle of tipis laid out like the small round stones of a medicine wheel. Figures came and went like ants: men bringing horses down from the mountains, back into the corral, women feeding the fires, dogs barking.

Four Winds descended with the Eagle and Silver Cloud. They could not be seen by Wahnistow and his warriors.

'Snake Eye lives, but his breath is worth nothing!' the women whispered, gathered at the door of the wounded chief's tipi. 'He cannot move a hand or foot!'

'His warriors have sworn revenge against the boy and the horse!'

'The Comanche will lay waste to the White Water band. Their anger is greater than before.'

And the men of Wahnistow's band brought back the horses, grumbling and cursing. 'Now we must travel into the mountains to track the boy warrior. We would rather stay by our tipi now that winter has come!'

'The Prisoner Woman is to blame. She hid the boy while the horse returned to carry him away.'

'She has paid the price,' another said.

Four Winds gasped.

'Has he put her to death?' one asked idly as he hammered a stake into the ground to repair the fence, with no more concern than if Shining Star had been a ground squirrel or a fox.

'At sunset, when great Iron Eyes emerges from his lair; that is the time to sacrifice the woman.'

So there was still hope. Four Winds let out his breath.

'She has not given a single cry, even though she is tied to the cedar pole within Wahnistow's tipi.'

'Perhaps he has cut out her tongue!' came the blood-curdling remark.

And the boy's chest grew tight again, and he ran invisibly from tent to tent to find his mother.

He found Shining Star where the warriors had said, bound to the pole in the centre of Wahnistow's tipi. The walls were painted with warriors wielding spears and the faces of wolves which were hardy and war-like in their habits. The chief's wolfskin headdress hung from a hook above the prisoner's head.

Four Winds' mother stood motionless. Her eyes wore a faraway look, dreaming of the time when she cleaned deerskins and fetched firewood from the forest while Swift Elk hunted their meat and Four Winds lay wrapped in warm fur and learned his first words: 'Father', 'Mother'.

When the girl, Black Tail Deer, took pity on the Prisoner Woman and brought her water to drink, Shining Star did not notice her.

Black Tail Deer had lifted the wooden bowl to

Shining Star's lips when Wahnistow strode into the tent. He swept the bowl to the ground and flung the girl aside. 'She has no need of water,' he said coldly. 'Nor of friends like you!'

Black Tail Deer struggled to her feet. 'I am Oglala Sioux!' she cried. 'We are sisters.'

'You are a fool!' Wahnistow grew angry. 'You seal your own death with these words.'

'I would rather die than live without Shining Star, here in the village of my enemies.'

The chief laughed. 'Easy to say you would rather die!'

Then Black Tail Deer ran to seize the knife from Wahnistow's wampum belt. 'Action follows words!' she gasped, ready to end her own life until Shining Star let out a sudden cry.

'She is a child of ten summers!' she reminded Wahnistow. 'Who has the knowledge to act wisely before fifteen summers have passed?'

The chief laughed again in his cruel, mocking way. 'The Prisoner Woman and the Prisoner Child defy Wahnistow. This is a tale to tell around the fire!' Casually he took two strides and seized back his knife with no more effort than if he had been flicking dust from his war shirt.

Black Tail Deer fell against the wall of the tipi, sobbing bitterly.

Then Wahnistow went away to amuse his warriors with what had just taken place.

The girl's sobs broke the muffled silence of the tipi, along with the sighs of Shining Star.

It was time for Four Winds to speak. 'You cannot see me but you can hear.'

At the sound of his voice, the woman and the girl were still as carved statues.

'I came here through the air, with the help of the Eagle and my dream horse. Trust me.'

Black Tail Deer ran close to Shining Star for comfort.

'Do not be afraid,' Four Winds whispered. 'The Great Spirit helps those who follow His way. He would not leave you to die.'

Hope was rekindled and Shining Star looked round eagerly. 'Then I may live?'

Her son untied the leather strap that bound her wrists to the pole. 'You and Black Tail Deer will come with me.' Rescuing one, he could not leave the other behind.

A wind rustled the flap at the tent door, and Four Winds knew that it was time to leave. So he appeared before them and offered his hands to Shining Star and Black Tail Deer and led them through the door into a whirl of snowflakes so thick that it was impossible to see ahead.

'The spirits have brought back the storm to hide us,' he said in a low voice. 'Here is the Eagle and here is Silver Cloud.'

The woman and the girl were afraid of the ghostly creatures. They hesitated, then pulled back.

But Eagle spread his wings and sheltered them from the snow. 'No harm will come to you,' he promised.

Then he carried Four Winds, Shining Star and Black Tail Deer through the air in a flurry of pure snowflakes.

They were gone from the village by the time the Blackfoot warriors had stopped laughing over the young Sioux girl's foolishness.

Then there was no more smiling, when they went to Wahnistow's tipi and found it empty.

EIGHT

'I will watch over you,' Eagle promised, after he had delivered the small group of travellers back on to the high ridge. 'Look up and you will see me.'

Four Winds thanked him.

'Be alert,' the sharp-eyed spirit warned. 'You must pass through the largest forest before you reach the highest mountain. There are bears and coyotes, and the servants of Iron Eyes: Stone Man and his wolf messengers.'

'I fear no spirit with you and Silver Cloud watching over me.' The boy looked ahead with hope. Soon, very soon, he would climb to the top of the world and find the feather that would save his People.

Shining Star listened to the brave words with pride and fear.

'Iron Eyes is cruel and treacherous,' Eagle explained. 'He is the most cunning of your enemies. He hunts alone at night and, like the wolf, he shows no mercy.'

'Listen well!' Silver Cloud advised. He knew that

eager pride was the weakness in Four Winds, as it was in most young creatures.

'The forest is dark, even in the day. There is no track to follow, nor stars to guide you.'

'Then there can be no enemies like Wahnistow living there.' Four Winds grew more confident. 'And Snake Eye's men will not follow, now that their chief has been struck down.' It seemed lucky to him that all their effort should be directed from now on in pitting their wits against Anteep and his spirits.

Eagle listened. 'Learn well from Silver Cloud,' he advised. 'And take care of Shining Star, your mother, and of Black Tail Deer, your Sioux sister, for we have risked much to save them.'

The boy promised with all his heart. He looked ahead to where their path must take them, across the bare mountain into a frozen forest that stretched as far as the eye could see.

'Go then,' Eagle declared. He spread his wings and prepared to fly away.

Four Winds felt a rush of wind from the bird's feathers. He looked up at Eagle and across to Silver Cloud. Then he smiled. For with these two to protect him, how could he fail?

MOUNT KIVIOQ

NINE

Silver Cloud led Four Winds, Shining Star and Black Tail Deer through the day into the night.

'We must make up for lost time,' he said. 'While Snake Eye and Wahnistow decide what they will do next, we can forge ahead.'

'The Blackfoot braves had recovered many of their horses from the mountain,' Black Tail Deer told them. 'The horses were hungry and cold. They came close for food and the men lassoed them.'

'So they will follow us,' Four Winds concluded. 'But we will be far away.'

'The snow will cover our tracks,' Shining Star pointed out. 'The tall trees will hide us.'

But Four Winds felt uneasy as the forest loomed. Eagle had issued a warning about the bad spirits who lurked in the shadows. Iron Eyes, the wolf spirit, was the one he feared the most. He was a servant of Anteep, with mighty powers to change the landscape and direct the weather, perhaps a shape-shifter like Yietso by Yellow Water, and more ruthless even than Thadodaho, the thunder spirit.

'Stay close,' he urged his mother and the girl as they entered between the first snow-laden trees. 'Never let Silver Cloud out of your sight.'

Overhead, the pines rose taller than any cedar, broader than the largest aspen. Their branches formed a roof through which no daylight penetrated. The air turned heavy with the scent of resin.

Shining Star took Black Tail Deer by the hand. 'Do not be afraid,' she said gently.

The girl gathered up her courage. 'I believe in the dream horse,' she whispered. 'His magic is strong.'

So they journeyed on into the gloom, pausing in small clearings to breathe in fresh air and to look up at the sky, then pressing on through the still, quiet forest.

Four Winds didn't like the silence. He preferred the sharp click of the horse's hooves on solid rock to the soft footfall on to pine needles; the bracing wind from the north to the unnatural stillness of the pine-scented air.

'The forest is full of eyes!' Black Tail Deer whispered what they all felt, but could not see. She looked longingly over her shoulder, only to discover that the way back out of the forest was now as far as the way ahead.

Shining Star thought of a story to help the frightened child. 'There were once two sisters,' she began. 'They lived alone in a lonely place, a long time ago, when tribes were few and the animal people were friendly to man.

'The name of one of the girls was Earth, and the other was Water.'

Four Winds relaxed as he recalled the story of The Girl Who Married the Star. It was one of his favourites, told by his mother around the fire.

'The animals brought food to Earth and Water. Bears brought nuts and berries, and bees brought combs dripping with honey. The girls lived in a lodge made of birch-bark, and their beds were mats woven of rushes.'

'I know this!' Black Tail Deer exclaimed. 'The girl called Earth sees a handsome young man in her dreams, and her sister says that she too has seen a handsome young man, who was a great warrior.'

'That is the one,' Shining Star said with a smile. Now the girl would forget about the watching eyes, and time would pass pleasantly.

' "Do you not think that the bright stars above us are the sky men of whom we dream?" Earth suggested. And an excited Water exclaimed that she chose the brightest Star in all the sky for her husband.'

' "And I," declared her sister, "choose for my husband that small twinkling Star!" ' Black Tail Deer ran ahead with the story. 'By and by the sisters slept, and when they awoke, they found themselves in the sky. The husband of Water turned out to be an old warrior with a shining reputation, but the husband of Earth was a handsome young man with no glory attached to his name.'

'And the girls were happy because the Star men were kind to their wives,' Four Winds joined in. 'One day the girls went out to dig wild turnips. The old warrior said to his wife, "When you are digging, you must not hit the ground too hard."

'The young warrior also warned his wife, saying, "Do not hit the ground too hard!" But Earth forgot, and she struck the ground hard with a sharp pointed stick. She hit so hard that the floor of the sky was broken and the poor girl fell through.'

'Two very old people found her lying in a meadow,' Shining Star went on. 'They kindly made her a wigwam of pine boughs and brought ferns for her bed. They nursed her as well as they could, but Earth did nothing but wail and cry. "Let me go to my husband!" she begged. "I cannot live without him!"

'Night came and the stars appeared in the sky. Only one little twinkling star did not appear, for he had lost his wife and had painted his face quite black.

'The poor wife waited a long time, but he did not come because he could not. At last she slept and dreamed that she saw a tiny red star in the sky that had not been there before. "Ah!" she cried, "that is Red Star, my son!"

'In the morning she found at her side a pretty little boy, a Star Boy, who afterwards grew to be a handsome young man and had many adventures. Red Star's guides by night through the pathless forests were the Star children of his mother's sister, his cousins in the sky.'

It happened long ago, in a time when the animal people were friends to men, Silver Cloud reflected sadly. Before spears were made, and a thousand buffalo were driven to their deaths in a *piksun*. Before any blood was spilled.

Perhaps the travellers had grown unwary, or maybe their lively voices had alerted the enemy that lay in their path. There was a thick part of the forest where high winds had blown and branches had fallen to the earth. Dead brush and smaller twigs had built up a barrier of jagged spikes and thorns between the trunks, and Four Winds decided that the only way through was to hack with knives.

So he began the task, slashing at brambles and busily thrusting aside dead wood. Then suddenly he stopped.

'What is it?' Shining Star asked.

'Nothing.' More eyes watching, soft breath, but nothing which he could see.

He worked on, irritated when thorns caught on the flesh of his arms, or brambles wound themselves around his legs. This was holding them up, and they had far to go.

The creature, when it pounced from a hidden branch, came at him with its jaws open and fangs exposed. It landed heavily, digging sharp claws into Four Winds' shoulders. The boy saw the tell-tale pale strips down its dark sides – wolverine!

This was an enemy to be reckoned with. Ferocious, strong and dogged, it could bring down a deer, or even a snowbound elk. Its teeth could crush through bone.

The wolverine's jaws snapped at the boy's neck, missing by a fraction. Seizing its front legs, Four Winds used all his strength to pull the creature from his shoulders and send it crashing to the ground. Youth aided him; his reactions were swift, his slim body lithe.

Winded, the animal cowered against a tree, gathering its breath for a second attack. Its black eyes glittered as it crouched in wait.

But then a second, still more dangerous foe appeared. The bear warned of its approach with a roar from deep in its throat. It thrust its way through the dense thicket, walking on two feet, gripping branches and tearing them down with its front paws.

Cowering by the tree trunk, the wolverine recognised the bear's approach. Its round ears flicked, then it turned and loped out of reach, content to watch and move in on whatever carrion prey the bear might leave behind.

Four Winds thought fast. 'Climb on Silver Cloud!' he ordered Shining Star and Black Tail Deer. 'Let him carry you to safety.'

They did as they were told, for there was no time to argue.

Soon the bear lumbered into sight. Raised on its hind

legs, it stood one and a half times the size of a man. Its thick brown fur was matted with burrs, its long muzzle trickling with blood.

Though frightened by the size and power of the bear, the boy regarded it with respect. The Bear gave the Sioux people powerful medicine, he stood guard over the Great Spirit, so he was not to be harmed without cause. Yet this she-bear was angry, and soon the reason grew clear, when Four Winds peered into the network of thorns and deadwood and discovered two cubs staring back at him.

Now he wished that he shared a language with the bear and that he could speak. 'Do not be afraid,' he would say. 'We mean you and your cubs no harm.'

But the mother did not understand why the travellers were here. She knew only that their winter den was under attack. So she came at Four Winds with slashing claws, surprisingly quick for a huge, thickset animal, forcing him back from the barrier towards the spot where the sly wolverine lurked.

Four Winds couldn't turn and run. The bear could outrun him and outclimb him, and besides, the sight of a fleeing boy would anger her more. 'Stand still and stand tall in the face of a bear,' his father, Swift Elk, had always taught him. 'Have the courage of a warrior and do not run away.'

So the boy drew a deep breath and let his knife hand drop to his side. He told himself that amongst all the tests he would face, this one was not so difficult nor so dangerous. And he looked the mother bear in the eye.

She stared intently back, then the growl in her throat fell silent. She dropped on to all-fours, padded forward, sniffed at the ground where Four Winds stood.

From a distance, Shining Star saw that her son had learned well from his father.

The bear was a huge creature, almost as wide as she was long. Her legs were thick as the trunk of a tree. Four Winds did not move.

She nosed in the earth by his feet, her thick fur carrying the sharp stink of the den which Four Winds had just disturbed. Then she padded around him full-circle, making the ground shake as she walked.

And the boy's head stayed up. There had been no need to threaten or fight. Patience and courage were all that had been needed. He had proved that he had both.

At last, the bear was satisfied and lumbered back towards her hidden den. The two cubs crept free of the tangle of branches and scampered between her legs, glad to be out of their cramped winter quarters. They rolled and turned head over heels, play-fighting with their front paws, then chasing each other around in circles.

Waiting until their mother had rounded them up and ordered them sternly back inside, Four Winds watched the disappointed wolverine lope off through the forest. He didn't like creatures that fed off carrion, letting others do their hunting for them, yet still he wouldn't willingly have sunk his knife into it, for he believed, as his grandmother had taught, that we are all connected and that, though each animal had its own shape, underneath their skin they were all People.

'We must leave the bears in peace and find another way around this barrier,' he told Silver Cloud and the others as he strode to join them. 'Perhaps we should climb higher up the hill, above the tree line.'

The dream horse disagreed. 'And be caught high on the mountain at night?' he queried. 'Your blood would freeze in your veins, you would die in the snow.'

'So we will walk down into the ravine.' The boy was forced to make a choice he didn't like because that way was rocky and the trees grew crooked. It would be a slow, difficult route.

However, there was no other way. Even if Four Winds himself was prepared to face a night in the open, there was no way he could put Black Tail Deer and his mother through such a trial. After all, the girl was slight and small for ten summers. She had hardly any flesh on her bones to keep out the cold.

So they trekked down into the valley, setting off small avalanches of loose snow as they went. The girl rode on Silver Cloud's back to allow her to rest.

'This is a dream!' she gasped, holding tight to the horse's mane. She slipped from side to side, laughing at the motion. 'How do I sit straight?'

'Press with your legs against the horse's sides,' Four Winds told her. 'And sit tall. Look straight ahead.'

Now she rode more skilfully. 'I am high off the ground!' she called. 'I can see far!'

'Don't shout so loud,' Four Winds warned.

And Shining Star smiled to hear how her son had become a big brother to the excitable girl.

The daylight, grey and heavy at the best of times, grew dimmer as they walked deeper into the ravine, where the steep sides closed in to a narrow channel giving just enough space for them to pass through. The streams that in summer would tumble down the almost sheer rock faces were frozen solid, hanging in jagged icicles as long as a man's arm.

Four Winds looked up to either side. He would have liked to spy Eagle soaring up in the leaden sky, but the bird was nowhere to be seen. He entered the final stretch of the ravine with an uneasy feeling, wondering what they would meet on the far side.

He clambered ahead to make sure that the gulley was wide enough for Silver Cloud to pass through, leaving the others waiting in the dusky light, promising to return without delay.

He had gone fifty paces ahead, picking his way around ice and boulders, pressed on both sides by the smooth, sheer granite cliffs, when a cloud of cold mist descended. The mist was so thick that he could no longer see where to put his feet, so he felt his way forward, his hands scraping against the rock until he sensed that the ravine was opening out and that there truly was a way through which they could pass.

Four Winds was about to turn back to deliver the good news when he felt a presence in the mist. Eyes in the forest. Hot breath. Creatures gathering. He peered ahead, knowing before he made them out that wolves were watching him.

They were lurking amongst the trees at the far side of the ravine, their grey coats merging with the mist and the silver white trunks of the aspens. Bigger and stronger than any dog, their pointed ears were pricked, their pale eyes fixed intently on the boy.

The largest wolf, and leader of the pack, padded forward. Here was easy prey: a solitary, half-grown boy. Climbing on to a rock, he threw back his head and howled.

Silver Cloud and the rest would hear this cry, Four Winds knew. They would probably press ahead through the narrow ravine to join him. That would make four of them against ten or twelve wolves. He decided to challenge and defeat the strong leader, in the hope that the rest would flee.

He drew his knife and climbed on to a ridge where he could be level with the lead male. Down below, the other wolves wove through the trees, encircling him.

This was a battle the boy didn't relish. Already

exhausted by the encounter with the bear, he wondered how many more enemies were hidden in this dark forest. Then the mist thickened and the wolves became mere shadows. The leader howled again, long and loud, answered by a cry from the top of the mountain.

As if in a cloud of freezing mist, the mighty spirit wolf, Iron Eyes, descended for the first time to view his human enemy. He came in wolf shape through the white mist; enormous and savage. His muzzle was black, his pointed ears outlined with white, a thick ruff of grey fur hung around his neck; wolf in every respect, except for his huge size.

As the spirit materialised, the boy recoiled. He wanted to run and hide like a child, but the spirit wolf's eyes held him. They were staring at him, mesmerising him, drawing him nearer.

And the Wolf saw that his enemy was not to be feared. This was a mere boy, sent on an impossible errand to bring the feather from the highest mountain. He was not armed with spear and tomahawk; he did not bring with him a band of warriors.

The eyes of the Wolf were narrow. They glowed pale yellow, with a hard, black point at their centre. Under their harsh gaze, Four Winds was helpless. He lost the will to fight.

Suddenly Silver Cloud burst through the ravine, carrying Shining Star and Black Tail Deer on his back.

Their arrival scattered the wolf pack and took Iron Eyes' gaze away from the boy.

Four Winds felt as though he had been released from an iron band that had encircled his chest. He took a deep breath and slid down from the rock to stand by Silver Cloud's side.

'I am Silver Cloud, messenger of Ghost Horse, servant of the Great Wakanda!' the horse announced. 'What business has Iron Eyes with us?'

The Wolf captured the dream horse in his gaze. 'I know who you are and why you are here. I am Iron Eyes, servant of Anteep. My business is to watch and wait!'

Silver Cloud fought the hypnotic stare. 'And ours is to travel on through this forest.' He set off between the aspens, carrying the woman and the girl, with the boy at his side. The huge, mist-shrouded figure of the wolf seemed to rise and float above them, melting into the branches then reappearing, first to their right, then to the left.

'Why is he waiting?' Black Tail Deer asked. Her voice fell away into a terrified sob.

'Because Anteep orders it,' Silver Cloud guessed correctly. 'Evil spirits take pleasure in making you afraid.'

From a nearby hill, the lead wolf gave his chilling howl. He threw back his head and bayed to the rising crescent moon.

'And will he always be watching?' the girl gasped.

She hid her face against Shining Star's shoulder.

'Always,' Silver Cloud answered quietly. 'Anteep's spirits are everywhere, in the air and the earth and the water.'

Four Winds clenched his fists as he walked, determined not to look up and meet the cold gaze of Iron Eyes and fall under their cruel spell. He found that he could think and plan as long as he took care to avoid looking into the spirit's eyes.

'Then how can we win our fight against him?' Black Tail Deer wanted to know. She asked the simple questions of a frightened young child.

'Because Wakanda's spirits are here too; all around us,' Shining Star reminded her. 'And if Four Winds follows the path of the Great Mystery, then he will succeed.'

Silver Cloud saw that the woman understood many things, and was wise. So he stayed silent until they were clear of the low mist and had left the wolves behind.

'Today has been long,' the horse said at last. The trees were beginning to thin, there were more clearings to allow in the very last of the sun's rays. 'We will rest, and begin again when the moon is high in the sky.'

These were welcome words to the others. So they found a sheltered clearing where the snow lay thin on the ground and they could find dry wood for a fire. Four Winds unwrapped the bark parcel of meat and berries given to him for his journey by the grieving

Burning Tree, and shared it between them. Thus, with full stomachs and weary limbs, they slept.

'Smoke!' Tall Bull said, pointing to a thin grey spiral that rose from the clearing.

'I will inform the others.' Spotted Tail leaped from the Comanche lookout rock and ran through the snow to the circle of horses and riders. 'The boy and his companions have made camp,' he reported.

The Wild Dog warriors listened gravely. 'Did Snake Eye hear this news?' one asked, stooping over a long travois pulled by a black-and-white horse. The sled was made of two cedar poles and a buffalo hide strong enough to carry the weight of the motionless chief.

Snake Eye looked up from the travois. His face was pale as death, still smeared with white and red war paint. His dark eyes smouldered with hate. 'The enemy is resting,' he whispered, tight muscles in his jaw clicking as he spoke. His voice was like the rustle of dry leaves. 'We move on!'

His scout, Spotted Tail, stepped forward. 'While the enemy rests, we should rest also,' he pointed out. 'Our horses are tired, we are cold and hungry.'

All around knew that Spotted Tail would not have questioned great Snake Eye's decision if their chief had not been struck down so that he could move neither arms nor legs. Horror was in their hearts as they looked down at the wretched figure.

'We will travel on!' Snake Eye hissed. Already he had defied Wahnistow, who had told him that the way ahead was hard and that a fresh snowstorm hung over the mountains.

'You will take your men to their deaths!' the Blackfoot chief had warned. 'Besides, you barely cling to life. What good does it do to pursue the boy now?'

But Snake Eye had not listened. His men had recaptured their horses and he had made them build a sled to take him through the forest. Only hatred kept him alive, and the desire to destroy the Sioux boy.

The Blackfoot warriors had stood silently and seen the Wild Dogs on their way. There was shame in letting their allies travel on alone, but Wahnistow had declared that he would not lead his braves to certain death.

And so Tall Bull, the strongest of the Comanches, and Spotted Tail, whose belt carried the most enemy scalps, had led the Comanches on their relentless way through the forest. The two men had much to prove now that Snake Eye lay helpless on his bed, for they knew that whoever led the Wild Dogs through this hard journey would soon become chief. For Snake Eye's life hung on the thread of bitterness and could not long be sustained.

'We travel on!' the helpless shell of their chief insisted. His voice rasped, his black eyes glittered. 'While the enemy sleeps, we will make our move!'

TEN

Out of the frozen forest into the icy wasteland Four Winds and his companions made their way.

The short sleep had refreshed them and given them new heart, even though they could now sense the huge, grey presence of the wolf spirit watching every move they made.

With Silver Cloud to guide us, we need not fear Iron Eyes, Four Winds told himself. *We have come through the forest, and now Mount Kivioq lies within our reach. All will be well.*

As they journeyed into the dusk, Shining Star asked her son about the life of the White Water People.

'Is it very hard?' she asked fearfully.

'No harder than the years you have spent as a prisoner of the Blackfoot,' he replied. Summers had come and gone; his mother had fetched water, fed fires and skinned deer as Wahnistow's slave.

'But our warriors are few?' she persisted.

He nodded. 'One Horn, Little Thunder and Three Bears remain,' he told her. 'Sun Dancer's life rests with the medicine man of the Cree People.'

'And is that all?'

'Besides me. I have made my vision quest to Spider Rock. I am a warrior too.'

His mother's heart quickened with pride and fear. 'You are young,' she reminded him.

'But my grandfather chose me for the quest, because I am the one he loves the most,' he told her.

'Ah, Red Hawk,' she said quietly. 'How is he?'

'He is chief still.'

'But sick?'

Four Winds nodded. 'White Deer tends him. But there is no medicine that will bring back his strength.' After thinking for a while, he took the lizard skin pouch from his medicine bundle and showed it to Shining Star. 'This is the gift you left me. Grandmother kept it safe and gave it to me before I set out on my first journey.'

She smiled softly. 'Your father gave this pouch to me when we were married. Before that, it was a gift from his father to his mother, and for many generations before that it has been in the family.'

'I never forgot you,' he whispered, walking alongside her while the girl rode the horse. 'You were with me in every step I took and every dream I dreamed.'

'My son,' she whispered.

They walked on into the white wilderness, the grey sky above them, towards the highest mountain.

'Here is where the boy rested,' Spotted Tail announced. He led the Wild Dogs to the sheltered clearing and showed them that the ashes from the fire were still warm. The lightly falling snow had not yet covered the footsteps of the departing travellers.

The Comanche scout stood over the low sled where Snake Eye lay. He folded his strong arms across his broad chest and spoke loudly. 'Let me ride ahead and kill the enemy,' he pleaded. 'I will take him by surprise and sink my tomahawk into his skull. I will return with his scalp.'

Some of the Wild Dogs murmured their approval. Spotted Tail would go like a fox through the woods. He would attack like a mountain lion then take flight like a bird, disappearing before he had really appeared.

But Snake Eye spat out his response. 'That is not how it will be!'

Tall Bull nodded, then spoke out. 'Listen to our great chief, Snake Eye, for his word is strong, though his body is weak!' He towered above the travois, taller than Spotted Tail, fierce rivalry flashing from his eyes.

Snake Eye's face was twisted with pain; his chest scarcely rose and fell to the rhythm of his shallow breathing. 'We will follow the trail,' he told his band. 'We are many and the enemy is few. I want the boy to be taken alive and the horse to be slain and sent back to the spirit world.'

More murmurs showed the Wild Dogs' unease.

'The dream horse cannot be killed, even if we thrust twenty spears into his chest,' someone pointed out.

'Ghost Horse protects him,' another said.

Snake Eye lay on his travois, helpless with rage. Snowflakes settled on his black hair and his smeared red face, and none of his warriors stooped to wipe them away.

'It is because we turned our backs on Anteep and his evil spirits,' Spotted Tail declared. 'By Yellow Water, when the false Matotope betrayed us and Silver Cloud went death-side, only to return again, you turned your back on Yietso, Anteep's servant, and declared that we would fight the White Water People without their help.' He cast a careless gesture towards the broken chief. 'This then is the result.'

'Perhaps, but Spotted Tail speaks unwisely,' Tall Bull argued. He stood at the head of the black-and-white horse which pulled the travois. 'We must do as Snake Eye says and capture the boy. The White Water People will see him brought back as our prisoner. They will watch us tie him to the cedar tree in our village, and they will understand that his quest is finally ended.'

'With whose help will we capture this boy, Four Winds?' Spotted Tail demanded.

There was a deep silence as the snow continued to fall.

Then Snake Eye spoke. 'With the help of Anteep, great ruler of the spirits and the source of all evil.'

There was a stir amongst his men. Many glanced around, as if Anteep himself might suddenly appear.

'Take out my medicine pipe,' the chief ordered. 'I will offer up prayers for the great Anteep to appear before us.'

Tall Bull acted quickly to fulfil the sick man's request. Unwrapping the chief's medicine bundle, he laid aside the wolfskin headdress and took out the ceremonial pipe. The other warriors formed a circle and watched the pipe being filled and lit.

'Each man must breathe in the smoke then pass on the pipe,' Snake Eye ordered in his rasping voice. 'Now, Tall Bull, place it across my chest, that I might implore the spirits to visit us.'

Responding to the urgency of the sick chief, the strong warrior knelt beside Snake Eye.

'Great Anteep, hear us!' Snake Eye began. His dark eyes moved restlessly in his drawn face, searching for a response to his call. 'I turned my face from you, and I have paid the price. For see how I am stricken. Now I ask you to show yourself to us, that I might once more pledge myself to the great powers of evil which you command!'

There was hush amongst the Wild Dogs, as night drew in and the grey sky darkened. Only the fading embers of Four Winds' fire lit the face of the sick man on the travois.

Then a wind arose and blew the embers hither and

thither. Red sparks flew into Snake Eye's face and whirled around the legs of his standing warriors. The men stared into the darkness, bracing themselves for whatever spirit might appear.

'I am your servant!' Snake Eye rasped. 'My painted warriors and their horses I offer to you.'

The pipe across his chest gave off the sweet scent of tobacco, which flew off in the whirling wind. '*Le na wanla ka nunwe*,' he chanted, closing his eyes as if in a trance. These painted horses may you behold. '*Mita sunke wakin yan iye ceca wanla ka nunwe*!' My horse like the Thunder Bird may you behold!

And then a mist followed the wind, so that the Wild Dogs could not see their own hands, nor the face of their stricken chief. But eyes were watching them, and wolves were gathering at the edge of the clearing. They could hear the pant of the animals and their loping stride, the crack of twigs and the soft brush of snow as it fell from low branches to the ground.

The howl of a wolf rose above the wind.

'We thank Anteep for these messengers!' Snake Eye cried. 'We follow the way of the wolf, we are not afraid.'

Through the mist the head of Iron Eyes slowly appeared. A startled brave fell to his knees and shielded his face from the spirit's cold gaze. Others met his eyes and straight away fell under his spell.

Only Spotted Tail and Tall Bull resisted the wolf spirit's force. 'Speak again!' Tall Bull urged Snake Eye.

'Anteep has sent his messenger; speak now!'

The wolf's head filled the sky, his eyes glittering like cold stars. His breath was the mist that filled the clearing.

'I recognise Iron Eyes, great messenger of Anteep!' the chief cried. 'You and your creatures of the night and the high, wild places will help us defeat Ghost Horse's messenger. We are Anteep's People, we will never again turn our faces from the forces of evil!'

The mesmerised warriors chanted their agreement. 'From this moment, we are the People of Anteep. Our hearts are hard as iron, we strike only in his name!'

'Anteep hears!' Iron Eyes whispered. 'He claims your spirits, He has you in His grasp!' The wolf's yellow eyes kept the watchers enthralled.

'And you will kill the dream horse?' Spotted Tail asked, looking directly at Iron Eyes and falling under his spell. He felt his strength drain from him, and all his power to act alone.

'Why have you not slain Silver Cloud?' Iron Eyes mocked, noting the many scalps hanging from the warrior's wampum belt. 'Can the spirit horse outrun your painted horses? Is his medicine too strong?'

'That is why we call on your help, great spirit,' Snake Eye admitted. 'A wolf may bring down a horse in the spirit world as well as this world of forests and frozen ice. Your jaws are strong, you are swift as the deer.'

In the background, the gathering wolf pack howled.

'Go then,' Iron Eyes said at last. 'And be bold. Know

that I have seen the boy and his companions: a woman and a girl. These you can easily defeat if I destroy the horse.'

And Snake Eye was glad. He knew now that spirit was set against spirit and that his fearful ally was stronger. The teeth of the cruel wolf would tear into Silver Cloud's throat. Evil would triumph.

Mount Kivioq seemed as far away as ever when darkness fell. Its pure white peak shone in the moonlight, seeming to invite Four Winds and his companions to travel on, even as their legs grew weary once more.

And the cold cut through their bodies like a sharp knife. Their fingers grew numb and the snow froze into their hair and into Silver Cloud's thick mane.

'How much further must we travel?' Black Tail Deer asked plaintively. Riding on the horse's back, a small, huddled shape wrapped in a blanket, she was faint and trembling in the driving snow.

Four Winds hardened himself to give an abrupt reply. 'Until we reach the mountain.' It was far far away, beyond a flat, frozen plain.

Shining Star reached up and touched the girl's cheek. 'Have courage,' she murmured.

But Silver Cloud knew that the child could go no further. She would die of the cold before the night was through. So he scanned the plain then took a course to the east.

‘Why have we come away from the north?’ Four Winds demanded impatiently. They were bearing away from Mount Kivioq, delaying their arrival. To the boy, every moment lost put his White Water People in ever greater danger.

‘You will see,’ the horse promised calmly.

Mystified, Four Winds resolved to trust his companion. He curbed his impatience and set his face to the east.

As they reached the flat land, the snow let up and their progress was quicker. The moon and stars lit their way and the wind softened, so they were able to take in more of their surroundings.

Despite the dangers, Four Winds could see that this was beautiful country. The land was locked underneath its pure white blanket, sparkling in the moonlight. Low ridges cast long blue shadows across the crisp crust of snow, whose undulating surface was disturbed only by the criss-crossing tracks of foxes. Narrow streams meandered across the plain, their banks encrusted with glittering ice, the water chilly beneath a clear, frozen sheet.

After a time, the boy made out a settlement built in the shelter of a ridge. It was a village, but not like one he had ever seen before, for there were no tipis gathered around a central cedar pole, but instead one long wooden structure, its curved roof lying under a deep weight of snow. Long, narrow boats were upturned and stacked by the side of the lodge, while thin plumes of smoke issued from the roof.

'What is this?' Four Winds asked.

'It is the home of friends,' Silver Cloud assured him. 'These are the Hodenosaunee People, meaning people of the longhouse. They will offer us a warm welcome.'

The boy turned to his mother, who said, 'I have heard of these clans from the north, of the Iroquois bands who gather maize and fruit during the summer months, who fish the great lakes, whose women run a council of peacemakers, so that the Mohawks and the Onondagas live in harmony.'

All was quiet as the travellers approached the longhouse. Then a dog set up an alarm which brought three men into view. Silver Cloud stopped and told the others to and stand wait. The men approached cautiously, but without anger. Swathed in crimson blankets, with their smooth hair parted to each side, and wearing heavy necklets of shells and beads, they came close to the visitors and took in the shivering girl astride the silver-grey horse, the woman standing patiently at her side, and finally the proud boy.

'I am Deganawida of the Bear clan, part of the great Mohawk nation,' the spokesman announced. 'We offer you the warmth of our fire and a rush bed to sleep on.'

Silver Cloud inclined his head. 'Help the girl, Black Tail Deer, and the woman, Shining Star,' he told them. 'But the boy and I must travel on.

ELEVEN

'We must part,' Shining Star said to Four Winds.

Of all the tasks he had faced, from the lonely vision quest to Spider Rock, to the recent parting from his grandfather, Red Hawk, this was the hardest of all.

The boy clung to his mother, as she embraced him. 'I will return,' he promised.

Tears ran down her cheeks. 'And I will wait.'

'She will be safe here,' Deganawida told Four Winds. 'She and the girl will live with us through the harsh winter, until you have accomplished your quest.'

'Stay here with us!' Black Tail Deer begged. She saw only danger and death on the way ahead, and already she loved Four Winds like a brother. 'Give up the journey and live happily here with Shining Star and me.'

Four Winds gazed down the longhouse which sheltered ten families of the Bear clan. Platforms at ground level housed bark bins and baskets where food and supplies were stored. Upper platforms contained tobacco and corn in more baskets, together with wooden bowls and skins for clothing. An urge to give in to Black Tail Deer's plea washed over him.

Give up the journey, stay here. Be warmed by the fires, fed with bread and meat. Live in peace with the Mohawk People; fish in their bark boats, hunt with their bows and arrows. Stay here with Shining Star, from whom he could not bear to be parted again . . .

He looked at his mother's face and saw that it was wet with tears.

'A blizzard is coming from the north,' a woman warned from amongst the group which had awoken and gathered around the visitors. 'Before morning, the skies will open and the wind will blow.'

'Stay until daylight,' Deganawida advised. 'Few can survive the driving snow and the howling gale.'

At least until morning, Four Winds thought. He turned to Silver Cloud with a questioning look.

The horse turned his head away.

'No. We must leave now.' The boy accepted his duty with a heavy heart. He must follow the Mystery and find the feather. Once more he hugged his mother and kissed her cheek.

Then he wrapped himself in fresh furs and blankets and shouldered his medicine bundle.

'I am with you in every step you take,' Shining Star reminded him. 'We are one, and cannot be divided.'

* * *

Deganawida, kindly chief of the Bear clan, known throughout the Hodenosaunee nation as The Peace Maker, sent his braves, Wounded Hand, Horn Cloud and Black Thunder, to accompany Four Winds and Silver Cloud on their journey.

In spite of the bitter cold, the three men went willingly.

'The Great Law tells us to cast away selfish acts,' Wounded Hand explained. He was a tall man, swathed in hide and furs, held in place by a wide, beaded wampum belt. 'We live under the shade of the Great Tree of Peace, its white roots spread strongly, its branches offer shelter.'

To Four Winds, as he faced the frozen north, this dream of peace seemed far off. He hugged the misery of recent separation from his mother close to him, and salt tears stung his face. Anger against Snake Eye and all his enemies swelled in his heart.

Ahead, the hilly land flattened out into a vast, level plain of pure white. So flat, in fact, that the boy turned with a questioning look to his three new companions.

Black Thunder understood his puzzlement. 'That is Lake Cayuga,' he explained. 'You must cross it to reach Mount Kivioq.'

'But where is the water?' Four Winds asked, seeing only flat land covered by snow. The wind whirled and whistled, driving banks of snow clouds across the horizon.

'Beneath the ice,' came the reply.

Four Winds stared at the wide expanse. He saw the rim where the snow-laden bushes and tall, spiky rushes ended and the smooth, frozen surface began, yet he still couldn't believe that winter could capture an entire lake in its icy grasp.

'How do we cross?' he asked.

'We walk. The ice is thick, it will easily bear our weight.'

Black Thunder was the first to step out on to the lake. His feet crunched on the crisp snow which covered the ice.

Four Winds looked on in wonderment. Surely nature could not permit that men should walk on water. Yet the ice did not crack, even when it took the full weight of a wary Silver Cloud.

'Come,' the spirit horse told him. 'There is no time to be lost.'

So Four Winds trod on the ice and walked on towards the mountain.

Meanwhile, the wind rose to a howl across the wide open space. It gusted from the north, full in their faces, almost sweeping them off their feet. With it came fresh snow, falling fast and thick, coating them from head to foot and obscuring the way ahead.

Large flakes blew into Four Winds' face. He stooped

to avoid them, but still they whirled into his eyes and against his lips. The cold cut through his body and chilled his bones.

'Walk!' Horn Cloud ordered sternly. 'Do not stop, even for an instant.'

Four Winds forced himself to obey. But his legs were stiff and his hands and arms grew numb. The snow blinded him. He staggered.

'Walk!' Horn Cloud repeated the command.

Strong arms supported him; words of encouragement penetrated the howling of the wind.

'The storm will soon pass,' Wounded Hand promised. 'Until then, you must keep going. Though you cannot see the mountain, it is still there. The end of your journey grows closer.'

'If you fall, all is lost,' Black Thunder warned him. 'The cold will overcome you, you will fall asleep and never wake.'

Four Winds heard dimly. Snowflakes froze on his eyelashes. All was blurred.

Then the three men and the horse surrounded him and formed a shield from the wind. They willed him to continue, out on the vast emptiness of the frozen lake.

'I will go on,' Four Winds muttered to himself. 'I did not fight and outwit the Wild Dogs and the Blackfoot in order to die in the snow!'

'Good!' His friends praised him and brought him through the blizzard.

★ ★ ★

'You have done well,' Horn Cloud told Four Winds when the storm had died. Now small flakes drifted gently from a clearing sky.

Black Thunder and Wounded Hand brushed the snow from him and offered him the sweet juice of berries to drink from a skin bottle.

But Silver Cloud did not relax. Instead, he pricked his ears and stared all around.

'What do you hear?' Wounded Hand asked. Though the Hodenosaunee had no knowledge of the horse, they trusted the boy's spirit guide.

'Wolves,' he replied quietly. 'Beyond the lake.' The Hodenosaunee men looked uneasily into the distance.

Four Winds went up to Silver Cloud and in turn brushed the frozen snow from his mane. 'Wolves will not defeat us,' he promised. 'We know our enemy. We follow the true path.'

They went on, more quickly now, crossing the ice and heading north, listening to the Hodenosaunees' advice about the land they were about to cross.

'It is the homeland of our friends, the Inuits,' Black Thunder explained. 'Soon we will hand you over into their care. Our task will be done.'

Four Winds was astonished to hear that this wasteland contained people. 'How do they live?' he demanded.

'The Inuit live well,' Black Thunder assured him.

'In summer they fish in kayaks, in winter they hunt the walrus. They live in houses made of ice. *Iyaiya-yaya!*'

'I will tell my People of this when I return to my homeland,' Four Winds decided. He asked Silver Cloud if he had heard of such wonders, but the spirit horse still scanned the horizon and did not listen.

'See!' Horn Cloud took Four Winds by the arm and drew him to one side. He pointed to a small group of figures across the lake. 'You did not believe us, but we told you the truth.'

Sure enough, the men in the distance had stepped on to the ice with long spears. The short, stocky men were dressed from head to foot in thick fur. Seeing the travellers, they changed course and headed towards them.

Horn Cloud greeted the Inuits as brothers as they drew near. He asked for news of their chief, Niountelik, and told them that all was well with his own People. Then he drew skins from the bundle on his back, preparing to trade them for the long Inuit spears.

Growing impatient, Four Winds made out for himself the high peak of Mount Kivioq appearing on the skyline as the snow clouds finally lifted. Their destination now seemed tantalisingly close, so he turned eagerly to his guides. 'We thank you for your protection,' he told them, feeling the blood course strongly through his veins once more. 'But now we must hurry on. My journey's end beckons me. With the help of Silver Cloud, we will reach it before nightfall.

Now it was the turn of the Hodenosaunee men to express surprise. 'The distance is too great,' Black Thunder protested. 'You must make camp with Niountelik and wait until daybreak until you complete your journey.'

But Four Winds vaulted on to the spirit horse's broad back and smiled down at them. 'Silver Cloud runs swift as the deer. He climbs like the mountain goat.'

'He will carry you on his back?' Horn Cloud asked.

The Inuit men murmured in their own language, making signs of astonishment.

The boy nodded. 'He is my spirit horse, the messenger of Ghost Horse. Without him, I could not have begun my quest.'

Then Silver Cloud tossed his head and Four Winds took hold of his mane. The boy felt the power of the horse, resting his legs against Silver Cloud's flanks, moulding himself to the width of his back. 'Wish us good fortune,' he said.

One of the Inuits stepped forward, saying something and pointing towards the shore of the frozen lake.

'Black Feather warns you about the wolves,' Horn Cloud explained. 'They have seen them gathering.'

Four Winds thanked him. 'Silver Cloud is faster than the wolf,' he claimed.

But before he had time to prove his boast, the wolves themselves appeared by the shore. They came silently out of the snow drifts, between frozen mounds, on to the ice; more than Four Winds could count.

The Inuits muttered angrily and held their spears in readiness. Horn Cloud and his brothers drew their long knives in preparation for an attack.

'Watch!' Four Winds told the frightened men. He had faith in his dream horse. Together they had survived worse than wolves.

So Silver Cloud set out towards the silent pack, alert to the dangers. Ears pressed against his head, he trotted forward.

Reacting quickly, the wolves spread out to encircle the horse and the boy. Their low, slinking movement drew warning cries from the men who watched.

But Four Winds was not afraid. He made his horse run full charge at the enemy, his intention being to leap clear of their snapping jaws.

Nearer now, the boy could see the glint of the wolves' eyes. Their breath was almost on him.

Four Winds leaned forward for the surge over the top of the enemies heads. There was one jump between him and Mount Kivioq.

But the ice proved treacherous. As Silver Cloud prepared to leap, he lost his footing and skidded sideways, tossing Four Winds from his back. The boy landed on his side and staggered to his feet clutching his shoulder.

At this, the Hodenosaunee and the Inuit came running. Spears flew through the air, finding their targets and laying low five or six of the attacking wolves. The creatures' blood stained the white ice.

But many more continued the attack. Three leaped at the spirit horse, teeth bared, tearing at his flesh. Two pounced on Four Winds, their claws piercing his beaded war shirt. Then it was a fight at close quarters, with the drawn knives of the Hodenosaunee striking out at the wolves and the spears of the Inuit hunters tearing into their flesh.

The battle was almost won. The wolves were being beaten back towards the shore when Iron Eyes showed his presence.

A huge shadow appeared on the ice, bringing with it a deadly cold mist. Pale yellow eyes glowed, white teeth glistened. The brave warriors fell back in dismay.

The wolf spirit looked down on the spilt blood of his messengers. His gaze was cold and cruel. 'You fight a puny battle!' he snarled at the men. 'What is one wolf brought down by your spears and knives? Or two or three? For every one of these, I have a thousand at my command!'

In the distance, invisible creatures bayed for blood, but Black Thunder and the rest stood tall.

'We will fight the servants of Anteep with all our strength!' Horn Cloud cried.

But Iron Eyes turned his mighty head and caught him in his glare. The brave Hodenosaunee staggered and fell to his knees. 'As for the boy,' he said scornfully, 'the anger and impatience in his heart make him weak. He will never reach the mountain because of it!'

The words hit home. Four Winds knew that bitterness against the Wild Dogs had twisted his actions and spurred him on unwisely, against good advice. The knowledge made him groan, as the faces of Red Hawk, White Deer, Shining Star and all those who depended on him flashed before his eyes.

And now Iron Eyes turned his attention to his chief enemy, Silver Cloud. 'You suppose that we are equal in might,' he sneered. 'The servant of Ghost Horse against the follower of the Great Anteep! Yet I have been chosen to shadow your every step, and now the time has come to show who is strongest.'

As their master spoke, the wolves drew back into a wide circle. Horn Cloud pulled Four Winds clear. There was silence as the wolf spirit faced the dream horse.

We follow the path of the Great Mystery! Four Winds told himself. *Ours is the true way.* This was the faith of his fathers. He believed in Silver Cloud.

But when the two great spirits engaged in battle, the sharp fangs and the cold fury in the eyes of Iron Eyes struck fear into him. What match were Silver Cloud's hooves against the claws of the giant wolf? How could the flight animal defeat the fierce aggressor?

By swiftness and clear thoughts, Four Winds reminded himself. He willed Silver Cloud to use his speed to escape Iron Eyes' jaws, glad when he saw his dream horse rise on to his hind legs and wheel away from the wolf.

Flee and return, Four Winds begged. *Bring strong medicine from Ghost Horse to overcome the wolf spirit. Seek the help of the sharp-eyed Eagle, call out the name of the Great Wakanda!*

But the evil gaze of Iron Eyes trapped Silver Cloud. Though the horse wanted to run, he could not. He froze like a carved statue, while the wolves bayed and howled.

Then Iron Eyes called upon Anteep. 'In the name of Evil and all the spirits who serve the Great Master, may you crack this solid ice asunder!'

Four Winds cried out and wrenched himself free from the grasp of Horn Cloud. He must stand beside the dream horse in whatever took place. As he ran to join him, he felt the frozen surface of the lake begin to shudder.

'Crack the ice!' Iron Eyes hissed.

The Inuit hunters cried out in fear. 'If the ice gives way and the water swallows us, we will all die! Run. Save yourself!'

Too late. Iron Eyes worked his magic and the thick

ice began to splinter. It cracked in wide, zig-zag patterns, like forked lightning in the sky. The edges slid apart, opening up a gap through which clear green water gurgled.

Four Winds looked down at the shattering surface. Silver Cloud still made no move, though the ice on which he stood tilted and rocked. The boy called out the name of Ghost Horse, but the wolf spirit mocked him.

'I have lain in wait!' he howled. 'I have seen how weak this boy warrior is! I have put before you many dangers and diversions to take you from the path. Those whom you believe to be your friends are your enemies in disguise. Even your family betrays you!'

Four Winds gasped. 'What diversions? Do you mean my mother, Shining Star?'

The wolf spirit howled again. 'Easily fooled! That was no more your mother than these wolf messengers lying slain on the ice!'

The words were more painful than a spear in the boy's side. They left him empty and gasping. His beautiful mother, Shining Star, with whom he had been lovingly reunited, was in fact a shape-shifting servant of Anteep!

Four Winds stretched out to Silver Cloud, but the dream horse slipped from his reach across the widening gap in the ice. His fingers grasped at air.

And the horse was still paralysed by Iron Eyes'

mesmeric gaze. Water rose up around his knees, then higher than his belly while the wolf spirit hovered over him.

'Is this the spirit who is as swift as the deer?' Iron Eyes mocked. 'Where is his speed now?'

The gap in the ice widened and Silver Cloud plunged downwards without a struggle.

'Where is his cunning? What defence does he offer against the might of Iron Eyes?'

The cold green water swirled over Silver Cloud's white back. For a moment his long mane fanned out across the surface, then his head too disappeared. The water closed over him without a struggle. Then there was stillness. Four Winds peered over the jagged edge into the depths and saw no sign of life.

TWELVE

Lake Cayuga was deeper than the deepest ocean. It had no ending. The green water went on forever.

So said the Inuits who had watched Silver Cloud plunge from view.

'Nothing can survive its icy depths,' the men had sworn, standing clear of the jagged gap in the ice. They had gazed in distress at the swirling water.

Wounded Hand and his two companions had tried to comfort Four Winds. 'Perhaps the dream horse will return,' he'd said, once Iron Eyes had torn the ice apart and Silver Cloud had disappeared. 'Wait here until tomorrow with our friends, the Inuits.'

'Yes, wait!' Iron Eyes had jeered. His image was fading into the mist, his yellow gaze losing its hold. 'For without your spirit guide, you might as well give up your quest!' In the background, his wolf servants had howled.

Four Winds had sunk to his knees, the sound of the ice splintering and cracking still echoing in his ears. Pitted against the power of Iron Eyes, his spirit guide had suffered a swift and easy defeat. Yet the boy had loved the horse's grace and beauty; the turn of his noble head, the kindness in his large brown eyes. He had placed all his trust in Silver Cloud.

So fresh grief had piled on other sorrows and made him bow his head to his chest, there on the shattered ice. The mighty Iron Eyes had vanished in the mist, taking his pack of wolves with him. The Hodenosaunee and Inuit braves had gazed sorrowfully at the boy across a widening gap.

Weighed down by sorrow, Four Winds had almost given up his journey once more. What hope was left, now that Silver Cloud had drowned? What was there to rely on, since the wolf spirit had mocked him with his foolish mistakes?

He recalled his mother, Shining Star – her warm touch and soft voice. All that had been false; an illusion created by the evil spirit to delay him on his vital journey. Nothing but shape-shifting and pretence.

'I am with you every step of the way,' his mother had whispered. 'We are one, and cannot be divided.'

Four Winds had believed in her, and now he had lost her forever. He stared into the clear green water.

'I am with you every step of the way!' a voice insisted, like a soft breeze on his face.

He breathed in the message. The band of sorrow around his chest began to loosen.

'We are one!'

He looked up at the clear sky, remembering how he had talked with Shining Star about his father, Swift Elk, and his grandfather, Red Hawk. She had recalled how she had left the lizard skin pouch for him on the night she was captured. The pouch had belonged to Swift Elk's mother, and had been passed on through the generations.

Surely this was a thing that no evil spirit could have known.

'We cannot be divided!' the voice murmured.

It was real. It was warm and human. To pretend otherwise had been part of Iron Eyes' cruel mockery. Hope rekindled in his heart.

So he stood up from the ice, a small, lonely figure, and waved farewell to his companions. 'I have the beaded shoes of my grandfather to give me swift passage,' he told them. 'And a necklace of wolf's teeth in my medicine bundle to protect me from the forces of Anteep. Mount Kivioq lies within reach. I will continue on my quest!'

Wounded Hand listened grimly. 'Iron Eyes will be watching,' he warned. 'He will not let you reach the top of the mountain.'

'Perhaps. But while there is a grain of hope in my heart, I will go on.' Shouldering his medicine bundle, the boy turned towards the mountain. 'I will look for Eagle in the sky, I will listen for the voice of Shining Star in the wind!'

Saying this, Four Winds stepped out towards the shore of the lake.

'Who would have thought that our chief would live through this blizzard?' Spotted Tail asked, as though in sorrow.

Snake Eye lay on his travois, deathly still except for the darting of his dark, angry eyes.

The Wild Dogs had kept hard on the trail of Four Winds and Silver Cloud until they had come to the end of the forest and the edge of the frozen lake. Now, short of food and with weary horses, many were questioning the value of continuing.

'Snake Eye lives, but his wisdom has deserted him,' one dared to murmur. 'He orders us to step out on to the lake, as if men can walk on water!'

'There were wolves in the forest,' another muttered. 'Those creatures can smell out the weak and the dying!'

The men stood around while their horses drank water, their sallow faces streaked with war paint, black crow feathers fluttering in their headbands.

Tall Bull broke in angrily. 'Fools; the wolves will not harm us. They hunt the boy and the silver horse, in the name of Iron Eyes and the Great Anteep. You are safe from their fangs!'

Snake Eye's strongest warrior was the only one to speak in favour of going forward. 'The enemy grows weaker,' he reminded the others. 'We only have to follow and overtake the boy on the mountain to know that our victory over the White Water band is secure!'

'Victory is ours in any case!' Spotted Tail protested. 'Red Hawk has only a handful of warriors, while we have a hundred. We can sweep into their village on horseback and destroy them without loss.'

There were more murmurs of agreement, until Snake Eye opened his mouth to speak.

'You can kill the White Water People, every man, woman and child, but still their blood will water the earth and a new nation will spring up to replace them, unless we destroy this solitary boy!'

The Comanches strained to hear the dry, urgent whisper that issued from the lips of their stricken chief. They were afraid of him, despite his useless limbs and the leather straps that bound him to the stretcher. Maybe they believed that strong medicine could still cure him and that he would soon stand up straight as before, wielding his tomahawk against those who had spoken against him.

'Understand this,' Snake Eye whispered. 'Four Winds went on his vision quest to Spider Rock with Matotope. The boy's prayers were answered. The Great Wakanda has sworn that the White Water Sioux will regain their homeland if the boy succeeds in his tasks.'

'Snake Eye does not have to remind us!' Spotted Tail retorted. 'But now you have taken the oath to serve

Anteep. Do you not trust his power to overcome the horse and the boy without our help?'

For a moment, Snake Eye's lids drooped and his eyes closed. His breath escaped as a narrow sigh. 'My life hangs on a thread,' he told his men. 'I cannot lift my hand to strike my enemy, but I will not let them escape!'

'It is because of the silver horse,' someone muttered. 'Snake Eye seeks vengeance against the one who struck him down!'

The men understood this. Until the scalp of the enemy hung from the belt of the injured man, he would not rest. It was the Comanche way.

'We cross the ice!' Snake Eye insisted.

Driven by revenge, the Wild Dogs set their faces to the north.

'You are young to travel this mountain alone,' the old man told Four Winds. He had emerged from a small, domed house made of snow which was perched on the lowest slope of the foothills leading to Mount Kivioq. Like the Inuits who had been hunting for walrus on the ice, he was dressed in fur, with a hood which encircled his wrinkled face.

Four Winds scarcely slowed his pace to speak to the stranger. An urgency to reach the top of the mountain and find the precious feather drove him on. 'Young limbs are strong,' he replied. 'All the better to climb to the summit.'

'Many have tried.' The old man stood in his path, which lay between high banks of snow. 'Few succeed.'

'And I will be among them,' the boy said abruptly.

'Not at night, under a crescent moon,' the stranger pointed out. 'It is dusk. The sun's rays have fallen to the west of the mountain.'

'I will travel by starlight.'

'You will encounter deep ravines, you will step into drifts which will engulf you.'

Seeing that the old man did not intend to step aside, Four Winds stopped. 'What is this to you?' he demanded.

'Young and impatient,' the old man tutted. 'I have seen many winters in these hills, and know that only those who act slowly live long.'

Checked by this reminder, Four Winds drew breath and nodded. 'I'm sorry. I see that you mean well. But my journey is urgent, I cannot stop to talk.'

'Then at least let me guide you and show you the dangers.' The old Inuit reached out a shaking hand.

Four Winds drew back.

'So young and full of suspicion.' The old man shook his head. 'And yet you have a grandfather like me, I'm sure.'

'Chief Red Hawk of the White Water Sioux,' the boy replied proudly and impetuously, and he missed the cold glitter in the old man's narrow eyes.

'And you respect your grandfather. You listen to his advice?'

'Always.'

'Because the child and the old man are close. One has just entered this world and the other is about to return to the Great Spirit. Therefore you must allow me to guide you. Besides, you will not succeed alone.'

Giving it some thought, Four Winds recognised that the old man's words were wise. No doubt there were dangerous crevasses ahead and other perils that Silver Cloud might have picked out for him. Besides, he was afraid to ascend the high white mountain without a companion.

And yet – there was a doubt. What was it that troubled him? What had the old man said or done that should raise these suspicions?

'Wait here,' the Inuit told him. 'I will fetch light and a stout stick to help us on our way.'

Four Winds watched him return to his strange house on stiff joints and trembling limbs. His body stooped forward, as if unable to support the weight of his head. And yet this ancient man was preparing to guide the boy up the highest mountain.

No, this wouldn't do. Waiting for the Inuit to disappear inside his shelter, Four Winds strode on alone and unhindered.

He climbed on in the fading light. At times the way was firm and smooth, at others the snow would give way and Four Winds would plunge waist-deep into a soft drift. Then sheets of ice would glint underfoot, sometimes many paces in length. These he would have to skirt around, choosing another slope, but always heading steadily towards the summit.

Alone in these clear heights, he cast from his mind the memory of beautiful Silver Cloud plunging beneath the water, of Black Tail Deer begging him to stay in the warm longhouse, of Sun Dancer struck down at twenty summers. Instead, he listened for the words that crowded the air – words that bound him to his forefathers, that carried the dream, the mystery, the gifts from generations unseen.

'We should know that all things are the work of the Great Spirit,' his grandmother's voice whispered. These were the things she had taught him from the start. 'He is within all things: the trees, the grasses, the rivers, the mountains, the four-legged animals and the winged creatures.'

The boy looked up and saw the shape of an eagle arc across the sky. His heart jolted, then soared to greet the bird. 'We should understand this deeply in our hearts, then we will fear and love and know the Great Spirit, and then we will be and act as he intends.'

* * *

'I knew you would not wait,' the old man said.

He had stepped out from behind a frozen waterfall. In one hand he held a long wooden staff, in the other a flickering dish of tallow that lit up his ancient face.

Four Winds gave a gasp of surprise. In spite of his creaking joints, the Inuit had overtaken him and stood on a snow ledge a man's length above his head. 'I thought you would slow me down,' he confessed.

'You were wrong. And unwise. Beyond this ridge is a sheer glacier and no way to reach the summit.'

The boy frowned. He had been made to look foolish, and now it seemed he was forced to rely on the advice of the old man.

'To you, this path seems the most direct,' the Inuit admitted. 'It follows the direction of the North Star, and many have made the same mistake. Most must retrace their steps into the foothills and begin again. Only I know how to cross the glacier.'

'Then show me,' Four Winds said eagerly.

'Not until you tell me the reason for your journey.' Slowly the old man came down from the ledge. 'There is a mystery here which I wish to hear.'

Still Four Winds could not rid himself of his doubts about this strange guide. 'Why must you know?'

'Am I guiding you to good or ill?' the Inuit replied. 'If ill, I will play no part.'

'That is fair,' Four Winds said. And quickly he told the old man of his quest to save his tribe.

'Very well.' The Inuit gave a grunt of satisfaction. 'Know then that I am shaman of my band, whose chief is Niountelik. I have strong medicine to help you to the summit of this, the highest mountain. Come to the ledge and I will show you.'

So they climbed together and looked down on a sheet of sheer ice which glistened under the night sky. It dropped into a ravine strewn with ice boulders, then rose again level with the first ridge. Looking more closely, Four Winds saw to his horror that other travellers had fallen foul of this treacherous place and plunged to their deaths. Now their corpses could be seen encased in ice, their bodies broken, pain etched into their frozen faces.

He realised then that he would never have crossed this frozen ravine, and he wondered how the shaman's power could be used to bridge the gap.

He did not have long to wait, however. Holding his staff high in the air, the old man called upon Coyote, his spirit guide, to help him in his task. There was a stirring of wind, a distant howl, and then the shaman launched his staff across the chasm.

In an instant the thin stick turned into a broad plank long enough to span the gap between the two ridges. It settled firmly in place; a strong and steady bridge to the far side of the ravine.

Startled, Four Winds put out a foot to test the magic structure.

'It is no illusion!' the old man laughed shrilly. 'This will bear the weight of twenty men!'

Reluctantly the boy edged forward. He felt the plank shift a little, then steady itself.

'Now you believe me.' Holding the tallow light out over the ravine, the old man urged Four Winds on. 'Be bold!' he said. 'This short cut will take you to your goal!'

Four Winds took three steps out on to the magic bridge. Beneath him, the glittering chasm opened up. If he missed his footing now, he would drop like a stone to his death.

'Good, good!' the shaman cried. 'Take courage, move on!' High above, Eagle soared.

Four Winds reached the middle of the bridge, afraid now to look down. His head was whirling, every step was torment.

'What is the matter?' his guide called. 'Why do you shake?'

At this, Four Winds felt the plank begin to tilt sideways. Quickly he dropped forward and lay full length, grasping the sides of the bridge. A glance behind told him that the old man was grinning and shedding his fur robes, growing taller and stronger until he stood high as a cedar pole, his shoulders broad and his hands huge.

Worse, the monster wore a hundred black and red feathers in his scalp-lock, his face was painted with fresh blood and there were green rings around his eyes. A huge raven, awful to behold, clung to the back of his neck and flapped its wings, so that the boy's heart quaked and he was sick with fear.

'I am Stone Man!' the shape-shifter gloated. 'Brought from the eastern plains by Iron Eyes!'

Four Winds felt the bridge tilt further and heard the wood begin to crack. A split appeared.

'You are easily tricked!' Stone Man roared. 'Who but a boy would place his trust in such a one as me!'

As the bridge cracked beneath him and his grip weakened, Four Winds gave a cry that echoed around the chasm, then rose skywards. At that moment, a winged shape swooped down. There was a rush of wind, the beating of powerful wings, a cry of rage from the shape-shifting servant of Iron Eyes.

Then, just as the bridge finally splintered apart, the boy felt himself swept into the air. Eagle's talons held him firm as together they rose to safety.

Down below, Stone Man seized his staff and flung it in fury after them. It arched high but missed its target. Four Winds heard it thud into the mountain, saw the monster seize it and throw it a second time. Once more, Eagle used the air currents to avoid the weapon.

And he flew with Four Winds high into the night sky, between the stars, to freedom.

THIRTEEN

'Be more wary,' Eagle warned the young warrior. 'Stone Man is a dangerous enemy. He travels the earth in search of victims whom he kills and then eats. He can shift into a hundred different shapes, his brain is cunning as the fox.'

Four Winds shuddered. Looking around, he saw that Eagle had set him down high on Mount Kivioq, within reach of the summit. 'Will Stone Man still pursue me?' he asked.

'Yes,' Eagle replied. The mighty bird rested on an icy promontory, its eyes bright as gold. 'He will not rest until he has sealed your body in the icy cavern. It is as Iron Eyes has commanded.'

'But we are high on the mountain.' Four Winds tried to reassure himself, though his head still spun from the sensation of flying through the dark heavens. 'We have left Stone Man far below.'

Eagle waited and watched. Then he spoke again. 'Beware of the owl and the blue jay, of the arctic fox and the bat which flits close by. It may be Stone Man in disguise.'

Four Winds breathed deeply and said that he would learn this lesson well.

'Be sure that you do,' Eagle said gravely. 'Once and once only I can save you in Silver Cloud's absence. The rest is up to you.'

So Eagle flew away, and now the boy was truly alone.

He climbed by the dim light of the new moon, seizing handholds in the ice and hauling himself towards the summit. He did not look back.

Ever upwards, where the air grew thin and he gasped for breath. Steeper and steeper, defying death.

'I am with you,' Shining Star whispered. 'We are one.'

Four Winds grew light-headed. It was as if a vast space had opened up inside him, as if the shining stars had entered his head, or as if his whole body had become one with them. A wonderful feeling, like music, like harmony.

'In the beginning,' his mother murmured, 'a boy, Tatqeq, and a girl, Siqiniq, stole a caribou skin and a firestone. Stricken with guilt, they changed into animals but were afraid of being killed. So they decided to turn into thunder and lightning instead. Now, when thunder rolls and lightning flashes, it is because the brother is rattling the dry caribou skin while his sister strikes sparks from the firestone.'

Words are all around us.

Four Winds climbed on. Footholds in the ice were few. The face of the mountain was sheer and smooth.

'We will sing a song.' Shining Star began a lullaby from his boyhood.

> 'We will sing a song.
> We will go down the current.
> The waves will rise;
> The waves will fall.
> The dogs will not bark at us.'

Warm sleep drifted towards Four Winds as he clung to the face of the mountain. A moment's rest would do no harm, before he climbed to the summit.

So he rested back into a crevice in the ice, sheltered from the wind. There was room to stand upright, time to gaze out at the mountain range where Kivioq towered above the rest.

The song drifted from his head and another voice entered.

'My son,' the man said.

Four Winds' head drooped, his lids began to close.

'My boy, Kola!' Swift Elk came to him in all the glory of his warrior days. Naked to the waist, dressed in doeskin trousers with trailing fringes, his black hair braided and decorated with white feathers, his father appeared. The skin of his chest was smooth and brown; there was a band of silver around his arm.

The boy opened his arms to embrace him.

'I have come life-side to protect you,' Swift Elk

explained. 'By the power of the great spirits, I have crossed over.'

'You will help me to reach the top of the mountain,' Four Winds sighed. His heart was full to overflowing.

'Here is my shield, my *wo'tawe*.' Swift Elk presented his son with a round, rawhide shield adorned with eagle and hawk feathers. Eagle brings you power of thunder, hawk brings you keen sight and swiftness.'

Four Winds took the precious *wo'tawe* and grew stronger. He drank in the sight of his dead father and gave praise to Wakanda. 'Of all the blessings in my fourteen summers, this is the richest,' he said softly. 'I will be strong, like my father, bold and sure. My eye will carry kindness, my heart will be wise!'

Swift Elk smiled. 'Come, I will lead you to the summit.'

The boy raised his head and opened his eyes. His father stretched out a hand to guide him.

'Come!' the warrior repeated. 'You have endured much, my son. I have been with you on your journey to the deepest mine. I have watched over you when you fought the Blackfoot and the Wild Dogs. I was at your mother's side in her days of slavery.'

Strapping the shield on to his shoulder and following his father across the face of the glacier, Four Winds looked up. Yes, he was within reach of his journey's end. The pinnacle shone white and glittering in the night sky.

'You are the true son of Swift Elk, grandson of the great Red Hawk,' the vision chanted. 'Pride is in my heart when I behold you!'

So the boy would not say that he was afraid to follow the path his father chose. He would follow in his footsteps, find the shallow footholds, grip the slippery ice with his freezing hands.

Swift Elk climbed ahead, careless of the danger. He glanced back, then waited.

Four Winds scrambled after him, slipping once and catching hold of a narrow ledge. His breath came shorter still.

'Soon!' Swift Elk promised. 'Have courage and you will reach the top.'

Struggling on, battered by wind, his fingers frozen, Four Winds trusted the words of Swift Elk. There was no one whom he trusted more deeply or admired so fully. His father, who had fallen at Thunder Ridge, fighting for the survival of the White Water band.

'Look up!' the vision urged.

Ahead, the jagged summit of Mount Kivioq held out the promise of success. But the stars shifted in the black sky and the boy's grip loosened. He could scarcely breathe.

'Here is a ledge for your feet,' Swift Elk pointed out.

Four Winds fumbled and found the place.

'And here is the next.' The vision offered his strong, warm hands to heave his son into position.

Gratefully Four Winds looked up into his father's eyes. Instead of kindness, he saw two dark hollows.

The face above set suddenly in lines as cold and hard as stone. The hands gripping Four Winds' wrists loosened.

There was time to glimpse the spirit's real face before he fell. The blood-red paint, the smudges of green around his hollow eyes.

Betrayed, the boy cried out. He let go of the monster's hands and plummeted down the mountain.

Whiteness surrounded him. Snow broke loose from the cliff and carried him down, cushioned him from the ice, yet half-smothered him. Down from the summit, slipping, sliding, tumbling across a glacier, down a deep chasm, with the avalanche gathering speed around him.

The sharp arrow of betrayal.

Head-first, clutching at nothing, falling without end.

Stone Man stood on the summit and raised both hands to Iron Eyes. 'Master!'

The wolf spirit looked on in satisfaction.

Down. Dreams shattered, hopes smashed. Whiteness.

Four Winds came to rest on a ledge. He knew that snow and boulders rushed on to either side, heard the great roar of its mass rolling down the mountain, like thunder, like the earth splitting open. A strong pressure crushed his ribs. He must claw and fight his way free of the avalanche.

But he could not breathe. The pressure increased. His hands were too weak to push aside the packed snow. He would die then in its cold embrace.

Then the snow above his head began to shift. It broke apart, letting in air, relieving the crushing weight on his chest. There was fresh air, a glimpse of the stars. A hand reaching down.

The boy reached out to his rescuer.

Hands tore at the snow and ice. The boy had been caught in an avalanche, but had come to rest. He lay underneath the debris, perhaps suffocating. With quick work, the boy warrior's life could be saved.

Four Winds felt himself lifted out of the snow.

Tall Bull scraped the ice from his face and saw that the boy enemy was still alive.

FOURTEEN

Tall Bull tied Four Winds' wrists and ankles with leather thongs. He slung him over his shoulder and descended Mount Kivioq.

Drifting in and out of consciousness, the boy was aware only that he had failed.

The treacherous vision of Swift Elk tormented him. Truly the power of Iron Eyes knew no bounds, if the spirit could even conjure the dead.

To bring his father back life-side and then inhabit his being was the worst cruelty; to turn good into evil and make the father betray the son. Four Winds' heart bled.

Soon Tall Bull reached the Comanche camp at the base of the mountain. When the strong warrior strode into the middle of the circle of hastily-erected tipis and threw the semi-conscious captive to the ground, yells of surprise and jubilation rang out.

'Anteep is mighty!' they cried.

'He has overcome the spirit horse, and now he delivers the boy into our hands.'

Tall Bull stood proud. While the rest had made camp

and rested, he alone had forged ahead. He had seen the avalanche sweep the boy down the mountain. He had dug him free and brought him to Snake Eye.

'To Tall Bull belongs the honour of putting the young White Water brave to death!' someone declared. 'How shall it be: by tomahawk or spear? By blade or arrow?

Four Winds knelt in the snow, his head bowed. A numbness had overcome all his senses; the Wild Dog spoke as if from a great distance. While his fate was being sealed by the blood-thirsty Comanches, he thought only of his failure to take back the feather to Red Hawk.

'What does Snake Eye say?' Tall Bull asked. 'How shall we kill the boy?'

The Comanche chief ordered two men to raise his travois so that he could see the enemy for himself. Thus propped up, his gaze levelled on the bound and bowed prisoner.

'A puny enemy!' he said in a hollow voice. 'I, Snake Eye, have survived many battles. I carry the scalp of twenty fully-grown warriors on my belt. I have the scars to prove my boldness. And yet this one weak boy and his spirit guide have robbed me of everything!'

'Except for the means of revenge,' Tall Bull insisted. 'Say now how the boy shall meet his end!'

The chief's eye darted around his circle of followers. 'By knife!' he could command, and his victorious warrior would take the carved weapon from his belt and strike the boy to the heart. Or, 'By spear! By the dread blow of a tomahawk!' And yet he could not bring himself to declare the way, as if striking the boy down and fulfilling his revenge would simultaneously slash the thin thread of bitterness which held the helpless chief life-side. So his eyes glittered and he remained silent.

Grandfather, I am sorry! Four Winds grieved inwardly. *I have been hasty. I have put my trust in the wrong places. I have not followed the Mystery. And now our People must die.*

My son! Red Hawk's voice came on the bitter wind. *You have followed the Way. You have been true.*

Then why have I failed?

Because Anteep is strong. Because the task was too great.

So our People suffer.

It is as it is.

Four Winds looked up into the dawn sky. High over the mountain, Eagle soared.

'We will take the boy back to our homeland!' Snake Eye declared.

A murmur of consternation ran around the group.

'Kill him now!' Spotted Tail insisted. 'What if he should escape? What purpose does it serve to delay?'

'He will not escape!' Snake Eye answered angrily. 'I am chief still. I want to carry him home in triumph and parade him before the White Water Sioux, see the suffering in the eyes of our enemy!'

Still the uneasy murmur persisted. Even Tall Bull was downcast.

Eagle soared but did not intervene. *I am with you every step of the way!* Shining Star whispered. A pink glow filled the sky as the sun rose in the east.

The boy proudly lifted his head. *I am Four Winds, son of Swift Elk, of the White Water Sioux. I am within the Hoop of Life, part of its Great Mystery!*

My son! Swift Elk called from death-side in his true voice.

'Father!'

And a swift shape rode the clouds. He returned on the wind, galloping through the air; silver-grey, dappled, silent.

Four Winds stared in wonder.

Do not be astonished. I became one with the green lake, Silver Cloud told him. *I was bubbles, white foam on the surface. I did not desert you!*

Once before, on the journey to the mine, the spirit horse had returned to Wakanda and been restored. Four Winds saw him surge through the air now, his mane flying free.

At first the Wild Dogs mistook the vision.

'A storm approaches!' Spotted Tail warned, rushing to close the doorflap of his tipi and gathering extra furs for protection.

The wind blew through the snowdrift, raising flurries and obscuring the dream horse. His hooves sounded like thunder in the morning air.

Silver Cloud came in a rage of snowflakes which

whirled around the Wild Dogs and drove into their faces. He struck out with his hooves, pounding them to the ground. Isolated one from the other by the blizzard, they fell.

Until Spotted Tail made out the shape of the horse and cried out in fury. 'Why did Snake Eye delay?' he demanded, rushing at Silver Cloud from behind, his tomahawk raised. The wind whipped his wild hair from his face as he savagely attacked.

But Four Winds rose, though still bound. He threw himself forward, thrusting Spotted Tail off balance, giving his spirit guide time to swing around and defend himself.

The last things the rebellious Wild Dog saw and felt were the white underbelly of the horse, the flailing hooves and their crushing, thudding weight.

Then others in the band grew afraid. Five of their number lay in the snow, their bodies already covered in a shroud of snow, killed by a spirit who had vanished under the green waters of Lake Cayuga.

'Silver Cloud can never be destroyed!' they cried.

And they began to flee; some on foot, others by horse, rapidly deserting their stricken leader, running to save their own skins.

Enraged, Tall Bull killed two of the deserters with arrows in their backs. But the snow helped others escape. Soon, only he and Snake Eye were left.

So the one loyal warrior was left face to face with

the spirit horse. But he was not afraid. He did not fear death, nor pain, but thought only of his honour as a Wild Dog Comanche. Future generations would say his name with respect; he had not run from his enemy.

From his stretcher Snake Eye watched the battle. He poured curses after those who fled. The fury of helplessness raised his voice to screaming pitch.

As Tall Bull faced Silver Cloud and lifted his bow and arrow level with the spirit horse's chest, Four Winds fell to his knees and rolled alongside one of the slain Comanches. With difficulty he seized a knife which lay by the enemy's side and managed to slice through the thongs which bound him. Then he sprang up and threw himself at Tall Bull, making the huge man stagger sideways.

'Come with me,' Silver Cloud ordered Four Winds, before Tall Bull had time to recover.

Snake Eye cried out more bitter prayers. 'May Anteep crush your bones! May you live like me, without movement in your limbs, forever cursed!'

The chief raised his head from the travois, his face contorted with rage. His mouth was dragged down by hatred, his breath came loud and rasping. At the mercy of the horse who pulled his sled, he cried out as it swung away from the carnage and turned to follow the others.

The sudden movement tilted the travois and frightened the horse further. It jolted forward off balance, dragging Snake Eye towards a ledge overhanging a sheer drop into a deep ravine. The chief let out a loud groan as fresh pain seared through his body.

Frenzied now, the black-and-white horse used all his might to pull and twist free of the shafts that tied him to Snake Eye. The sled was flung closer towards the edge, skidding on ice, sliding into danger.

The Comanche's scream of agonised rage made Tall Bull turn.

He began to run after the travois, plunging deep into drifts and stumbling over the half-hidden corpses of his dead brothers.

'Kill the boy! Destroy the dream horse!' Snake Eye screamed in rage.

The travois slid to the brink, carrying Snake Eye head first. It swung out over the empty space and for a split second balanced there.

Tall Bull raced to save his chief.

Slowly the end of the sled tipped down.

Tall Bull flung himself along the snowy surface, reaching out, grasping, clutching at nothing.

The sled vanished over the edge.

Snake Eye screamed in fury as he plunged to his death.

To die in hatred; that was a terrible thing.

Four Winds heard again and again that final cry. He saw the drop into oblivion. Snake Eye's bitter face, with its dark, glittering eyes, would haunt him forever.

But now the boy and Silver Cloud could ascend Mount Kivioq once more. Tall Bull was grieving over his dead chief and carrying the news to his cowardly brothers. Meanwhile, Four Winds rode on Silver Cloud's back in a swift final climb.

'You held faith with Wakanda and the Great Mystery.' The horse's praise filled the boy's ears. 'In the worst of times, you did not lose hope.'

So Four Winds' spirits were high as they faced the final test.

Until Iron Eyes rallied his forces and brought his full might against the travellers.

The distant howling of wolves from below brought the first warning. As always, the powerful servant of Anteep announced his presence.

A high-pitched, faint cry that infiltrated the brain and made the hairs at the back of Four Winds' neck stand up. Wolves in the foothills, padding through the snow with pink tongues lolling, or heads raised and howling at the dawn.

And then the familiar mist, rolling up the snowy slopes, soon enveloping the boy and his dream horse. Four Winds breathed in its icy breath.

'Stay on my back,' Silver Cloud told him. 'You and I are one.'

The horse set off up the mountain fast as the wind. He rose above Iron Eyes' mist. But then the wolf spirit sent white fog from above, and his yellow eyes materialised ahead of them. His huge head grew visible; his long white fangs and shock of grey-white fur.

'It is time to settle scores,' Iron Eyes said. 'This game no longer amuses me.'

Four Winds clung to his horse's neck and avoided the evil spirit's gaze.

'If death is a game, and torture amuses you, then you are truly the servant of Anteep,' Silver Cloud replied. He took to the air, rising clear of the snowy slopes, through the wolf spirit's mist.

Iron Eyes sprang after him. Wolf against horse. Hunter against hunted.

Four Winds held his breath. They were circling the summit of Mount Kivioq; he was looking down on his journey's end.

Iron Eyes pursued them, low and swift. His jaws snapped at them, his breath hot on the air. Silver Cloud swerved and escaped.

Speed alone wouldn't be enough, the boy knew. He had seen a wolf bring down a deer; that was the way of the animal kingdom.

Besides, Iron Eyes called in other weapons. He drew dark clouds down on them, and made thunder which shook the heavens. Lightning forked through the air.

The flash of electric light threw Silver Cloud off course. He reared up then veered away from the mountain, pursued by a crash and roll of thunder. The boy clung to the horse's neck, moulding his body to his guide.

Then lightning attacked them from every side, darting through the sky, splitting it apart; above, below, to left and right. Blinding and deadly, the forks were aimed at Iron Eyes' enemy.

But Silver Cloud swerved and galloped on. The lightning did not strike. Though thunder deafened them, the boy and the horse wove their way through the storm.

Then, when the force of nature's anger was spent, Silver Cloud swept down towards the summit of Mount Kivioq. The wolf pursued him with snapping jaws.

'Hold tighter!' Silver Cloud commanded. He strained every muscle to outrun Iron Eyes.

Still the wolf snapped at their heels.

'I will land on the top of the mountain,' the dream horse decided. 'Have your knife ready. Trust me in everything I do.'

So they alighted on the very peak. Iron Eyes surrounded them with his mist and hovered overhead.

'I am exhausted,' said the horse. 'I cannot defeat you with speed. I must rest.'

And the wolf mocked him. 'Ghost Horse sent a poor servant to defend the boy on his quest. A creature without weapons, who lacks strength. You are no match for me, servant of the great Anteep!'

Secretly Four Winds drew the precious knife of his grandfather, Red Hawk, from its sheath.

'Still I will not give you the boy!' Silver Cloud said defiantly. 'You must come and take him from me!'

'With my sharp claws in your neck, you will soon give in!' the wolf spirit gloated. He prowled forward with glaring yellow eyes, lips pulled back to expose his deadly fangs.

Holding fast to the horse's mane, Four Winds trembled.

Silver Cloud stood firm. He waited until Iron Eyes stopped and crouched low, ready to spring.

Then Four Winds lifted the knife above his head. He brought it down, slashing at the enemy as he pounced. There was blood on his hand as Iron Eyes fell back.

'A hidden knife is as good as a wolf's jaws!' Silver Cloud cried. He commanded the powdery snow under Iron Eyes' feet to turn to sheer ice, and they watched their weakened enemy begin to slip away from them.

The wolf's eyes flashed. He slid into the snowy wastes, falling, gathering speed, caught up in a rising flurry, howling as he went.

Nothing could stop him or the power of the gathering avalanche.

Four Winds' hand trembled. He dropped the knife. It had done its deadly work.

FIFTEEN

Four Winds stood on top of the world. He looked out across a snowy mountain range tinged pink by the rising sun. He looked up at the sky.

'Eagle has guarded us well,' Silver Cloud said.

The mighty bird soared high in the heavens.

'This is our journey's end.' Here, on the summit of Mount Kivioq, the loneliest place on earth, Four Winds drew a deep breath.

The sun rose and made the snow sparkle. The boy shielded his eyes.

'You must find the feather,' Silver Cloud urged.

Then the boy faced a new and bitter truth. He saw that no birds nested here in the icy peaks. It was too cold and exposed even for the hawk and the eagle, too far from the scuttling pikas, voles and mice that formed their prey.

Nothing lived.

'Search!' the vision horse told him.

So Four Winds walked the ridge that formed the summit of the mountain. He looked under ledges, behind snow-covered boulders; in every nook where a bird might find shelter. There was nothing but glittering ice and dark blue shadows.

To have come so far and endured so much! Four Winds slid down the far side of the ridge, out of sight of his spirit guide. He sat cross-legged and stared down at the endless, jagged mountains.

And then a thought stole upon him: there were certainly no feathers to be found on Mount Kivioq, but what if he were to take his medicine bundle from his shoulder, unwrap it and take out an eagle's feather? There were feathers enough in the bundle: a soft brown hawk's wing feather, white, downy ones from an eagle chick. He could pick one out, wrap up the bundle and return to Silver Cloud with his prize. Who then would know the difference?

Overcome by temptation, Four Winds untied his precious bundle. The contents spilled out. There was his lizard skin pouch, bestowing long life because the lizard had *wakan* powers and was hard to capture and kill. There was a plait of silver-white hair from Silver Cloud's mane, a tiny swallow's head because the bird could fly swiftly without alighting. Then there were herbs to place inside the nose and mouth if Four Winds fell ill, and lastly an eagle plume from Red Hawk's headdress; a gift to enable its owner to run faster and more easily.

This was the object which the boy picked up with

trembling fingers. He stared at its perfect structure, the central spine and the brilliantly interlocked fronds, at its black sheen and finely pointed white tip.

Was this not a feather from the highest mountain? Had he not carried it here and would it not pass examination amongst his brothers of the White Water band? Surely, after all the hardships, one small, well-meaning lie would be forgiven?

Four Winds let the idea take tight hold of his mind, like the tendril of a choking plant winding its way up a great tree trunk and finally squeezing the life out of its host.

Keeping the eagle feather to one side, he carefully rolled the other objects back inside the rawhide case. Then he stood holding the feather.

Who will know? he asked himself.

And what could be worse than returning without a feather and so condemning his People to oblivion?

And yet. The boy tore his gaze from the feather and looked up at the sky. Eagle swooped in a low arc, then rested on an air current and rose again.

And yet. 'I am always with you,' Shining Star whispered.

They would know that he had lied. Silver Cloud would take one look into Four Winds' eyes and would turn away forever.

And yet.

Torn, the boy followed the flight of the eagle.

Then he cast his grandfather's precious feather on to the wind and watched it whirl away.

'Your mind is free. Your spirit is pure,' Silver Cloud consoled him. The spirit horse knew the boy's every fleeting thought, and had feared in his absence that the great lie would take hold. If Four Winds had chosen to take the false eagle feather back to his People, Silver Cloud would indeed have forsaken him.

'But I have failed my grandfather, Red Hawk,' Four Winds sighed. 'I had rather stay and freeze here on Mount Kivioq than return empty-handed.'

Silver Cloud understood. 'It is as it is. Wakanda sees all.'

The boy stood by the horse on the summit, hollow and exhausted. 'It is as it is,' he agreed.

And he stretched out both arms towards the golden sun, feeling its warmth on his face.

And Wakanda sent soft snow drifting from the blue sky. It fell gently, floating on the wind, settling with a light touch on the boy's cheeks.

Four Winds felt it melt to water, which mingled with his tears. He caught the snowflakes on the palm of his hand, gazed and saw them transform to the lightest, purest of soft white feathers.

He gasped and turned to Silver Cloud.

And the spirit horse commanded the boy to climb on to his back. Together, they took the feathers home.

ONCE HE WAS A WARRIOR

'You will see a sorrowing People,' Burning Tree warned Four Winds.

The girl had greeted them at the entrance to the high winter camp of the White Water band; Four Winds, Silver Cloud, Sun Dancer, Black Tail Deer and wonder of wonders, Shining Star. The woman and the girl had stayed with their Hodenosaunee friends. On Four Winds' safe return to the longhouse, the boy had fallen into his mother's arms and many tears had been shed. They had travelled on together and been reunited with the young warrior, Sun Dancer, cured by the powerful medicine of the Okeepa People. The small band had completed the final stage of their long journey in a mood of quiet celebration. They arrived to find Burning Tree waiting at the entrance to the small ring of tipis. Her face was strained; there was no smile on her lips.

At first, Four Winds thought she still sorrowed for her slain brother, Running Fox. 'Our enemy, Snake Eye, is dead,' he comforted her. 'The Comanche Wild Dogs have scattered and fled.'

The girl bowed her head. 'You must talk with your grandmother, White Deer,' she said softly, leading them forward.

The tipis were covered in snow; the dogs lay under the shelter of the door flaps. Smoke rose through the smoke holes.

White Deer emerged from her tipi. 'My son,' she murmured. Then, with eyes full of tears, she embraced Shining Star. 'I have cared for the boy since you went away,' she told her. 'He has grown into the warrior that you see now.'

The old woman did not show surprise that the young woman had come back from the dead. 'Going always brings return,' she said.

Her hair hung in white braids. Her face was lined. In her long life she had seen many wonders.

'At dawn, when soft snow fell, Red Hawk left the life-side and rejoined the Great Mystery,' she told them. 'He could not carry his burden further.'

Four Winds felt a great emptiness. His grandfather was dead.

Weary of this life, waiting for his grandson's return, the old man had taken his last breath.

The boy opened his palm and showed White Deer the small collection of soft white feathers.

Burning Tree saw and went to tell One Horn, Little

Thunder and Three Bears. Two tasks were complete; a third and final journey remained.

'You are brave and true.' White Deer smiled through her grief. 'Your grandfather was once a great warrior. His name carried from ocean to ocean, across this wide land. Now the name of Four Winds will also be known.'

Feeling the weight of sorrow balance against the joy of success, the boy asked to be taken to Red Hawk's funeral stand.

He went alone with his grandmother, White Deer.

She showed him the four tall poles draped with buffalo skins, feather banners and round shields. The poles supported a platform which carried his grandfather's dead body. A rough wooden ladder rested against the funeral structure, and Four Winds used this to ascend to the platform.

It was as if the old man slept. He wore his war shirt and many-feathered headdress, his wampum belt and his fringed moccasins. His arms were folded across his chest, the hands curled into loose fists. All around, a cold wind played.

'We offer you to the Lord of Life,' Four Winds murmured. 'Before we bury you in the burying ground, we will set your spirit free.'

The breeze disturbed the shields hanging from the platform. They knocked against the poles with a hollow sound.

'I have brought a feather from the highest mountain,'

Four Winds told his grandfather in a broken voice. 'I have succeeded in my task.'

Below the funeral stand, Silver Cloud came and waited.

'Tomorrow I set out for the furthest ocean, to bring a breath of wind,' Four Winds went on. 'It is as Ghost Horse wishes. Silver Cloud will guide me. Your People will not be cast out. For your sake, we will survive!'

The wind passed over Red Hawk's still features, disturbing only the black and white feathers of his headdress.

Then Four Winds unclasped the fingers of his grandfather's right hand. In the palm lay a small, glittering object: the diamond from the deepest mine. Beside it he placed a soft white feather from Mount Kivioq.

'Believe in me,' he whispered. 'Watch over me and your sorrowing People.'

The wind carried Red Hawk's spirit across snowy ridges, to the warm valleys of the White Water River.

Going always brings return.

And so the old man went home.

PART THREE

BAD HEART

PROLOGUE

We stand, great warriors,
In the circle.
At dawn all storm clouds disappear.
The future brings hope and glory,
Ghost dancers rise,
Five hundred nations.

White Deer sang Red Hawk's spirit song in a clear voice.

The boy, Four Winds, sat amongst the listeners and gazed up at his grandfather's wind-battered funeral platform.

'This is the song that Chief Red Hawk kept in his heart,' White Deer said.

'At dawn all storm clouds disappear.
The future brings hope and glory.'

Four Winds knew that she had learned the song at his grandfather's death. The old man had passed it on with his dying breath. It spoke of peace and a prosperous future.

White Deer addressed the shrouded figure on the high platform. 'Though you have passed from life-side and joined our only son, Swift Elk, your spirit is in the song. We are within the Hoop, the great Circle of life and death, and we hear your voice, mighty chief of the White Water tribe.'

A north wind tugged at the crimson banners and feathers draped from the platform. It raised the grey shroud to allow a glimpse of old hands crossed in prayer, a loved face sleeping its final sleep.

'Ohhh . . .' A sorrowful murmur passed among the White Water People. There were tears. Four Winds felt his own eyes blur.

'Ghost dancers rise,
Five hundred nations.'

White Deer sang through her grief. She stood still and straight in the wind. 'This is your spirit song, kept in your heart. We cling to your wise words which offer hope. We are White Water Sioux, one of five hundred nations. Our brothers are the Cheyenne and the Apache, the Blackfoot and the Comanche.'

'No!' The women, the warriors and the children would not accept the Wild Dog Comanches as brothers. These were the warriors who had driven the White

Water band from their homeland; the reason why they starved and shivered on the mountain as winter tightened its grip.

Four Winds called up a memory of Snake Eye, leader of the Wild Dogs, falling to his death on snowy Mount Kivioq. The angry death of a bitter man; tumbling, sliding, crashing out of sight, still calling for revenge. Horror and hatred had sat in the boy's heart as he'd watched. And yes; he was too young and hurt to be able to call the Comanches brother.

'In time,' White Deer insisted. 'For together, the nations are strong, and divided we are weak.'

Then she sang the spirit song over and over, until the children crept away to the tipis and huddled together for warmth, and the women went to gather wood for the fires before more snow fell.

Four Winds stayed with the four warriors, One Horn, Three Bears, Little Thunder and Sun Dancer. His mother, Shining Star, fetched a deerskin blanket for White Deer and wrapped it around her frail shoulders. The old woman sang on, grieving and giving thanks.

'You must set out on your third journey,' Three Bears told Four Winds.

'You must fetch a breath of air from the furthest ocean,' One Horn reminded him.

The boy replied with the slightest movement of his head.

'The spirit horse will guide you,' Little Thunder encouraged.

Four Winds felt that his heart must break from grief at the death of his beloved grandfather and the weight of the task he had yet to undertake.

Sun Dancer turned his gaze from the shrouded corpse high on the platform to Four Winds, on whom their hope for the future rested. 'It is as Red Hawk commanded,' he said quietly. 'He chose you, the youngest among us, to make three journeys, because you were the one he loved the most.'

Four Winds nodded. He looked up at his grandfather and he heard his voice.

'We are the invisible ones, the People of the Sky, the People of Dreams whose voices cannot be bound by pain or death.

'We are the People of Prayers who stand small before the great Wakanda, Creator of all things.

'We pray that the strand of time that we hold up to eternity might not be cut and our words slip into silence. We stand, great warriors, in the Circle.'

LIFE-SIDE

ONE

'The children are hungry,' Burning Tree announced when the singing and grieving were done. She was a young woman with sorrows of her own to bear, since her brother, Running Fox, had died at the hands of the Wild Dogs. Now she came to the five warriors to beg for food.

'They must eat what they can find,' Little Thunder told her. 'Berries and roots, the meat of the jack rabbit, fish from the stream.'

'The birds stole the berries. The roots are already frozen into the ground,' Burning Tree replied. 'We are too weak to hunt the rabbit, and ice as thick as my hand covers the water in the stream.'

Little Thunder knew this, but, being young, didn't care to admit his hopelessness.

'Is there still grain in the store?' Three Bears asked.

'Enough for seven days.'

'And after that?'

'Nothing.'

'I will hunt for rabbit,' Little Thunder decided, ready

to seize his bow and arrow. 'I cannot hear the children cry and do nothing.'

'One rabbit will not feed many children,' Three Bears pointed out. He was strongest of the remaining warriors, one who thought before he acted.

'And none will feed no one.' Little Thunder went into his decorated tipi, hoping to shame the others into action. 'Yours are the children who cry from hunger, not mine,' he said rashly. 'I have no wife to worry over, no sons and daughters to protect.'

Three Bears shook his head. 'That is a lucky thing, for what wife could rely on a hothead who rushes out on to a snowy mountain in search of a solitary jack rabbit?'

Then One Horn stepped into the argument. 'My daughter and my daughter's children bear the big bellies of hunger,' he acknowledged. 'It is many weeks since they tasted meat.'

His words fell into silence. Now that Chief Red Hawk was dead, One Horn was the warrior with the most honour in battle, the one who wore the most ermine pelts on his war shirt.

'We must hunt for bigger prey,' the new chief decided. 'We will go down from the mountain into our White Water home, where the deer and the buffalo pass the winter.'

'Yes, and face a hundred Wild Dogs on horseback, who will cut us down as a sharp blade scythes through corn,' Sun Dancer reminded him. The young brave's own memory of savage hand-to-hand combat with the Comanches was still fresh in his memory.

'Snake Eye is dead. Perhaps the purpose of the Wild Dogs is blunted.' Four Winds offered a faint hope.

But One Horn shook his head. 'Revenge sits in their hearts. No, if we go into the valley for buffalo meat, we must travel in darkness, without a sound, and return as swiftly with food.'

'Oh, now I am sorry that I came with my complaints!' Burning Tree cried. She was small and slender amongst the men, her shoulders wrapped in a woven shawl, her long black hair bound into one thick braid which hung to her waist. 'I would not send our warriors into such dangers!'

'Death hounds us from all sides,' One Horn replied. 'So while Four Winds sets out on his third and final journey, Three Bears, Sun Dancer, Little Thunder and I will call upon the spirit of the buffalo and hunt him in the valley.'

Little Thunder's objections continued. 'And so we leave our women and children without men to guard them! The Comanches have scouts posted all around our village. They will see how it is when we have gone.'

'We will defend ourselves.' Burning Tree held her head up high. 'My brother, Running Fox, taught me to fire an arrow straight and true!'

'Call the buffalo spirit,' One Horn said finally.

Death surrounded them. The choice was hard.

The warriors gathered around the cedar tree in the centre of the village. They wore their buffalo-skin headdresses and danced to the beat of Cochise's drum.

Four Winds felt the weight of the headdress bear down on his bare shoulders. He bore his tomahawk high above his head and stamped his feet hard against the frozen earth in time to the drum.

'The boy wears his grandfather's headdress like a man,' White Deer commented from among the group of woman and children who watched.

'He joins the Buffalo Dance but he will not hunt,' Shining Star sighed, thinking of his journey to the furthest ocean. 'He is like his father, Swift Elk, in the dance.'

Four Winds whirled and stamped, calling the buffalo up the mountain. He had painted white stripes across his chest and smeared his face with streaks of blue. '*Le maka wecicon kin*,' he chanted. 'This earth I have used as paint. Great buffalo, give us meat for our food, skins to clothe us and build our lodges. You are our only means of life!'

This was his first Buffalo Dance. He had joined the men while his boyhood friend, Cochise, sat cross-legged and beat the drum.

'Kola, you have thirteen summers like me,' Cochise

had complained while Four Winds prepared for the ceremony. 'Why then should I not be a warrior too?'

'Do not call me Kola,' Four Winds had chided. The chalk stripes were wet across his chest, the blue paint dried hard on his face.

'That was your name when we played by the tipis,' Cochise had reminded him. Envy made him argue. 'It means "friend". Now you are a warrior, does that mean we are no longer brothers?'

'We are different,' Four Winds had replied. He had glanced at Cochise and seen a young face, unmarked by experience. Clear eyes untroubled by bloodshed, a mouth too ready to pout and sulk. 'I have travelled to the deepest mine and the highest mountain.'

'I would be a warrior too,' Cochise had insisted. 'I would dance around the cedar pole, I would hunt the buffalo.'

'Then you must ask One Horn if you might make your vision quest. Without it, you cannot fight or hunt.' Four Winds had lifted the heavy headdress and placed it over his head. 'Come, buffalo, and give us meat for our food.'

Cochise had seized the drum and angrily begun to beat. 'I have thirteen summers,' he had grumbled, 'and yet I am left behind with the children!'

Then the dance had begun, and Cochise's complaints were forgotten.

Four Winds felt stifled by the weight of the buffalo

head. He prayed that the creatures would stray from the plains up as far as the snowline, so that the White Water warriors need not risk the dangers of descending into the valley.

'*Tate ou ye topa kin!* The four winds are blowing,' Sun Dancer cried. 'May they bring the great buffalo to us here on the mountain!'

The five dancers turned and pranced.

'We will use your hide for shields and moccasins, your hair for headdresses and rope, your horns for cups and fire carriers,' Little Thunder promised. 'If you come, our children will not starve!'

White Deer stared into the valley, craving the sight of buffalo. She saw only bare aspen trees weighed down by snow and water frozen in the streams.

'The wind cuts like a knife,' Shining Star murmured. A young child crept close and wrapped himself in her skirt for warmth. She heard him whimper, and lifted him into her arms.

Then the dance was over, and One Horn, Three Bears, Little Thunder and Sun Dancer were ready to leave.

'Let me come with you!' Cochise begged. 'I can fire an arrow straight as any man. I will track the buffalo. I will cut the meat from the bones.'

One Horn shook his head. 'Your time will come,' he promised.

The boy trotted after him. 'Let me go with you now!'

'When you are older.'

'I am the same age as Four Winds.'

'In summers, perhaps. But you are not yet ready.' One Horn was firm. 'Cochise, I will hear no more.'

The new chief strode away, calling for his warriors and taking swift leave of his wife, Two Moons.

'And we too must part,' Shining Star told Four Winds. She led him to her tipi and the sweat bath which would purify him before his journey. Lemon grass fed the flames which heated the water. It filled the air with a sweet scent.

Then Four Winds opened his heart to his mother. 'I am afraid of this journey,' he told her.

'I am afraid for you, my son,' she replied.

A thin trail of blue smoke twisted upwards towards the smoke hole. The tipi was dark and safe.

'I have fought many battles for my People.'

'You are weary?'

'My bones ache. My spirit is heavy.'

Shining Star sighed. 'You have seen the evil of this world.' The evil of Anteep, great lord of the Underworld, and of his many servants; those spirits summoned by him to defeat Four Winds on his quest.

'When I was young, I thought the world was pure and good,' Four Winds confessed. 'But now I know that Anteep is strong.'

You are still young, Shining Star thought. She knelt beside him and bathed his face. 'There is a balance which we call *hozho* between good and evil in this world,' she assured him. 'A harmony amongst all things.'

Four Winds longed to believe her, and the hopeful words which Red Hawk had passed down through his spirit song. Yet the good man perished beside the bad, and his beloved White Water People were pushed to the edge of extinction.

His mother saw what he was thinking. 'I know full well that the buffalo days have gone and that our people have fallen into poverty. But we are rich in family and songs and beauty.'

'We have lost the best of our warriors.' Red Hawk, Swift Elk, Black Kettle, Running Fox. The list was long. Of fifty, only five were left.

Shining Star saw that her son's heart wavered on its path to seek out a breath of wind from the furthest ocean.

'I would give my life to keep you safe at home,' she admitted softly. 'I long to say that your final journey will not be necessary, that you have done enough, that One Horn can bring back meat for our children and defend our band by his strength and cunning alone.'

Four Winds shook his head. 'It would be a lie.'

'And so I cannot say it.'

There was silence as the smoke twisted upwards and the lemon grass crackled in the flames.

'Every moment you are gone I will wish you back with us. My dreams will be filled with fears, in my waking time I will dread the arrival of the owl with news that will break my heart.' Shining Star went to the door of the tipi. 'And yet you must go,' she sighed.

Four Winds put on his buckskin shirt, his grandfather's beaded moccasins, and tied his medicine bundle around his shoulder. 'I have Silver Cloud to guide me,' he reminded her.

'You see; we are rich in beauty.'

The creature waited by the cedar tree, tied by no rope, but standing patiently. He was built for flight, with long legs to carry him over obstacles, a long and graceful neck down which his silver mane flowed. His head was shaped like the deer's, yet not so fine; his back was broad to carry her son.

Shining Star stooped and picked up a necklace made of porcupine quills and carved beads made of bone, strung on a thin leather thong. 'Each quill is a prayer for your safe return,' she whispered. 'The carvings are signs for your protection.'

'I will wear it as long as I live,' Four Winds promised.

There was a world of things she wanted to tell him, but time for only one. 'Kola, you are strong as the hope you carry with you.'

The wind blew hard and cold as he lifted the tent flap.

'Do not lose hope, as I did not lose hope when I was a slave to Wahnistow and the Blackfoot people. Even at the worst of times, when stars blazed across the daytime sky and disease and death swept through the villages, a flame flickered in my secret heart. I heard my dead husband, Swift Elk, and saw you, my son, in my dreams.'

Four Winds saw the tears roll down his mother's cheeks. 'I hear you. And now, wait for One Horn to return with food. Be with White Deer in her grief, tell her we will go down from this frozen mountain to bury Red Hawk in his homeland.'

He turned and walked across the frozen ground towards Silver Cloud.

'It is as the Great Spirit wills,' his mother murmured, feeling as if a sharp blade stabbed her in the heart with every step he took.

TWO

A breath of air from the furthest ocean.

A long, hard journey after the worst of farewells.

Silver Cloud read the boy's pain as they descended from the mountain. The spirit horse bore Four Winds on his back away from his village.

Why was I chosen? Four Winds wondered.

The burden was heavy at the start of this, his third and final quest. He remembered his life before he had become a warrior; fishing in the White Water river, collecting honey, playing and listening to stories inside the tipis as the wind and rain rattled at the dewcloths.

I knew nothing except the names of the creatures we hunted for food and the sweet berries we picked, and I loved the life I lived, he thought. *I climbed trees and swam in the rapids, and I was not afraid. But now the future of my tribe rests on my shoulders. It is much for a boy of thirteen summers to bear.*

The horse took him through the snow, northwards into the great plains which stretched to the lakes as big as seas, where men sailed in boats made of bark and lived in long wooden houses.

The boy carried his medicine bundle slung across his shoulder. His black hair was braided; he wore a thin band of plaited leather across his forehead, and three eagle feathers like a plume at the back of his head. The precious quill necklace was tied firmly around his neck.

Why was I chosen? he asked himself over and over again.

There was flat land as far as the eye could see, more vast than the boy's mind could imagine.

The air was warmer now; the pale grass swayed like a silver sea. Flat and sweeping, with swallows soaring overhead. Bleached, rustling, open space, without a landmark. The horizon a straight line, the sky a pale, indefinite blue.

Behind them the mountains were still visible; greyish blue and disappearing in the mist. There in the foothills, One Horn and his men would hunt the buffalo when darkness fell.

It seemed to Four Winds that he had been journeying for most of his life. And yet the task had only been set by Ghost Horse when the berries were ripening on the bushes, before the snow had fallen on their mountain refuge.

As the dry grass swished like silk around Silver Cloud's legs, the boy allowed his mind to dwell on the moment at Spider Rock when he had received the vision that would mark him out for this quest.

He had fasted by the sacred rock and, while the spirits had refused to visit Matotope, the treacherous and cowardly shaman, they had appeared before this pure boy of thirteen summers. It had not been the Fox with the gift of cunning, nor the Elk to give him courage, nor the Wolf for hardiness, nor the Owl for wisdom.

'*Wanma yanka yo!*' he had called to the sky. 'Behold me!' And a creature had appeared, whose name he did not know. Its large, dark eyes had watched him calmly. It had spoken at last.

'I am swift as the Deer, strong like the Buffalo, brave like the Elk. I will not fail you.'

He called himself Silver Cloud. A spirit sent by Wakanda, in the shape of Ghost Horse himself. A guide for the boy who would become a warrior and live like a man. *I will not fail you.*

And now the weight of doubt lifted and Four Winds remembered why he had been chosen.

'Tell me about the ocean,' he said to Silver Cloud.

The war drum beat loud in the Wild Dogs' camp.

Tall Bull was stripped to the waist; his hair hung unbraided down his back. In his left hand he carried the Comanche medicine shield, painted red and hanging with eagle feathers. With his right he raised a tomahawk high above his head.

The drummer beat savagely on the skin drum as the

smoke from the fire rose thick and white. The sound drove the Wild Dog warriors into a frenzy of angry shouts.

'Behold, Anteep!' Tall Bull cried. 'Lord of all Evil, we call you to witness this passing of the medicine shield through fire!'

The smoke billowed around the circle of painted warriors; Red Wing and Wolf, Lightning Snake and Night Raven; men with wild, knotted hair interwoven with thin braids, with silver discs in their ears and narrow black streaks on their white painted faces. Their medicine man, Old Eagle, sat closest to the fire in his cap of buffalo fur.

'Anteep, protect us!' Tall Bull chanted. Four times he passed the shield through the smoke. 'Guide us in our revenge!'

The warriors bayed like wolves.

'Bring us revenge for the death of Snake Eye, our great chief!' Tall Bull pleaded. 'And for Spotted Tail, who died with him on Mount Kivioq. Deal cruelly with our enemies, the White Water Sioux, and help us drive them from the face of this earth!'

The drum beat and the men howled. The smoke rose and Old Eagle thumped the butt of his spear against the ground.

'Send us your spirits, oh great Anteep! Your shape-shifters and your monsters, your death-dealers with the sharp claws and strong jaws, your bone-crushers and fire-makers, and every creature who will bring destruction to the boy, Four Winds!'

'He sets out on his third and final journey,' Old Eagle muttered, as if in a trance. 'The silver dream horse accompanies him.'

'We have horses as swift as Silver Cloud!' Tall Bull claimed. As the new chief of the Wild Dogs he had much to prove. 'This time we will not fail.'

'Red Hawk is dead, but his voice lives on,' Old Eagle reported.

Tall Bull raised the shield high over his head, his lithe body arching backwards. 'The White Water Sioux are few and the Wild Dogs are many. We build our tipis in their homeland, we fish in their river and hunt their buffalo. Now we will capture them and put to death every man, woman and child who bears the name of White Water Sioux!'

His words drove the warriors into a crouched, stamping dance, their faces set like cruel masks, their eyes glittering from the orange flames.

Old Eagle looked up at Tall Bull. 'We have failed twice,' he reminded him quietly. The shaman judged well how to goad Tall Bull into savage action.

'Once because we turned our backs on the great Anteep, and twice because Snake Eye's body was weak and bitterness clouded his brain!' Tall Bull declared.

'The boy who makes the journey for the Sioux is stronger than he looks, wiser than his years.'

'My brain is clear, my body strong!' Tall Bull turned his back on the warning words. He held the decorated shield before him, raised his tomahawk and joined his warriors in their savage dance.

'The ocean is a beautiful place,' Silver Cloud told Four Winds. 'It is larger even than this great plain.'

'What colour is it?' the boy asked.

'The colour of the sky.'

'Then it is blue?'

'As azure when the sky is blue, then milky white like a pearl when clouds shield the sun, murky grey during a storm. And it is always moving in and out from the shore, following the course of the moon.'

Four Winds' eyes grew wide in wonderment. He had only ever studied the movement of the river of his White Water homeland. 'How does water flow backwards?' he asked.

'The ocean ebbs and flows. It is part of the Mystery,' was all Silver Cloud would tell him.

'And what of the fish in the sea? Are they big or small?'

'Some are as small as an aspen leaf,' the horse replied. 'But some are ten times the size of the buffalo.'

Wonder turned to disbelief in Four Winds. 'There is no creature on earth bigger than the buffalo!' he insisted.

'In the ocean there are whales that spout mighty plumes of water high in the air. There are dolphins that talk, and octopus without a tail but with eight long arms; crayfish with claws sharper than the scorpion's sting.'

'Now I *know* you are telling me stories that even a child would not believe!' Four Winds declared.

'You will see!' Silver Cloud promised. 'And the best of all when we arrive at the edge of the earth is the wild sound of the ocean as it crashes on to the shore. It is like no other sound I know.'

'One Horn and his warriors have left the village!' Black Thunder, the Wild Dogs' scout, galloped along the river bank carrying his urgent message to Tall Bull. 'They seek buffalo to feed their children. Only the women remain!'

The Appaloosa mare which carried the scout was lathered with sweat. She sucked air through her wide nostrils, her sides heaved.

Tall Bull greeted the news with satisfaction. 'Great Anteep, we thank you!' he cried. He stopped the war dance and bade the drummer be silent. 'Now is the time to ambush the White Water warriors! They travel by foot. Before morning their scalps will hang from our wampum belts!'

Black Thunder slid from his horse. 'There is a better plan,' he insisted. 'While One Horn is away from his village, let us ride our horses up the mountain. We will seize the women and children without a fight.'

Lightning Snake overheard the scout's eager suggestion. 'Where is the honour in that?' he asked. 'I would rather fight man to man, than spill the blood of women!'

Black Thunder wheeled around. 'Who talks of spilling blood?' he scorned. 'No; the women are of more use to us alive. For amongst them are White Deer, widow of Red Hawk, and Shining Star, mother of Four Winds!'

Tall Bull nodded. 'Black Thunder truly carries the Comanche cause in his heart,' he said warmly. 'For if we take these women prisoner and send a message to the boy that his mother and grandmother are bound to the cedar tree in the heart of our village, then he will not continue with his quest!'

'His failure will ensure our success!' Black Thunder promised. 'I have thought much about this as I rode down from the mountain. It is as Anteep wishes!'

Though it was a plan thought out by another, Tall Bull was not vain. He would reward the scout with ermine pelts and claim him as his brother. But he, Tall Bull, would make sure that the main honour fell to himself when the boy, Four Winds, gave up his quest.

'Seize the women,' he ordered his warriors. 'Let the foolish White Water men hunt the invisible buffalo!'

He strode for his horse; a brown-and-white creature painted with bold, red, zig-zagging stripes, its mane decorated with feathers, its broad back draped with a red banner to show that its rider was chief. Then he paused. 'Seize everyone!' he insisted. 'Let no one remain. Kill the dogs and burn the tipis. Bring the women down from the snow without harm.'

Old Eagle, the shaman, stretched his thin lips into a smile. It amused him to hear a Wild Dog chief issue the order to take prisoners, not scalps. 'Snake Eye seeks a more bitter punishment!' he chided.

But Tall Bull was a match for the old man's cruel humour. He did not rise to an argument which would have delayed the plan. 'He shall have it,' he promised grimly. 'When he sees Four Winds fail in his quest, when we torture the boy in full view of his mother and grandmother, then Snake Eye will have his revenge!'

Cochise watched thirty men mount their painted horses.

He stayed well-hidden behind the tall log pile at the edge of the Wild Dogs' village, but his body trembled at what he had heard. His breathing was shallow and quick.

He had come down from the mountain, telling no one, gathering his courage to creep into enemy territory. His plan was to spy and take back news so his people would praise him, and the women would tell One Horn that Cochise too deserved to be a warrior.

But now his courage deserted him and he stayed hidden as the Wild Dogs followed Tall Bull out of their village.

How could he, one boy, carry the news of their imprisonment and Four Winds' impending torture to White Deer and Shining Star?

And yet this knowledge was precious, if only he could outrun the Comanche horses and return to his people in time to warn them!

I am White Water Sioux! he told himself. *If Four Winds can face the wolf spirit, Iron Eyes, and outwit him, then I too can overcome our enemies!*

But his heart beat hard against his ribs and his mouth was dry. A black dog came sniffing out the smell of fear at the wood pile. Cochise cowered out of sight, trying to plan his escape.

There *was* one way that he might take, but it was dangerous. The logs were stacked amongst pine trees, in the shadow of an overhanging cliff. This granite cliff was part of a rocky slope, too steep for horses, which led to a ridge, running unevenly on to the mountain where the White Water band had been forced to take refuge after the Comanches had driven them from their homeland.

The dog came closer. It would soon attract the attention of those who stood and watched the departure of Tall Bull and his men.

Cochise knew that the difficult climb would give him an advantage over the raiding party. It took him as the crow flew back to his village, whereas the riders would have to follow the river in a long, winding loop around the back of the mountain. They would then have to double back and scale the slope from the south.

I can do this! he told himself. *May Wakanda give me the feet of the Goat and the swiftness of the Deer. May he give me the courage of the Elk!*

Taking a deep breath, he began to slither along the damp ground away from the logs. He heard the dog stop and listen. If it discovered him, all would be lost.

So Cochise took a pine cone from the bed of needles, aimed, then threw it high in the air. It disappeared among some low branches, then tumbled down, distracting the dog, who went to investigate the noise.

Quickly, the boy continued his secret progress towards the cliff. Crawling on his belly, he reached the undergrowth at its foot. He glanced back to make sure that no one was watching, then sprang up and found the first handholds in the rock.

Cochise was light and nimble. He climbed the damp, dark overhang by grabbing at roots and finding crevices wide enough for him to slither up. Then, when he came to the overhang, he clung like a bear cub to its mother's belly, trusting the tangled tree roots to bear his weight. Soon he was out from under the cliff and scrambling freely up the next slope.

Now he felt he could make it back to his people before the Wild Dogs arrived. He would tell White Deer of the enemy's plan; she would know what to do.

He ran eagerly towards the ridge, careless of the loose

stones under his feet. The stones rolled down the steep slope and rattled over the overhang. The black dog barked.

Old Eagle looked up towards the ridge and saw the Sioux boy fleeing into the mountains.

THREE

There were buffalo all around. More than Four Winds could count, as far as the eye could see. They thronged the plain, the life-givers.

Four Winds slid from Silver Cloud's back and let the horse drink. They had reached a river which wound across the flat land like a silver snake. Here was water and food; a land of plenty.

And yet the White Water People starved in their mountain exile. Four Winds frowned, then stooped to splash his face with cold, clear water.

The dream horse drank and rested. 'Is it any wonder that the Comanches wished to possess such a land?' he asked, standing quietly at the water's edge. 'Strangers will always covet it, as surely as the sun will come up tomorrow.'

'It is beautiful,' Four Winds agreed. He looked up at the sun and saw that it had already sunk low in the sky. On the far river bank, a small herd of white-tail deer cast long shadows as they came to drink.

'Once, the world was made entirely of water,' Silver

Cloud told Four Winds. 'Everywhere was ocean, even the place where we stand now.'

The boy smiled. 'Then man would have been born with fishes' tails, not legs!'

'You may smile, but there was only water, and the only creatures were birds that swam on the ocean, and Isakata'te, the Old Man, who oversaw everything.'

Four Winds squatted and listened. The deer were peaceful, no danger was present. He hoped that he and Silver Cloud would travel through the night, making good progress under cover of darkness.

'Isakata'te sat on a log,' Silver Cloud went on. 'He was lonely, so he persuaded the birds to swim down to the depths of the ocean and return to tell him what they saw.

'A red-headed bird dived down and saw earth below the water, but he could not bring any back to the Old Man. Then a blue-feathered bird followed and he managed to return with some mud caught in his webbed feet.

'Then Old Man rolled the mud between his hands and it grew so large that he let it drop back into the water and he was able to stand on it. And wherever he stepped, more land was formed, and gave rise to the mountains and plains. And so the world was created.'

Four Winds listened contentedly to the old tale. He pictured an azure blue world of water, imagined diving into its bottomless depths to find friends who would relieve his loneliness. 'Old Man needed others,' he commented.

'All creatures do, even the spirits.'

Then Four Winds went and circled his arm around Silver Cloud's neck. 'You are my friend and my guide,' he confided. 'As you promised never to fail me, I swear not to desert you. Love sits in my heart.'

Silver Cloud lowered his head. 'So you like this strange creature, the horse?'

'*Nagi Ksa pa wan.* Wise spirit.' Four Winds ran his hand through the horse's mane. 'Your coat is silver like the morning mist, your dark eyes see what is invisible.'

Cochise felt that his legs would carry him no further. His ribs ached, his throat was raw, as he approached his village. Now he could see the tipis and the thin trails of smoke drifting from the smoke holes. Medicine bundles swung in the wind; all was snowy and silent.

Cochise broke his stride. Was he too late? Had Tall Bull and his braves already arrived to carry out their plan?

Then Burning Tree appeared in the doorway of White Deer's tipi, carrying a water container on her shoulder and shivering as she came out into the cold air. She saw Cochise stagger towards her, dropped her burden and ran to support him.

'Put your arm around my shoulder,' she told him. 'Are you hurt? What is the matter?'

'I have been amongst the Wild Dogs. They mean to come and capture us all!' he gasped.

The young woman helped him into the centre of the circle of tipis. His arrival had brought out others, who crowded round to listen.

'Catch your breath,' Burning Tree insisted, ready to chide the boy for running off and being disobedient. As yet, she didn't understand his warning. 'Why do you bring us new problems when we already carry more than we can bear?'

'Tall Bull and thirty warriors are coming!' Cochise cried. 'Where are White Deer and Shining Star?'

Burning Tree pointed to the old woman's tipi. 'But do not disturb them. They have troubles enough.'

Ignoring her, the boy wrenched himself free and ran to the tipi. 'You must run and hide!' he told the two women. 'Before the Wild Dogs take you prisoner and force Four Winds to return!'

Shining Star heard the urgency in his voice and saw the look of anguish on his face. 'Come!' she said to White Deer. 'We must flee this place.'

But the old woman was weary of life. 'Since Red Hawk has departed from life-side, I have no wish to stay in this world,' she confessed. 'Let the Comanche Wild Dogs do as they please with me.'

Her answer made Cochise cry out in frustration.

'Make her understand!' he pleaded with Shining Star. 'Say it is for Four Winds and all the White Water People that she must flee!'

Shining Star nodded. 'What the boy says is true. The Wild Dogs do not care about the women and children left here. They will capture us and kill most. But they will keep you and me as hostages, to lure Kola back from his quest. Is this not so?' she asked the boy.

Cochise nodded. 'Come!' he pleaded. 'Tall Bull is not far behind!'

Then Burning Tree hurried into the tipi. 'There are many horses coming up the mountain!' she warned. 'They are decked for war, the warriors carry spears and tomahawks!'

White Deer wrung her hands. 'I have lived long,' she wailed. 'I have beheld wonders. I have lived according to the laws of the Great Spirit!'

'And it is His wish that you should come with us now,' Shining Star explained gently. She raised the old woman from the ground and made her lean on her arm. 'We will hide from the Wild Dogs and send them away empty-handed.'

'Hurry!' Burning Tree urged.

By now, all the women and children were gathering blankets and the remains of their food stores. 'We will go separately into the forest, leaving many trails,' they decided. 'The Wild Dogs will not know which to follow.

Then we will hide our trails with brushwood. Perhaps the snow will fall and cover our tracks.'

The women agreed hastily, bidding the children not to cry. 'Tall Bull will come and find you if you make a noise!' they whispered, hurrying off between the pine trees.

'Come!' Shining Star urged White Deer. She wrapped the old woman in a heavy shawl and bound her feet in strong hide.

'You have done well,' she told Cochise. 'One Horn will hear of this!'

'I will carry White Deer into the forest!' he offered, seeing that the old woman stumbled.

'Must I leave my husband, Red Hawk?' White Deer wailed, looking up at the tall funeral platform.

'He is with the Invisible Ones. He looks down on you, even now!' Shining Star said. 'Now do not risk the life of your grandson, Four Winds, by this delay!'

The sound of horses' hooves carried loudly on the wind.

So White Deer submitted. She was taken up into the arms of Cochise, light as a bundle of sticks, weeping softly.

The tent flaps of the empty tipis blew open, the fires died. The White Water women and children vanished like ghosts.

* * *

Four Winds and Silver Cloud had travelled on from the winding silver river. They journeyed across the plain, surrounded by deer and buffalo. The gold disc of the sun had almost met with the flat horizon.

'Soon it will be dusk and we will meet with the Pawnee people,' Silver Cloud predicted.

'Are they men of good will?' Four Winds asked, keeping a careful lookout. Here, on the flatland, there was little chance of sudden ambush.

'They are the Morning Star band. They live in peace and make no enemies.' The dream horse seemed unconcerned, perhaps even eager to meet the strangers.

And they appeared as the dream horse had predicted; a line of ten men on horseback on the western horizon, walking steadily towards the travellers. The sun sank behind them, turning the clear sky pink, draining the plain of colour.

Silver Cloud picked up speed, taking the most direct route to meet the Pawnee warriors.

'*Maka akanl wicasa iyuha el!*' the leader declared. Peace on earth! 'May Tirawahat, the Supreme Being of the Pawnee universe, go with you!'

Four Winds felt easy in the Pawnee presence. 'I am Four Winds of the White Water Sioux,' he announced.

The spokesman bowed his head. His hair was swept upwards and back from a strong face, free on one side, braided on the other. He wore a green feathered plume at the back, and a tunic with ermine-strip fringes. 'I am

Northern Fox,' he replied. 'I hear what the ground says. The water says the same thing, and the grass all around us. They say, "The Great Spirit has placed me here to welcome strangers. Take good care of travellers and do each other no harm!" '

Four Winds smiled. 'The earth here is plentiful. I am heading north and west to the furthest ocean in search of a breath of wind which will save my people.'

Northern Fox dismounted from his white horse, gathering his braves around him. Then he invited Four Winds into the centre of their circle. 'We have heard of your journey,' he confided. 'And of your battle against the Wild Dog Comanches.'

The boy said little, but accepted the meat and bread which his new friends offered.

'You are young,' Northern Fox commented.

'I am grandson to Chief Red Hawk, who has gone from life-side.'

The Pawnee warriors bowed their heads.

'Your grandfather's name is known from ocean to ocean as a man of peace,' Northern Fox said quietly. 'He met with my father, White Buffalo, and with other Pawnee chiefs. Throughout the Plains, among the Lakota and Blackfoot, the Mandan and the Crow, Red Hawk's name was revered.'

Once more Four Winds' eyes filled with tears. 'Then I am not alone on my journey,' he murmured.

Northern Fox waited for the boy to master his grief.

'We will make camp with you here,' he offered, for no matter how strong Four Winds' heart was and no matter how great his determination, he would need sleep before he continued.

But Four Winds shook his head. 'My spirit guide will carry me on through the night,' he explained. 'The children of the White Water People are starving, the women are left without protection. I must hurry to complete my quest.'

The Pawnee leader asked more questions, then came to a rapid decision. 'We will ride south and seek out your mountain village,' he told Four Winds. 'We carry a little food to give to the children, and we ten warriors will guard the women until One Horn returns.'

Gratitude poured from Four Winds' heart. 'You are my brothers.'

'And you will become a great warrior, like your grandfather, Chief Red Hawk. Your name will be passed from mouth to mouth, as far as the great lakes to the north,' Northern Fox predicted. His heart softened towards the slight youth with the great purpose. There was courage in the set of his shoulders, and yet he was so young and afraid. A boy alone on the great plains.

'Follow the North Star,' Northern Fox advised. He took out a scroll made of thin hide from his medicine bundle and unrolled it for the boy to see. He pointed to a large cross near the centre of the chart. 'Here is the North Star, and beyond it the stars of the Great Bear. To reach the furthest ocean, you must find the position of the stars in the sky and follow this course which I mark in red.'

Four Winds watched closely, comparing the crosses on the chart with the stars just now appearing in the sky. He marvelled how a people could chart the heavens and find their way according to the stars, while his own tribe used the mountains and rivers as their guides.

'Here, take it,' Northern Star ordered, after he had finished marking the course with his stained forefinger.

Four Winds accepted the chart graciously, rolling it once more and tying it to his own bundle.

'Tomorrow, when the sun rises, you will meet a deep river with clear green water, running swiftly,' Northern Fox explained. 'You must cross the water, keeping the sun behind you. The further west you travel, the hotter the sun will become. But before that, the night will come again. The stars will guide you once more, but take care, for with the darkness comes frost, and you will not be expecting it.'

Four Winds mounted on to Silver Cloud's back. 'For this help and the help you are about to offer my people, we are forever in your debt.'

The ten Pawnee braves nodded gravely. 'Go with Wakanda,' they murmured, turning their own horses and travelling south under the stars.

★ ★ ★

No smoke rose from the tipis when Tall Bull and his Wild Dogs galloped up the mountain into the White Water village. The angry chief reined his horse to a halt. He knew in an instant that the women and children had fled.

'Find them in the forest!' he cried.

The riders urged on their tired horses, but soon the undergrowth grew too dense for them to continue on horseback, so they leaped to the ground and continued the search on foot.

'Here is a trail!' Lightning Snake cried. He and Night Raven smashed through the bushes, blundering past the entrance to a cave which was carefully concealed with brushwood. Inside the cave, two White Water women and three children crouched low and held their breaths.

'There is a dog from the village!' another of the Comanches called, pointing to a shape lurking between two tall pines.

'No, it is a coyote!'

Dusk was falling and the light played tricks with their eyesight. Heavy grey clouds were beginning to produce flurries of light snowflakes.

'Never mind the animals, find White Deer and Shining Star!' Tall Bull cut back the snowladen bushes with his tomahawk. 'We cannot let women and children trick and cheat us!'

'How did they know of our plan?' Night Raven

demanded. 'Did the Eagle fly ahead with a warning? Do the servants of Wakanda see and hear everything?'

Hiding in a deep crevice in the granite rock, shielded by a fallen tree trunk, Cochise smiled to hear the enemy guess wrongly. He turned to White Deer, whom he had carried to safety. 'They will not find us,' he promised. 'Soon they must give up the search and return by night to their own village. Then we will creep back to the warmth of our tipis!' The old woman shook her head. 'There is danger everywhere,' she warned.

Shivering in the cold, thin air, the hidden White Water People watched through frozen branches as the enemy slashed and cut their way through the thorn bushes. Then at last Tall Bull called his warriors angrily out of the forest, back to the empty village, where they were met under the cedar tree by a hunched figure on horseback.

The chief of the Wild Dogs recognised the newcomer. 'Old Eagle, what brings a man of your years up the mountain in the snow?' he demanded.

The shaman returned the mocking question with a false smile. 'I see these chicks have flown the nest!'

'We have no need of a medicine man's wisdom to tell us this!' Tall Bull retorted. He kicked at the embers of the fire outside One Horn's tipi.

'A young Sioux scout is to blame,' Old Eagle told him. 'He hid in our village and overheard everything.

He climbed like a young bear cub up the steep side of the mountain and warned the women!'

Tall Bull kicked again and sparks flew up from the embers. He glanced wildly round the deserted village, noting that the tipis looked ghostly white in the gathering dusk.

'Burn them!' the thwarted Wild Dog chief snarled. 'Let us see how long the women stay in hiding once we set fire to their houses!'

So his men thrust sticks into the dying fire and took flame with them, visiting one tipi after another and torching each in turn. Soon the orange flames licked greedily up the sides of the tents. The Wild Dogs' savage faces were lit by the unnatural light.

From the forest, Shining Star was among the first to see the flicker of flames in the distance. She crept out of her hiding place and stared down towards the village.

When Cochise joined her, he gasped and almost cried out, until she held up a warning hand. Slowly other women emerged to witness the destruction of their homes. They held their hands up to their faces in horror.

'The White Water tipis burn well!' Tall Bull cried, raising his tomahawk above his head. His warriors threw flaming torches high in the air. Flames crackled and roared, fanned by the wind. Sparks flew into the night sky.

From the high, frozen forest, the women wept silently.

FOUR

Cheered by the help of Northern Fox and his Morning Star band, Four Winds charted his course by the stars.

The night sky shone with a thousand pin-pricks of white light. The unending plain spread out before him like a silver sea. Alone in his quest, lulled by the peacefulness of his surroundings, Four Winds let himself dream of the time when he would return with the breath of air from the ocean. He would ride back on Silver Cloud, swift as the wind. One Horn would greet him as an equal, the Comanche Wild Dogs would admit defeat and the White Water People would walk down from the mountain to reclaim their homeland.

'We have far to go,' Silver Cloud said, as if to check the boy's racing thoughts.

'And friends to support us,' Four Winds countered. He thought of his brothers, the Pawnee warriors, travelling south through the night with food for the children and protection for the women.

'But there are hidden enemies.' The dream horse knew that too much confidence would make the boy careless. 'This plain might seem empty and silent, but we are surrounded by spirits. They are within all things; the earth and the grass, the moon and the stars, even in the wind.'

The reminder made Four Winds more thoughtful. He drew out the chart of the stars and decided that they must head more to the west. His senses grew more alert and, when a jack rabbit sprang up from under Silver Cloud's hooves, his hand went to the knife hanging at his side, as if the grass hid a deadly enemy.

Hours passed and the air grew cold. Four Winds wished that they could stop to light a fire, but there was no time, and anyway these open, grassy spaces did not provide wood for fuel.

'Tomorrow the sun will burn you,' the dream horse predicted. 'We will rest from the heat then.'

So, with freezing fingers and the wind of the vast plain drumming against him, Four Winds urged the horse into a gallop, following the stars of the Great Bear towards the far-off ocean.

'What will the mighty Tall Bull do, now that the women and children have tricked him?' Old Eagle asked.

The medicine man had lived through many battles, had seen land won and lost. It amused him to observe the new chief thwarted.

'What would the great Snake Eye have decided?'

Night Raven demanded of Old Eagle. He, like others in the raiding party, doubted Tall Bull's wisdom.

The medicine man closed his eyes and inhaled smoke from the burning tipis. 'I can speak for our dead chief, for I hear his voice in the night sky. 'He says that we must forget the women and return to our village. When the sun rises, we must send many men after the boy and the dream horse.'

Tall Bull rounded on the shaman. 'This message is false! You think only of your own comfort. You are an old man longing for the warmth of your bed; you do not truly listen to the Invisible Ones!'

Old Eagle grunted and turned away, but Night Raven argued on. 'Tall Bull does not accept the wisdom of others, yet he gives us poor direction. What should we do? Do we let the flames from the tipis die away and wait in the snow for the women to appear? Shall we send scouts to gather our brothers who hunt the scalps of the White Water warriors? How much time do we waste before we pursue the boy who is our true enemy?'

Challenged in front of his warriors, anger burst from Tall Bull. In a swift movement he drew his knife from its sheath and slashed the blade across Night Raven's cheek. Blood sprang from the wound.

The other men looked on in silence.

'Night Raven must know that I am chief of the Wild Dog Comanches!' Tall Bull declared. He stood head and shoulders above the one who had dared to challenge him. His shoulders were broad, his face rough, as if hewn out of rock.

Night Raven felt the blood trickle down his face on to his neck, but he would not put up his hand to stem the flow. Instead, he stared boldly back at his angry chief.

'Know too that there was no warrior more loyal to Snake Eye while he lived. When we drew him on a travois through the snow to Mount Kivioq, when his body was a useless husk and he could move neither hand nor foot, even then I followed his command!'

Night Raven lowered his gaze to the ground under the force of his new chief's glare.

'But I am chief now. Old Eagle, you live in the past if you imagine that the voice of Snake Eye from beyond life-side can outweigh my command!'

The shaman gathered his buffalo-skin cloak around him and withdrew into the background.

'And Night Raven, next time you question me, the blade will cut deeper!'

Tall Bull's low voice carried up the mountain like thunder.

From high above, the White Water women heard the argument. They watched their tipis burn and did not venture down.

Dawn crept into the sky and still the White Water village was deserted. Though chilled to the bone, the women followed the advice of Shining Star to remain in hiding until the Comanches grew tired of waiting and returned the way they had come.

Only Cochise chose to ignore the danger of making his way out of the forest, creeping under cover of darkness from his hiding place to the outskirts of the ring of smouldering tipis. After all, he had proved he was an able scout. He could move like a ghost through the trees, his footfall deadened by the soft snow.

'Ten of us will remain here,' Tall Bull decided at last. 'Night Raven, you will stand guard by the cedar tree, while the others return to search the forest by daylight. Ten of us will ride off in search of One Horn and his buffalo hunters. Lightning Snake, you will lead this group. The rest will come with me. We will follow the boy and the spirit horse, capture them and ride back to our village. We will meet there before two suns have risen.'

The chief strode among his men as if challenging anyone to disagree. None did, and even Old Eagle listened without comment.

Cochise heard the plan. It seemed now he must split himself in three to take warnings to Shining Star, One Horn and Four Winds! It was more than one boy could do.

'In the name of Anteep and the spirits of the Underworld, we will carry out our purpose!' Tall Bull vowed. 'We will avenge Snake Eye and sweep the White Water Sioux from the face of the earth!'

Cochise's heart pounded as he tried to think clearly. He must leave the women to fend for themselves. They were like the redwing hawk, looking down on the enemy from a height, able to run and hide again when Night Raven's men came looking. And both Shining Star and Burning Tree would lead wisely.

But what of Lightning Snake's party of ten men, sent in search of One Horn and the three warriors? They deserved to be warned. Cochise might easily slip away and find the hunters; if not on foot, then by stealing one of the nearby horses belonging to the Wild Dogs.

Then again, perhaps four strong warriors could defend themselves against ten Wild Dogs in a raiding party. One Horn had won many such battles in the past. Whereas Four Winds was one boy alone on his long journey.

Yes, that was where his help was most needed, Cochise decided. He didn't stop to think of the great distance already forged between him and Four Winds, nor that Silver Cloud was swift. All he knew was that the success of the quest now rested on him.

A weak sun had appeared in the eastern sky as Cochise began to slither through the snow towards the herd of tethered horses. The creatures huddled together for warmth, their backs to the boy, their moist breath clouding the cold morning air. In the pale daylight, their plaited manes and painted war stripes were dull, and their proud heads hung low.

Cochise knew he must act swiftly, before Tall Bull's men had time to organise themselves into three groups and follow the chief's commands. So he raised himself and zig-zagged from rock to rock and tree to tree, insubstantial as a shadow.

'Remember that the enemy has the protection of Wakanda and Ghost Horse!' Old Eagle called upon the Wild Dogs to be cautious. 'That is why the boy they call Four Winds has survived two journeys. He made his vision quest to Spider Rock, and now he follows the true way of Wakanda!'

'But Anteep is stronger!' Tall Bull proclaimed. 'He has the spirit called Waktcexi, the great water monster, lurking by the western shore. He has Kannuck, wolf spirit, and Gunarh, killer whale. The caves of the seashore are guarded by great Tlenamaw, the monstrous dragon, and strongest of all is Bad Heart, dread Bear Prince, whose claws are like knives and whose jaws crush the bones of his prey like so many weak reeds growing by the water's edge!'

The Wild Dogs murmured and jostled, more eager now to pursue their quarry.

So Cochise took a great risk, leaving the cover of the rocks and running in a line as straight as the crow's towards the horses. He chose a grey mare whose colour would help him merge into the landscape as he galloped away, coming up from the side, untying her and sliding on to her back before the other horses had time to recognise what was happening. Then he seized the reins of plaited leather and turned his mare away from the herd, kicking her sides as he'd seen the Comanches do.

The horse responded by breaking free of the herd. She charged wide of the burnt-out village, in full view of the war party, raising cries of astonishment from the Comanches. Cochise clung tight with his legs, using his lithe body to stay balanced. The drumming of his heart sounded like thunder in his ears, and yet his courage did not fail him as he used the reins to guide the mare down the mountain into the valley of his homeland.

The Wild Dogs soon overcame their surprise when they saw that the enemy was a single boy unused to riding a horse.

'There is your spy!' Old Eagle cried. 'Not once, but twice he tries to outwit you!'

Wolf and Red Wing were fastest to react, seizing their horses ready to pursue the interloper.

But Tall Bull held them back. 'Let him ride on ahead of us!'

Wolf wheeled his horse to one side, making him prance and rear up in his impatience.

'See how the boy flies on your horse, Lightning Snake!' Old Eagle found his usual twisted pleasure in the unexpected theft.

This time no one questioned the chief's decision.

'Let him believe that he has tricked us once more.' Tall Bull folded his arms and calmly watched Cochise's progress. 'We will wait until he is out of sight, then we will pick up his trail and follow him.'

'For how long, before you capture him and take his scalp?' Lightning Snake demanded.

Tall Bull cast a sideways glance. Then he gazed back into the valley, watching the boy and the horse cross the river and head west, away from the rising sun.

'Until he leads us to Four Winds and the dream horse,' he replied.

As the sun rose high in the sky, the sighing grass of the plain gave way to the dry dust of the desert. The only plants were spiked cacti and a dry weed that would uproot itself, form itself into a ball and be scattered by the wind hither and thither across the path of Four Winds and Silver Cloud.

'It is as I said,' the dream horse reminded the boy, who complained of the scorching heat. 'Now is the time to find shade and to rest.'

Though eagerness to reach the ocean shore surged through every vein, Four Winds had to accept the horse's wisdom. His mouth was dry as the red dust all around, his face ran with sweat. So he pointed to a small outcrop of rock surrounded by tall cacti, suggesting this as a safe shelter.

Silver Cloud agreed. 'The fruit of this plant contains

sweet juice,' he told the boy. 'But take care; the thorns contain poison.'

Slipping from the horse's back into the shade of the rock, Four Winds sighed. 'Who can live in this bare desert?' he complained.

'The mighty condor,' the horse replied. 'He sails the air current with the vulture and the eagle. They hunt the deer gathered at the water holes.'

'And do people call this their homeland?' Four Winds looked out at the unending dust, broken by tall fingers of rock. Then he turned to concentrate on cutting a pear-shaped fruit from the nearest cactus. Avoiding the long black spikes, he sliced the golden fruit away from the green stem.

'Look at the rock behind you,' Silver Cloud told him. The horse seemed alert to distant sounds. His ears were pricked and he held his head high.

Unnerved by the reply, the boy studied the rock. At first he saw nothing unusual; only a rough surface with sand gathered in the crevices. What was he looking for, he wondered.

Then he made out a pattern. It had been scratched into the rock by a sharp tool; the shape of a man, except that the figure had giant wings.

'This is the bird chief of the Miwok people,' Silver Cloud explained. 'Their shaman wears the wings of the giant condor. With the bird's help he may suck poisons from the bodies of the sick.'

Four Winds saw then that the scorching desert was home to many men, and that the land was good. 'Where is the water?' he asked.

'Deep under the ground. The Miwoks must dig to quench their thirst.'

With his finger, Four Winds traced the image of the man-bird. He thought how it must be to live in the heat, with no water running across the surface of the land. 'Do the Miwoks see us now?' he asked.

'Every moment since the rising of the sun,' Silver Cloud answered. 'For it would be a foolish people who let strangers cross their homeland without keeping careful watch.'

Try as he might, Four Winds could see no sign of the Miwok scouts. Then he listened; nothing but the hot wind brushing the tumbleweed across the dust. 'Are they friends to the White Water Sioux?' he wanted to know.

Silver Cloud turned away to the east. 'They let us pass in peace,' he remarked.

'What do you hear?' By now, Four Winds could read the horse's body signals well. He knew that the arched neck and pricked ears meant that Silver Cloud was listening intently.

'One horse with a rider.'

'Coming this way?' Climbing to the top of the rock, despite the glaring heat, Four Winds used the high point as a lookout to scan the flat eastern horizon.

'Swift as an antelope,' the dream horse confirmed. 'See; in the far distance!'

The boy shaded his eyes and tried to focus, but a heat haze shimmered all around and he could make out nothing distinctly.

'A grey horse with a boy rider,' Silver Cloud reported. 'The mare has travelled far. They are following our trail.'

At last Four Winds could make out the horse and rider.

'She bears the war stripes of the Wild Dogs.'

'Then the boy is a Comanche scout!' Four Winds declared. He leaped down from the rock, ready to ride out and challenge the stranger.

But Silver Cloud went ahead, leaving Four Winds in the shade of the rock. Until now he had seemed unconcerned, but as he trotted full circle around the landmark rock, he grew agitated. When he returned to the boy, he brought bad news.

'More horses and riders come after the first,' he reported.

'Then we must go on.' Four Winds' first thought was to outrun the mystery followers. But when he looked back over his shoulder, he saw the exhausted grey mare stumble and go down on her knees. Her rider was thrown forward against her neck, lost hold of the reins and somersaulted over her head to the ground.

For a moment, the boy lay stunned in the dirt. Then he raised his head and slowly pulled himself up into a sitting position. It was then that Four Winds recognised him.

'That is Cochise!' he told Silver Cloud. He began to run out into the open desert to help his friend.

'Wait!' Silver Cloud easily overtook Four Winds and stood between him and Cochise. 'You are eager to invite danger. Be more cautious, for things are not always what they seem.'

'Why is Cochise following us? Why is he on a Comanche horse?' Four Winds demanded. 'I must reach him to find out the answers!'

So the dream horse allowed Four Winds to climb on his back and carried him to the dazed rider whose horse had by now fled to a safe distance. The mare stood dejected and quivering in the full heat of the midday sun, looking to the east.

Four Winds found Cochise winded and clutching his arms around his ribs. He was covered from head to foot in the red dust of the desert. 'What news do you bring?' he asked, sliding to the ground and offering his hand.

'They have burned our tipis!' Cochise gasped. 'The women have fled to the forest!' He had ridden since dawn and not stopped for the heat of the sun.

Four Winds' heart shuddered and missed a beat. 'What of my mother, Shining Star?'

'Alive,' Cochise told him. 'And so is your grandmother, White Deer. But the Wild Dogs hunt them in the forest like deer. The women must silence the crying children for Tall Bull shows no mercy.'

Again Four Winds' heart almost stuttered to a halt. 'Where is One Horn?'

'Still hunting buffalo, but pursued by the Wild Dogs,' Cochise reported. 'This is why I stole the horse; to carry this news to you!'

Four Winds nodded. He had raised Cochise to his feet, but the boy still stooped forward from the pain in his ribs.

'You risked much,' he said gently.

'To be a warrior is my only wish,' Cochise confessed. 'I will not sit at home like a child!'

Four Winds looked into his friend's eyes and saw the strength of Cochise's will. 'I understand,' he murmured, remembering the time when he had demanded to go with Matotope on his vision quest, and the sorrow of White Deer as he had rushed to leave his childhood behind. But no one remained alive in Cochise's family to counsel the boy and steady his rash ambitions.

As Cochise struggled to take a deeper breath, his face creased with pain. 'There is more!' he gasped. 'Tall Bull and ten of his men will pursue you across this desert to the furthest ocean!'

More riders! That was what Silver Cloud had said. The sound of more horses' hooves carrying across the flat land; more danger to Four Winds on his quest.

And now Four Winds looked out towards the eastern horizon, and what he saw was what he most feared.

Across a hot plain of shimmering red sand, standing still and silently watching, was a group of warriors on horseback.

The boy turned desperately to Silver Cloud. 'Are they Miwok?'

'The Miwok do not have horses.'

'Then they are Comanches?'

Silver Cloud bowed his head.

Cochise staggered free of Four Winds. 'I am to blame! They have followed me!' he cried in an agony of guilt.

'They would have found us anyway.'

'But not so soon!' Cochise would not be consoled. Instead, he reeled out into the desert, as if to ward off the enemy with his bare hands.

And now Four Winds must make a hard decision. He could spring on to Silver Cloud's back and race like the wind away from Tall Bull and his men. He would escape, but it would mean leaving Cochise to die in the desert at the hands of the Wild Dogs; something he could not do.

'Go!' Cochise declared when he saw Four Winds hesitate. 'Do not be afraid for me. I will take my chances with the enemy!'

Four Winds pulled him back towards the grey mare which had carried him. 'Silver Cloud will make the horse understand that she must bear you to safety!' he explained. 'You must set off to the north, take a different path. It's me who Tall Bull will pursue.'

'No, I will stay with you and fight by your side!' Cochise struggled against Four Winds' strength, while Silver Cloud rounded up the Comanches' mare. The grey horse let him approach, then quietly followed him back to the boys.

'We must act swiftly,' Silver Cloud told Four Winds.

Staring back across the desert, the boy saw that Tall Bull had ordered his men to bunch together and set off at a gallop towards them. The horsemen raised a cloud of red dust that trailed behind them as they advanced.

'Ride away!' Four Winds forced Cochise on to his mare's back, but still his friend refused to go.

'I will fight until there is no breath in my body, but I will not run away!'

Shaking his head, Four Winds sprang on to Silver Cloud's back. He heard the Wild Dogs' horses' hooves thunder towards them, could see the red-and-white war stripes down their sides.

'Then come with me,' he told Cochise. 'And be prepared to die!'

FIVE

What chance had two boys against ten strong warriors?

Silver Cloud and the grey mare set off at a gallop, but the sound of the Comanches' approach did not fade, and a swift glance over his shoulder told Four Winds that if anything the enemy was gaining ground. By now he could make out Tall Bull at the head of the group, his face set in harsh lines, his body leaning forward and his legs gripping tight to spur on his horse.

Four Winds understood that Cochise's horse was exhausted and could not pick up speed. Again, he heard his friend urge him to go on without him.

'Make the dream horse carry you through the air!' Cochise gasped. 'He can use his powerful medicine to escape from Tall Bull.'

'It is as Ghost Horse wishes,' Four Winds replied hastily. He knew by now that the spirit power did not rest at his fingertips and that there was no point in calling upon supernatural forces at will.

As the Comanches narrowed the gap between them,

Cochise grew more desperate. 'But Silver Cloud is your spirit guide, he has sworn to protect you!'

'He has sworn loyalty,' Four Winds said. He tried to be calm and trust his horse.

But now the chief of the Wild Dogs ordered his men to fan out and form a semi-circle behind the boys. Still they gained ground, galloping flat out, with their war banners flying from the long shafts of their spears.

'We are like buffalo driven to the piksun!' Cochise cried.

Piksun. Blood kettle. The word sent a shudder through Four Winds. He imagined a thousand buffalo being driven down a narrow channel to the edge of a sheer cliff, where they fell to their deaths and their hunters moved in for easy pickings. That was the piksun; only now he and Cochise were the buffalo.

'We will try to reach that ridge to the north!' Four Winds decided that the rocky outcrop was their only chance of finding cover from the Wild Dogs. So they guided their horses and spurred them on, knowing that their lives depended on outrunning Tall Bull.

But now the chief gave the order for his men to fire, and a shower of arrows rained all around Cochise and Four Winds. The arrows landed harmlessly, but soon another volley was fired, and this time one grazed the flank of the grey mare, who reared and wheeled off to the right.

Four Winds saw what had happened and turned to

follow. This was leading them diagonally across the right flank of the Wild Dogs' U-shaped formation, making them an easier target, but Four Winds did not hesitate.

Tuwa nape cinahon opa kte sni ye! He who flees from danger shall not be admitted! This was the White Water Sioux's cry.

More arrows rained down as Four Winds leaned sideways to grab Cochise's reins. Gradually he steadied the runaway horse and drew her back on course for the ridge. But he saw that the flesh wound slowedher down, and so he urged Cochise to take hold of him around the waist and slide into position behind him.

'Silver Cloud will carry us both!' he promised.

Gasping and frantically clutching at Four Winds' deerskin war shirt, Cochise scrambled from his own mare to sit behind his friend. The grey mare stumbled and slowed, then was lost in a cloud of red dust.

Now Four Winds gave all his energy to willing Silver Cloud to reach the ridge. Those rocks meant shelter and possible safety; the chance to hide and perhaps lose their pursuers. 'Pray to the Great Wakanda!' he murmured to Cochise.

And even with two riders to carry, Silver Cloud ran more swiftly than any of the Wild Dogs' horses, so that Tall Bull cried angrily, 'Do not let them escape! Death to the boy who entered our village! Death to Four Winds, and so Snake Eye will be revenged!'

Silver Cloud raced on. Four Winds felt Cochise's arms

around his waist. He saw the ridge more clearly. There was a line of tall, crooked cacti in the centre, and to the left of them a second line of horsemen.

More Comanches; he and Cochise were running into a trap!

Four Winds closed his eyes and felt his throat constrict. Then he opened them again to look more closely.

A band of warriors looked down on the chase. Their arrows were loaded into their bows, their strings pulled taut. They did not move.

Not Comanches! As Silver Cloud bore them closer, Four Winds saw the upswept hair and eagle plumes of his friends, the Pawnees. Northern Fox and his Morning Star band; allies against the Wild Dogs, who had first sent help to the women, then had ridden on in search of One Horn and his three warriors. They had brought them on horseback here into the desert to rescue their boy-warrior.

'See!' Four Winds pointed.

One Horn, Three Bears, Sun Dancer and Little Thunder sat with drawn bowstrings, waiting to unleash their arrows on Tall Bull and his Wild Dogs.

'Draw back!' Tall Bull commanded, seeing that they were outnumbered.

The Wild Dogs reined back their horses and watched helplessly as Silver Cloud carried the two boys up the ridge into the arms of their friends and brothers.

But Red Wing questioned the order. 'Are we cowards that we hold back from this fight?' he demanded. 'We are so close to hunting the boy down. Why let him go now?'

'Because we wish to live to enjoy our revenge!' Tall Bull replied. 'We will withdraw and wait. Soon Four Winds and his horse must continue their journey alone. Then we will strike!'

'Soon? What does Tall Bull mean by this?' Rage made Red Wing cry out. 'How many times must we wait? I say we act now and risk an honourable death!'

'What is honour without victory?' Tall Bull mocked. He watched the silver horse draw near to the top of the ridge, saw One Horn lower his bow and raise a hand in greeting.

'I will not let him go!' Red Wing muttered, aiming his weapon. 'In the name of the mighty Anteep, may this arrow find its mark!'

There was the sound of the arrow being released and the loosening of the string. Neither Cochise nor Four Winds looked back.

It flew through the air straight and true.

Four Winds heard a soft thud, felt Cochise's grip loosen from around his waist, caught the gasp and the quiet groan as his friend slid to the ground.

Cochise fell face down, a Comanche arrow lodged deep between his shoulder blades.

* * *

The Pawnees and the small band of White Water warriors answered Red Wing's cowardly attack with a hail of arrows.

Two found their mark, then Northern Fox gave a signal for an advance down on to the desert floor. Meanwhile, One Horn and Four Winds dismounted and went to help Cochise.

The boy lay without moving, spreadeagled on the rocky ground.

Quickly One Horn snapped the shaft of the arrow, leaving the point embedded in the boy's back. Then he turned him and supported him in his strong arms.

Four Winds leaned forward and gently wiped the dirt from Cochise's face. 'See now what has happened,' he murmured.

Below them, Northern Fox led the attack against the Wild Dogs, who scattered in many directions.

Cochise's eyes were open but he did not move.

'Drink this water,' One Horn urged, taking out a leather bottle and tilting it towards the boy's lips.

But the water trickled out of the corner of his mouth.

'See what has happened!' Four Winds whispered again. 'Why didn't you ride to safety?'

Cochise stared into Four Winds' eyes. 'He who flees from danger shall not be admitted.'

Four Winds gazed back, slowly shaking his head. 'You are among the bravest of the White Water Sioux.'

Cochise smiled. Then his head fell sideways against his chief's shoulder.

'The spirit has left him,' One Horn said.

Four Winds wept for his friend; for the soft thud of the arrow as it found its mark, for the loosening grip and for Cochise's courage in death.

'Come!' One Horn commanded. He had seen three Comanches ride wide of the main battle and head towards them on the ridge. Cochise's body hung limp in his arms as he carried him into the shade of the tall cacti.

Red Wing and two young warriors charged the ridge. They had seized their chance as soon as Northern Fox had led the charge on to the scorching plain, cutting away from Tall Bull and sweeping upwards on a single-minded mission to destroy Four Winds.

And the daring plan had caught everyone by surprise, so that the three Comanches were upon their quarry before One Horn and Four Winds were ready to defend themselves. They rode at full gallop, slicing their tomahawks downwards, tearing the air with their high war cries.

One Horn and Four Winds reacted swiftly by taking out their knives. They dodged the tomahawks and darted to one side, spinning round, ready to face Red Wing once more.

'Lasso the silver horse!' Red Wing yelled, seeing Silver Cloud rear up and strike out with his hooves.

'Drag him away and put a spear through his chest!'

One of his accomplices obeyed, snaking his rope over the horse's head and dragging him down the far side of the ridge.

Now One Horn and Four Winds faced two riders, their faces savagely painted, their tomahawks raised high above their heads.

As they charged a second time, One Horn stood firm, feet planted wide apart, with Four Winds at his side.

'Do not weaken!' One Horn muttered.

Four Winds braced himself. He saw the two horses come straight at them, their nostrils flared, their ears flat against their heads. Red Wing's painted face was fixed in a snarl, his eyes wide with fury as he closed in on his prey. Then, with the horses' hot breath upon them, still standing fast, Four Winds saw them swerve apart. In that moment, One Horn reached up, seized Red Wing's arm and pulled him to the ground, while Four Winds caught at the leg of the second rider and unseated him.

Then it was hand to hand; a fierce test of strength and suppleness, tomahawk against knife.

Four Winds used his speed to evade the enemy's heavy blows, darting in close to wrestle his weapon to the ground. As the Wild Dog scrambled after his tomahawk, Red Wing slashed out sideways and knocked Four Winds' knife from his hand. But then One Horn caught Red Wing's wrist and pressed his arm against a rock. There was a crack; Red Wing yelled out in pain and went reeling and stumbling down the far side of the ridge.

Then One Horn ran and trapped the other Comanche's arm beneath his foot. The man's fingers could almost touch his tomahawk where it lay, but he could do nothing to grasp and use it.

'Take the nearest horse and ride away from here!' One Horn told Four Winds.

The Wild Dog writhed and twisted on the ground; Red Wing was nowhere to be seen.

'What of Silver Cloud?' Four Winds asked.

'Trust Wakanda that your spirit horse will find you, but you must go now, while you have the chance!'

So Four Winds ran towards Red Wing's frightened Appaloosa, trapped its reins underfoot, then moved in to leap on to its back. Down below, the Comanches under Tall Bull put up a strong fight against the Pawnees and the Sioux.

'Bury my brother, Cochise!' Four Winds begged, reining his new horse to face west.

One Horn nodded. 'Ride hard,' he ordered. 'Cross water when you find it. Leave no trail.'

Four Winds waited only to say one last word. 'I will find the ocean,' he promised. 'I will bring back a breath of wind!'

'Go quickly.' One Horn bade him farewell. '*Wakin yan iye ceca*. Go like the Thunder Bird. Do not look back.'

SIX

The stolen horse was eager to escape the battle. He galloped west, leaving behind the war cries and the clash of weapons. Four Winds looked straight ahead, trusting the White Water warriors and their Pawnee friends to hold the Wild Dogs at bay.

Cochise was dead. The truth hit Four Winds afresh. A boy born in the same summer whose haste to follow in Four Winds' footsteps had led to this. Cochise had not gone on his vision quest to gain a spirit guide; in his impatience he had broken the cycle and gone into battle unguarded. Wakanda had not been able to help him. But still, Four Winds wept for the boy with whom he had played. And he cursed Red Wing for his cowardice.

Meanwhile, the flat desert gave way to gentle hills and the first trees that Four Winds had seen for many hours.

There must be water nearby, Four Winds realised. Then he recalled that Northern Fox had predicted that he would come to a river on the second day.

Soon the bare ground gave way to sparse grass and the return of thorn bushes and tumbleweed. The hills grew steeper, the trees taller and straighter.

I have crossed the desert, Four Winds thought, glancing behind in the hope that Silver Cloud would be following. But there was no graceful creature shadowing them at a distance. When he came to the river, he and the Appaloosa would have to cross it unaided.

And gradually the air changed. No longer dry and hot, it became cooler and fresher; something to breathe in deeply. The wind carried the scent of flowers.

Soon, Four Winds thought; perhaps over the brow of the next hill, they would come to the river. The horse too seemed to sense it, picking up speed again on the downhill slopes and toiling hard up the following incline.

Yes, there was water, and it was very close. For the first time, Four Winds realised how dry his throat was. His lips were cracked; the skin on his face was pricked and stung by the sharp, dry sand of the desert. So now every step was wearisome, as hill followed hill, until at last they crested a ridge and saw the river below.

It looped lazily across the floor of the valley; a wide, slow-flowing silver stream which attracted birds and animals of all descriptions. Four Winds made out mule deer drinking in the shade of an aspen copse, and ducks floating downstream on the current. The high sun reflected in the water, whose surface was rippled by a light breeze.

Four Winds breathed in deeply. He set the Appaloosa on a straight course for the water, and it was not long before they approached the bank and both the boy and the horse began to drink greedily. The Appaloosa lowered his head and took long, noisy sucks, while Four Winds waded into the water to drench his whole body before he cupped his hands to drink.

Once his thirst was quenched, he began to consider how they should cross the wide strip of water. He knew from his journeys with Silver Cloud that the horse could swim, and so he decided to lead the Appaloosa a short way along the bank to where the current seemed slow and easy. He slid on to the horse's back and squeezed his sides.

Instead of going forward, the stolen horse refused to move. Four Winds frowned and squeezed again. 'Go!' he urged.

Still the horse dug in his heels and braced his legs.

So the boy gave him a sharp tap on the rump with the free end of his reins. The animal jerked and took his first step forward.

'Silver Cloud would do this without hesitating,' Four Winds muttered. It was vital for him to cross this river and continue his journey. 'Why isn't he here with me?'

he asked impatiently. 'I need him to guide me to the ocean!'

Reluctantly the Appaloosa edged into the river. He stopped once to paw at the water with his front hoof, raising a great splash and attracting the attention of the nearby deer. Fighting with his head to gain control of the reins, he only went on when Four Winds kicked hard.

Then they were out of their depth and the horse was swimming strongly. They were halfway across the river, making good progress. Refreshed by the cool water, the boy looked ahead to the far bank.

But suddenly everything changed. There was a hidden undertow in the deepest part of the river; a powerful downward current that pulled the horse off course and swept him downstream. The Appaloosa struggled to keep his head above water, but the undercurrent dragged him down. Four Winds felt himself lose contact with the horse, then he too was having to fight the current, striking out with his arms and legs, trying to swim to the bank.

But he went down, deep under the surface. Water swirled all around; he touched the bottom, kicked with his feet and raised a cloud of mud. He kicked again and shot back to the surface, gasped in air and resumed his fight to survive.

Where was the horse? Four Winds glanced downstream and saw him reach calmer waters. He realised that he too must let himself be carried by the current to the same spot, then he would be able to regain control.

So he let the water take him like a log down rapids, bobbing and turning in the unseen force of the current. The sky seemed to spin above him, and below the current gripped him and invited him to a watery death.

Then at last, as suddenly as it had taken hold, the river let him go. Four Winds had followed the Appaloosa to the point on a bend where the current slackened. Seizing his chance, he struck out for the bank and soon found himself able to rest his feet on the pebbly bed, then drag himself clear.

Four Winds crawled on to dry land and shook himself like a dog. His carelessness made him angry; he should have taken heed of the horse's fear of the water and chosen a different crossing. But luckily they were both safe. Except that when he looked more closely at the Appaloosa, he saw a wide gash on his front leg and blood pouring freely over his hoof.

The boy held back an impatient sigh and approached the injured horse. No doubt he had knocked his leg against a jagged rock; the wound would need packing with herbs from Four Winds' medicine bundle and strapping tight.

'I am to blame,' Four Winds confessed as he quietly approached the horse and led him up the bank. Then he unrolled his bundle and took out the dried leaves which would prevent fever in the wound. He laid them skilfully against the raw gash then bound it tight with a strip of soft doeskin. The horse stood quietly, seeming to understand that the treatment would lessen the pain.

I will be less hasty in future, Four Winds promised himself. *I will listen to the silent language of the animals.*

Meanwhile, the Appaloosa lowered his head and started to graze the fresh green grass. This gave Four Winds time to consider his situation. What if the horse could no longer carry him? The creature's legs were slender and the gash was deep. He walked now with a stiff limp. Would it be fair even to try to ride him on towards the ocean?

And yet One Horn and Northern Fox might not be able to hold off the Wild Dogs forever. Perhaps more of Tall Bull's men were following close behind and would soon arrive at the scene of the battle. They would then outnumber the Sioux and the Pawnees, and there would be great danger for the White Water warriors. In any case, there was no time for delay.

Frowning deeply, Four Winds approached the Appaloosa. The horse tossed his head; *Keep away!*

The boy tried again. This time, the horse moved quickly out of reach. It was no good; the creature himself had decided that he would carry Four Winds no further.

There was only one thing left to do; Four Winds must continue his journey on foot. So, slinging his bundle over his shoulder, he turned his back on the grazing horse and set off uphill to the next ridge.

Silver Cloud watched from a distance. It was mid afternoon, the sun was past its high point.

He had seen Four Winds force the Appaloosa into the river at a point where the current was strong. *Has the boy learned nothing during our journeys to the deepest mine and the highest mountain?* he wondered.

He had kept his position on the hill as the undertow had seized hold of the swimmers, had watched them vanish below the surface and reappear, swept like logs downstream. He had noticed the blood pouring from the gash on the Appaloosa's leg and seen the boy delay his journey to treat the wound.

Four Winds has a kind heart, he thought. But a kind heart alone would not lead to success in the task he had undertaken.

Then, when the dream horse saw the boy toil up the hill alone, he softened towards him. This showed more than a kind heart. For a boy of thirteen summers, he had courage and determination more than most.

Four Winds strode on, his face set towards the west, never faltering; a tiny figure in a vast landscape.

So Silver Cloud set off at a gallop towards Four Winds, his mane and tail streaming behind him, his long legs working in perfect grace and harmony.

Hearing the approach of hooves, Four Winds took

cover in a nearby thicket. Thorn bushes scratched his hands and face as he peered out and saw Silver Cloud appear on the horizon. He stepped out gladly, with a broad smile of greeting.

'You will not get far by foot,' Silver Cloud said. He had stopped some way away and was intent on chiding the boy.

'Where have you been?' Four Winds challenged. 'Why did you stay away for so long?'

The horse ignored the question. 'Did you think that you could finish the third and most difficult journey on the Comanche horse?'

'What choice did I have? One Horn fought to save my life. He bade me ride away on the Appaloosa.'

'You imagined that I had deserted you?' Silver Cloud lifted his proud head. 'And yet I swore that I would not fail you!'

Four Winds wondered at his spirit guide's aloofness. 'I kept faith with you,' he swore. 'Even when the Wild Dog threw a lasso around your neck and threatened you with his tomahawk, I knew you would not be defeated.'

'Is it keeping faith to flee on an enemy horse?' Silver Cloud demanded.

Four Wind's reply came from the heart. 'Yes, because my quest is lifeblood to our tribe. It is more important than breathing to me!'

Silver Cloud understood. He bowed his head and

came close. 'You were wise,' he conceded. Then, 'Was the Appaloosa swift as the wind when he carried you towards your journey's end?'

'Swift, but not swift as the wind,' Four Winds replied.

'Was he strong as the buffalo?'

'Strong, but not like the buffalo.'

The horse was satisfied. 'Climb on my back,' he told Four Winds.

The boy smiled and did as Silver Cloud bade him.

'Death to One Horn!' Red Wing proclaimed. His right arm hung useless at his side, the bone snapped by the chief of the White Water warriors.

Tall Bull scowled across the circle of men sitting cross-legged at the heart of the Comanches' temporary camp.

'Brave words!' he sneered. 'But what are words without action, and what action can a warrior with only one arm carry out against the enemy?'

Red Wing hung his head and was silent.

'This is what happens to those who act alone, without the blessing of their chief!' Tall Bull declared. 'Now Red Wing must return in shame to our village and sit with the women around the tipis!'

The injured warrior stood abruptly and left the circle.

Tall Bull accepted a pipe from Old Eagle, the shaman, and drew smoke deep into his chest. 'Today you fought well,' he told his men. 'But the Pawnee and the Sioux fought better.'

Old Eagle smiled scornfully. 'They call on Wakanda. Their cries are louder than our prayers to Anteep!'

Tall Bull passed on the pipe. 'Our scouts have ridden out in search of Lightning Snake, who is lost in the desert,' he said. 'When the sun rises again, we will be many!'

Old Eagle shook his head. 'It is not enough. You must make Anteep send his spirits to defeat the boy and his dream horse. You may gather braves as numerous as the buffalo on the plains, but man alone is not strong enough!'

With the eyes of his band upon him, the chief held the gaze of the wizened medicine man. 'We have called upon Anteep,' he reminded him. 'What more can we do?'

'Call again.' Old Eagle's voice was dry and thin, like autumn leaves. 'While you fought in the desert, I have performed a ceremony and spoken with the Evil One. I bring a message. Ignore it and you will fail!'

Tall Bull frowned deeply. It brought a bitter taste to his mouth to ask advice from the cunning old man. And yet, this shaman held the trust of all the tribe. 'Speak!' he grunted. 'Tell us what it is that Anteep would have us do!'

Still smiling, Old Eagle leaned towards the chief and whispered in his ear.

SEVEN

'I am Tall Bull, great chief of the Wild Dog Comanches!'

The warrior raised both arms to the empty sky. He had sought a lonely place, in the shadow of a tall rock, far from the scene of the last battle. He had built a fire on top of the rock and passed his hand three times through the flame.

'There will be no victory without pain!' Old Eagle had whispered this warning. 'The fire will show your resolve to speak with the spirits. It is a severe test which you must not fail!'

'I am not afraid.' Tall Bull had bowed his head. He had followed the ways of his tribe and told no one of this secret meeting with the spirits, merely saying that he must walk out to the rock, as Old Eagle had bidden him. 'There will be fire,' he had warned.

'But the Sioux enemy will see our smoke,' Wolf had protested. He knew that the battle was not yet won. One Horn and his Pawnee allies had merely withdrawn in order to regroup.

Tall Bull had defied the challenge. 'I have sent scouts

to fetch more Wild Dog warriors from the mountains and the plains. Soon all our men will be reunited here on this desert. Meanwhile I will follow the wisdom of Old Eagle.'

The shaman had pulled his woven blanket over his head to hide his lined features. *Tall Bull may be a mighty warrior*, he had thought; *tall as a tree, strong as a buffalo. But even he must bend to my will!*

And now the Wild Dog chief was reaching upwards with hands that had endured the flames. Smoke from the scented fire curled around him and rose high into the blue sky.

'Why does Tall Bull delay?' Three Bears asked.

Sun Dancer had spotted the spiral of smoke, and brought his fellow warriors to witness it. All except their chief, One Horn, who talked with their new Pawnee friends about the route which Four Winds must take to reach the furthest ocean.

'Why does he not move in quick pursuit of the boy and the horse?'

Sun Dancer and Little Thunder shook their heads uneasily. The young men had fought the battle in the desert with great fury and courage; they had been reluctant to withdraw and even now would prefer to sweep down from their ridge in a fresh attack.

Three Bears surveyed the empty desert basin. 'Perhaps the Wild Dogs await more warriors,' he guessed. He was wise in the ways of war.

'Then we should strike before they come!' Little Thunder declared. 'At all costs we must prevent the Wild Dogs from picking up Four Winds' trail.'

The three men's uneasiness grew as they stood and watched the distant smoke.

'Perhaps this is a trick.' Sun Dancer spoke for them all.

'The Wild Dogs are cunning. Maybe they built the fire to deceive us, making us believe that they have not moved off in pursuit of Four Winds.'

'Then we are fools!' Little Thunder cried. He strode off to speak with One Horn.

But Three Bears shook his head. 'We have not heard the Wild Dogs' horses move off to the north,' he reminded Sun Dancer. 'Besides, their hooves would have raised clouds of dust.'

The younger warrior frowned. 'Waiting is hard,' he sighed. He thought of Four Winds travelling alone, of the still unknown fate of the women and children they had abandoned on the mountain above the White Water homeland.

Three Bears gazed at Tall Bull's smoke. 'We must be wise,' he insisted. 'Come, we will build a funeral platform for Cochise. We will deck it with banners and feathers. The boy died bravely and deserves this tribute.'

* * *

Tall Bull had built the fire to call upon the spirits to gather.

'Oh, mighty Anteep, hear me! I accept the wisdom of Old Eagle, and I call in the name of Snake Eye, whose death must be avenged!'

The high sun dazzled him and beat down upon his bare head.

'I call out the names of your servants, great Anteep, for we know that without their help we will not succeed!'

The chief's voice grew higher as he stood legs apart, arms outstretched.

'Come, Kannuck, the great Wolf spirit, cousin of Iron Eyes. Come, Sisiutl, the double-headed serpent with your darting tongues!'

Tall Bull waited. He saw the smoke from his fire gather in a huge cloud over his head, blotting out the sky. It filled his lungs and stung his eyes until they watered.

Then, among the curling fumes, the first of Anteep's servants appeared. Kannuck showed himself; a creature in the shape of a wolf, only ten times the normal size. He hovered in the smoky air, yellow eyes gleaming. Sisiutl followed, a snake with two horned heads, hissing and spitting venom as he came.

Almost staggering from fear, Tall Bull nevertheless welcomed them. 'The power of Anteep is strong. What can you do for us, oh mighty Kannuck, in our journey towards revenge?'

'I can fly through the air, swifter than the speed of light,' the Wolf spirit replied. 'I lurk in the darkest forests, I tear my enemies limb from limb.'

'And great, two-headed serpent, who are you?' Enveloped in smoke, the Wild Dogs chief appealed to the more terrifying of the two visions.

The snake's tongues darted towards the man. 'I am Sisiutl, servant of Anteep. I can show a human face. I am greedy for flesh; my hunger is never satisfied.'

Tall Bull embraced his arrival. 'What else?' he asked eagerly.

The serpent decided to toy with the Comanche chief. 'Watch,' he said, descending to the rock and coiling himself around Tall Bull's feet.

The man recoiled in horror. Instinct made him take out his knife then stoop to hack at the scaly monster. But he felt his arm freeze in mid air and he saw his hand turn grey and dusty. His whole body fell motionless, so that try as he might, he could not take a step, and the cage of his paralysed ribs began to crush the air out of his body.

Sisiutl waited until he heard his victim begin to choke, then slowly uncoiled his body and slithered away. 'Thus I can turn a man to stone,' he hissed, 'or to white foam on the waves of the ocean!'

Struggling to regain his breath, Tall Bull acknowledged the serpent's power. 'I thank Anteep for sending you, but still Old Eagle bade me call on the most powerful servant of all!'

'It is as Anteep wishes,' Sisiutl and Kannuck conceded. They stood to one side and waited for Tall Bull to address the Lord of the Underworld.

'Great spirit!' he cried. 'The time for our revenge runs out, as sand trickles through the fingers. The boy, Four Winds, nears the end of his final journey, and still the forces of Wakanda protect him. Now I, Tall Bull, chief of the Wild Dogs, come to you. My band has sworn to serve you and to die in your cause. Is this not enough?'

As the smoke from the fire thickened, a strong wind rose. It swept the chief from his feet and hurled him against the pinnacle of rock, where he slumped to the ground.

'Know that you must not question Anteep!' Sisiutl hissed. 'It is in His time that the boy will be overthrown; not at a moment of your choosing!'

Raising himself, Tall Bull went on in a more humble manner. 'You are the source of all Evil and I beg forgiveness for my impatience. I stand now and await your command!'

Slowly, the wind eased. Time passed and the sun beat down. At last, the Comanche chief turned to the two spirits on the rock. 'What must I do?' he pleaded.

'Wait,' Kannuck said.

'Watch,' Sisiutl instructed.

* * *

Along the ridge, Tall Bull's warriors kept their eyes fixed on the rising smoke. They longed to know which water monsters, cannibals and giants would be sent to help them carry out their revenge.

'Perhaps Yietso will return,' Lightning Snake suggested.

But others said that a monster who had already been defeated by Silver Cloud would not be their choice.

'The boy heads for the ocean,' Night Raven pointed out. 'Our best hope lies with Waktcexi, who lives below the water, and will not let our enemy pass by.'

Meanwhile, they grew angry at Old Eagle for causing this delay.

'What need was there for Tall Bull to perform this ritual?' Red Wing demanded. 'The sun sinks in the west while the spirit horse carries the boy to his journey's end and we sit idle.'

'It is because the old man needs to rest,' Lightning Snake jeered. 'He does not have the taste for revenge that we, his brothers do.'

Old Eagle's mouth twisted with contempt. 'You know nothing of a shaman's ways,' he retorted. 'You think only of blood and the scalps that hang from your wampum belts!'

The sun set, casting an orange glow across the desert. Tall Bull's face was hidden in deep shadow. The two evil spirits faded so that only their eyes gleamed through the smoke. And only then did Anteep provide the answer.

As Tall Bull scowled into the dying fire, Wolf commanded him to seize an ember and hold it aloft as a torch in the dim light. 'Look to the west!' he cried.

The chief seized the charred end of a twisted branch. He felt dazed by the smoke and the long, lonely wait.

But gradually he was able to make out a change in the dusk sky. It seemed that clouds were rolling towards them, thick and heavy, hiding the sunset. Shadows deepened as the clouds advanced, like a dark blanket drawn across the landscape. And then the wind returned, and with it a crashing sound as of waves beating the shore.

Tall Bull heard it and cowered against the rock. As the sound engulfed him, the air grew bitterly cold. A wet mist surrounded him, settling on his warm skin like the touch of death's hand. Then, with the ever-increasing roar of water, a shape began to materialise out of the clouds, towering over the man so that he sank to his knees with the flaming branch still held aloft.

The huge creature grew clearer in the glow of the torch. Its bulk was dark and massive, its eyes small, its snout black. Tall Bull shuddered.

But when the beast shaped like a bear opened its jaws to reveal long teeth that could rip into flesh, he turned away in terror, ready to flee. Then Sisiutl and Wolf stood in his path and made him stay.

'You have got your wish!' the snake spirit hissed. 'Anteep has sent you the most feared of his spirits!'

'But beware!' Kannuck warned. 'The Great Spirit has awoken his dread servant from kutenai, the long sleep of winter. He has called upon him to serve you against his will. Know then that you must not anger him, for he will kill with a look, such is his power!'

Tall Bull trembled and bowed before the mighty spirit.

The creature threw back its head and snarled. It stank of its winter den, its black fur matted, its claws shining cruelly in the torchlight. Above the roar of the wind and the crash of the waves, it spoke to the Comanche warrior.

'I am Bad Heart, leader among the spirits of Anteep! My powers cannot be defeated by any man, nor by the strongest of Wakanda's servants. Since the world began I have ruled the western shore!'

The Wild Dog chief threw himself down upon the rock in front of the Bear spirit. 'I will serve you!' he vowed. 'I will praise Anteep!'

'You must do more than this,' Bad Heart said. His voice was low as thunder.

'What then?' Tall Bull asked eagerly, craning his neck to see the spirit while he remained face-down on the ground.

Bad Heart towered over him. 'Anteep demands your life for this,' he growled.

Tall Bull caught his breath. 'When must I die?' he asked. 'Now, or after the boy is defeated?'

'Who can tell?' Bad Heart told him. 'But you must swear now to sacrifice yourself for this cause!'

For a moment Tall Bull rested his face against the hard rock, then he raised himself to his feet. He raised his head proudly. 'Anteep is a stern master!'

'This is the price of the Wild Dogs' revenge.' Bad Heart's hot breath filled the air. 'Ask your medicine man, Old Eagle, for Anteep spoke with him when the sun was high. He was the one who made this bargain!'

And no doubt the wily shaman thought that the life of their new chief was a small price to pay, Tall Bull thought bitterly. No wonder too that Old Eagle had whispered his instructions with a cold smile.

'Well?' Sisiutl demanded. 'What is Tall Bull's answer?'

There was a long silence. Anger and fear flitted across Tall Bull's stern face. 'I will die when I see the body of the boy,' the chief agreed.

Bad Heart stared at him, looking deep into his soul. 'Then I will wait for you by the ocean,' he said. 'Do not waste time, for the boy and the horse have travelled far.'

Then the sound of the waves faded and the wind died, leaving Tall Bull alone by the pinnacle of rock.

BEYOND LIFE-SIDE

EIGHT

Four Winds had left his friends far behind. He rode his spirit horse through the night, with only the owl in the sky and coyotes in the bush for company. But he could unfurl the map which Northern Fox had given him, and read his course by the stars.

'How far must we travel before we reach the ocean?' he asked Silver Cloud.

The horse galloped swiftly by the side of a stream which glinted silver in the moonlight. He swerved around boulders and ran through the shallow waters. 'The world is bigger than you know,' was his reply.

And Four Winds had to be content. They rode hard until the sky grew light and a fresh challenge faced them.

The boy had become used to passing through green valleys and over gently sloping hills. Their progress had been smooth, with no sign of pursuit by Tall Bull and his band.

But as the grey light of dawn revealed the way ahead,

Four Winds saw that the gentle landscape was ending and that they must cross another empty desert.

His heart sank. 'Is there no way around?' he sighed, surveying the flat, featureless landscape. But he knew from Silver Cloud's silence that they must take the straight course.

'Drink,' his guide ordered him, when they approached the last stream. The horse himself lowered his head and took his fill.

So Four Winds dismounted and took up cool water in his cupped hands. As he stooped beside the horse, he saw his own image reflected in the smooth surface; his face pale and determined in the morning light, his braided hair swinging free of his hunched shoulders. It was his own face, he knew, yet there was something in the image that disturbed him; a tenseness in his smooth jawline, the shadow of fear present in his dark eyes.

'I am older and more weary,' he muttered. 'My friend, Cochise, died for me.' Then he dipped his hand into the water to break the reflection into a hundred small ripples.

The desert was hotter than anything Four Winds had so far experienced. The sun blazed down, turning the ground to powdery dust, draining every last drop of moisture from the red earth.

By midday, though he conserved his energy by riding Silver Cloud safely and steadily, the boy was exhausted.

'We must find water,' he insisted. 'Did you tell me that the Miwok tribe must dig deep beneath the desert earth to find it?'

'Yes, but they have a wisdom about this land that we lack,' Silver Cloud pointed out. 'Perhaps we might dig up the whole desert as far as we can see, and still fail.'

'Then we need the help of these people,' Four Winds decided. 'Did you not also tell me that they watch us as we cross their homeland?'

'There is always a scout,' the horse agreed.

The boy straightened his slumped body and stared around. 'How can we call him?'

'We cannot. He will come when he is ready.'

'Does he know that I am faint from thirst?' the boy sighed.

'He watches,' Silver Cloud insisted. 'He will choose his time.'

Four Winds raised his hand to shade his eyes. A heat haze shimmered on the western horizon. Above, the sky was an intense, clear blue. He gazed north, east and then south. 'Do you hear any sound?' he asked.

'I hear the wings of the eagle beating the air. That is all.'

Once more Four Winds turned to the west and this time he spotted the huge bird flying towards them. The sight raised his weary spirits; Eagle was lord of the air, a watchful spirit, loyal to Wakanda. 'Soon all will be well,' he murmured, imagining the moment when once more he would dip his hands into cool water and raise it to his cracked lips.

So he wasn't surprised when soon after a solitary man on horseback appeared in the west.

'Here is a Miwok brave come to guide us to water!' he declared, steering Silver Cloud to meet him.

From above, Eagle soared over the vast, baking expanse of desert, watching the two riders draw closer together.

Four Winds' eagerness increased. Had not Silver Cloud told him that the Miwok were peaceful people? And here was the proof; a warrior dressed in strange clothes and carrying no weapon. He was a small man wearing a tall, colourful headdress, with many long strings of beads around his neck. His torso was bare and painted white, with a zig-zag pattern across his chest. Nearer still, the boy saw that the stranger was smiling broadly and that his small eyes were mere wrinkled slits after many years of living in the blazing heat.

'I am Kuksu of the Tolowa band of the great Miwok tribe!' he announced. 'And you are Four Winds; grandson of Red Hawk, famed warrior chief of the White Water Sioux!'

Four Winds bowed his head. 'Did Northern Fox's scout bring this news to you?'

'As you say, Northern Fox,' Kuksu agreed. He unslung the leather water-carrier from his saddle and offered it to Four Winds. 'Drink,' he invited.

Quickly Four Winds tilted the bottle and swallowed. He felt the cool water refresh his mouth and travel down his throat. 'I thank Kuksu!' he gasped.

The stranger smiled. 'Give water to your horse,' he suggested.

But when Four Winds dismounted, Silver Cloud turned his head away. So the boy drank again, then handed the container back. 'Have you ridden far from your village?'

'Half a day,' Kuksu said. 'Our scout to the south sent a message. His news was that a boy and a horse were riding west into the desert. It is a desolate place. Many strangers die here. My chief, Helin, sent me to meet you with water and an offer of shelter and rest.'

The Miwok's horse pranced sideways as his rider spoke. It was brown and white, sturdily built, with a white mane and pale eyes. It seemed impatient with Kuksu, shaking its bridle and edging away from Four Winds and Silver Cloud.

'Where is shelter from the sun?' Four Winds asked. It seemed to him that there could be no shade for many hours.

'If you know the desert as we, the Miwok, know it, then there are places to rest from the midday sun,' Kuksu informed him. 'Though your journey is no doubt important, I would advise you to seek such a refuge.'

Four Winds received the words gladly. They made sense, knowing that the Comanches who must by now be in pursuit would also need rest when the sun reached its height. 'I am travelling to the ocean,' he confided to Kuksu. 'The great Wakanda guides me in the shape of this, my spirit horse.'

'Then you will not fail,' Kuksu said. 'For the power of Wakanda is strong.'

'He has carried me through two journeys,' Four Winds said proudly. 'My grandfather chose me as the one he loved the most. Now old age has taken him beyond life-side, and all the hopes of my people rest with me on my final quest.'

Kuksu listened attentively. 'Come,' he said. 'Follow me.'

So Four Winds took his wise advice.

'I carry many years on my shoulders,' Kuksu went on, turning his horse and riding slowly north. 'And yet I do not have a grandson to share my stories with. Red Hawk was fortunate.'

Four Winds smiled at memories of his grandfather.

'Stay out of that cave,' Red Hawk would warn when he took the boy to hunt deer. 'If you go in, Uwulin will get you!' And Four Winds would rush home to his grandmother's tipi and ask her to describe the monster of the cave.

'Long ago, the bird and the animal people lived well,' White Deer would say. 'But then came Uwulin, a great giant from the north who began to eat people. He was as big as a pine tree, and his hands could hold ten men at a time.'

Then Four Winds would cry out and cover his ears. From that time he would never go near the cave his grandfather had warned him about.

He smiled now at his innocence, and then felt sad because it had gone forever. He rode beside Kuksu, noting the tall headdress decorated with many tiny woodpecker scalps and the heavy necklace made from beads and deer hooves. The old man's arms were scrawny, but his belly was round from plentiful food. 'Tell me your stories,' Four Winds invited.

'There are stories in the stones we tread upon and the sky above our heads,' Kuksu said. 'See the eagle. He is the messenger spirit who takes your wishes to Wakanda.'

'Eagle guides me away from danger,' Four Winds replied. 'He saved me on Mount Kivioq.'

'And the bear who lives in the mountains by the western shore; he is inhabited by the dead spirits of wicked shamans. His heart is bad. He digs a cave on a lonely summit where he lays in wait for travellers.'

'I will take care not to pass by his cave,' Four Winds assured the old man, warming to him as they talked. *Wakanda is good to send me such friends*, he thought.

But soon the heat of the sun began to drain him once more. He could not tell how far they had come, nor whether they strayed from the course he must eventually take. He felt dazed, as if his body scarcely belonged to him.

'Soon we will reach my village,' Kuksu promised. 'My people live in domed houses covered with dry grass. You do not see them until you come upon them, but they are there.'

'The desert offers a hard life,' the boy muttered, wishing that his head would clear. The horizon seemed to shimmer and shift, making him dizzy. And he sensed that Silver Cloud was walking unwillingly alongside the brown-and-white horse, perhaps because he too was achingly thirsty and exhausted.

'It is the life that we have been given,' Kuksu remarked. 'Come, my village is a few hundred paces east from here. Soon you will rest.'

Four Winds studied the desert, but saw no domed houses. Instead, the land seemed to blur and rise up towards him, so that he swayed to try and keep his balance, but instead slipped from Silver Cloud's back. As he landed, his legs buckled and he dropped forward on all fours.

Kuksu dismounted slowly and stooped to check the boy. He didn't touch him, but let him recover enough to raise himself to his feet. 'You can ride no further,' he said. 'Rest here. Sit, take off your shirt and cover your head. I will lead your horse to water and soon return for you.'

Four Winds nodded. He tried to lick his lips, but there was no moisture in his mouth. 'Go with Kuksu!'

he gasped at Silver Cloud. 'Let the Miwok take care of you.'

'I will stay,' Silver Cloud argued. 'Remember that Red Hawk told you always to keep me at your side.'

'But my grandfather did not know that we would crave water in the desert.' Four Winds wished that his words would come more easily. His throat rasped and burned. 'You must take the chance and drink!'

'And follow behind a stranger to a village we cannot see?' Silver Cloud retorted.

Kuksu watched and waited. 'Will the horse come?' he inquired.

'He will not follow,' the boy explained. 'He is too proud.'

'Then I will lead him,' Kuksu decided, taking a rope and going forward to slip a noose around Silver Cloud's neck.

Four Winds only dimly made out what was happening. He saw the old man approach the spirit horse more nimbly than he had expected, seizing his chance to slide the lasso over Silver Cloud's head and pull the noose tight. Silver Cloud pulled away, but Kuksu held on with surprising strength. So the horse reared in anger and struck out with his hooves.

Then, as if out of nowhere, Kuksu was wielding a knife, raising it against Silver Cloud and lunging forward with stabbing movements.

Four Winds cried out. 'Stop! The horse is the messenger of Wakanda. Do not strike him!'

'He resists me!' Kuksu called back. The old man's painted body twisted and turned in his struggle to overcome Silver Cloud.

The boy gathered his strength. Shakily he stood up, but could manage only two or three steps before he collapsed once more. He saw the blade flash in the blinding light, saw Silver Cloud finally pull free.

'This is no old man of the Miwok tribe!' the horse declared. 'His strength is that of ten men!'

And now Kuksu shed the robes and headdress. He was changing shape and colour, his limbs dissolving, his long body writhing.

Four Winds shuddered. He crawled for the knife which had dropped to the ground.

'Fool, I have led you deeper into the desert!' the shape-shifting monster said to Four Winds. 'I planned to abandon you here. But your horse is wiser than you are!'

Four Winds watched in horror as the monster took the form of a two-headed snake. Its tongues flickered towards him as it spat out its words.

The boy's hand closed over the knife, but he had no strength to stand and fight. Meanwhile, Silver Cloud reared up, then struck out at the enemy. His hooves came down within inches of the serpent's slithering form.

'I am Sisiutl, servant of Bad Heart!' he hissed as he twisted clear. 'You will die of thirst here under the burning sun, and I will rejoice in your death!'

Four Winds groaned and fell forward. He had been too quick to trust the stranger on the horse. And yet Eagle had soared overhead and Four Winds had taken this as a good sign. Nor had Silver Cloud warned him of the danger.

'You are no match for your enemies!' Sisiutl mocked, raising himself to his full height. His body shone green and golden; the slits of his black eyes glittered. 'Now that Tall Bull has sworn to forfeit his life to defeat you, there is no hope for you!'

Silver Cloud reared again to strike the serpent. Once more the snake twisted clear.

'Your journey ends here in this desolate place!' Sisiutl jeered. 'Even though your spirit horse would not abandon you, he lacks the strength and the time to carry you to safety. The sun bakes the earth. There is no escape.'

Dazed and confused, Four Winds collapsed forward. He cursed himself and his lack of wisdom.

'I will take this news to my master,' Sisiutl declared. 'I will say that the boy fell easily for my trick, and that his spirit guide did not help him. Now he is meat for the vultures, and his People must give up hope.' These were the monster's final words, for, as Silver Cloud attacked again, Sisiutl turned away. He dazzled them with his shining scales, rising from the ground and hovering in the air. Then quickly he disappeared, leaving behind only his discarded robes and the knife in Four Winds' trembling hand.

NINE

Four Winds closed his eyes but he could not cut out the glare of the sun. It pricked his eyelids and made the darkness inside his head swim with darting orange sparks.

I will die now, in the heat of the desert, he thought. *And all the battles I have won and the struggles I have gone through will have been in vain.*

Silver Cloud came and stood over him, giving him shade. 'Do not despair,' he said quietly.

'I need water!' the boy gasped. Then, 'Did you know that Kuksu was not who he seemed?'

'There was doubt in my mind,' the dream horse confessed. 'Though the old man was generous in his actions, and he talked as a member of the Miwok tribe would talk, there was one thing wrong. Think of what I told you as we entered the desert.'

'That the Miwoks were peaceful people and that they were watching us as we passed through their homeland,' Four Winds recalled.

'And what else?' Silver Cloud prompted.

'That they do not have horses!' Four Winds remembered in a flash. And yet Kuksu had appeared on horseback on the shimmering horizon. 'You suspected, yet you let me trust him!' he said bitterly.

Silver Cloud stayed silent, taking the full force of the sun's rays to protect the boy.

Then Four Winds was sorry. 'It was my mistake. Many times you have warned me not to rush into trusting strangers. Beside the swollen river near the village in the rock, I have seen the helpless girl, Gilspa, change shape before my eyes. And Anteep has fooled me on Mount Kivioq by sending Stone Man to send me hurtling down the icy slopes. And yet still I let the evil spirits lead me into danger.'

'These are the cunning ways of Anteep,' Silver Cloud said. 'You need a clear head to see evil in what appears good, and your body cried out for water. You saw only Kuksu's leather bottle, heard only his promise of shelter.'

Revived a little by the shade provided by his horse's body, Four Winds gazed out at the flat expanse of stone and sand. 'The monster mocks me and says I must die. But while there is breath in my body, I will not give in!' he declared. This was the moment Silver Cloud had been waiting for.

'If you have the strength, climb on my back,' he said. 'Though the desert is vast, it is not endless, and the real Miwok people may still come to the rescue.'

Try as he might, though, the boy could not raise

himself. So he unslung and unrolled his medicine bundle and spread out its contents, picking out herbs to restore a little of his strength. First a sweet leaf to chew which would clear his dazed thoughts, then a bitter powder ground from roots by his grandmother, White Deer. This would bring back energy to his weak limbs. He swallowed the medicine, rolled up his bundle and waited.

Soon Four Winds felt the power of the herbs surge through his body. He sat and gave thanks to White Deer for her skill in preparing the medicines, then he stood and slowly eased himself on to Silver Cloud's back. 'With you to guide me, I will not give in!' he declared.

'And now at last I can call upon the spirits,' Silver Cloud sighed. 'A lesson learned the hard way is remembered for a whole lifetime, and I do not think that in times to come you will place your trust unwisely.'

'Yes, call the spirits,' Four Winds pleaded.

So the spirit horse summoned the kachinas of the air to bring clouds into the cruel blue sky.

'Come, spirits who have the wellbeing of the boy, Four Winds, at heart! Oh, bringers of rain, come!'

Riding slowly in the intense heat, Four Winds stared anxiously at the sky. At first it seemed that Silver Cloud's appeal had failed, for no cloud appeared on the horizon. But then the boy thought that he saw a white haze begin to form, and soon the haze thickened and rose to weaken the glare of the sun.

'Welcome!' Four Winds murmured.

The white clouds rolled towards them on a light breeze. They shaded the dry desert land, deadening the garish colour, bringing coolness.

And the boy turned his face to the heavens, waiting for the first drops of moisture. He felt the wind, the gentle motion of Silver Cloud. There was a cold splash on his cheek, followed by another. He tasted rain.

Tall Bull had gathered his Wild Dogs from the plains and the mountains. They were thirty strong; a force equal to the Pawnees and the remnants of the White Water tribe who kept a close watch.

'One Horn and his allies will be our shadows on this journey,' Tall Bull warned. 'They will follow where we go.'

'Then let us fight once more, and this time we will add their scalps to our belts!' a young brave named Black Buffalo cried.

But his chief held up his hand to silence him. 'We must go forward and pick up the boy's trail. Let One Horn watch and wait, like the mountain lion stalking his prey. Let him pounce; then we will stand and fight!'

The firm authority in his voice silenced Black Buffalo.

Old Eagle stood to one side, pleased with the bargain he had made on the Comanches' behalf. The shaman had no liking for the new chief; he had preferred Snake

Eye, who had been lean and cunning, like Old Eagle himself. Tall Bull relied instead on brute strength and willpower. So it had amused Old Eagle to talk with the spirits and barter his new chief's life for success against the White Water Sioux.

'Anteep will demand a high price!' Tlenamaw had warned. He had come to Old Eagle in the shape of a dragon, breathing fire; foremost among the Evil One's messengers.

'Name it!' Old Eagle had replied.

'Nothing less than your death.' The monstrous dragon had laughed as he named the cost.

Old Eagle had scarcely paused to let the news sink in. 'Did Anteep name me as the sacrifice?'

'He wants the life of the most evil member of your band,' Tlenamaw had replied. 'One who lies and cheats and is without respect or courage.'

Old Eagle had bowed his head to conceal a mocking smile. 'But I am not the most evil,' he had argued. 'Anteep needs the life of one who trusts no one, who leaps to violence, and bends other men to his cruel will!'

'Who then?' Tlenamaw had asked.

Old Eagle had paused to weigh his reply. 'It is Tall Bull, our chief. His hands are red with spilt blood. His soul is already pledged to Anteep.'

'Send him to the rock!' the dragon had commanded. 'Let Anteep judge for himself.'

And now every Wild Dog there knew that their shaman had sent their chief to visit the rock and that Tall Bull had offered his life to their cause. Awestruck, they were ready to follow his command.

So they prepared their horses with fresh war paint and feathers, then set off in a tight group, galloping behind Tall Bull out of the green valley into the arid desert.

Far out to sea, the waves swelled. Soundlessly they rose and fell, approaching the rocky shore. Seabirds soared overhead, calling out with sharp, piercing cries. The mighty waves tossed driftwood back and forth, sucking at the stony seabed, throwing themselves at the black cliffs lining the coast. A weak sunlight reflected from the water, picking out the crests of the swelling waves.

Then the water hit the shore. It smashed against the land, first furling into banks of white foam, rolling and breaking, racing and frothing, running between rocks down deep chasms, then pulling back and relentlessly rising again.

Sisiutl rested on a clifftop, staring down at the ocean. Nothing on land was as powerful as the sea, which continued for ever and had no end. The monstrous serpent saw the might of the waves and recoiled.

Slithering away, he went along the cliff in search of Kannuck.

'What news do you bring?' the spirit demanded,

standing guard before a great, dark den that overlooked the vast ocean. The giant wolf's hackles stood out thickly on his neck; his yellow eyes glared.

'My news is for the ears of Bad Heart only,' Sisiutl replied proudly. 'I come from the desert especially to speak with him.'

'He sleeps,' Kannuck warned. His role was to guard the great bear spirit and take messages to him in his den. 'It is better to tell me what Bad Heart should know!'

Sisiutl hissed and rose up, his eyes sparking with anger. 'Let me past. I am here myself and will have no one speak for me!'

As the argument between the two evil spirits flared, there was movement from inside the den. Quiet and slow at first, the noise soon grew louder: the sound of a beast shifting, twigs snapping under his great weight, an animal beginning to emerge.

Sisiutl and Kannuck fell silent and waited.

Bad Heart's den was hidden inside a vast cave where sunlight never penetrated. It was lined with brushwood and dried grasses, its entrance blocked by sturdy branches.

'You have woken him from a deep sleep,' Kannuck warned Sisiutl. 'Beware his anger!'

'He will not be angered by the news I bring!' the snake boasted. But in his heart, he was afraid.

Wolf slunk silently to one side as the chief servant of

Anteep emerged. Bad Heart breathed heavily as he made his way out of the cave. He brushed aside dead wood, advancing on all fours towards the light.

'Who disturbs my sleep?' he snarled, raising himself on to his hind legs as the weak sun greeted him. 'Where is Kannuck? Who dares to wake me?'

'It is I, Sisiutl!' the snake spirit announced. He held his ground, though Bad Heart's massive form filled him with terror.

The bear curled back his lip and showed his teeth. 'What news?' he demanded.

'The boy, Four Winds, is dead!' Sisiutl said.

Bad Heart came closer to the serpent. 'How did he die?'

'Of thirst. I deceived him and led him deep into the desert.'

Bad Heart listened closely. 'What of the spirit horse?'

'He was present, but did nothing to help the boy.'

'Did you kill Silver Cloud and send him back to Wakanda?' As Bad Heart probed more deeply, he saw that Sisiutl's answers were weak and suspect.

'I did not need to overcome the horse. The boy hovered on the brink of death. No magic could save him.'

Then Kannuck crept forward. He spoke low and urgently into Bad Heart's ear.

The bear turned on Sisiutl. 'Kannuck has spoken with Raven,' he snarled. 'Raven flies faster than the wind. He came from the desert especially to talk with us.'

The snake spirit tried to writhe away from Bad Heart, but Kannuck blocked his path.

'Four Winds was alive when you left him?' Bad Heart asked.

'Barely,' Sisiutl answered. The chill of the waves crashing on to the rocks below reached him and made him tremble. 'It was a slow death. He could not fight, or even stand.'

'You are a fool!' Bad Heart's anger exploded from him. He swiped at Sisiutl with his massive claws. 'Raven spoke of clouds in the desert. Rain fell and watered the land where the boy and the horse rested. They did not die!'

Kannuck fell back again as Bad Heart advanced on the serpent. He prowled in a wide circle, watching Sisiutl's every move.

'You are a proud and boastful spirit!' Bad Heart snarled. 'And pride has made you blind to Silver Cloud's power. It was an easy matter for him to call upon the kachinas and bring rain.' He forced the snake back towards the edge of the cliff.

'I will return to the desert!' Sisiutl promised as fear gripped him. 'This time I will not fail!'

'You will not fail because you will not return,' Bad Heart said in a cold voice. 'Though you have the cunning of your kind, though you can shape-shift and deceive, still you cannot outwit your enemy.'

Bad Heart's scorn cut deep and the snake cowered low on the ground.

'There is no place for followers such as you,' Bad Heart went on. 'I have many who would serve me.' With this he called out the name of Matotope.

Kannuck lurked by the entrance to the den, while Sisiutl was humbled.

A spirit in the shape of a man strode along the cliff. His shoulders were broad and his face was bitter.

'Matotope, I have brought you from beyond life-side to serve me!' Bad Heart declared.

The spirit held aloft his war shield and spear. 'I greet you in the name of Anteep!'

'Give me a reason to hate the boy, Four Winds, and his spirit horse, Silver Cloud!' Bad Heart demanded. He towered above his fellow spirits.

Matotope's face darkened with anger. 'When I was life-side I was shaman to the White Water People. But Red Hawk cast me out of my village and left me alone on the mountain, where wolves roamed.'

'Because you betrayed him with false wisdom!' Bad Heart mocked. 'Your only concern was to remain as medicine man, even though your powers had long deserted you.'

Matotope scowled. 'Bad Heart is wisest of all Anteep's spirits,' he muttered. 'True, I lied and deceived, but all the more reason to hate the White Water band and pledge my support to Snake Eye and his Wild Dogs.'

'A traitor,' Bad Heart sneered. 'A man in whom no one could place his trust!'

The evil shaman held his head high. He wore a band around his head decked with three eagle feathers. His narrow face had hawk-like features. 'Did Bad Heart bring me back from death-side merely to mock?' he demanded.

'I brought you here because hate is lodged in your heart. You will not be careless. You will be cunning and greedy in your revenge; a fit servant to stand in the place of Sisiutl!'

Matotope bowed his head in acknowledgement.

Then Bad Heart turned to the snake. 'You will return to death-side, but it will not be an easy journey,' he warned.

Sisiutl lay on his belly, unable to escape the wrath of his master. 'Send me back, but do not make me suffer!' he begged. The bright green and gold of his once splendid scales had faded to brown.

'No longer so proud!' Wolf sneered.

Bad Heart was deaf to Sisiutl's pleas. His savage spirit had no room for mercy. He seized the serpent, his bear's claws cutting deep into Sisiutl's soft flesh, as he writhed helplessly in his grasp. Still raised on his hind legs, Bad Heart strode to the edge of the cliff and glanced down at the white foam swirling around the sharp rocks.

The snake felt a violent wind tear at him as his life force drained in Bad Heart's grasp. Pain tore at his body.

Then he was falling, released from the sharp claws, but wheeling and dropping through the cold air, as if for ever, until at last he hit the icy water and sank out of sight.

Then Bad Heart raised his massive head and howled at the sky. He looked down on the restless waves without compassion for Sisiutl, who must now struggle from the bed of the ocean on a long, dark journey to regain his place beside Anteep.

Then the all-powerful beast turned back to Kannuck and Matotope. 'The boy leaves the desert, carried towards the ocean by his spirit horse.'

'We are ready!' they swore.

'He seeks a breath of air to take back to his tribe.'

'We are ready!' they said again.

Bad Heart looked east, beyond the hazy sun, as if searching the sky. 'Then let him come!' he cried.

TEN

For White Deer it was the worst of times. Her husband was dead, her tipi burned, and she must hide with the women in the snowbound mountains.

And yet she held Red Hawk's spirit song in her heart. The White Water People were great warriors; the future would bring hope and glory once more.

'Mother, there are women from the Morning Star tribe waiting by the tipis,' Shining Star reported.

White Deer sat on a blanket inside a cave. She had lost count of the days.

'They have brought food,' Shining Star said gently. 'Their chief, Northern Fox, who is ally to Four Winds, has sent them.'

'What of the Wild Dogs?' White Deer asked.

'Gone,' her daughter by marriage answered. She knew more; that the Comanches had given up their search of the forest only to ride off and join Tall Bull in pursuit of Four Winds. But the young woman did not wish to add to the old woman's woes. 'Come,' she said. 'The children will eat at last. We can leave these caves.'

They emerged into a weak sun which scarcely filtered through the thick pine branches. Burning Tree met them and helped lead White Deer down the mountainside.

A tall Pawnee woman greeted them by the burned village.

She embraced White Deer. 'I am Silver Moon, wife of Northern Fox. Your women are sisters to the Pawnees, we love your children as our own.'

The old woman wept tears of gratitude. 'We are all within the Circle of the great Wakanda,' she sighed. Then she took a little food and drink.

'The Wild Dogs have driven you to a desolate place,' Silver Moon said, gesturing towards the charred poles of the burned tipis. A northern wind tore at the tatters of the skins which had once formed the walls.

'We have seen much suffering,' White Deer agreed, her slight shoulders stooped now, her limbs stiff and aching. 'Such is life.'

Then the Pawnee women wrapped her in warm deerskin blankets while Burning Tree and Shining Star ate the food which the children and the other women had left. After this, several of their new friends, following White Deer's wishes, carried the shrouded body of Red Hawk down from the funeral platform, into the valley which had been his homeland. They buried him there, and chanted songs which set his soul free to return to Wakanda.

'We laid him in that beautiful valley of winding waters,' they told the grieving wife.

'He loved that land more than all the rest of the world,' White Deer sighed. 'The White Water land is the land of his fathers, and a man who would not love his father's grave is worse than a wild animal.'

That night, in the village of the Morning Star band, the White Water women gathered around a fire.

'Our children sleep, they are safe,' they murmured, grateful that the Pawnee women had brought them here.

'Except for Cochise,' Burning Tree sighed. News had come via the Pawnee scouts of the boy's death in battle.

'And my grandson, Four Winds, who is no longer a child.' White Deer stared into the embers. She pictured him as a boy of one summer, cradled in his mother's arms. Then when he was old enough to listen to her stories of how the world began; a child full of questions and laughter.

Tears ran down her wrinkled face, as ice melts during a thaw.

'Let the tears flow,' a voice said.

White Deer knew her dead husband was present by the fire. She closed her eyes to hear him speak.

'Sorrow invites peace along with it,' Red Hawk reminded her. 'As surely as the sun rises in the east after the dark night of the spirit.'

'I know this, my husband,' she murmured.

The women who sat with her remained silent.

'Tears heal the wounds,' the old chief said, 'as long as you keep hope in your heart.'

The beloved voice calmed White Deer. 'It is as you say; we must not give up hope, and while you watch over us, we are strong.'

Then Shining Star leaned across and touched White Deer's hand. 'Ask Red Hawk what he knows of Four Wind's journey,' she begged.

'Do you see our grandson on his quest to the ocean?'

'He continues,' Red Hawk said. 'The way is hard, there are dangers still to come.'

The women around the fire sighed. 'He is one boy against the Comanches. It is beyond our belief that he can succeed.'

The ghostly voice grew stronger. 'The strength of all our people lives within the boy,' he reminded them. 'All our warriors who have gone before, through the generations, join to give Four Winds the courage he needs. Do not forget the sacrifices of Swift Elk, my son, of Running Fox and Black Kettle, and many before them.'

The sighing women fell silent.

'We do not forget,' Shining Star said. 'Is Four Winds prepared for the dangers still to come?'

Then the spirit of Red Hawk drew the fearful woman apart from the others. 'Your son makes mistakes. He is not wary of strangers.'

Shining Star sprang to Four Winds' defence. 'It is a good fault! The fault of those who are pure and still close to childhood.'

'It is hard for Silver Cloud to watch him follow the wrong path,' Red Hawk continued. 'But the spirit guide must wait for Kola to learn wisdom and earn the right to be truly called warrior.'

Shining Star wrung her hands. 'May Wakanda protect my son!' she cried.

The dead chief took pity. 'Listen. When the wind is cold, and all we have are faded memories and great gaunt vistas before our eyes, that is when we must remember that we were put here by the creator, that we did not come here except by his wish. We love our homeland because we were born there, and until we return, the Circle of life is not complete.

'Your son, Four Winds, understands that he is not one boy against the forces of Tall Bull and Anteep, but one small part of our nation's journey back to that homeland. He looks out across the desert in hope. Even now he approaches the mountains and the ocean beyond.'

Shining Star accepted the wise words. She sat once more beside White Deer and looked eagerly towards the western horizon.

Four Winds and Silver Cloud came out of the desert into the foothills of the western mountains. The boy had not slept or rested for many hours, certain that the Wild Dogs would have regrouped after the battle and must by now be close on his trail. However, he knew also that One Horn and his new allies would hinder the enemy whenever they could.

Despite his exhaustion, Four Winds rode hard. He was one with the horse, settled into Silver Cloud's smooth rhythm and finding a perfect harmony with the graceful creature. Boy and horse in a vast, empty landscape, galloping towards the ocean.

'This is beautiful country,' Four Winds said.

All around, young trees grew fresh and strong, their silver bark bearing black markings, their delicate bare branches reaching towards a pale, clear sky. And there were many animal tracks leading down to small streams, and sometimes the deer themselves drinking there.

The scene was so peaceful that Four Winds found it easy to forget that danger might lie hidden on the way ahead. Yet he kept himself alert, for he had learned that what seemed innocent could hide great harm.

So he kept a watchful eye on the fox that bolted from his den across their path, and on the small lizards basking on sunny rocks, and the blue jays calling from the branches.

'There is a lake ahead.' Silver Cloud slowed to a trot. 'The easier path lies to the south, but the most direct way is by the northern shore.'

Soon Four Winds could see the stretch of calm water

in the valley below. 'We will ride to the north,' he decided when he saw three long, narrow boats moored on the southern side. A meeting with strangers would hold them up, and besides they might be enemies in disguise.

So Silver Cloud took him along the rocky shoreline, splashing through shallows and trotting across pebbles rounded and smoothed by the water's gentle action. The surface of the lake sparkled. All seemed well.

But as the horse and rider came to an indent in the shore, two boats emerged from the tall reeds. Each boat carried three men with braided hair and doeskin shirts. They paddled with flat, broad oars crafted out of wood and the boats were made from strips of beautiful silver bark from the trees which Four Winds had seen growing nearby.

Startled, Silver Cloud rose up. He backed away on two legs, making Four Winds tilt forward to keep his balance. The six men rowed on, cutting swiftly across the smooth water. They called out a warning in their own language to the young stranger. One man pointed to the suddenly darkening sky.

'What is happening?' Four Winds called back. He felt Silver Cloud plunge down on to all four feet, then stagger on the stony ground. 'What is the matter?' he said again to the horse as the men rowed on without replying.

'They are afraid,' Silver Cloud answered.

'Of us?' The boy could not believe that six men would flee from one rider.

'No. Look at the sun.'

Four Winds raised his gaze to the dull sky, expecting to see clouds and a gathering storm. Instead, hemet with a puzzling sight. The sky was clear, but the sun was weakening in strength, its dazzling disc diminishing.

The sun, the life-giver, was disappearing in the middle of the day!

Fear seized Four Winds. How could the sun depart from the world? For a moment he wanted to run and hide, as a child would run to its mother's skirts.

And all around, as daylight faded, the animals grew alarmed. Birds left the sky and took refuge in their nests, grazing deer huddled miserably together, while wolves, coyotes and other creatures of the night prowled from their lairs to howl at the vanishing sun.

'Is this how the world ends?' Four Winds cried. He had never seen or heard of such a thing. 'Is Wakanda angry, or has Anteep vanquished him?'

'This is certainly the work of Anteep,' Silver Cloud replied.

Darkness seemed to swallow the last rays of the golden sun, which existed now only as a sliver of light against the black sky. One point on the crescent shone like a diamond, growing dimmer, and then eclipsing completely.

'Wakanda save us!' Four Winds pleaded, slipping to

the ground and falling to his knees. He lifted both arms to implore the sun to return. In the black sky, owls hooted and from the forests the wolves bayed on. Silver Cloud was a ghostly figure at his side.

'Sun and moon are eclipsed,' the spirit horse said. 'The heavens yawn open to unleash evil on the world!'

The boy groped in the pitch blackness. 'Is our quest ended?' he gasped. What worth was there now in attempting to save the lives of the small White Water band, when all life on earth was extinguished?

For how could plants grow to nourish Wakanda's creatures without the sun? And without grass on the great plains to sustain the buffalo, how could His people build tipis or find meat to eat?

How could men live in perpetual night?

'While we have strength we go on!' Silver Cloud insisted. 'What would you do; lie down and die?'

In his terror, Four Winds backed into a boulder, fell and crashed into a bush. He sent small creatures rushing noisily into the open blackness. Further away, the men in the boats ceased their frantic rowing and cried out to their own spirit guides.

Fear was everywhere, like a cloak that suffocated the world.

'Wakanda, send the stars into the sky!' Four Winds pleaded. 'In the name of my dead father, Swift Elk, and my grandfather, Red Hawk, bring us light!'

And at his call, though the sun remained invisible,

two stars appeared in the heavens. They twinkled dimly, growing stronger and moving towards the lake.

So Four Winds called out the names of all the dead White Water warriors; the men whom he had celebrated since childhood, the spirits who were with him even now. More stars appeared and lit up the darkness. 'Black Kettle!' Four Winds called as his sacred list ended. 'Running Fox and brave Cochise!'

And now the brightest star of all appeared, close at hand, and Cochise's voice said to Four Winds, 'Beware Kannuck. Beware Matotope.'

And through the great darkness of the eclipse, in the shimmering light of the stars, the boy saw Kannuck prowl from the mountains towards the lake. He saw Matotope, the evil shaman, slink along the shore.

'Matotope is returned from beyond life-side!' Cochise breathed in his friend's ear.

Cruel Matotope with his wolfskin headdress, wielding tomahawk and spear. A shadow man with scalps hanging from his wampum belt, bent to Anteep's will, sent by Bad Heart to capture the boy and finally bring him to his ocean den.

'I hear you!' Four Winds answered. He shuddered as the evil spirit stopped and listened.

And then Matotope stalked on through the day that had turned to night.

ELEVEN

In the pale, pure light of the stars, the men in the boats paddled back to find Four Winds and his horse.

'Boy!' they called. 'Come with us! We will give you shelter from the great disaster that has befallen the world.'

Four Winds thanked them. He marvelled that in the midst of their terror they had thought of him. 'I must travel on,' he said. 'For I am Four Winds, grandson of the great chief, Red Hawk, who has sent me on this journey.'

'We have heard of Red Hawk's plight,' the leader of the boatmen replied. Under the starlight his face was grey, his hair jet black. 'I am Smohalla of the Nez Percé people. My father was Wallowa, friend of the White Water scouts who travelled west.'

'It is sad to meet under such bad times,' Four Winds said. 'I recall that Red Hawk talked of Wallowa and his beautiful white horse, Winter Spirit.'

'Are you not afraid to journey on in this great darkness?' another of the Nez Percé fishermen asked.

'Why not return to our village and hide until the sun returns?'

Once more Four Winds thanked the men. 'This is Anteep's work,' he reported. 'The Evil One sends night to cloak the earth and prevent me from reaching the ocean. His servants, Kannuck and Matotope, hunt me through the darkness.'

'And will the world end now?' another demanded, breathless with fear.

Four Winds searched hard and found courage deep within himself. 'No!' he declared. 'In the name of Wakanda, I will find the great water beyond the mountains and evil will be defeated!'

Then Smohalla ordered his men to row to the shore. He leaped from his shallow boat and embraced the boy. 'You teach us to defy Anteep,' he said humbly. 'We will call to our sky chief, He Who Sits on Top of the Mountain, creator of sun and earth. We will sing the Song of the Sky Loom!'

So Four Winds agreed to wait while the Nez Percé performed their ceremony.

'It is a Sun Song,' one of the fishermen explained as they moored their boats among the reeds.

Four Winds nodded. 'Their words will banish the darkness!' he told Silver Cloud.

'Perhaps,' came the uneasy reply. 'Or maybe Matotope will strike, or Kannuck pounce under cover of night!'

As the Nez Percé braves prepared to dance, the boy

weighed the risks. 'I will trust Smohalla,' he decided. 'For to rush on through the unnatural night holds more dangers than remaining here for a short time.'

'Beware Matotope!' Cochise's voice breathed on the wind.

Four Winds stared at the aspen trees, at shadows that moved and branches like thin fingers reaching for the stars. He saw the treacherous shaman behind every black boulder; crouching, waiting, choosing his moment.

Meanwhile, Smohalla's men gathered into a circle by the shore of the lake. They raised their arms and began to chant.

'O Mother the Earth, O Father the Sky
Your children are we, and with tired backs
We raise our voices to you.'

The men swayed, their upturned faces etched with life's troubles. But their voices were strong, banishing the fear they had felt.

'Then weave for us a garment of brightness;
May the warp be the white light of morning,
May the weft be the red light of evening,
May the fringes be the falling rain,
May the border be the standing rainbow.'

Four Winds searched the shadows for a glint of

Matotope's spear. Silver Cloud listened to every rattle of the dry reed heads and every breath of wind in the trees.

Smohalla led the chant to its conclusion.

'Then weave for us a garment of brightness,
That we may walk where the birds sing
That we may walk where the grass is green,
O our Mother the Earth, O our Father the Sky!'

'The spirit approaches!' Silver Cloud warned.

Four Winds looked among the tall reeds where the boats were moored. He made out a slight movement; nothing more than a shadow. Then he caught sight of a stooping figure, shoulders hunched, creeping low among the reeds.

The boy drew his knife from its sheath. He would fight hard with his grandfather's weapon; he would defy the treachery of Matotope.

The spirit's eyes met his across the unnatural darkness. They were empty hollows, for good shines through the eyes.

Four Winds shuddered. The eyes told him that Matotope had truly sold himself to Anteep. He made ready to run into the water and fight.

'Bring us light!' Smohalla and his brothers implored. Then their chant began again.

And, gradually, the darkness began to fade. Four Winds found that he could make out the knife in his hand, and the cruel, mask-like features of his enemy.

Matotope raised his hand to shield his face from the dawning light.

'Creature of the dark!' Four Winds cried. 'I am ready to fight!'

But the shaman let out a savage cry. He cursed the sun as it appeared again in the sky.

'Weave for us a garment of brightness!' Smohalla called loudly, above the snarling anger of Matotope.

A sliver of golden sun showed quickly, bright in the sky, bringing back the day. The wolves of the forest slunk away; the mountain lions retreated to the shade.

And Matotope ran from the shore of the lake, covering his face, hurrying to reach a low mist which had gathered in the reeds. His figure grew ghostly and insubstantial, until the mist swallowed him completely.

Then the Nez Percé braves rejoiced. 'He Who Sits on Top of the Mountain has great power!' they cried. 'And we learn true courage from the boy who seeks the ocean!'

Four Winds' heart beat fast. He had faced the evil of Matotope and for the present he was safe.

'Let us help you now,' Smohalla insisted. 'Our people know of a way by river through the mountains to the sea. It is quicker than travelling by land, and it will mislead your enemies.'

Four Winds listened carefully, then nodded. He relaxed and his heartbeat slowed. 'Tall Bull will seek our trail by land,' he agreed. 'They will lose many hours searching for tracks that don't exist.'

'Then come in our boats,' Smohalla invited.

By the new light the boy could see that the leader of the Nez Percé was young; dressed for hunting and fishing, not for war. His buckskin shirt was heavily fringed and beaded in red-and-blue zig-zag patterns across his chest. Four Winds smiled in gratitude, then turned to Silver Cloud. 'What will you do if I ride in the boat?' he asked.

'I could gallop through the mountain passes,' the spirit horse suggested. 'We could meet once more on the ocean shore.'

Silver Cloud shook his head. 'My grandfather told me never to leave your side. Where you go, I must go with you.'

'Good!' The horse was satisfied. 'Then I will swim across the lake and downriver, taking Smohalla as our guide.'

It was settled. Four Winds waded through the shallow water to the nearest boat and climbed in. It rocked from side to side, then steadied. Meanwhile, the spirit horse stood to one side, until the Nez Percé had stepped in after Four Winds, taken their oars and begun to paddle steadily into deep water.

Edgy at first, the boy looked down into the still, green

lake. He saw the weeds swirling below the surface, and fish swimming silently by. To their side, Silver Cloud kept up a steady, even pace.

Then the motion of the boat steadied the boy's nerves. He rested his hands on either side of the bark boat, glad of the strong sun on his face. Soon they were far from the shore, cutting swiftly through the smooth surface, accompanied by the rhythmic splash of the oars.

'Your horse is one to be prized,' a brave named Utamilla said. He sat behind Four Winds, rowing strongly. 'He has grace and strength, his grey-blue coat is dappled and beautiful.'

Then Four Winds learned that these people loved their horses, whom they rode to hunt deer and to travel on to the plains to trade skins with the Pawnees.

Utamilla described with pride his own horse, Bluejay. 'He is swift and he never stumbles. My father gave him to me after my first vision quest at the cave of Tca' Mogi. We pass by the cave at the point where the lake meets the river. I will show you,' he promised.

Four Winds looked ahead and saw that they were coming to the western edge of the lake. A range of low, rounded hills lined the shore, where there were deep indentations.

'The water from the ocean washes into those caves,' Utamilla explained. 'Sometimes Waktcexi, the water monster, rides on the tide. He brings with him the giant, Natliskeliguten, and the cannibal woman,

Atata'tiya. Once, a woman chief of the Wishram tribe was turned into stone at the entrance to Tca' Mogi. You will see her eyes carved into the rock, for she still watches over this sacred place.'

The boy took in what he was told. All around he felt the invisible people who had gone before. Turning to his new friend, he asked him to point out the exact spot.

'Here, where the mountains meet the lake, there is a dark arch rising from the water.' As he spoke, the men in both boats stopped rowing and floated silently towards the shore.

Four Winds saw the dripping entrance and the huge eyes carved into the rock. He heard the slap of the water and an echo from inside the dark cave. 'Can you reach this place by land?' he asked.

'No. For my vision quest I came alone by boat. I entered the cave and waited two days and three nights. Many times the ocean flowed in and the cave was flooded. I climbed higher and crouched on a narrow ledge, fasting and seeking my vision. On the third day, Coyote appeared to me.'

A gasp escaped from Four Winds. The White Water People feared Coyote, despite his cleverness.

Utamilla smiled. 'Before the world was born, Coyote destroyed a great monster with a trick. First he persuaded the monster to swallow him, then he stabbed him in the heart and killed him. He cut the body into pieces and flung them to the Wind gods. The pieces became the different tribes of men. Then Coyote shook the blood from his hands and created the Nee-Mee-Poo, our ancestors, the noblest men of all.'

'And Coyote is your spirit guide?' Four Winds saw that Utamilla was favoured among his people. 'You are a great warrior?'

Utamilla's smile broadened. 'I am the third son of our chief, Sun-Goes-Down. I have nineteen summers, and yet I have not tasted the blood of battle.'

'I envy you,' Four Winds sighed. He imagined the calm, easy life of the Nez Percé. 'With your boats and horses you live in a land of peace and plenty.'

'There are fish in the lake and berries on the bushes,' the young brave agreed. 'We plant corn and the sun ripens it. Wakanda is good.'

'Do you know that I am pursued by Tall Bull and the Wild Dog Comanches?' Four Winds asked as the men resumed their rowing. He saw now that these peaceful people had put themselves in danger for his sake. 'Tall Bull's anger will be raised against you when he discovers that you have carried me across the water.'

Utamilla listened, then spoke urgently with Smohalla. The two men agreed that they must quickly return to Sun-Goes-Down with this news.

'We will prepare to defend ourselves,' Smohalla declared. 'Tall Bull shall not pass through our homeland unhindered!'

So they rowed swiftly to a point on the shore where a river ran out of the lake towards the ocean. They held the boat steady to let Four Winds shoulder his medicine bundle, then wade to the bank. Then they saluted him, turned their boats and headed back across the lake.

Four Winds watched them go. 'Now we are alone again,' he said sadly to Silver Cloud, who had waded out of the water and stood beside him.

'But the ocean is near,' the spirit horse reminded him, showing him where the river wound its way through the low mountains. 'The river will soon widen and meet the sea,' he promised. 'We will go silently through the willows, watching, avoiding the shadows. The sun will go down and by the time it rises again in the east, we will have reached our journey's end!'

TWELVE

Tall Bull stood by the eastern edge of the lake, his face dark and brooding.

'The trail has gone cold,' Lightning Snake insisted. 'We have followed the boy faithfully, out of the desert into these mountains, but then the sun disappeared from the sky and chaos came. Since then, Four Winds and his spirit horse have vanished.'

'Perhaps the monsters of Anteep descended and destroyed the enemy during the great darkness,' one of the Wild Dogs warriors suggested. He was weary and wished to return home.

'Our task is done!' another said. 'The boy is death-side. The spirit horse has returned to Wakanda in defeat.'

Their chief stared out across the smooth lake. 'You talk like children. If this were so, do you not think that Anteep would let us share his victory?'

'He did not warn us that the sun would vanish from the sky,' Lightning Snake pointed out. 'He let us grow terrified. I for one believed that the world had come to an end.'

The Comanches recalled how their horses had reared and thrown their riders, how they themselves had tried to hide in caves and behind boulders, crouching and crying out for mercy from the evil spirit whom they served.

'The power of Anteep is great,' Tall Bull reminded his warriors. 'We must serve him, even though he confronts us with danger and the unknown.'

Still his men murmured, but none dared argue outright, for Tall Bull's face was full of anger.

Night Raven sighed. 'We must continue,' he agreed. 'But even our best scout, Lightning Snake, cannot find the trail that we need.'

'It ends here among the reeds.' The scout pointed to the trampled mud where the Nez Percé oarsmen had taken Four Winds into their canoe not long before. 'The boy and the horse are strong swimmers. Perhaps they hope to confuse us by crossing the water.'

Tall Bull nodded. 'This is the homeland of Sun-Goes-Down, chief of the Nez Percé people; men who fish in this lake from boats made of bark and who hunt deer on its shores. They are no friends to the Comanches, for many summers ago, our brothers stole the wife and horse of Sun-Goes-Down's father.'

'Then why do they let us pass through their land?' Lightning Snake wondered. He could not understand men who did not desire to hang the scalps of their enemies from their wampum belts. He glanced round to make sure that there were no watchful eyes observing them from the distant shore, or from the nearby willows.

'Who knows the minds of the Nez Percé?' Tall Bull replied. He had no time to waste on the peace-loving tribe. Instead, he gave orders for his men to split into two groups and follow the shores of the lake. 'We must find where the boy and the horse emerged from the water,' he declared, confident that they would soon pick up the trail again. 'Before night falls we will have them in our sights!'

So the Wild Dogs set off along the water's edge, urging their horses on, eager for the shedding of blood.

Matotope waited for the night. He wore his buffalo robe, painted with his exploits in battle.

During his life, the shaman had killed three enemy chiefs, and eight scalps hung from his belt. On his head he wore the feathers of owl and wild turkey, with a carved wooden knife to show that he had fought in hand to hand combat with a great Blackfoot chief.

These war trophies had been won in the days when Matotope was a true warrior, before his shaman powers had deserted him and he had betrayed Red Hawk and his White Water People. Now though, they had become emblems of his disgrace. The robe hung raggedly around his stooped figure, and the once splendid headdress was tattered. Etched into Matotope's face were bitter lines. Death dominated his thoughts.

I have sold my spirit into slavery, he told himself as he gazed down to the sea. After the mighty change from day to night and the sudden ending of the eclipse, Bad Heart had recalled the shaman to the entrance of his cave. 'Your time has not yet come,' the bear spirit had informed him. 'You must wait until darkness falls before you can fulfil your revenge!'

Bad Heart's tone had mocked him, as if to say, 'You are my creature. Your futile bitterness amuses me. When I say that you must wait, I see anger burn within you, and yet I know that you will rush to embrace any agony at my command!' For it was true that evil spirits experienced pain, just as any man during his lifetime.

Now Matotope considered the price he had paid for betraying his people and binding himself to Anteep. Condemned to suffer forever, he could only appear life-side at the command of one of Anteep's servants. *I exist as a prisoner bound to the cedar pole*, he told himself. *I cannot take a step without permission from the Evil One, and I must go through flame and flood to fulfil his cruel desires.*

And yet there was a glimmer of satisfaction still to be had. Dead himself, he could deal the most brutal of deaths to his enemies. His knife could cut deeper than any blade known to man. The grasp of his dead hands was superhuman, there was poison in his breath, and his tread was more silent than the mountain lion's.

'I will have my revenge!' he cried at the swelling sea. 'I will trap the boy, Four Winds, and send him hurtling to his death. And with him will die the hopes of the White Water Sioux!'

'Matotope makes a fine promise!' As darkness fell, Bad Heart prowled heavily from his clifftop den. The stones disturbed by his feet rolled and fell into the ocean. 'And yet the moon is not yet fully risen in the sky. Bats still flit from tree to tree.'

The shaman nodded. 'Dusk is soon followed by deep night,' he said through clenched teeth, as if every moment of delay caused him pain.

'You must go from here to the lake in the mountains,' Bad Heart told him. 'I wish you to speak with Tall Bull and guide him to this shore.'

'But the boy approaches!' Matotope cried. 'Do not send me inland to talk with the Wild Dogs. I wish to be here when Four Winds finishes his journey and realises that we, the enemy, are here to greet him. I must confront him face to face and enjoy the exact moment of our victory!'

Bad Heart snarled and stood on his hind legs. He towered over the shaman. 'I will send you hurtling down with those stones if you delay!' he warned. 'Fetch the Wild Dog chief to this place by any means within your power. And do it swiftly, for I am certain that his desire to see the boy fail outweighs even yours, Matotope!'

Scowling, the shaman was forced to bend to Bad Heart's command. 'Let me at least be present when the boy dies!' he pleaded.

The bear heard, but he dropped on to all fours and turned away. 'Bring Tall Bull,' he repeated. 'Night has come. I hear the footfall of a single horse. May Anteep's will be done!'

THIRTEEN

It was midnight. A strong, salty breeze swept along the clifftop. Waves swelled and broke into cool white flecks of foam that carried in the tide until they melted on the black rocks below.

Four Winds took a deep breath. At last he had reached the furthest ocean.

After a long time, he slid from Silver Cloud's back. Taking his medicine bundle, he unrolled it and found a small leather bag filled with red dust. This was precious earth from his White Water homeland. He poured the dust into his palm and let it trickle on to the rock in the outline of a small circle which he then stood inside. Looking up, he saw that the moon was full and that the stars seemed very big and close.

'I have walked the path of the heart,' he said aloud to the sky. 'I have spoken to the Great Mystery and found my place within it.'

For answer, the sea roared.

'I am one with the world!' Four Winds declared.

Silver Cloud stood at the cliff edge. He saw that the

boy was pure in his belief, that the cruelty of Anteep had not poisoned his heart. And the horse felt sad that his time with Four Winds was almost ended.

Four Winds drank in the silver light of the moon. He saw his friend, Cochise, amongst the stars.

'I thank Wakanda that I have lived through many dangers,' he murmured. 'O Great Spirit, you gave me Silver Cloud as my guide, and for this I also thank you.'

The boy's gratitude moved the horse. He lowered his head and snorted gently.

Then Bad Heart, who had all this time watched the travellers' arrival at the ocean, called upon the monsters of that western shore.

'I name Tlenamaw, the dragon who breathes fire, and Gunarh, killer whale of the great ocean!'

Flames appeared in the forest beyond the mountains as the sleeping dragon awoke. Tlenamaw's tongue licked at the tall pines and swallowed them in bright flames. Black smoke billowed into the night sky; sparks reached the stars.

Then the dark ocean heaved. Mighty Gunarh rose from the depths, his grey, smooth bulk huge beyond imagining. One flick of his tail brought him to the surface, where he spouted water high into the air. Opening his mouth, he swallowed a thousand fishes, before turning slowly and heading towards the rocky shore.

'Next I call upon Adee, great Thunder Bird, to rise

from his lake high in the mountains.' Bad Heart summoned the most terrifying of Anteep's sky servants.

Adee beat his wings and thunder rattled through the night air. Lightning flashed from his beak. This was a bird who could carry a buffalo or even a whale in his talons, so great was his strength. And he came towards the ocean to crush Four Winds between his beak.

'Come Yehl, the raven of the night!' Bad Heart cried.

The black bird flew eagerly, ready to trick and deceive the puny enemy.

And as Bad Heart gathered his spirits from far and wide, so Matotope went to fetch Tall Bull from the lakeside.

'We two will travel on the wind,' he told the chief of the Wild Dogs. 'Your warriors will follow on horseback.'

Tall Bull protested. 'My braves are weary. They have travelled far and fought in the desert. Why not bring them by your magic to the ocean shore?'

'I do not have the power,' Matotope said impatiently. 'Does Tall Bull wish to witness the defeat of his enemy, or not?'

So the Comanche Chief reluctantly agreed to part from his men, and the shaman called the wind.

At first the strong gusts tugged at the limbs of all the Wild Dog Comanches. They held their ground, until gradually the wind closed in on Matotope and Tall Bull, whirling in a tight circle, faster and faster, until the cyclone tore the two figures from their feet and drew them into the air, hurling them up over the final mountain range towards the great western sea.

'We are almost ready,' Bad Heart said. The night hid his monstrous spirits, who waited by land and sea.

Tlenamaw, covered in black scales, with eyes bright as burning coals, lurked in a cave at the foot of the cliffs, close to Gunarh, who lay submerged on the sea bed. Adee hovered in the air, his huge wings casting a shadow over the moon, beating slowly in a low, thundrous roar.

And Yehl, perched on the furthest finger of rock, surrounded by crashing waves, took delight in his sight of an unsuspecting Four Winds and Silver Cloud who joyfully gave thanks to Wakanda on the next rocky headland.

Bad Heart rose on to his hind legs. 'In the name of Anteep, we will crush this enemy!' he declared. 'Though many spirits have failed, in the yellow water by the deepest mine, and on the pinnacle of Mount Kivioq, still we will succeed.'

A strong wind blew from the mountains in the east and brought Matotope and Tall Bull to the cliff edge. Matotope's thin face was skull-like in the darkness, his figure a mere bundle of bones, beside the brutish strength of Tall Bull.

The Wild Dog chief landed on the rock. He regained his balance and crouched low, ready to defend himself from the huge bear spirit.

'Put back your knife!' Bad Heart snarled. 'It is a foolish courage that challenges the might of Anteep's servant!'

Still Tall Bull gripped the knife in his fist. Alone in the black night, he did not trust the shadowy figure with the huge open jaws, whose teeth glinted yellowish white, and whose claws showed the sharpness of ten bare blades.

So Bad Heart struck out with his talons and swept Tall Bull's knife from his grasp. The metal rang out as it hit the bare rock.

The Comanche chief felt pain tear through him, and saw that the flesh on his right hand was torn to shreds.

'Let he who has most to lose from the boy's victory be the first to challenge him!' Bad Heart cried. The cruel spirit made it clear that he would enjoy the spectacle of the wounded man's struggle with Four Winds and Silver Cloud.

'Remember that failure brings disgrace,' he warned. 'Your braves will despise you and cast you out. You will be condemned to wander in the wilderness, as once Matotope was cast out by Red Hawk and the White Water tribe.'

Tall Bull felt the smart of the insult. Without saying a word, he took his tomahawk in his left hand and crept along the clifftop towards Four Winds and his spirit guide.

★ ★ ★

'You must descend to the shore,' Silver Cloud told Four Winds. 'Until you reach the water's edge you cannot complete your quest.'

Four Winds gazed down the sheer cliff. Way below, white foam smashed against the rocks, but the moon was hidden now, and there was the sound of thunder in the distance. He could see no possible way down to the shingle beach.

So, with his head spinning, he turned to his spirit horse for advice. 'Must we travel further along the cliff until we come to a path?' he asked.

'The rocks drop sheer into the ocean for many hours to both north and south,' Silver Cloud explained.

'Well then, I must grow wings like the eagle!' Four Winds exclaimed. 'Or else you must carry me through the air.'

But Silver Cloud shook his head. 'That is not the way.'

'What then?'

'Look harder.'

Frowning, Four Winds steeled himself to peer over the edge. He made out footholds in the rock, and sparse bunches of sea oats clinging to narrow ledges which would serve as handholds. 'In daylight I can climb down,' he decided. 'But at night, without the moon and stars, it is too difficult.'

Then another problem jumped into his mind. 'You

cannot climb with me, either by night or by day!' he gasped at Silver Cloud.

'No; you must go alone,' the horse replied quietly.

'But you are my guide. I must never leave you.'

'I will be watching over you.' Silver Cloud's tone stayed calm and firm until a light sound disturbed him. He pricked his ears and flicked them this way and that. Then he trotted a few steps in the direction of the noise.

Alerted, Four Winds fell silent. Now he too heard small stones peppering down the rocks and guessed that someone or something was approaching. Still he wasn't prepared for the appearance of a crouching figure from behind a boulder some twenty paces from where they stood.

'Four Winds!' a voice called.

The boy spun round to see a second man standing on a rock.

Both were warriors, wearing feathered headdresses and carrying weapons, but the night hid their identities. Four Winds drew his knife in readiness.

'Beware your enemy, Tall Bull!' the second man cried.

Then Four Winds recognised the voice of One Horn, chief of his tribe. 'My brother!' he called, turning his back on the first crouching man. 'You have found me in my hour of victory!'

'We have followed close on your heels!' One Horn hissed. 'We have used the boats of our friends, the Nez

Percé. Our brothers, Sun Dancer, Little Thunder and Three Bears, are not far behind!'

'Beware Tall Bull!' Silver Cloud warned, as the other brave sprang forward.

Cursing One Horn, the Wild Dog chief hurled himself towards the boy. 'You are within my grasp!' he snarled at Four Winds. 'This time your friends cannot save you!'

With horror the boy saw that his enemy's face was twisted with pain. He noticed the dark glistening blood which dripped from Tall Bull's right hand. Then the Wild Dog was almost upon him and Four Winds had to leap to one side. Tall Bull brought down his tomahawk but struck only rock.

Then One Horn rushed in to grapple with Tall Bull. 'Did you think that the White Water People would let you leave the desert unhindered?' he cried, grasping Tall Bull's left wrist with a hand so strong that it could snap a lesser man's wrist like a young sapling.

One Horn shook the Comanche's weapon from his grasp. 'We have followed you step by step through the mountains. We have rowed across the lake without being seen. Now my men hide in the trees and await your slow and stumbling riders!'

Savagely, Tall Bull twisted out of One Horn's embrace. He drew a knife from his belt and slashed wildly at his enemy.

In the darkness Four Winds saw the blade flash. He

darted forward with his own knife, but the two heavy bodies were once more locked in close combat. For fear of stabbing One Horn, Four Winds held back.

And now One Horn was forcing the knife out of Tall Bull's hand. He thrust him back against a boulder, his massive forearm jammed under the Wild Dog's chin, throttling him and spreadeagling him helplessly, pinning him to the rock.

Four Winds heard the dry rattle in the man's throat. He saw his arms flail and then drop to his side as if life had left him.

The roar of the gathering storm grew louder as Thunder Bird flapped his wings. Yehl croaked and flew up from the rocky promontory. Bad Heart viewed the fight from afar with scornful curiosity.

'The Wild Dog has found his equal in the White Water chief!' he mocked. 'There is a weakness in him despite his desire to serve Anteep. He will pay the price!'

Meanwhile, the dragon Tlenamaw stirred in his cave and breathed fire and thick smoke into the maze of underground fissures and tunnels in the ancient rock.

As Tall Bull slumped in his arms, One Horn let him drop to the ground. 'Such a death is fitting for a treacherous dog who drove our people from their homeland!' he declared, turning his back on Tall Bull and raising both arms to the night sky. 'May his bones never be returned to the great plains of his birth, may his spirit never rest!'

Then Four Winds saw the beaten man draw his black bulk together. As if returning from the dead, his face savagely distorted, he staggered towards One Horn, who stood at the cliff edge.

The boy gave an incoherent cry. He ran to One Horn and, with all his might, pushed him sideways.

It was too late for Tall Bull to stop himself. He lurched, but his blurred vision did not keep pace with Four Winds' action to save his brother. So, in unwitting sacrifice, he threw himself at the space where his enemy had stood, met nothing but air and went hurtling over the edge, down into blackness.

Falling, flailing, screeching, Tall Bull's heavy body plummeted into the ocean.

Four Winds, One Horn and Silver Cloud gazed down. The roar of thunder drowned Tall Bull's screams. The white spray swallowed him and the mighty tide carried his broken body out to sea.

FOURTEEN

Yehl flew to Bad Heart with the bad news of Tall Bull's death.

'Tell Thunder Bird to descend,' the bear spirit said. The sacrifice of Tall Bull amused him, but now it was time to carry out Anteep's will.

The raven soared high in the sky to carry his message.

'My brother!' On the cliff edge One Horn embraced Four Winds. 'I hold you in my heart as my own son. Your courage on these long journeys surpasses all that I have seen in many battles during my long life!'

Four Winds felt his chief's strong heart beat against his own. Tears came to his eyes. 'Without Silver Cloud I would have failed in my first journey,' he confessed. 'He brought me loyalty and love.'

The spirit horse stood in silence at the boy's side. His dappled grey coat shone luminous silver under the night sky.

'Now I must go alone down to the seashore,' Four Winds explained to One Horn.

'And how will you capture this breath of air from the furthest ocean?' the White Water chief asked anxiously. A wind was gathering force, bringing storm clouds from the mountains. One Horn shivered at its approach. 'How will you contain such a thing?'

The boy shook his head. The unspoken question had been with him from the beginning. 'I will not know until the moment arrives,' he replied. 'Wakanda alone holds the answer in his hands.'

'Let me climb down the cliff with you,' One Horn begged.

But a new threat had begun to emerge from the very ground beneath their feet. At first it was a wisp of smoke issuing from a narrow crack in the rock. Then another appeared, and another.

Silver Cloud's nostrils widened in fear.

'What is happening?' Four Winds cried out. It seemed to him that the smoke came from nowhere, curling around his feet and creeping along the surface of the rock. Then a spark flashed from a crevice. It died in an instant, replaced by others, then by a small burst of yellow flame.

'The earth is burning!' One Horn gasped.

'This is the work of Bad Heart's monsters,' Silver Cloud guessed. He trotted to a ridge and looked east to the mountains, then west to the sea. 'Gunarh lies in wait beneath the ocean,' he warned the two frightened warriors. 'He lurks offshore but he cannot come on to the land to harm us.'

'Then where is the fire coming from?' Four Winds implored. 'And why is the thunder roaring in our ears?'

As he spoke, more flames shot into the air, making One Horn leap to one side. The sudden burst of light revealed the terror the brave warrior felt at the mysterious eruption.

'Climb on to my back!' Silver Cloud ordered in a voice full of authority. One Horn obeyed, then the spirit horse spoke rapidly to Four Winds. 'Begin your descent!' he urged. 'Let me fight the spirits of flame and storm. Think only of fulfilling your quest!'

A great flame leaped into the sky and the rock began to split apart. Silver Cloud carried One Horn high above Four Winds' head.

Panic seized the boy. 'How will I succeed?' he cried out, as smoke blinded him and the heat of the flames scorched his face.

Silver Cloud soared free of the land. He circled and returned to the boy. 'You are so near your journey's end,' he called. 'Seize this moment to take your people home!'

'I will try!' Four Winds answered, dodging the flames and reaching the very edge of the cliff. He looked down at the foaming sea.

'Answer truthfully, what do you feel?' Silver Cloud demanded.

The boy stared out to sea. Waves rolled and broke, bank after bank, relentlessly crashing against the shore. Behind him, the flames still flared from deep inside the rock.

'I am afraid!' Four Winds confessed. But he swiftly lowered himself over the edge of the cliff and sought his first foothold.

'Overcome your fear. I will not fail you,' Silver Cloud promised before he took One Horn to the safety of a high ridge.

'You are asking too much of the boy,' the chief of the White Water band protested.

The spirit horse let the man slide from his back. 'It is not I who asks it,' he reminded One Horn. 'Remember that Red Hawk chose his grandson for this quest because he was the one the old man loved the most.'

The memory of his dead chief quietened One Horn. 'May Wakanda be with us,' he murmured.

Then Silver Cloud returned alone to the heart of the flames. He stood firm as the earth cracked and he looked down into the depths at Tlenamaw breathing fire.

The dragon monster had made the core of the earth boil. He pushed the molten rock up through a thousand fissures, sending it bubbling bright red and smoking to the surface. He rose with it, his black scales shining, clawing his way through the lava.

Now that he knew his enemy, the horse did not

flinch. He stood unharmed, his white mane flying, his beautiful neck arched proudly.

Tlenamaw rose to the surface. He climbed out of the widening fissure, clawing at the rock and still breathing flames.

On the ridge, One Horn cowered away from the sight of the monster.

But Silver Cloud struck out at the scaly dragon with his hoof. His challenge drew Tlenamaw across the cliff, lumbering clumsily on his hind legs, certain that his fiery breath would soon defeat the horse.

Instead, Silver Cloud withstood the attack. 'False fire cannot harm me!' he declared. 'I defy Tlenamaw and all of Bad Heart's creatures.'

Angrily the dragon pursued his opponent across the rock. Behind him, lava bubbled to the surface, running into hollows and dripping from ledge to ledge. The monster's eyes glowed with fury as the chase went on.

Meanwhile, Four Winds picked his way down the cliff. He could smell the sulphurous fumes of the volcanic fire and see the glow of Tlenamaw's flames, but the lava did not reach him as he descended to the shore. His feet reached for bushes and ledges that would support his weight, while his fingers grasped the wild sea oats. Sometimes he would slip and his heart would thump, then miss a beat as he recovered his hold. Often, he was within a hair's breadth of losing his footing and crashing on to the jagged rocks that lined the shore.

From high on the mountain Bad Heart watched. 'Tlenamaw allows the horse to draw him away from the boy,' he muttered to Matotope, deciding that it was time to enter the fray. 'But at least Four Winds has no defence when he reaches the shore!'

So the evil bear spirit led the shaman down the mountain, entering a cave and using tunnels through the rock. They waded unharmed through molten lava, crossing vast underground caverns then creeping on all fours through shallow tunnels. Acrid fumes choked Matotope, so that he had to stop. When he recovered he found that Bad Heart had forged ahead out of sight.

'Wait!' the shaman called out. Alone under the earth, surrounded by hissing red lava and thick black smoke, he shook with fear.

His own voice returned as an echo.

'Bad Heart!' He begged for guidance.

'Heart – heart – heart!' came the fading echo.

Cursing, Matotope was forced to find his own way through the maze of tunnels, stumbling on, knowing only that he must keep on heading down until with luck he reached sea level.

'I will not serve Bad Heart any longer!' he swore to himself. 'I will stay out of danger until the struggle against Four Winds is won. Then, when I return death-side, Anteep will be none the wiser.'

With this plan in mind and bitterness clouding his mind, Matotope sensed a breath of fresher air.

Immediately he followed it, choosing a fork in the tunnel, hoping that it would lead him to safety.

Four Winds paused for breath. Below him the roar of the sea grew louder, while high overhead thunder clouds gathered. He closed his eyes and prayed that Silver Cloud would carry One Horn to a safe place and then return to defeat the flame-breathing monster.

He opened them to a flash of lightning which tore through the black sky. For an instant the world appeared a brilliant white, then was plunged back into darkness. Thunder boomed. Terror clutched at Four Winds. The thunder was so loud that he felt it would shake him from the cliff face. And a wind arose, driving the smoke and ash from the volcanic outpouring over the cliff edge. It enveloped him and made his descent even more dangerous than before.

Still he struggled on. He was so close now to his journey's end. He must fix his mind on that alone. Step by step, falteringly, Four Winds went on.

From the shore Bad Heart watched the boy.

He had come swiftly through the caverns and tunnels ahead of Matotope, and now waited at the sea's margin.

Under the constant flash of lightning and the roar of thunder he prowled the jagged rock, calling for Gunarh to appear.

'Thunder Bird shakes the world!' he told the killer

whale, who rose out of the ocean to speak with his master. 'And Tlenamaw melts the very rock on which our enemy stands. Now I ask you, great Gunarh, to make the waves as high as mountains and to send them crashing against the cliff. Sweep Four Winds from his feet and smash him on the rocks. Drag his body down into the depths of the ocean, never to be seen again!'

'I will do this,' Gunarh replied. 'I will swim out to sea and push the waves to the shore. It will be terrible to behold.'

The creature turned with a flick of his giant tail, shooting a powerful jet of water into the air. Then he surged out to sea to do Bad Heart's bidding.

A fork of lightning drew Matotope to the end of the tunnel. He felt his way, scrambling like a coyote on all fours. At last he had found his way out.

But he emerged not at the foot of the cliff as he had hoped, but halfway down the sheer face, on a ledge wide enough to find a foothold and peer down at the restless sea.

With a horrified intake of breath, Four Winds saw the treacherous shaman appear below him. Blackened by the smoke from the molten lava, slyly edging on to the ledge, Matotope didn't realise that he had been seen.

But Bad Heart too noted the furtive movements of the figure on the cliff. He saw what was in the shaman's mind. 'He thinks he can escape danger by hiding until the battle is won,' the bear spirit told Yehl, who had alighted nearby. 'Cowardly in life, this creature from death-side continues his treachery!'

The mocking croak of the raven pierced the roll of thunder that swept down from the mountain.

Four Winds remained still. He wanted to recoil from the black figure crouching below, and at the same time he wished to climb down and confront him in the name of the White Water People whom he had betrayed. Overcoming his disgust and fear, he found his next foothold.

Matotope heard the boy's movement and looked up as a flash of lightning illuminated the cliff face. He saw Four Wind's lithe figure and the glint of the knife in his belt. 'Come then!' he cried suddenly. 'And I will steal the glory from under the nose of Bad Heart and his monsters!'

Four Winds heard him speak in his old voice of betrayal and a steely will to resist coursed through his body. 'You are ten times worse than Tlenamaw with his breath of fire, for you were once our brother!'

Snarling, Matotope reached up to grasp the boy's leg. He caught hold and pulled with all his might. Four Winds gripped the rock with his fingers, then he kicked with his free leg, knocking the shaman to one side. He loosened his grip and lowered himself quickly on to the ledge.

But Matotope had recovered himself. He crouched

low then lunged at the boy, ready to tear at him with his teeth and crush him in his superhuman grasp.

Four Winds defended himself with his grandfather's knife. 'In the name of Red Hawk, you will not succeed!' he cried. He forced the shaman back into the entrance of the tunnel from which he had emerged.

For a moment the boy faced the hated enemy. He saw him prepare to lunge forward, to use his weight to knock Four Winds off the ledge and send them both plunging on to the rocks below. But then, in the pitch black of the stormy night, a sudden blast of smoke belched from the tunnel, and after it a burning river of lava. With an almighty leap, Four Winds bounded clear and clung to the rocks above the tunnel.

Matotope screamed as the red flood swallowed him. He felt pain over every inch of his body. The lava rose to his waist, flowing round him, reaching his chest, freezing his outstretched arms in a gesture of terror. His face was set in an expression of unspeakable terror.

Then Tlenamaw sucked the crimson river back into the bowels of the earth, sweeping the shaman from sight.

Bad Heart saw and was satisfied. 'For those who desert Anteep there is no punishment too great,' he said.

Trembling, Four Winds continued his descent.

'I am with you, my son.' The voice of his mother spoke gently to him.

'Kola, *tuwa nape cinahon opa kte sni ye!*' Friends, whoever runs away shall not be admitted! His father, Swift Elk, and his grandfather, Red Hawk, spoke together.

'I will face whatever is to come!' he promised.

And as he spoke, Silver Cloud returned. 'Love sits in my heart,' he said. The spirit horse watched the boy climb down to the shore, shielding him from the wind of Thunder Bird's wings.

Then the wind changed. No longer from the mountains, it swung in from the west, driving the waves against the shore.

'Be ready,' Silver Cloud warned. 'For Bad Heart has not finished with us yet.'

But now all Four Winds knew was that he was within reach of his goal. Soon he would step down on the shore. He would breathe a breath of air from the furthest ocean. Eagerly he scrambled down, deafened by the water's roar.

And at last he set foot on the wet black rock.

'I give thanks to Wakanda!' he declared, arms raised as lightning flashed and waves rose high as mountains far out to sea.

Then Bad Heart showed himself, towering above the boy and his spirit guide, blacker than the night, taller than the tallest pine tree. He opened his mouth to show his savage teeth and leaned back his head to let out a deep and blood-chilling growl.

'Climb on my back,' Silver Cloud said to Four Winds. Together they would face Bad Heart.

The boy felt the hot foul breath of the bear spirit upon him. He looked into the evil eyes and did not flinch.

Overhead, Thunder Bird sent forks of lightning from his open beak, while out to sea, great Gunarh turned and drove the waves higher.

'You have reached your final moment!' The voice of the bear spirit rose above the thunder. 'Think now of all you leave behind: life and friends, brother warriors, a mother who will grieve for you, a grandmother who will starve in the icy wastes of winter!'

'No! I will take back a breath of air!' Four Winds swore, not knowing how he would carry such a thing. 'With the help of my spirit guide, I will save my People!'

Then the high waves rolled in towards the shore; massive, glistening banks of water topped with white spray. They broke far out, crashing and booming against the promontories, swirling into the caves, rising still higher as another bank formed.

Bad Heart towered over his enemies. 'You cannot defeat the water of the world and Gunarh who drives it before him,' he gloated. 'Soon it will engulf you and drag you down, as it took Tall Bull and an army of lives before him.'

A mighty wave approached the shore. Four Winds looked up at a wall of water. He clutched Silver Cloud's white mane, feeling himself grow small, seeing his hands disappear, sensing that his body was melting to nothing. He became invisible, changing to foam, flying free in the night air. And he rose above the huge tidal wave unharmed.

But Bad Heart watched in terrible fury. He roared to the dark heavens, cursing Thunder Bird and Gunarh for letting Four Winds escape.

He heaved his massive bulk on to an outcrop, facing the great wave, crying out to Anteep, 'Master, I will try again! Though the boy and the spirit horse have melted before my eyes, I will find them and pursue them through eternity.'

Anteep was silent and unforgiving. The wave rose and broke, came crashing down on Bad Heart and drowned his plea.

The bear looked up at the curling wall of black water. He saw that the heavens had lightened and that Thunder Bird had withdrawn. Stars shone and the moon cast its calm silver light.

Too late Bad Heart begged to be given another chance.

He did not notice Yehl rise and flap away, carrying this news to the creatures of the underworld.

The wave broke. It smashed down on Bad Heart and engulfed him, swept his huge body from the rock, thrust him underwater in a whirlpool of foam.

Down he went, down and far out to sea. He had

failed Anteep and was banished for ever from this world.

The sea grew calm and the stars continued to shine.

Returning to his own shape, Four Winds saw that smoke no longer issued from the rocks and the storm had ceased. He stared at his own white palms, steady now, and then out across the smooth ocean.

'We have won our victory,' he said with a sigh.

Silver Cloud did not deny it. 'What do you feel?' he asked the boy whom he had guided. It was the second time he had posed this question, but now the reply would be right and harmonious.

Four Winds looked up at the glorious stars. 'I feel peace and love,' he whispered.

'Take a breath,' Silver Cloud said quietly.

Four Winds filled his lungs with the air of the ocean.

And the spirit horse took the boy home.

HOMELAND

Springtime. The worst of the winter had passed, though snow still clung to the peaks of the mountains in the west.

Women prepared food over bright flames and stretched deerskins between wooden frames. Girls brought bowls of boiled fat and tools made of bone for the women to scrape and treat the hides. Others hung strips of deer meat on poles and dried them in the sun, ready for the time when the snow would fall again.

'What are you doing?' Shining Star asked White Deer, who sat outside her wigwam.

'I am making moccasins for your son,' the old woman replied. 'Three hard journeys have worn out the shoes given by his grandfather, Chief Red Hawk.'

Four Winds' mother examined the fine beadwork. 'Make them bigger,' she advised. 'For your grandson shoots up as an aspen sapling in the bright sun.'

Then she went with fresh herbs for Four Winds' medicine bundle.

'*Tate ou ye topa kin*,' he told her when she discovered him looking far out across the plain. 'The fourwinds are blowing.' The White Water River wound by his bare feet; the sun shone down on his smooth breast.

'I feel a soft wind from the east on my face,' she murmured.

'*Tate ou ye topa kin. Sunka wakan wanzigzi an welo.* The four winds are blowing. A horse is coming.'

'I do not hear a horse,' Shining Star said.

Each morning Four Winds came to the river to look for Silver Cloud. Wherever he was, by night and day, he longed to see his spirit guide once more.

'No,' the young warrior agreed, hanging his head. Then he turned to his mother, this beautiful lover of her land and people, and of the quiet nights full of voices in the damp, heavy air, of fireflies and the smell of pecan trees, of the land crawling with tarantulas and creeping with rattlesnakes. 'You are right,' he murmured.

Shining Star took his hand. 'The horse you seek returned to Wakanda when your final journey ended and he had brought you back in triumph. You breathed the air of the ocean over us, which was new life to us, and we returned to the land of the White Water People.'

He remembered with pride. 'The Wild Dogs slunk like curs across the river.' Leaderless and ashamed, they had retreated far into the east.

Then he also recalled the courage of his friends and

the sacrifices they had made. 'I listen to the voice of Cochise when night comes,' he confessed. 'It comforts me.'

'The air is crowded with words.' Shining Star could hear her husband, Swift Elk, in every rustle of the aspen leaves and murmur of water running past smooth pebbles at the river's edge. 'He sings to me of the future and of your children still unborn. He makes me seek tomorrow!'

Four Winds smiled. 'We move in many worlds. We thrive.'

Shining Star did not say that it was thanks to his courage, but she smiled back then left him by the river.

She returned to the village and their chief, One Horn. 'Four Winds is ready to go on his second vision quest,' she told him.

One Horn heard. 'He seeks Silver Cloud?'

'Parting always brings return,' she reminded their wise leader. 'My son would see his spirit guide and talk with him once more.'

One Horn thought for a long time. He gazed around the village of new tipis, saw that his People worked hard and fed well. Children were born into plenty. 'Prepare the fire of lemon grass for Four Winds' inipi,' he told Shining Star. 'And may the blessings of all the White Water People go with him.'

So Four Winds went to Spider Rock and fasted for four days and nights. He sat cross-legged on a ledge in that sacred place.

On the fourth night Silver Cloud returned.

'Love sits in my heart,' the dream horse said softly. 'I will never leave your side.'